e-times Go

ed to pack her suitcases almost before she learned
nd. Born to a military family, she has lived in the
d States, Puerto Rico, Portugal and Brazil. In
on to travelling, Tina loves to cuddle with her pug,
, spend time with her family, and hit the trails on
orse. Learn more about Tina from her website, or
nd' her on Facebook.

Danvers grew up in a rural community surrounded
rmland. Although her town was small, it offered
y of scope for imagination, as well as an excellent
y. Books allowed Julie to have many adventures
r own home, and her love affair with reading
ever ended. She loves to write about heroes and
nes who are adventurous, passionate about a cause,
ooking for the best in themselves and others. Julie's
ite is juliedanvers.wordpress.com.

HOW TO WIN THE SURGEON'S HEART

TINA BECKETT

CARIBBEAN PARADISE, MIRACLE FAMILY

JULIE DANVERS

MILLS & BOON

Published in Great Britain 2021
by Mills & Boon, an imprint of HarperCollins*Publishers* Ltd,
1 London Bridge Street, London, SE1 9GF

www.harpercollins.co.uk

HarperCollins*Publishers*
1st Floor, Watermarque Building,
Ringsend Road, Dublin 4, Ireland

How to Win the Surgeon's Heart © 2021 by Harlequin Books S.A.

Caribbean Paradise, Miracle Family © 2021 by Harlequin Books S.A.

Special thanks and acknowledgement are given to
Tina Beckett and Julie Danvers for their contribution
to The Island Clinic miniseries.

ISBN: 978-0-263-29766-9

06/21

MIX
Paper from
responsible sources
FSC C007454

This book is produced from independently certified FSC™ paper
to ensure responsible forest management.
For more information visit www.harpercollins.co.uk/green.

Printed and bound in Spain
by CPI, Barcelona

HOW TO WIN THE SURGEON'S HEART

TINA BECKETT

MILLS & BOON

To my kids for always supporting me. I love you!

PROLOGUE

NATE EDWARDS STOOD on the tarmac, a tiny cloth doll clutched in his hand, awaiting the Medicine Around the World plane that would whisk him away from Saint Victoria and the aftermath of the hurricane that had wreaked havoc on the small Caribbean island. His thumb rubbed across the doll's rough cloth, trying not to picture the tearstained eyes of her parents as they presented the gift to him. But their faces were forever burned into his memory. As was the dark-haired child who had been so very sick. And yet she'd managed the tiniest of smiles for him. With the island's hospital obliterated by the fury of the storm, there had been little hope of saving her.

But God, how he'd wanted to. How he'd fought for her.

The phone in his pocket pinged.

Hell. His team had had only the most rudimentary supplies to work with during their stay. How, then, could cell phone signals still get through?

He pulled the phone out of his pocket, glad he'd charged it before packing for the trip home.

His mom's name appeared at the top of the screen.

Glad you're coming home today. We have a big surprise waiting for you! Your father and I can't wait for you to see it.

A sense of dread filled his gut. He'd hoped by coming to the island he could circumvent their plans and buy himself a little more time to explain things to them. And then there was Tara, who had been hinting about settling down once he finished specializing. Except so much had changed. He tucked the doll under his arm as a bead of sweat rolled down his temple. He typed back.

Please don't do anything until I get there.

He had no idea how he was going to tell them that he had no intention of joining their practice. After his trip to Saint Victoria—which they hadn't approved of—the last thing he wanted to do was practice plastic surgery on the rich and famous.

One of his colleagues came up beside him. "Nate, we just got the results back on your patient's mystery illness."

Too late. Marie had already passed away. Still he forced himself to ask. "What was it?"

"Schistosomiasis. It must have damaged her liver and intestines beyond repair. That's why she was so jaundiced. She had to have had it for a while."

A parasite found in water had killed her? He closed his eyes. That possibility had never even crossed his mind. They'd had to send samples via water courier to a neighboring island, but he'd known in his heart it was too late. It should make him feel better to know there was nothing he could have done. Instead he just felt…empty. And now he had to go home and face his parents and Tara.

He forced himself to meet the eyes of his colleague. "Thanks for letting me know."

"You're welcome." Peter clapped him on the back. "Not your fault."

"Thanks."

What else could he say?

Just then his phone pinged again, the screen lighting up and drawing his attention to the words that were printed there.

Too late. It's already done.

Three smiley faces appeared at the end of the phrase.

She was right. It was already done. All of it.

Marie. This trip. His decision about what to do with his future.

Maybe Tara would understand. Maybe she'd even want to join him.

He stuffed his phone back in his pocket and cradled the worn doll in his palms.

Because he was coming back to this island, someday, and he was going to use his training to do something good. Something worthwhile.

If it took every penny he had.

CHAPTER ONE

SASHA JAMES GROUND her teeth as she waited for the shuttle that connected The Island Clinic with Saint Victoria Hospital. She was surprised the man hadn't taken his fancy helicopter instead. After all, he was the one who'd paid for Saint Victoria Hospital to have the helipad installed. And for The Island Clinic's. His own little kingdom.

"Not fair, Sash. You know good and well he's done a lot for the island over the last three years."

But how long before he got bored with playing the part of a philanthropist?

She rolled her eyes. It would not do to make an enemy of the man, because without a doubt, she would come out on the losing end. Everyone she'd talked to idolized him.

Especially those wealthy women who had vacation homes here on the island. There were rumors that some of them had their eyes set on dating him. That a few might have done just that. Except the clinic's chief of staff was apparently not interested in deeper relationships.

Sound familiar?

The shuttle, with The Island Clinic's picture emblazoned on the side, pulled up to the doors of the hospital's main entrance. Why had she been appointed as the one to meet Mr. Big Wig?

Because they were short staffed and Sasha had no immediate surgeries scheduled. Basically, she'd drawn the short straw. It was also why Dr. Edwards had offered to come over from the clinic.

The door to the back opened and a couple of people got off the shuttle, followed by a man who must be Edwards in black jeans and a matching polo shirt.

She'd expected Armani and had gotten *Men in Black*, instead. Great.

Maybe he'd decided to dress down for the Saint Victoria crowd.

There she went again.

Pushing through the glass door, the heat outside swept across her cheeks and made her clothing want to stick to her skin. She hurried to meet him halfway down the sidewalk. "Dr. Edwards? I'm Sasha James. Nice to meet you."

"You, as well."

A quick smile appeared, forming a crease on the left side of his face, one which disappeared in the blink of an eye. With black hair swept back from a strong forehead and an even stronger chin, the man's features were swoon-worthy. Fortunately, Sasha was no swooner. Not anymore. Her gaze traveled a little further down, where the swell of biceps was noticeable under the sleeves of his knit shirt. How in the world had he gotten those? Warmth washed through her belly, and her hand instinctively went there to push back the tide. It didn't work.

She had to admit his appearance didn't immediately scream wealth and privilege, the way she'd expected it to. The way Austin's had done. There was no softness to his jawline, no paunch around his middle—not that her former boyfriend had had either of those things. Maybe, like Austin, this man spent hours exercising to keep himself fit. But she didn't think so, and underneath that rugged veneer there was something that said this was a man not to be trifled with.

Well, that was okay. She'd already met his type during her time at Harvard. Rich men were a dime a dozen there. And they were not always who they seemed, as she'd discovered.

She had to admit though, Dr. Edwards had done quite a bit for the island, had taken in a lot of Saint Victoria's hardship cases. Courtesy of The Island Clinic's wealthy clientele.

Okay, now that she had Dr. Edwards, she wasn't quite sure what to do with him. And she'd been too peeved by the request to meet him to ask. "Did you know where they wanted you?"

"Wherever you need me."

Her palm pressed even harder against her abdomen as the graveled tones turned the burner up on whatever was happening inside her.

"Dr. Edwards, I think—"

"Nate. Please."

She didn't want to call him Nate. Didn't want to be on a first-name basis with the man, despite the fact that she called almost everyone else by their given name. This just seemed…different. "I think I'll stick to Dr. Edwards if it's okay with you."

He lifted his shoulders in an easy shrug, although she was pretty sure there was a tension to the movement that hadn't been there moments earlier. "That's fine…

Dr. James." His lips curved as he added her title, making her realize how strange she was acting.

But it wasn't an act. She had no idea why he was even here. What could he do, exactly? Did he practice actual medicine anymore? Or was he just a showpiece for the clinic?

"Marcus...er... Dr. Warren," too late she realized she'd used the other doctor's name making a mockery of her reticence to calling him Nate, "worked in the ER. It's where our biggest shortage of staff is. If you're up to it."

"I'll do my best to keep up." Again that smile rolled across his face, that crease making her shiver. Was he making fun of her?

Her hand finally dropped from her stomach and curled into a ball next to her hip. "I'll walk you over, since I'm helping out there, as well." Today was her scheduled day off, but there was no way she was going to sit at home while everyone else in the ER struggled to cope.

"Thanks, I appreciate that."

In silence, they walked down the tiled corridor toward the small hospital's emergency room. Dr. Edwards threw her a look.

"What?"

"Nothing." His smile this time was a bit cooler than it had been. "How long have you been at the hospital?"

"A little over three years."

"Do you specialize?"

That made her hackles rise all over again. "I'm a surgeon, so yes. Why?" Did it matter to him what she did? If so, she might not be able to refrain from giving him the "we're all equal here" speech that she'd had to give to more than one person over the last couple of years.

"No reason. I just don't think we've met before, and I thought I knew most of the staff over here."

She didn't tell him that she made herself scarce whenever she heard that Nate Edwards was coming over to the hospital. She hadn't realized how much she'd prejudged him until right this moment though. Everyone she knew always spoke of him as if he could do no wrong. Maybe that was why. It had rubbed her up the wrong way, somehow. The man was not a god. He was a mortal just like everyone else.

But where she'd expected to meet an abrupt, pompous ass who thought he was better than everyone else, she was seeing something different. Either the man was a good actor…or he wasn't as much of a jerk as she'd painted in her head. She wasn't sure if that was a good thing or bad.

She'd give him the benefit of the doubt. For now. But she was going to reserve final judgment until she saw how he was with actual patients. The island's population, that is—not the wealthy ones from his fancy clinic.

"I don't think we have met. I'm in surgery quite a bit, so we've obviously missed each other." It was true, but she was well aware of the fact that she was fudging it just a bit. He was at the hospital once every week or so, normally to pick up a patient or check on one who had been discharged back to Saint Victoria Hospital.

"Obviously."

The way he said it made her squirm, as if he was glad not to have met her before this. Was she being that unfair? She wasn't trying to be.

Wasn't she? Didn't she guard her heart a lot more now that she was older and wiser?

They arrived at the ER to a chaotic scene. An ambulance had just pulled into the bay. Sasha glanced around and didn't see any other doctors. "I'll help with whatever's going on here, if you want to check in."

"Checking in can wait. I'll see if they need a hand."

They both hurried over to where the EMTs were sliding a gurney out of the ambulance.

"What have you got?" she asked.

"Possible heart attack."

For a split second her own heart froze. Then she forced herself back into action as the patient's vital signs were read off. Nate was leaning over the man, a stethoscope magically appearing in his hand. The patient was unconscious, his breathing loud and raspy. His color didn't look good either.

They rushed him into a room. And got to work with the help of a nurse, putting leads on his chest and firing up the EKG machine.

Sasha glanced at the readout. His heart was beating but there were some telltale signs coming across the machine. "I'm seeing hyperacute T's." The T waves were taller and more pointed than normal. It was one of the first signs of a heart attack.

"I see it. Let's get some blood readings and get some tenecteplase ready, just in case. Who's the cardiologist on call?"

The use of TNKase was still controversial in some circles, but in this case she agreed with Nate's assessment.

The nurse said, "Let me check." Two minutes later, she was back, a frown on her face. "Dr. Holloway is in emergency surgery and expected to be there for another couple of hours. I can try to call Dr. Benson at home."

"Damn." The word slid out before she could stop it. Their patient was at a critical stage. "It'll take him a half hour to get here."

Nate stripped his gloves off and pulled out his cell phone. "We're care-flighting him to The Island Clinic."

As he made the call, relief battled with irritation at the way he'd taken over. Just because he was chief of staff at The Island Clinic didn't give him the right to make decisions for Saint Victoria Hospital. But she knew he was right. Either they were going to have to treat the patient here in the ER and hope for the best, or they were going to have to rely on the specialists at the clinic, who were all top in their field. Nate had made sure of that.

She managed to grit out, "I agree."

Ha! Since he was already hanging up his phone, it hadn't really mattered what she thought. It was a done deal.

"Let's get him ready for transport."

For once she was glad for the helipad. By ambulance, the trip would have taken close to forty-five minutes, since the clinic was located on the southeast corner of the island. By helicopter it would only take seven minutes. She'd heard that magic number repeated over and over again. Another source of irritation.

They bundled everything they needed and got him to the double doors just as a low rumble signaled the chopper was headed their way. "Greg will be on that flight."

"Greg?"

"Sorry, Greg Morris. He's one of our cardiac care

doctors. Since we're needed here, we won't be able to go with the patient."

"Okay." She looked at him. Really looked at him, seeing him not as just another rich man, but as a doctor who wanted what was best for his patient. *Their* patient. She put aside her negative feelings. At least for now. "Thank you. Seriously."

He nodded. Met her gaze.

"This is what I envisioned The Island Clinic being used for. To serve the island's best interests."

She hadn't really believed that, and still wasn't entirely convinced, but for the moment she was putting aside the idea that he'd only come here to cater to wealthy clientele and was using Saint Victoria Hospital as some kind of tax write-off. Maybe it was why she'd so studiously avoided him. She didn't want her suspicions to be confirmed by meeting the man. She'd be more than glad to be wrong, in this particular case.

A few seconds later, her thoughts were only on getting the patient into the chopper and handing him off to the cardiologist on board. Then with a quick wave, the door to the helicopter closed, and they were off. She stared at it until it was out of sight then turned her gaze back to him.

"You'll let me know how he does."

His head cocked. "Sure. If you really want to know."

"Of course I do." Was he doubting that she cared about her patients? That stung. But she knew that she'd been less than welcoming toward him when they'd met.

"I could let you know…" There was a pause. "But better yet, why don't we go see him as soon as our shift here is done. If you don't have plans, that is."

She hesitated. She'd never been to The Island

Clinic—had kind of made it her mission to avoid thinking about it…and Nate. But she couldn't very well tell him that. And to turn him down would seem churlish. And definitely unwelcoming. She could pretend she had a dinner engagement, but that would be yet another fib on top of her claims that she'd been in surgery so much that she'd never had a chance to meet him. She'd always prided herself on trying to do the right thing, so here was her chance to prove that. Besides, she hadn't had a date in a long, long time, something he'd easily be able to check, if he listened to the rumor mill at the hospital.

"Thanks. I'd like that."

"What time is your shift over?"

"I wasn't really scheduled today to begin with. But I'd say around five o'clock. Barring any emergencies like that last one." Hopefully there'd be no hitches and the next shift's doctors would make it in. Life at Saint Victoria Hospital could be chaotic and unpredictable, even on a good day, but she could think of nowhere she'd rather be than here at the hospital.

A call came in saying another ambulance was on its way in, so she forced her mind to return to work as she and Nate rushed back toward the ER.

Five o'clock came, and Nate realized he was exhausted. But it was a good exhaustion. He'd done his fair share of work since becoming a doctor, but over the last three years, running The Island Clinic had taken up most of his time. So he didn't often deal with emergencies like he had over the last several hours. As tired as he was, he welcomed the opportunity to get back in the thick of things. And he could see ways that the clinic had helped Saint Victoria Hospital in the glimpses of new equipment he noticed here and there. In the helipad that had whisked their heart attack patient to the facility on the other side of the island. But there was so much more to be done. So many people left to help.

If he'd given in to his parents and stayed at their facility, things would have been very different. For this hospital and for him personally. Because he'd probably be married to Tara and have a couple of kids by now.

But he hadn't stayed, and Tara had wanted no part of coming here. And it was for the best. Especially after realizing all any of them cared about was...

Stop. Just stop. He snapped his gloves off and tossed them into a nearby receptacle, just as he spotted Sasha across the space, laughing at something the male nurse next to her had said. He tensed without knowing why.

She was good at what she did. Prickly...but good. He wasn't sure why she'd been so against using his name. He'd thought maybe she held herself aloof from everyone, but no...over the day she'd called almost everyone by their given names. And every time she had, he'd tensed, seeing that flash of a smile she gave person after person. And watching the easy way she was with all of her colleagues, the way that full bottom lip formed a fake pout when someone suggested something she didn't like. Hell, his insides had shifted and quivered like some kid who was high on hormones.

And she was having a good old time talking to the man on the other side of the room...

So it was just him she didn't like. Why?

Because he was an outsider?

Maybe. He'd worked hard to fit in, but he knew at the heart of it, The Island Clinic was probably seen as a place where the wealthy came to have procedures in seclusion. And there was a lot of truth to that statement. But most of the people he'd talked to knew the main purpose of those clients was to have a steady flow of funds that would supplement Saint Victoria Hospital's shortfalls—which were sometimes huge. At those times, basic supplies could run dangerously low. Like during Hurricane Regan, which had decimated parts of the island. And his clinic wasn't just there for the wealthy. It was there for anyone who might need it. Like their heart-attack patient.

Not only that, but the clinic provided free additional training for any of the hospital's staff who might want to rotate through for a month or two. That was one of Nate's biggest sources of satisfaction. He saw it as a win-win arrangement.

He caught Sasha's eye, and like magic, her smile disappeared, that sexy lower lip straightening in what looked like disapproval as she regarded him. So maybe not everyone felt that way about The Island Clinic. If he wasn't mistaken, she didn't like him or his clinic. And he had no idea why. But she said something to the man she'd been talking to, throwing another smile and touching his arm before turning away.

His gut squeezed again. *Knock it off, Nate. It doesn't matter to you who she talks to. Who she's involved with.*

His parents had disapproved of him coming here. Had been angry that the pretty new plaque they'd made for their surgery center—the one with his name added to theirs—had had to be taken down and replaced. They'd talked about their disappointment and asked him how he could embarrass them like that. How he could disappoint Tara.

He hadn't meant to embarrass them. But he'd also

never asked to be a part of their thriving practice, either. He had still had two years of his specialty training, but he'd made the decision that it wouldn't be in plastic surgery.

And when he'd told them he was using his trust fund to start The Island Clinic, they hadn't said a word, but their stony silence said it all.

They hadn't contacted Nate in the three years since he'd established the clinic. Not to see how it was doing. Not to ask how he was. And he had no idea if Tara even still worked at his parents' clinic.

To realize that those he cared about could turn their love off like some kind of spigot had done a number on him. Or maybe they hadn't wanted children at all. A thought that had plagued him for the last year. He'd had a series of nannies who had cared for him during his early childhood, since his mom had wanted to get back to work as soon as possible. When he looked at all the evidence with new eyes...

He wasn't going to think about that right now, since Sasha was now standing in front of him looking up with a frown.

Had she said something to him? "Sorry, my mind was wandering. Are you still good to go with me to the clinic?"

"I said I would."

And she kept her word, even if it was the last thing she wanted to do. She hadn't said it outright, but the arms folded across her chest, the stiff stance said it all.

Hell, why had she agreed to come, if it was so distasteful to her? But he was too tired to challenge her or ask what was wrong. He'd done that ad infinitum with his parents and Tara after that publicity fiasco when they'd unveiled that plaque on their center less than a half hour after his flight had arrived in the States. Tara had been standing at his side and had looked at him in stunned silence when he'd shaken his head no. But no amount of explanation or sharing his heart had seemed to penetrate the united wall of ice they'd erected…the one that found them on one side and Nate firmly on the other. He'd finally given up, breaking it off with Tara and no longer trying to get through to his parents.

He wasn't anxious to expend that kind of emotional energy ever again. Especially on someone he didn't even know. If she didn't want to come, she could just say so and be done with it. "Okay, ready? We'll use the shuttle, if that's okay. Unless you'd rather use the helicopter. It'll only take a moment to call for it."

Her eyes widened, before narrowing again. "No, I'd rather save the chopper for those who actually need it. The shuttle will be fine. Or we can use my car."

He had a feeling the less he asked of her, the better. "Let's take the shuttle, then."

Her nod had him less than sure. But again, he wasn't going to grab a shovel and try digging down to what she really meant. Because he might find that hole was a lot deeper than he had time for.

Sasha went to get her purse and to finish the last of her reports, while he went and grabbed a coffee. By the time she returned, the shuttle texted him, saying they'd arrived at the hospital.

There were three banks of seats in the back of the shuttle. He waited for her to choose one of them and then sat across the aisle from her. He wasn't going to pretend they were chummy or even friends. Because they weren't. But he damned well wasn't going to sit here in silence. He'd had enough of that to last a lifetime.

"So you've been at Saint Victoria Hospital for three years?"

She turned dark eyes on him, her lashes thicker than they had a right to be. Each blink of her eyes found his gaze tracing their path. His jaw clenched.

"Yes. Once I finished up my residency, I came back to the island."

Saint Victoria was small enough that there weren't large universities or medical schools on it. "Where did you study?"

"Harvard."

The word came fast, taking him by surprise. So much so that it took him a few seconds to process it and drum up a reply. But he didn't have time to give voice to it.

"Surprised?"

He was. But maybe not for the reasons she expected. "It's just a huge university."

"Yes, it is. And if you're wondering how I paid for it, I received a full scholarship." Her chin was tilted up as if expecting him to challenge her right to study there.

"I wasn't wondering."

Her eyes closed for a second, those lashes he'd noticed casting shadows on her cheeks. "Sorry. I'm just used to that being one of the first questions I get asked around here."

To have received a full ride at the prestigious university meant that Sasha had had top grades in all of her classes as well as on her entrance exams. He was surprised she'd chosen to come back here. She could probably practice medicine anywhere she wanted to.

Why wouldn't she come here though? He'd chosen

to, hadn't he? But he didn't care about prestige or about practicing at one of the top teaching hospitals. He just wanted to help people.

"You didn't want to stay in the States?"

She stared at him for a second before glancing away. "I thought about it for a while. But things didn't work out, so I came back home."

Didn't work out? Like at another hospital?

"Where did you do your residency?" Harvard didn't run its own hospital like Johns Hopkins did, so they partnered with other hospitals to provide places for clinicals and residencies.

"I actually did mine at Beth Israel. They place a lot of emphasis on community care, which Saint Victoria Hospital does as well, so it seemed like a good fit." She tilted her head. "Where did you study?"

"Johns Hopkins. I did my residency there, as well."

"What made you want to become a doctor?"

He was asked that on a regular basis, but it was a tricky question. He'd originally gone into premedicine because his parents had expected it of him. He'd given in mainly to explore whether it was an option for him or not. He'd been surprised to find that he loved the classes. Loved his teachers. And loved the science of medicine.

What he didn't love was the greed that sometimes went along with it. He'd met people who went into medicine as a way to build wealth, or a reputation or to climb the social ladder. He used to think his parents had gone into medicine for altruistic reasons. And to now look at them in the cold light of day... Well, he was a little more cynical about that than he'd once been.

He decided to give the easy answer, because the true

explanation was more complicated than he wanted to get into right now. "I had relatives who were doctors, so it seemed the obvious choice."

Her frown told him that what he'd said had hit a sore spot.

"So you didn't really want to be a doctor? Why be one, then?"

The tricky question became even more convoluted. "In the beginning I wasn't sure where the separation between my wants and others' expectations was. But now? Well, I can't imagine anything I'd rather be than a surgeon. And you?"

One shoulder went up. "That's easy. It was because of my dad."

She'd said it so easily. As if it didn't bother her at all. That intrigued him enough to nudge for a deeper explanation.

"Your dad?"

"He…well, he died of a heart attack when I was fourteen." Her eyes glistened with what looked like deep emotion. "There was nothing in place at that time for true emergency care. People had to be flown to a neighboring island. My dad never made it that far. He died right after arriving at a nearby clinic."

Nate shifted in his seat, reaching across to place his hand over the one she'd curled around the armrest of her chair. "I'm sorry."

The tenseness he'd been aware of in her while dealing with their patient suddenly made sense. Her need to know how he was doing. If the man had stayed at Saint Victoria Hospital, it would have been easy for her to check up on him. But at The Island Clinic, it would entail a phone call, and very probably, an explanation about why she wanted to know. No wonder she'd agreed to make the trek across the island.

Her next murmured words were soft. As if she were talking to herself. "It was a long time ago."

But not long enough to snuff the spark of grief that appeared in her eyes when she talked about him. "Your mom?"

"She's doing fine. She's a chef, actually."

"She's still in Saint Victoria?"

"It's her home. Where else would she be?" As if she'd had second thoughts about her answer, she amended it. "This is where she was born. Where she got married. She can't imagine living anywhere else. When I thought I was going to get... Well, when I was thinking of remaining in the States, she wouldn't consider moving there. Sometimes things work out for the best, since I later decided to come back home."

Sometimes things did work out for the best. Like his deciding not to join his parents' practice? Like not caving to Tara's demands that he remain in the States? Yes. He could see now how unbearable that would have been for him. While they were perfectly happy doing what they did, Nate would have felt stifled and trapped. Maybe the estrangement was for the best. It had given him a clear road to do what he thought was right, without the constant need to run things by them, like he'd had to when he was a teenager.

It was easier this way. Right? Being alone?

He realized his hand was still covering hers. He pulled away, sitting back in his seat, just as the long driveway to The Island Clinic appeared on their right.

A sliver of pride went through him when he spotted

the large bronze statue out front. Marie would have approved of it, he was sure.

Glancing at Sasha, he said, "Welcome to The Island Clinic."

CHAPTER TWO

SASHA STOOD IN front of a modern white building that would rival some of the hospitals she'd seen in the States. It was on a smaller scale, but still a stunning sight on her little island. She suddenly had second thoughts about coming here.

The helipad, complete with the helicopter that had whisked their patient away, was a short distance from the building. There was a pristine asphalt driveway leading to a pair of double doors.

"*Bon Bondye,*" she whispered. It was at times like this that her English failed her, the island's French Creole coming to the forefront. But it fit so much better than simply saying *Good God*.

Nate murmured something to the shuttle's driver before coming to stand beside her. "You've never been here before."

"No." What else could she say? She'd heard it was beautiful, but that would be an understatement. It was sitting a short distance from the beach, and there was a long boardwalk that meandered from the back of the building to a white sandy shoreline, the waters calmly licking at it.

She squinted when she spotted something else. A

lone figure stood down there, staring out toward the sea as if in deep thought. There were some bright umbrellas and lounge chairs scattered along the area.

Saint Victoria Hospital, on the other hand, was on the interior of Williamtown and boasted no such vistas. But then again, the staff didn't often find themselves with enough time on their hands to enjoy sights like this one.

Off to the side, there was another wing, painted in sand tones. Each of the three-story windows had a wrought iron balcony and matching table and chairs. "Is that the clinic's hotel?"

Sasha had heard it had added some accommodations that rivaled the island's own five-star Harbor Hotel.

"Yes. As you saw, the trip here from Williamtown is quite a drive. We wanted relatives to be able to stay close and for patients to be able to convalesce nearby. Would you like to see one of the rooms after we check on our patient?"

She hesitated, before saying, "Sure." It wasn't like she could just say no without sounding ungrateful for what the clinic had done for Saint Victoria Hospital. And she had to admit, she was curious about what the facility had to offer.

They went in, and Nate checked in at the desk, then came back. "They put him up in ICU. They were able to dissolve the clot and are now working to get him stable enough to put a couple of stents in."

"That's wonderful." She'd been half afraid he might have died en route. But surely Nate would have gotten a call, if that had been the case.

"Greg is really good at what he does."

She knew he didn't mean it as a criticism of the staff at Saint Victoria Hospital, but it was hard not to bristle all over again. She forced herself to breathe through it and gave him a smile. "I'm just glad that flying him over here gave him a good chance for survival."

"It did. They expect him to make a full recovery, as long as something unexpected doesn't happen. His family has arrived and will stay at the clinic's hotel while he recovers."

She didn't want to ask, but felt she had to, since she didn't want them to find themselves saddled with a huge bill. "Most of the islanders can't afford to stay in fancy hotels. Maybe I can help pay for some of it."

Nate's brown eyes cooled, like they had at Saint Victoria Hospital. "They won't be charged for staying. That's part of what we're here for."

She'd offended him. Not what she'd meant to do at all. But after her experience with Austin… Well, he never once thought about the fact that not everyone could afford the luxurious things he had. Why had she ever thought her ex could fit in with the people on Saint Victoria? Not that there weren't different socioeconomic levels here, like there were everywhere else. But only now did she realize how unequally matched they would have been.

It would be like her dating Nate.

The thought made her pause. Not that it was likely to happen. And since she'd made that mistake once before, she was now inoculated against men like him. One move in the wrong direction, and her immune system would come charging in to shut her down. Especially when it came to someone like Nate.

Although he seemed to understand the island in a way that surprised her. Warmed her. Her antibodies sat up and took notice and were readying themselves to intervene, should she do something stupid. She just hoped they arrived in time.

"I'm sorry. I just wasn't sure how it worked."

"The clinic is here for the island's hospital, not to make money off it. The patients we bring in from the outside, along with the gala, are what keep us afloat and give us the ability to help those in need."

Friends had told her time and time again that she had the wrong idea about the clinic, her friend Patty in particular, but she just hadn't been able to shake her preconceptions. Maybe it was time to start listening.

"I haven't been to one of the galas yet, but I've heard they're quite elegant."

"They are." He glanced at her. "Why don't you come to one of the planning meetings?"

"Oh, I don't know, I'm not sure you'd want my opinion."

He smiled in a way that made her stomach do a flip-flop. "I think your opinion is exactly the one we need. We actually have a meeting tomorrow night, if you're free. It's here in the conference room."

"Please don't feel like you have to invite me." The last thing she wanted was to be the token islander.

"I don't normally do things because I 'have' to. I truly do want to know what you think. Especially since you haven't been to any of the previous galas."

"I'll think about it. What time?"

"Six-thirty. We'll have dinner there, since a lot of folks will just be coming off their shift."

So the committee was made up of people working at the hospital? Not some kind of outside party-planning organization? "How many people will be there?"

"I don't know. We invite everyone." He sent her a

look. "From both Saint Victoria Hospital and The Island Clinic. Whoever wants to come is welcome. You didn't know that?"

Modi. So it wasn't even just the clinic that made the decisions. "I guess I never thought about it."

"There are posters up at the hospital. I made sure of it."

Sasha had blocked out so much of the stuff about The Island Clinic that she must have chosen not to read those posters. It also made her realize that his invitation wasn't about Sasha being who she was, but about the fact that he wanted a wide range of ideas and opinions. Her knee-jerk reaction that told her to come up with an excuse not to be at that meeting fell by the wayside. "I'll try to come."

"I'll look forward to seeing you there."

They made their way up to the second-floor ICU, and Nate swiped his nametag across a keypad. The doors opened, and he waved her through. "You have to have security clearance to get in?"

He nodded. "We have everyone from high-ranking public officials to actors who come to the clinic. No one wants a picture of themselves at their most vulnerable flashed across the tabloids."

"Of course not. I didn't think about that."

The intensive-care unit was ultrahigh tech, on a scale like she'd had at Beth Israel during her residency. "What's our patient's name?"

Saying *our* gave it an intimate feeling for some reason, even though she'd used that phrase countless other times. It had to be because she'd been so resistant to meeting Nate…to working with him.

"Bill Waddel. He's in the second room on the right."

They moved toward the door, which was closed. Nate opened it and peeked in, then nodded to her that it was okay.

The man was asleep, but unlike so many who probably filled these rooms, he wasn't intubated and the number of tubes was minimal, given what he'd been through. She went to the head of the bed and noted his lips were no longer as ashen as they'd been when he was at Saint Victoria Hospital. And the heart monitor was showing a nice sinus rhythm. The *T*-waves weren't as tall or pointed. "I'd say the damage to his heart was surprisingly small, given what it could have been."

The situation could have become catastrophic if they hadn't transported him. His family might be sitting in a very different kind of room than the fancy hotel that adjoined this building.

"I agree. Greg thinks the stents he'll put in will keep the blockage from happening again. He's hoping to do the procedure tomorrow."

"That's great." The man's family wasn't here at the moment. "He's allowed to have visitors in here, isn't he?"

"Yes. His son went out to the beach to meditate, according to the front desk."

The lone figure she'd seen staring out over the water? Maybe. She looked at Nate. "Thanks for lending a hand today. The outcome might not have been the same, if you hadn't been there."

He frowned. "The hospital knows they can always refer anyone to us."

That might be so, but Sasha was ashamed to admit that she might not have been so quick to send him over. Not out of pride or arrogance, but because it simply would not have crossed her mind to call for the helicopter. But it would from now on. She didn't have to like Nate. Or The Island Clinic. But she would be negligent if she didn't take advantage of every opportunity afforded her patients. "I'll make sure to keep that in mind. Thanks for letting me see him."

He smiled again. "All you have to do is call the front desk. I want there to be collaboration between our facilities. No turf wars. Okay?"

She laughed at how well he'd read her. But maybe that wasn't such a funny thing. Hopefully he hadn't read the small jolts of attraction she'd felt from the time he showed up at Saint Victoria Hospital. Surely not. Even she hadn't been sure of what she was feeling. "Okay."

"Do you want to see the rest of the clinic?"

"I'd love to." And for once she meant it.

By the time they reached the wing with the hotel, Sasha's senses were swimming. If The Island Clinic had been here when she'd been ready for her residency, she could have probably done it here. And then stayed here to work afterward. But she'd learned a lot at Beth Israel and wouldn't trade that experience for the world. Or her time at Harvard, even if it had resulted in a broken heart and a vow to never be duped so easily again.

In reality, she hadn't been duped so much as dumped by a man who'd placed a lot less value on their relationship than she had. He was rich enough to have women standing in line to have a chance with him. She wasn't sure why she'd thought she was any more special than those others. Except the fact that she'd been young and naive of the way things worked in Austin's sphere.

He'd seemed so caring. So willing to take on the

world. At least at first. But all his talk of coming to Saint Victoria had been just that. Talk.

The experience had left her cynical and untrusting, painting everyone with the paint dipped from her ex's bucket.

Including Nate? Almost certainly, since she'd avoided him like the plague for the last three years.

"Lydia said Room 201 is vacant."

"Sorry?"

He frowned. "I was going to show you one of the rooms."

"Oh, of course."

She was being ridiculous. What had she thought he meant? That he was taking her there for reasons other than showing her around?

No, she'd learned the hard way that she was nothing special. Nate could have his choice of sleeping partners.

And given the chance, would he choose to sleep with…?

No. He wouldn't. And neither would she.

She followed him down a hallway painted in muted greens with pendant lights that were modern, but elegant. Her shoes sank into luxurious carpet, her toes curling as they wondered what it would feel like on her bare feet.

Decadent.

Just like the clinic's founder.

Even her *manman*, who believed in simple tile that was easy to clean, would be amazed at how this felt. "Do you rent rooms to tourists, as well?"

"No. The island already has a hotel that does that. I wouldn't want to take business from them. This is just for patients and their families."

"I see." She mentally ticked another box on the list of things that surprised her. "Do you have enough patients to fill this up?"

"At times. But it's not something we're aiming for. For the most part our patients have come to us as a result of word of mouth. Or if they hear about the gala and attend. We do house attendees here, if they choose to go that route. It's one of the few times we're at capacity."

"I can imagine."

They found Room 201, and Nate again used his key card to open the door. "Does that get you in anywhere you want?"

He glanced at her, that same crazy half smile curving his lips. "No. Not anywhere."

Something about the way he said that made her shiver. Her toes curled again, and this time, it had nothing to do with the carpet.

He pushed the door open and motioned her to precede him. She did and was surprised when he didn't shut the door behind them. She was grateful, though, since her thoughts had been ricocheting into some pretty questionable territory.

The room was furnished with the same deep carpeting. Two large beds, covered in what looked like down comforters, were housed in a surprisingly large space. The air conditioning was set cooler than what she was used to, but if it was true that they had A-list patients, they would probably expect no less—especially with those warm bed coverings.

He didn't say anything, so Sasha went over to the window and looked out. The room had a spectacular view of the sea and the beach. There was no sign of the man who'd been there when they'd arrived. Was he back in his hotel room with his family? Or were they with Bill?

She didn't even know if that was the same man Nate had been referring to.

"This is gorgeous."

"Yes. I agree."

His voice was a little closer than it had been. And for a second time, she was glad that door had been left open. Not because she was afraid he might try something, but because she was afraid she might lose sight of what lay outside that room. Because in here, everything felt magical. Unreal. As if fairy tales might actually exist in real life.

She'd thought that once before. But it had turned out to be a lie.

"Sometimes you don't realize how things look to people who aren't from here. But this view… It's like something out of a magazine."

"Saint Victoria is beautiful. It's easy to become blind to the beauty around us, when we see it day after day."

"Yes. It is." She glanced back to see him watching her. "Is it okay if I go out onto the balcony?"

"Yes. Of course."

She unlocked the door with fingers that were shaking slightly. Because of him? Or the view? Maybe a little of both.

The balmy sea breeze slid over her face, beckoning her closer. Going over to the rail, she laid her arms on the black ironwork. The scent of salt and all that lived in the water was intoxicating. She leaned her head back and breathed deeply. She could only imagine the battle between worry and being bewitched by this locale families might experience. Maybe even Bill's son. This would be the perfect place to meditate. To relish being alive. Nate came beside her and leaned a hip on the railing as he turned to look at her. "It's a nice spot, isn't it?"

"I think nice might be the understatement of the year. It's amazing. I'm so glad The Island Clinic was able to build here."

She was surprised to find it was the truth.

"Really? I got the feeling you weren't all that thrilled with us being here."

"Dr. Edwards, I just—"

"Nate. Please."

The way he said it, made her heart twist. She really was being unreasonable about it. And in her attempt to maintain her distance, she could see that she'd probably come off as ridiculous.

"Okay. Nate…" Except saying his given name…out loud…made whatever she'd been about to say vanish. So she just stood there, taking in his casual clothing that was now rumpled in a way that was somehow wonderful. The hard lines of his body were more visible now, and she was having a difficult time looking away. Her gaze trailed up his face, noting there were dark circles under his eyes, probably from the stress of the day. She imagined he put in long hours most every day. A little far removed from the lap-of-luxury living she'd pictured him in over in this corner of the island.

"Not so hard, after all, was it?"

"W-what?" Had he read her thoughts?

"Saying my name."

Her senses went on high alert as an image of her whispering his name in an entirely different way scurried through her head, only to run away when she tried to catch it and banish it. Instead, the two beds in the room behind her seemed to taunt her, to remind her of how long it had been since she'd been with anyone.

She cleared her throat. "Maybe I was being a little silly when we met. I'd just heard stories…"

"Stories?" His frown was back. "Such as?"

Um, not happening. Because the words *delectable* and *delicious* had been interjected time and time again. "Nothing bad."

That line in his face played peekaboo. "I find that rather hard to believe."

"That nothing bad was said?"

He made a sound of assent. "Are you saying *you've* never had an unkind thing to say about me?"

Ugh. She'd had lots of unkind things to say. Patty had called her on it numerous times. But then again, her friend was a newlywed, still caught up in the early stages of love.

Her lips twitched. "Maybe you'll have to work on changing my mind."

"Is that a challenge… Sasha?"

The shock of hearing her name on his tongue washed over her like the waves of the sea. Warm. Sensual. Snaking up her calves, edging over her hips and making her nipples tighten.

Some dangerous part of her brain sent the word "Maybe" from her mouth before she could stop it.

And when his hand moved from the railing and slid up her forearm, she was powerless to stop from leaning toward him, her eyes closing.

"That's one challenge I might have to accept." The low words made the sensuous fog that was slowly enveloping her body thicken.

Kiss me!

Thank God she hadn't said the words aloud, but she'd definitely sent them out into the stratosphere. But his mouth didn't cover hers. After several agonizing seconds, she opened her eyes.

She found him staring at her, a muscle working in his jaw. Then he let go of her arm. "I'm sure you're tired, especially since this was supposed to be your day off."

"I—I..." Her mind scrambled for something witty to say. Something that didn't make her look as much of a fool as she felt. "I am. I should probably head home."

"You'll still come to the meeting?"

That was about the worst thing she could think of at the moment. Her reaction to him had been electric. Crazy. She'd been so sure he was going to kiss her.

But obviously that hadn't been on his mind. Or if it had, he'd thought better of it.

Smart on his part.

She took a step backward, only to find herself trapped by the metal portion of the balcony. Instead, Nate moved away, motioning for her to go through the doors where those two big beds sat. Beds that she'd seen herself writhing on moments earlier.

God. How stupid was she?

Hadn't she already fallen into that trap once before, of falling in love with someone with power and money?

Well, she wasn't going to do that again. From now on, her heart was going to be on guard against Nate's good looks. Against his low voice, against that seductive dimple in his cheek.

And most of all. She was going to be on guard against herself.

CHAPTER THREE

"BUT WHY DO you need to bring in an outside catering service? Why not use something from here on the island?"

Sasha could feel everyone's eyes on her the moment she spoke. She'd vowed to herself that she'd not say anything, especially since misreading his signals last night had made it hard to sleep. Hard to even contemplate attending tonight.

For the most part, she'd sat quietly. But she couldn't stop herself from asking the question.

Nate moved back to the podium, his eyes meeting hers. Something flashed in his gaze, and she wasn't sure if it was curiosity or irritation. "Okay, tell me what you would do."

"I would hire local DJs or musicians, contract food and services from here, play up what we have to offer. If you're hoping to bring in outside contributions, then you make this personal—memorable—rather than just another of a hundred fund-raisers that they've attended in the past."

His face remained passive, and she floundered a bit, wondering if maybe she was wrong. Nate had been doing this just fine, without her help for the last three years. And if what she'd seen of the clinic was anything to go by, then he'd been successful beyond anyone's wildest dreams. But he'd wanted her input, right? Had asked her to come. The least she could do was give him what he was asking for.

"And you know of a company here on the island that can provide services on a large scale? We're hoping to host between eight hundred to a thousand guests. I'd asked around before and from what I understood, there isn't a catering service that does events of this size."

She swallowed. Okay, so maybe she didn't know what she was talking about. And he was probably right about there not being a catering company that specialized in massive events. But surely it was just a matter of multiplying people, resources, waitstaff, etc. If what Nate said was true, and he was doing all of this for Saint Victoria, surely the folks here would want to be involved in that. It wasn't just a matter of having a telethon or television spot and expecting people to start pulling out their checkbooks. This should be a partnership between those on the island and those from the outside who wanted to help.

Nate shouldn't be carrying this on his own.

"Have you already contracted with an outside catering company?"

"We've had bids from several places. Tonight we were going to choose one of them."

So maybe it was too late. Maybe this was something that should be talked about for next year, not this one. But, her mom was one of the best organizers around and a super cook. If she asked her to round up people to cook and decorate, she had no doubt that Tessi James could get it done. She already made cakes for local weddings and food for several restaurants. If you got five or ten people like her, they could easily cover that kind of project. And if Nate rejected her idea outright? Well then, her opinion of him would drop back to what it had originally been: a rich man who had the money to throw at things, like caterers and fancy accoutrements, but didn't want to actually roll his sleeves up and work alongside everyone else.

And maybe she could get her weird attraction to him back under control.

Except he'd worked beside her at Saint Victoria Hospital to save Bill Waddel's life.

That gave her the courage to speak up yet again. "What if we could pull together a team from here on the island to do that? The caterers are going to decorate, as well?"

"Yes. They would bring in all of their own equipment and china."

China. Okay, so she hadn't thought about that. Enough for eight hundred to a thousand people?

She licked her lips. "Would it be possible to put off making the decision for a couple more days? I know someone who I think could organize something on this scale."

Nate crossed his arms over his chest. "You do? Can I have a name?"

Okay, it was now or never. And he certainly had a right to know. She only hoped he didn't see this as her wanting to throw business her mother's way. In actuality, she needed to ask her mom before she committed her to something, which was why she'd asked for a couple of days. "Tessi James."

Murmurs went up around the room, and she glanced

around to see nods and smiles from some of the folks from Saint Victoria Hospital. Many of them knew her mother from catering their own baby showers, weddings and family celebrations.

Nate's eyes were scanning the room, as well. "I see some of you know who this person is and…" His gaze swung back to her. "Tessi James. Would she happen to be any relation to you, Dr. *James*?"

Oh, this was exactly what she'd been afraid of. "Yes, she's my mom. But…" She turned to those in attendance. "How many of you have used my mom for your events?"

Hands lifted from all over the group. Probably twenty people.

"I see." Nate addressed Sasha again. "And you think she could pull off a formal event for this many people?"

He uncrossed his arms, his hands dropping to land on hips that were far too lean for comfort. Hips she'd imagined moving over hers on one of those hotel beds. His fingers tightened and her mouth went dry as shocking scenes of those hands closing on her flesh strobed through her head in snatches that were erotic beyond belief. She lost her train of thought for several scary seconds.

Clearing her throat, she managed to find her voice again. "It…um…depends what you mean by formal. If you're talking formal by Saint Victoria standards, then yes. But that might not look like what you're used to." She heaved a breath and forced her eyes back to his face. "I would venture to say, however, that it will be memorable and special…and it won't embarrass you."

Nate's brows went up. "That never even crossed my

mind. I was merely talking numbers, not whether or not your mother was capable of hosting an event."

"Which is why I'd like a day or two to talk to her. To talk to you, to see what you've done in the past and what you're hoping to accomplish at this year's event."

Was she crazy? She actually wanted to meet with him…alone? After last night? After the thoughts she'd just had about him?

And by committing her mom to having a part in the planning process, she'd committed herself to meeting with him on more occasions. So much for guarding her heart.

"Okay, let's put it to a vote. If you would like to explore keeping the catering local, raise your hands."

Every hand in the room went up, even people she didn't recognize, who probably worked here at The Island Clinic, most of whom had been brought in from other countries.

Her chest tightened, and her attitude took another slight shift.

"It seems it's unanimous. I'll give you three days to explore this avenue. But I'd like to meet with you after we're done here to discuss the particulars, okay?"

The way he said that made her shiver. She wasn't sure if he was angry or amenable to her suggestion. But she guessed she would find out soon enough.

Nate had been at Saint Victoria Hospital again today, so he had to be exhausted. She hadn't worked with him, this time, but she had caught glimpses of him every so often. She'd been relieved to be away from him. That encounter in the hotel room had been…

Fabulously sexy. If they'd actually kissed, maybe she could have put it behind her and moved on. As it was, she was picturing him doing a lot more than just kissing her.

But she knew how easily things could go from fabulous to horrifying, so she was better off not having any of those thoughts come to fruition.

He was waiting for her response. So she said the only thing she could think of. "Yes, of course."

While the meeting continued, revolving around timing and guest accommodations, she sent a quick text to her mom.

Hey, how do you feel about getting a catering crew together to serve one thousand people? Formal, islander style.

There was a pause, then her phone vibrated.

When?

Ha! Her mom had not batted an eye. Just like Sasha had suspected. Her fingers moved over the phone's keypad.

About a month away.

Let me check with some people and look at my calendar, but I think it's doable. When do you need an answer?

After Sasha's dad died, her mom had thrown herself into her little business, and had made a name for herself in terms of catering and party planning and cake decorating.

In just a couple of days. It's for The Island Clinic's yearly gala.

I'll get right on it and have an answer by Monday, if you can get me the details.

Whew. Sasha had wondered if she'd opened her big mouth before engaging her brain…which she had, but her mom was covering her back. I'll text you when I get home and can come by the house tomorrow, if that's okay.

She had the day off, although if the hospital got too busy, she was willing to work through it. There was no word yet on when Dr. Warren would be back to work. Hopefully his family member was doing better.

See you then. Mwen renmen ou.

Love you too, Mom!

The meeting dismissed soon afterward, with people going their separate ways. Patty Cohen sidled up to her. "Good idea suggesting your mom head up the catering. Will she do it, do you think?"

Sasha laughed. "I was being bad and texting her during part of the meeting. If her calendar is clear, and she can get enough help, I think she'll agree to do it."

"That's really great. And I'm glad you decided to come to the meeting, for once." The exasperated face Patty made was totally fake.

Her friend had been trying to coax her to be more involved with things that went on at The Island Clinic for quite a while and hadn't understood why Sasha was so resistant to the idea. Or why she'd taken a dislike to its chief of staff.

Well, even Sasha couldn't understand it. It probably had something to do with Austin and the pain he'd inflicted on her. Five years of dating, and just when she'd been expecting a marriage proposal, she'd gotten a breakup text instead, saying he'd decided to go on staff at a large New York hospital.

He'd had the audacity to conclude with an invitation for her to *drop by*, if she were ever in New York. They could get together for drinks. She was pretty sure she knew what the invitation entailed: sex with no strings attached. So much for his talk of coming to Saint Victoria to work.

It was the first time she'd realized how big a rift there was between her and some of her wealthier classmates. And it had been just in time for her to leave for Beth Israel. Everything about her experience at Harvard had been tainted by what Austin had done.

It had probably also tainted her view of Nate and his clinic.

"I'm glad I came too."

Patty took a step back. "Looks like you're being paged, and Dax is waiting for me at home, so I'm going to head out. We need to have lunch. It feels like we haven't gotten together in ages."

Her friend's whirlwind romance with an old flame had been the talk of Saint Victoria Hospital. But from the look of it, her friend was deliriously happy. And she was genuinely glad for them both.

She glanced to the side to see that Nate was standing a short distance away, waiting for her.

"It's been busy with Marcus gone. Hopefully he'll be

back soon. But yes, let's plan lunch once my schedule clears out a bit." She gave Patty a quick hug and then said goodbye, moving toward Nate.

She threw him an apologetic look. "I hope I didn't mess anything up with my suggestion. And really, I probably had no right to make it, since I haven't been to any of the other meetings. Or any of the galas."

"It's why I asked you to come. I did see you texting during the last part of it."

So he had noticed. "Sorry, I was texting my mom. If there wasn't any possibility she could do it, I was going to withdraw the idea."

"I thought that might be it. It was a good idea, and I'm not sure why I didn't check any further when I was told there wasn't a caterer large enough to handle it."

Because he knew one way of doing things, and it was hard to think of what you didn't know. She was pretty sure it really had been just an oversight, rather than a snub. "What you don't know, you don't know."

"Thanks for that. I never want to seem like a bulldozer coming in and running over people." He tilted his head. "And I somehow get the idea that's what you've thought of me."

Time to tread lightly. "Maybe. I'm hoping I was wrong about you."

His mouth quirked. "I'm hoping you were wrong too." He glanced at the phone in her hand. "So what did she say? Your mom, I mean?"

"She's going to check with some folks and said she'd have an answer to me by Monday."

"Good. I set another meeting for Tuesday. Can you have some ideas back to me before then?"

"How about if I bring her in to meet with you that morning, if she's free?"

He nodded. "She can do it that quickly?"

Sasha laughed. "You might not be a bulldozer, but my mom has been known to flatten anyone who gets in her way."

"In that case, remind me never to stand in her path. Seriously, though, it won't leave her much time to get a menu and plans in place. Can she do the cutlery and so forth?"

"I think so. I'll need to know exactly what she needs, if you have time to give me a rundown."

"Yes, let's go back to my office. Most of the paperwork is in there, and they need to clean the conference room."

Sasha turned and noted there were people already stacking chairs and picking up discarded coffee cups. "Oh, of course."

A frisson of excitement went through her as she followed Nate down the hallway. She hoped it was due to the idea of helping plan a small part of the gala, but she was pretty sure most of it had to do with the man himself. She'd dreamed about that almost kiss last night. Except it hadn't stopped at a kiss. It had turned hot and wet and wicked. Her face heated and she was glad, very glad, he wasn't looking at her right now.

At the very end of the hallway, Nate used his key card to open a door on the right and stood back to let her move past him. She walked in, and frowned, all thoughts of her dream disappearing. His office was huge, with a long leather sofa and seating area off to the left, and a heavy wooden desk and matching leather chairs to the right.

The carpet was the same thick pile as what she'd seen in the hotel and cushioned her every step. Thank God, because her feet were killing her.

He must have noticed her reaction, because he moved around to grab some file folders from the desk and motioned her toward the seating area. "I meet with people in here all the time."

She could imagine he did. How better to coax checkbooks to open than to meet them in a place where things looked like they did in their own fancy offices.

But it also was a reminder of how different they were. Of how alike he and Austin were. Both presented themselves as wealthy philanthropists. Austin's was just a thin, shiny layer that didn't go more than skin deep. And Nate's? Well, the jury was still out on that.

The bottom line was, she and Nate were from two different worlds, and she'd better stop dreaming about the man before she did something stupid. Or got hurt all over again. So she paid careful attention to the things in the room. Custom artwork that looked to be done by local artisans decorated the walls. On a set of shelves behind the sofa were colorful bottles that probably contained various types of liquor.

As if reading her thoughts, he said, "Would you like something to drink?"

Suddenly she did. And since she'd come to the clinic via the shuttle, she'd be taking it back home again, which meant she wouldn't have to drive. It also made her realize the vehicle would probably be making that trip just for her. "I hate to ask the shuttle to come back—"

"I'll take you back to the hospital. Or you can stay in one of the guest rooms here."

Like in Room 201? The one he'd shown her yesterday? No. She wouldn't be doing that. "I'd appreciate the ride, if that's okay."

"I am the one who asked you to stay after class, so it's the least I can do."

That made her smile. "I was the one who volunteered up my mom. But thank you. And I'd like a glass of red wine, if you have it." It had been a long day, and she could use something to help her unwind a bit.

"I do." He went over to the seating area and reached into a small glass-fronted refrigerator. Ah, a wine cooler.

While he retrieved a footed glass and a tumbler and fixed their drinks, she walked around the office. Her big toe twinged as it hit the end of her shoe. These were coming off as soon as she got home.

Something on a shelf behind his desk caught her eye. Something that didn't match the rest of the sumptuous surroundings. The discomfort in her feet disappeared as she moved closer.

A small cloth doll sat on top of a book that had been tipped on its side. Its hair was cut from pieces of brown yarn and stuck up in all directions, and the undyed muslin of the body and dress were simple. It looked like a doll that some of the moms on the island fashioned for their daughters. She couldn't picture him buying something like this.

She studied it. The facial features were embroidered, and the black shoes were stitched from felt. There were smudges of what looked like dirt here and there and the thread on one of the shoes was fraying. Her eyes widened. This doll had been played with, not purchased from one of the island's tourist shops.

She realized that the clinking of glassware had stopped and when she looked at Nate, she saw he was watching her with a glass of amber liquid in his hand. He took a sip of it. Then another.

"This is an interesting doll. Did you know that mothers here sometimes make these for their daughters? I had one when I was younger. I probably still have it somewhere, in fact."

"Yes. I knew." He took another sip of his drink and came over to her with the glass of wine. His eyes were not on the doll. They were on something off to the side.

Her curiosity got the best of her. "Where did you get it?"

A muscle worked in his cheek, looking much like it had last night. A sense of foreboding came over her, and Sasha thought for a minute he wasn't going to answer her question. Then he said, "It was given to me. Let's go talk about the gala, shall we?" His hand gestured toward the sofa on the other side of the room.

He'd made it about as plain as it could be. He didn't want to talk about the doll. But why? Well, that was his prerogative, and this time, she wasn't going to butt in where she wasn't welcome. With one last glance at the lonely figure on the shelf, she took her wine and walked back over to the couch.

People had asked Nate about Marie's doll before, and he'd always responded to them without hesitation. But when he'd noticed Sasha studying it, a rock had suddenly gathered in the pit of his stomach. It was the last thing he'd wanted to talk about after the meeting about a glitzy fund-raising gala, even though a portion of the money would go toward awareness of schistosomiasis, including water testing and prevention, as well as antibody tests and treatment.

So he'd snatched at the excuse to talk about something else. Anything else. But the second Sasha's face had closed in on itself, he knew he'd been blunt. Too blunt. But unless he wanted to go into a full-scale explanation, it was too late to rectify his mistake.

She sat on the couch, stiff and unyielding, and held her phone tightly in her hands. "So tell me about the meals you've had in the past."

He hesitated, the need to confide in her sneaking up on him again. He shook his head to rid himself of the impulse. Sitting in the chair across from her, he opened one of the file folders he'd brought over. In it were pictures from the past three galas. All three of them very different, but each of them elegant in its own way.

"These are shots from our other events. It doesn't have to look exactly like these though."

Sasha took the pictures from him and studied them, turning some of them sideways when the perspective changed. A movement caught his eye. She was methodically raising the heel of her right foot in and out of her shoe. She lifted it for a second or two before wiggling it back down. Up again, then pushing it back down.

Her feet hurt. She'd probably been in those shoes all day, and now he'd asked her to stay in them even longer. Well, technically she'd asked to speak with him, but still…

"Sasha." He waited for her to look up before he finished. Her dark eyes met his, a question in their depths. "You can take your shoes off, if you'd like. Your feet look like they're bothering you."

Her nose squinched up in a way that made his stomach twist. "I was trying to be subtle, but yes, they're new and it was stupid of me to have worn them today."

"No one will see you in here." He smiled. "It will be our little secret."

She blinked, eyes holding his. "Are you sure?"

"Sure that it will be a secret?" He nodded at the sheaf in her hands. "I promise it won't end up in that file folder."

Sasha laughed and the sound tickled something in his chest, and he let the weight of Marie and that doll slide away. At least for a few minutes.

"Okay, then, as long as you promise."

"I do."

She slid her feet from the shoes, using one to push the footwear to the side. Then she let them sink into the carpet, her toes actually curling into it and tightening on the fibers. Parts down low tightened, flickered to life.

Damn. Time to talk about something else.

Before he could, though, Sasha sighed. "Thank you. This feels heavenly."

Yes, it did. And it had nothing to do with the carpet. "I've been known to stretch out on it, when my back is hurting."

Her brows went up. "You have back problems?"

"Just the normal twinges from age." He'd fallen from a swing set as a child and every once in a while his L2 vertebra ached.

"Age…righ-h-ht."

The way she drew the word out forced a laugh from him. "It's either blame age or stupidity for it."

"Stupidity?"

"Let's just say jumping from a swing into a mud puddle doesn't always go as planned. It's all in the landing. And this one wasn't good."

"Ouch." Her head tilted. "I can't picture you swinging."

For some reason the last word caught his attention in a totally inappropriate way. A funny retort came to mind, only she might not find it nearly as funny. "For good reason. The only place I swing nowadays is on my hammock."

"Hammock? You have one?"

"I do. The catering team actually borrowed it for one of the galas. There should be a picture in there somewhere."

He moved to the couch, anxious to shift his thoughts in another direction. She handed him the snapshots and he sifted through them, finding the one he was looking for. "Here."

Sasha leaned closer to look at it to study the scene. Rough wooden pillars that were made to look like tree trunks boasted snaking vines and twinkle lights. His hammock was strung between two of them, layered with pillows and some kind of throw blanket.

"I love that. Something like this would be very doable for my mom. It wouldn't look exactly like this, obviously, but a tropical theme would really fit with Saint Victoria."

"Yes, I think this was my favorite gala."

"I can see why."

Her toes shifted in the carpet yet again, sending a sudden shaft of heat through his midsection. Her toenails were bare of polish and looked clean and natural. She was completely different from Tara. But then again, his former girlfriend had to maintain a polished appearance for his parents' clinic.

Not that Sasha lacked polished. She just didn't need it. There was a beauty about her that…

He cleared his throat. "So you think your mom can do this?"

"I don't *think* she can. I know she can. She's amazing."

Her mom wasn't the only one who was amazing.

Sasha's eyes came up, and he realized he hadn't responded to her statement. But right now, he wasn't sure he could come up with anything coherent. "Are you worried, Nate?"

He was. But it had nothing to do with the gala and everything to do with her. And the crazy jolt he always got when she said his name. Maybe it was because she'd made such a big deal about not using it. But, more likely, it was the way her velvety tones wrapped around the sounds, holding on to them before releasing them into the air.

"No." He paused. "Are you?"

Her thumb brushed across the glossy surface of one of the prints. "I…wasn't."

"Until now?"

She nodded, the tip of her tongue coming out to moisten her lips. That's when he knew. She felt the change in atmosphere, just like he had. It was the same sensation he'd gotten on the balcony last night.

Maybe it would keep happening every time they were in a room together. Unless he did something radical about it. Something to quench the sparks that were starting to sting the lining of his chest.

Maybe one kiss would put it behind him, just like

it had with any other woman he'd been with since he'd broken things off with Tara.

Or maybe it would be like that accident on the swing, where what he'd thought would happen when he jumped ended up turning into something he'd never do again.

Wasn't that the same thing? Either way, he'd try it once and be done with it.

He set down the picture he was still holding in his hand, and took the ones she had. Then he stood to his feet, reaching for her hand.

When she placed her fingers on his palm, it was as if an electric current surged through him, holding him fast in its grip. It was there when he closed his fingers around hers. It was there when he slowly pulled her to her feet.

And it was still there when his palms cupped her face, his thumbs sliding over it in a way that mimicked what she'd done with the photo a few minutes ago.

Suddenly he realized this was nothing like jumping from a swing and misjudging his landing. This was going to be far more dangerous. But like that foolish decision to leap out into the air, it was already too late to reconnect with the swing. All he could do was sail into space, and hope he survived the fall.

CHAPTER FOUR

His face was inches from hers. But he wasn't moving any closer. Not so his fingers, which were brushing across her skin in a way that drove her wild.

Please, please don't pull away this time.

The second his gaze landed on her, she shuddered. The molten depths of his pupils said this was nothing like last time.

"I just needed to see," he muttered. "Just needed to know…"

Then his mouth was on hers, and her world turned inside out.

She wasn't sure how this had happened. One moment they'd been talking about the gala. But when he'd come to sit next to her, her heart had started drumming in her chest as fear and anticipation swirled to life inside her. Fear that this was going to end up like last night. But anticipation that it might not. Maybe this time…

And it was better than even her sexiest dream. His mouth was plastered to hers as if he couldn't get enough. And the feel of it was shattering and amazing all at once.

His hand sank into her hair, his fingers closing around it. But it wasn't to control. It was as if he needed to anchor himself somehow. And she relished it, relished the reality of his arms around her.

His lips left her mouth, trailing to her ear, nipping at the lobe and making her shiver.

"Nate…" The whispered word came out before she could stop it. But he'd talked about lying on the floor, and right now, the carpeting seemed so inviting. How easy would it be to just sink down and have him follow her. Cover her body with his…

Images flooded her mind, causing parts of her to soften in readiness.

Or there was the couch.

Her hand went to the back of his head, drawing him back to her mouth. She opened, and his tongue accepted her silent invitation, sliding in and filling her, making her whimper with need.

A sudden loud knock at the door shocked her into immobility. Then she realized what it was and wheeled backward, their mouths coming apart, hand in her hair sliding free.

The back of her hand went to her mouth, trying to yank her brain back from wherever she'd left it.

His eyes speared hers. "Hell, sorry, Sasha. I…"

"Answer it."

The reality was, if he said anything to her right now, she was likely to burst into tears.

Giving her one last glance, he strode over to his desk, standing behind it before he told whoever it was to come in.

The door opened and a face she didn't recognize glanced her way for a second before looking back at Nate.

"We have a chopper coming in bringing a patient

who has severe injuries to his arm and leg after being pulled into a piece of machinery. The leg was almost severed...he's lost a lot of blood and right now and Dr. Sizer is on vacation, so—"

"I'm on my way. Get him as stable as you can and grab an operating room."

"Thanks."

The man withdrew.

"Sorry, Sasha, I need to—"

"I'm coming with you. I'm a surgeon and you might need some help." The temptation to just fade away into the night was strong, but she wasn't going to leave a patient in need. Besides, Nate was her ride home.

And that kiss? Not something she was going to think about right now.

He hesitated for a minute before nodding and saying, "Thank you."

It was then that she realized that her feet were still bare and her shoes were somewhere behind her. God! Hopefully the man at the door had been too busy to notice, or too concerned about the patient to care.

And right now, that's exactly what she needed to be. Too concerned to care.

Nate glanced at Sasha as she stuffed her feet back into her shoes, remembering they were hurting her. But he really did need the help. Grant Sizer was their trauma surgeon and this was his field. But Nate had dealt with some pretty traumatic injuries.

They went down in the elevator and out onto the surgical floor.

"Operating room three," one of the nurses called out as they hurried by.

Side by side they scrubbed in at adjoining sinks. Side by side they entered the room and allowed two surgical nurses to glove them up.

Nate went over to the table and took over from the ER doctor who had been overseeing the process of keeping the man alive.

"What have we got?"

"Severe spiral lacerations to the right arm, and the right leg is basically held together by the bone. Much of the soft tissue has been sliced all the way through. We've clamped the arteries." He looked at him. "We're going to need several hands on deck for this one."

He glanced at the IV pole next to the man's head, where a pint of blood was already hung and dripping.

"Dr. James is a surgeon from Saint Victoria Hospital. If you can find me a microsurgeon, we'll tag team it."

"I've got one on call now."

"Good." He glanced at Sasha. "Can you take a look at the arm, while I tackle the leg?"

"Of course."

"We'll need a couple of sets of instruments."

One of the nurses stepped forward. "We're ready for you. We have other surgical nurses on standby if needed."

His hospital had always run like clockwork and this was one of those times that he was extremely grateful it did.

He moved to the patient's leg and assessed the injuries. It was bad. And just like the other doctor had said. There were huge slashes in the midthigh through which pearly bone was visible. The bone had probably prevented the limb from being completely severed. He could handle reattaching the large swaths of muscle and skin, if they could get the microsurgeon to work on the smaller vessels and nerves.

"How are you up there?"

Sasha glanced up at him, her eyes sharp and aware. Thank God they'd barely had any alcohol. That kiss had interrupted all of that. Strange that he should be grateful for something that never should have happened, but he was.

"Several deep cuts, but they haven't reached the bone. Lots of work to piece everything back together, but I can do it."

Thank God she'd stayed. "Thanks, Sasha. Go ahead and start."

She nodded at him, her eyes crinkling above her mask as she smiled. "I already have."

It was then that he noticed the needle and suture material in her hand.

Time passed in a way that was surreal whenever he was in surgery. It both dragged and sped by as he sutured by rote. The microsurgeon had arrived within fifteen minutes of being called and they both worked on different sections with the other surgeon doing the finer work and Nate doing the bulkier repairs. Periodically he glanced up at Sasha and saw her eyes fixed on what she was doing, the concentration on her face intense as she worked silently, calling out for different instruments periodically.

As he put the last suture in place, he glanced up at the clock and saw six hours had gone by.

And Sasha was nowhere to be seen. The arm was neatly bandaged, so she'd finished it all by herself.

They woke the patient up, and thankfully he regained consciousness fairly quickly. After losing almost half of his blood volume, there'd been the fear of brain damage. But he responded to simple questions with a nod. Then he was wheeled away into recovery.

Ted Daly, the microsurgeon, clapped him on the back. "Good work. I think we saved his leg. I didn't even see his arm. How bad was it?"

"Not nearly as bad as what we had, from what Dr. James said."

Ted glanced his way. "Did she already leave?"

"I'm not sure. She's from Saint Victoria Hospital, came here for the meeting on the gala."

"Right. I thought I recognized her. I liked her ideas of using local businesses."

"Yes, so did I." He mused, glad that everyone seemed positive about those suggestions. But right now, he was wondering where she'd gone. Had she asked for the shuttle to come after all?

He didn't want her to leave without trying to figure out what had happened between them in his office. Or at least figure out where to go from here. How to backtrack and not let this interfere with their working relationship, since with her mom's involvement in the gala there was bound to be some overlap.

"Well, I'm headed home again. If you see Dr. James before I do, please thank her. She probably saved us a couple more hours of work tonight."

If he saw her before Ted did? Was the man going to seek her out?

And if he did? It should mean nothing to him. Nothing at all.

"I will. See you tomorrow."

Ted's brows went up. "I think you mean today."

The man was right. It was almost four in the morning. "Right. Go home and try to get some sleep."

"You, as well. See you."

With that, they parted ways, both stripping off their PPE and heading out the doors.

Nate turned toward the nurses' desk to ask if they'd seen Sasha, passing the waiting room as he did. He glanced over there just as he went by, then backtracked when he saw a familiar profile. She had her arm draped over the back of the chair next to her and her head rested in the crook of her elbow. He thought at first she was asleep, but she lifted her head and looked at him.

"How is he?"

"He woke up. Seems conscious. We won't know fully about his leg for a couple of days, but it pinkened up once the blood flow was restored to it."

"That's good. I wondered."

"Ted asked me to thank you. I'll add my thanks to his. The repairs to his arm went okay?"

"Yes. The damage looked worse than it actually was once I started working."

Her feet were out of her shoes again.

"How are they?"

She looked up at him. "Sorry?"

"Your feet. They were hurting before, and that was before you stood on them for six more hours."

"They'll survive." Her teeth came down on her lower lip. "I hate to ask, but would it be okay if I stayed in the hotel? The thought of getting up and walking on them again isn't thrilling, and I hate to ask you to drive forty-five minutes one way."

"Of course. Do you have to be at the hospital this morning?"

"No, not until the afternoon."

"Okay, let's get you checked in and you can get some sleep. And I'll take you home sometime after lunch."

She sighed. "Thank you."

"No, Sasha. Thank you. We'll discuss the other… stuff after we've both gotten some rest."

Her glance met his before skipping away. "I appreciate that."

She put her shoes on yet again, wincing this time as she did so before getting to her feet. "I'm ready. Can I just ask one thing?"

"Sure."

"Can you ask for a room other than 201?"

Room 201? Oh, hell, it was where they'd stood on the balcony. The first time he realized he wanted to kiss her. That time he'd been able to take a step back.

He wasn't going to acknowledge he knew what she was talking about though. Instead, he simply said, "Sure. That won't be a problem."

Then without another word he turned and led the way to the elevator, which would take them to the ground floor. And the hotel.

CHAPTER FIVE

HE WAS SUPPOSED to meet with Tessi James and Sasha today and talk about the possibility of catering it locally. He glanced at the shelf where Marie's doll was and was tempted to take it down and stuff it in a drawer. It was probably what had led to that ill-fated kiss. Something that never should have happened. But to do so felt sacrilegious, almost—as if protecting his own comfort was more important than the reality of what had happened to that little girl.

And why hadn't he shared its meaning with Sasha? Maybe it was just embarrassment that he hadn't been able to recognize what was wrong with the child. But it truly had been too late, even if he'd figured it out. Her liver had failed and there was no bringing her back from it.

So he left the doll where it was, and waited for the knock on his door that would signal Tessi's arrival. Five minutes after the appointed meeting time, he glanced at his phone with a frown. They were late. Had Tessi decided it was too big a project to take on? Had Sasha told her what had happened between them and talked her into backing out? Hell, why hadn't he talked to her about what had happened?

Because he hadn't had the chance. She'd disappeared before he'd even gotten back to the hospital. The hotel said she'd left at nine that morning, taking the shuttle back on one of its regularly scheduled trips.

So maybe neither Tessi nor Sasha was coming. Thankfully, he hadn't yet responded to any of the prospective caterers from the States.

As he was looking at his text messages, the phone in his hand rang, and he almost dropped the thing.

Dammit! What is wrong with you? Shaking his head and sighing, he pressed the button to answer. "Nate Edwards here."

"I'm sorry, Dr. Edwards, but I think your appointment is here."

"Good. Send them up, please."

"Um…there are like twenty people here. Do you want them all in your office?"

He blinked. Glanced at his office. He could hold ten people easily in here, but twenty? He had no idea anyone other than Tessi and Sasha were coming. "Can you direct them to the conference room at the hotel, if nothing is scheduled there?"

A few seconds went by. "I don't see anything. Okay, I'll send them over."

Marie's doll wouldn't be an issue after all. Nor would meeting Sasha in a place he'd made such a huge mistake. He had never kissed a colleague here or anywhere else. And he was going to make sure his little lapse of judgement never happened again. Still, he couldn't help but ask. "Is Sasha James with them?"

"I'm not sure who that is—"

"It's okay—I'll just meet them over there."

After shutting the door to his office, he made his

way over to the hotel wing and sure enough, there was a small crowd of people walking in that direction. And Sasha *was* with them. A weird sense of relief washed over him.

He unlocked the door and let them through, wrapping his fingers around Sasha's wrist to hold her back for a second. He realized that was a mistake when his fingers tingled from the contact. Hell, he'd thought the kiss might somehow satisfy whatever strange curiosity he'd had toward her. Evidently that wasn't so.

He forced out, "What's going on?"

"I'm as surprised as you are. But my mom thought you should meet the people who would be working with her on this project—if you decide to go that route. They're from small businesses all over Williamtown."

Not the time to have things out, though, so all he could do was make the best of it.

"I'm officially impressed. Can you make introductions?"

"Sure."

Her voice was stilted and formal, and he let go of her, his fingers curling in an effort to remove the sensation. But it was still there, along with a pressure in the center of his chest. The last thing he needed to deal with was his unusual reaction to her.

With her hair pulled back and small diamonds in her earlobes, she looked cool and chic and not at all affected by his touch.

Sasha led him over to a woman he immediately recognized as her mother. Tall and slender, the similarities between them were uncanny. If he didn't know any better, he'd say this was Sasha's sister rather than her mom. It gave him a glimpse of what she would look like in the future.

Not that it was something he needed to know.

"Mom, this is Dr. Edwards. Dr. Edwards, this is Tessi James."

"Call me Nate, please. Sasha does. Normally, that is." He wondered if their kiss had somehow set them back a few steps. Or maybe because of how abrupt he'd been in his answer over Marie's doll. Whatever it was, he missed hearing his name on her lips.

"Okay, Nate. Everyone calls me Tessi, so you might as well too."

He forced his attention away from the woman's daughter. "Great. So who have you brought with you today, Tessi?"

As the woman introduced each member of her entourage, Nate found his attention kept returning to Sasha, who was fidgeting next to him. Okay, maybe she wasn't as unaffected as he'd thought. Or worse, maybe that kiss had made things unbearably awkward for her. He could talk to her after this, and see if he could fix things. Or maybe take her out to lunch, depending on how long the meeting took. He wasn't sure why he felt the need to make things right, but the thought of things staying like they were... Well, he didn't like it. And he had no idea why.

"Nice to meet all of you. Let's pull some chairs into a circle, and you can tell me what you have in mind for the fund-raiser."

There were two florists, ten people from various food industries in Williamtown, a couple of people from janitorial services and the rest were a jumble of party planners, organizers and a company that provided plating and cutlery.

He hadn't been lying when he'd said he was impressed. When Sasha had said her mom cooked and made wedding cakes and the like, he'd had his doubts over whether she could handle an event of this size… but with all of these people? He could see it unfolding before his eyes. And they would probably save quite a bit of money by having everything sourced locally.

Tessi and her group had pictures on their phones of what they envisioned doing with the event.

"Wow. You pulled all of this together in this short a period of time?"

Tessi nodded. "Between us, we have decades of experience to draw from."

"Can you send these to me?" He gave the group his cell phone number. "With your permission I'll print some of these off and present them at the meeting tonight. If you're sure you're all available. Tessi, if you could come and represent your group and answer any questions…?"

"Yes, of course." She gave him a grin. "We've also drawn up a budget of expenses for you to look over."

"Yes, I'll be happy to."

They talked a bit more about the particulars. An hour later, he was convinced. And satisfied. He sent Sasha a smile and mouthed, "Thank you."

She smiled back and nodded.

They stood and Sasha hugged her mom and thanked the rest of the crew, telling her mom that she wanted to stay behind and talk to Dr. Edwards for a few minutes but would see her at home later this evening. Then they were gone.

Nate turned to her. "So we're back to Dr. Edwards and Dr. James, are we?"

Her mouth quirked to the side. "No, I just don't want my mom to get any funny ideas."

"Does she get ideas about all the men you're on a first-name basis with?"

"No, of course not, but we're not simply on first name…"

Her voice trailed away, reminding him that, like him, she probably didn't kiss every person she worked with. For some reason, that sent a burst of warmth through him. Although he remembered her talking to a male nurse at Saint Victoria Hospital, and at the time had wondered if there was something between the pair. But she wouldn't have kissed him the way she had, if that was the case. Right?

He decided maybe it was better if they didn't go back to his office after all. Especially after what had happened there. He could think of somewhere a whole lot safer.

Glancing down at her feet and seeing casual sandals that went with her long gauzy skirt, he asked. "Are your feet all recovered?"

She wiggled her toes. "Yep, as good as new."

"How do you feel about a walk on the beach then? We can talk as we go."

"Sure."

Was it his imagination, or did she seem relieved that he hadn't suggested his office?

Nate pushed through a nearby exit, guiding her over to the long boardwalk that led away from the hotel.

Strolling along it, she glanced at him. "So did you really like what they had to say?"

"Are you kidding? It's fantastic, better than I'd even hoped."

She smiled. "There's even a DJ here in town who can probably do the music, if that's something you'd be interested in."

"Yes. I'd love to talk with him or her." He looked out over the sea. "Your mom has quite a bit of influence here."

"I don't know that it's influence as much as having grown up with most of those people. It's a little different here than in Boston or New York or any of the big cities in the States. There are fewer people moving in and out, so friends and neighbors spend a lifetime getting to know each other."

He liked the thought of knowing a group of people that well. At least the idea of it. How well could you really know anyone? He'd grown up with his parents, only to discover how little he understood them. And how little they understood him.

Shaking away that thought, he came to the end of the boardwalk and stepped out onto the sand.

"You're going to ruin your shoes," she murmured.

He glanced down at his shiny black dress shoes. "They've been out here more than once. As long as you don't throw me into the water, we should be good."

"Throw you into the water? Really?" A lightness came into her voice that made him relax. Maybe they'd get through that incident in his office unscathed after all. She was really the most surprising woman. Some of the women he'd been with had been quick to try to get a second date, but Sasha hadn't done anything to indicate she wanted anything from him. Not a kiss. Not anything else.

Their eyes met. Got hung up. And he wondered if he was somehow wrong.

Then she stepped onto the beach and moved away from him. He stopped to strip his shoes and socks off, carrying them in one hand.

"You come out here often," she said.

"Why do you say that?"

"Your feet are as tanned as the rest of you."

Her assessment was right on target as far as him liking to be out here.

"I do sit and watch the ocean sometimes, but not here."

"Where? Another beach?"

"No, I'll show you. It's about a fifteen-minute trek, though, do you have time?"

"I do, actually."

They walked until they arrived at a sheltered cove that none of the hospital staff knew about. As far as Nate knew, he was the only person who ever came out here. It was around a curve and well hidden from anyone walking along the beach. "This is the spot."

Sasha moved closer to the water. "It's beautiful. I can see why you like to come out here." Lowering herself onto the sand, she kicked off her sandals and stretched her legs out in front of her, tossing her skirt over them. She'd polished her toes this time and the bright fuchsia drew his eyes toward the high arch of her foot— the smooth, silky-looking legs below the white fabric. She was gorgeous. And he was beginning to think her beauty really was more than skin deep. Working with her on the accident victim had shown him that she was skilled and caring, jumping in to help even when she could have left to go home.

The discovery made him uneasy. Because it put that kiss in a completely different light. And Nate liked categorizing things so that they fit neatly into the box he'd made for himself. Of things he did and didn't allow himself to think or do.

He was glad he'd suggested coming here rather than inviting her out to lunch like he'd planned to. The sound of the water lapping at the beach was soothing. And he didn't really want anyone to hear what he had to say.

"I think I owe you an apology."

"You do? About what?" Her head turned toward him, face registering her surprise. "And please don't say it was about the kiss. It was a mistake. I think we both realize that."

He pulled up short. Okay, she'd beat him to it. He should be elated. But instead, something made him change tack and pretend the kiss wasn't even important enough to discuss. "No, not about that. I was kind of short with you that night."

"You were? I don't remember you being short."

Was it possible he was mistaken? Or was she just saying that? Well, either way, he'd started down this path and he was going to see it through to the bitter end. And he realized it was true. He did want to explain why he'd acted the way he did.

"You asked about that doll on my shelf, and I cut you off."

"Ah. That. You had every right to. I was prying, even though I didn't mean to." She blinked, then a frown puckered her brow. "Oh! Do you have a daughter?"

Her glance went to his hand. Damn. "No. I'm not married. I certainly wouldn't have kissed you if I was. And I don't have any children, here or in the States."

Did she really think he was someone who would cheat on someone? That stung and he wasn't sure why.

"And… I'm prying again."

"No, you're not. Really." He just hadn't expected her to jump to that conclusion. "The doll belonged to a patient."

"And she gave it to you? How sweet. Those dolls are normally treasured possessions."

Yes. They were. This was going to be harder than he'd thought. "No. *She* didn't give it to me. Her parents did. Afterward."

She looked at him, head tilting. Then the softness of her face changed in an instant. "Oh, Nate, I'm so sorry. I had no idea."

"She was one of my patients when I was here with Medicine Around the World. It was after Hurricane Regan and was my first time on the island."

"That was a terrible time for Saint Victoria. So many businesses and lives wiped out. Parts of the island still haven't fully recovered. Was your patient injured in the hurricane?"

"No. At least that wasn't why her parents brought her to me. She had a persistent fever, was jaundiced and was very ill. Saint Victoria Hospital was in shambles at the time, and we only had rudimentary medical supplies with us. I treated her for hepatitis, but she just got worse. And the blood work I sent off didn't get back before she…"

Sasha's hand reached over and gripped his. "How awful. Did you find out what it was?"

"Yes. And that was the kicker. She had schistosomiasis."

She blinked, and there was a long pause while she stared at him. "God, Nate. That was *you*."

Confusion ran through him before a sense of horror kicked him in the gut. Were people talking about the foreign doctor who let a young child die?

Her hand squeezed his. "Not long after the hurricane, there was a campaign to test the water and try to find out where there were concentrations of the parasite. And doctors looked carefully at any case of swimmers' rash or symptoms of hepatitis or unexplained infections. They actually found a couple of children in a family with the chronic gastrointestinal form of schistosomiasis and were able to treat them with praziquantel. Both children lived. It's not as common in Saint Victoria as it is in some of the other tropical climates, but obviously it can kill. Even here." She leaned closer, and bumped his shoulder with hers. "You may not know it, but you're probably the reason those two kids are still alive."

Nate had actually sent his own money to the island anonymously asking it to be earmarked for the prevention and treatment of schistosomiasis.

"It was my first time out of the country as a doctor, and I'd never seen a case before. I always felt if I'd identified it earlier…"

"You couldn't have known and it would have been too late by then, anyway. Our island was struggling on a lot of different fronts at that time." Her fingers twined with his. "Believe me—her parents would not have given you that doll if they weren't extremely grateful to you. If they felt you hadn't done everything possible to save their child."

"I would have done almost anything to save her."

"I think you did everything you could have." She studied him. "What was her name?"

"Marie." A hard twinge went through his jaw, and he forced his teeth to unclench. He didn't often say her name out loud.

There was silence for a few seconds, then Sasha said, "I'm glad you kept her doll."

"It's a reminder. She's why I came back to Saint Victoria."

"I'm glad for that too." Her voice lowered. "Even if it was for those reasons."

Was she really? He'd gotten the idea she wasn't thrilled about him being there. Actually, she'd pretty much admitted it to him. And although he should have been able to let it roll off his back, her prickliness when they'd first met had bothered him. And he wasn't sure why.

Was she changing her mind about him? Maybe. They were back on a first-name basis again. And he felt better after confiding in her.

Just then a sound hit his ears and a rogue wave rushed toward them before he could warn her, sloshing over their legs and knocking Sasha flat on her back. She sputtered, and he went to yank her upright before realizing she wasn't struggling, she was laughing.

"*Bondye mwen*, what just happened?"

He leaned over her, chuckling at the look on her face. "*Bondye mwen*, indeed."

"Sorry, the language just slips out sometimes. You know what it means?"

"After three years, I should. Besides, *my God* kind of comes through in any language. And I like those little slipups." Maybe because he'd pretty much had that same thought. Only it hadn't been about the wave. It was about how she looked right now, with her hair plastered to her head and her skirt… Hell, the thing was almost transparent.

Her eyes widened and she sat up in a rush. "Oh, no. Your shoes."

"What about them?"

She waved her hand. "Well, one is here and one is… down there."

"Ah, hell." He leaped up, hearing her laughter as he jogged down to the low point of the water where his errant shoe was tumbling in the surf. He snatched it up, just as another wave crashed over his knees almost knocking him down. He looked up at where she was sitting and saw she'd made no move to stand up. She was holding her stomach as laughter poured out of her.

Suddenly, he felt carefree, loved that she could just get flattened by a wave and laugh about it rather than getting angry at her clothes being soaked. He tried to picture his mom in this kind of situation.

She definitely wouldn't have been doubled over in mirth.

Reaching her side, he grabbed his other shoe and then her sandals and threw them out of the sea's reach. Then he dropped back by her side. "So you find that funny, do you?"

"Yes. Very." The laughter came again. "If you could have seen yourself running toward the water, your pant legs dragging around your ankles. What kind of chief of staff are you, anyway?"

"A very wet one. I could ask the same of you." He leaned closer, murmuring, "What kind of doctor are you?"

The question hung in the air for a few seconds, before she said, "The kind who can laugh at herself."

"Really? It seems you were laughing more at me, than at yourself."

Her brows went up. "And you have a problem with that?"

"No. No problem at all." In fact, he liked it. Very, very much.

This time the kiss wasn't impulsive. Wasn't a spur-of-the-moment thing. He'd thought about it. Thought about all the reasons why it was a bad idea. And then Nate Edwards leaned over and did it anyway.

It was even better this time. The kiss. The setting.

The laughter.

She hadn't laughed that hard with a man in…well, forever.

It made having his mouth on hers that much sweeter.

He laid her back in the sand and followed her down, and right now she didn't care if the water rushed up and covered her head. If that happened, she would keep on kissing him for as long as she could hold her breath.

The heat of his body penetrated her wet clothes, her skin, reaching the innermost part of her. Sasha did not kiss men she barely knew. But here she was, rushing into uncharted territory, just like that wave that had crashed into them.

Only this was more powerful than that wave. And unlike Nate's shoe, it was unlikely she was going to catch herself before she tumbled into something even more dangerous. Something that wouldn't be as easy to pull free from.

But right now, she just didn't care.

Wrapping her arms around his neck, she pulled him

closer, her tongue touching his, tasting coffee and mint and…Nate.

One of his legs slid between hers as he closed the gap between them, and something nudged against the outside of her thigh. Her insides melted.

She wanted him. Here in the sand, under the sky.

"Sasha…"

The sound of her name made her open her eyes. His were deep and dark and full of all of the things she was feeling. Another wave went over her, sliding between their bodies, the juxtaposition of the cool water and the heat of his skin making her nipples pucker.

He kissed her again as the water receded. It was long and drawn out, making her breathless for more. Then he pulled away slightly. "You're going to drown if we stay here."

"Mmm, I can hold my breath for a very long time. So I don't think I care."

"But I do."

He stood, and she was just about to protest, when he reached down and swung her up in his arms. "Oh!"

"Yes, oh." He chuckled before walking with purpose down toward the water, moving sideways in a way that avoided them taking the brunt of the waves.

A heady sense of need went through her. He wasn't stopping. He was doing the opposite: making it possible for them to do more. Feel more. Explore more. He carried her farther out in this private slice of paradise, until the water covered her bottom and sent delicious sensations through her. Then he set her down on her feet.

He kissed her. Recklessly. With a passion and fervor that rivaled anything she'd ever felt before. Then he slowly turned her away from him, facing the shore as his fingers edged under her light top, under her bra, palms sliding over her breasts in a way that drove the air from her lungs. She pushed into his touch, with a soft cry, glad it was muted by the sounds of the sea. It didn't matter. No one would see them here. Her hands rounded his strong thighs and closed over his butt, dragging him closer, until he was nestled tight against her.

Nate leaned down and nipped at her ear. "You're driving me crazy, Sash."

No crazier than he was driving her. She hoped he had a condom somewhere on him, although she felt like she would die if she didn't have him however she could get him.

One of his arms dipped beneath the water, coming up under her skirt and bunching it around her legs. His fingers found her lacy undergarment and he slid against her, making her instinctively move toward the hard heat she felt behind her. He pushed against her, groaning as his fingers found her, brushing over that sensitive part of her and cupping her.

"Do you want this, sweetheart? If you don't, please tell me now."

"Yes. I want it." The words came out with a need that almost made her cringe. Until he growled against her ear, pushing her panties down her legs.

She stepped out of them not caring if they were lost forever to the sea. It seemed kind of fitting since she was finding herself lost to it too. Then his fingers were on her flesh, teasing, squeezing, trailing across her folds and blotting out every other thought but what was happening to her. He dipped inside her with a suddenness that made her clench around his finger.

Yes. She wanted it. Way too much.

"Hell. You're going to have to help me."

He withdrew and somehow, from his wallet or his pocket or some secret place pulled a packet above the water and handed it to her. She pivoted toward him as she ripped the packet open and handed him the wrapper. He shoved it in his pocket just as her hands slid beneath the surface of the water. When she found him, he'd already released himself. All she had to do was. Slide. It. Slowly. On.

It was heavenly. Warm and heavy and, oh, so hard. She could explore him forever.

But as soon as she'd sheathed him, his hands scooped beneath her thighs, lifted her onto his hips. She twined her ankles beneath his butt.

With one palm pressed against the small of her back, he used his other hand to find her, entering her with one swift deep thrust.

"Ahh…" She pressed her face against his neck, panting against his skin as she absorbed the sensation of being stretched. So very full.

"Okay?"

"Yes. Oh, yes."

Supporting her butt, he began to move, thrusting slowly, the water providing the perfect medium for them. The push and pull of the waves echoed what was happening inside her. She licked salt from his neck, murmured in her own tongue against his lips, before allowing herself to slide back into the water, her body buoyed by the salt and sea currents.

She could see him above her moving, eyes on hers. The sight was hypnotic. She couldn't see where they were joined but could see the muscles under his shirt contract with each forward movement, could feel the result inside her.

"Sasha, I need…to…touch you." Each word was punctuated with a short thrust that made her push against him.

A luscious pressure was building inside her. "You are, Nate." She took a breath. "Just keep doing what you're doing."

His hands squeezed her ass as he pulled her harder against him with each stroke. Her legs tightened around him, adding her own rhythm in an effort to keep up with the demands of her flesh.

Suddenly one of his arms slid under her back, and he supported her, leaning forward and taking her nipple into his mouth, then sucking hard. She held on to his shoulders to keep herself from going under as she watched his mouth work its magic on her, his hair wet and dark and wild.

As wild as she felt inside.

She moved against him, the friction against sensitive areas of her body making any hope of drawing this out impossible.

Using her legs, she pumped herself on him, going faster and faster, watching as his head came up, eyes glazing.

And then she was there, her body tumbling and crashing and exploding, as a keening cry erupted from her throat.

Nate's own cry joined hers a few seconds later as a frenzy of thrusts drove her even higher.

And then it was over. She lay on top of the water for a few seconds, her breath heaving, trying to push through the thick layer of sludge that seemed to have taken over her brain.

With one hand still behind her waist, he used his other hand to pull her upright until she was resting against him.

Neither one of them said anything for a few minutes. Then Nate eased free, and she closed her eyes in an attempt to blot out the truth: it was over. And she had no idea what to say.

He saved her from having to come up with something. "Are you okay?"

"Yes." She moistened her lips, almost dreading to hear his response. "You?"

"I think I just destroyed something."

She blinked at him in shock before realizing he was smiling. She smiled back at him, having no idea what he was talking about. "You did? What?"

"You were worried about my shoes. But neither one of us thought about this. Well I did. But I didn't care at the time."

He reached behind him and up out of the sea came his wallet. And it was streaming with water.

And suddenly she was laughing just like she'd been on the beach. This could have been the most awkward moment ever. And all Sasha felt was gratitude that he'd come up with the perfect icebreaker, even if his wallet had paid the price. She leaned forward and hugged him, putting every ounce of feeling she had into it as she thanked him in the only way she knew how.

And then she set her feet on the ground, and turned and trudged slowly toward shore.

CHAPTER SIX

SASHA DIDN'T MAKE the next gala meeting that night, even though her mom did, bringing with her an impressive presentation that Nate added to what they'd already sent him. And as it had been at the last meeting, the vote was unanimous that they let Tessi James's team head up the food and decorations. All they had to provide were the venue and the speakers. And that was the easy part.

And although he was glad things had gone in Tessi's favor, his mind was on the woman's daughter during most of the meeting.

She'd seemed to be okay after their…*don't say it*… But the words *sex on the beach* surged through his mind anyway. He barely refrained from rolling his eyes in front of everyone.

Maybe she wasn't okay though. And he had something in his office that belonged to her. He just wasn't quite sure how to get them back to her. He could mail them. But that seemed worse than handing them to her in person, somehow.

Except how? And where? Was there even a comfortable way for that exchange to take place?

He could just throw them away, but then she might

wonder what had happened to them or worry that they might wash up on the shore somewhere.

He adjourned the meeting, and as far as he knew everything was set in place for the gala.

Tessi came up to him afterward, and he tensed, wondering if Sasha had talked to her about what happened. He forced a smile.

"I just wanted to say thank you for letting us do the food and service for the fund-raiser."

"I should be thanking you. And Sasha, of course. She's the one who ultimately thought of it."

The woman nodded as if her thoughts were elsewhere. "She hasn't had it easy. First her dad and then that fiasco with Austin."

"Austin?" Nate knew about her dad and his death, but the other name wasn't familiar.

The woman frowned. "A man she dated at Harvard. He was rich and pretended to like her. But as soon as he got what he wanted—a job at a prestigious hospital—he dumped her. After five years of dating."

Shock rolled through him. She'd never mentioned having a relationship with anyone while in medical school. And somehow it seemed inappropriate to be talking about this with her mother. Especially since a wave of guilt had just knocked him for a loop.

Did she equate him with this Austin person?

No. They'd never talked about dating. And she'd acted like what had happened was all in good fun. But maybe it wasn't. Maybe on some level she expected him to...

To what?

Start a relationship with her? He hadn't dated seriously since Tara. And he'd had no desire to do so.

No. He thought over what had happened, and there'd been no hint that Sasha felt anything more for him than physical attraction. Which was good. Because that's all he felt for her too.

Right?

Of course. They barely knew each other.

And yet he'd told her about Marie. He told other people about the doll, but he rarely discussed it in the kind of detail he'd shared with her. And he'd never told Tara about it at all.

And Sasha had never once mentioned Austin.

"I'm sorry. I had no idea that had happened."

"She doesn't talk about it." Tessi's eyes closed. "And she would be very angry if she knew I'd shared it with you. I'm sorry. Would you mind…?"

"I won't say a word."

"Thank you so much. I don't even know why I said anything." Even as she said the words, worry lined the woman's face.

He tried to erase the concern. "You have a very special daughter."

"I know. I only wish she knew how much people think of her."

Nate thought of her entirely too much. But he needed to make sure that stopped here and now. She'd already been hurt by one man, who according to Tessi had toyed with her emotions and then cut her off without a word. Kind of like his parents had done with him?

Well, he had no intention of adding his name to a list of people who had hurt her.

So what was he going to do about it?

Maybe talk to her. Go have that lunch they'd never had. And do what? Lay her undergarment on her salad plate?

Hell, he shouldn't even be thinking about that with her mom standing right in front of him.

So he just added his own thought to hers. "I wish she did too. But people like Sasha aren't normally aware of just how important they are."

"That's the truth." Tessi smiled and reached up to pat his face. "But I have an idea that you do."

Then she turned and walked away, leaving Nate standing there in shock. Had Sasha said something to her after all? Or was her mom simply reading signs that weren't there.

He was going to go with the latter. And if he was the one giving off some kind of vibe he was going to have to cut it off at the knees. And if it was Sasha?

Well, he was going to have to make sure she understood exactly where they stood. And that was nowhere.

One of the nurses came in and interrupted his thoughts. "Mr. Blankenship would like to meet with you and talk about his wife's skin cancer surgery."

"Of course. I'll be right there."

Merriam Blankenship was an award-winning actress who'd starred in countless movies. She was at the height of her career, only to have it almost sidelined by a melanoma diagnosis on her left cheek. With what could be a disfiguring surgery looming on the horizon, she'd chosen to come to The Island Clinic to have the removal and reconstruction done. Nate and the plastic surgeon who worked out of the clinic had warned them it could take up to a year. Tendrils of the cancer had infiltrated the bone below it and it was going to be tricky to get clean margins, much less leave a smooth symmetrical result. There would be bone and skin grafts, and there was always the risk of nerve damage.

But this was what he was here for. Their plastic surgeon was one of the best in the world. And the Blankenships had already poured a huge sum into the Saint Victoria Foundation. The cost of privacy, they'd said. Nate had laid the base for that private foundation, using his own trust fund. The least he could do was guarantee the Blankenships got what they wanted.

His parents were top in the plastic-surgery field, and maybe he should have consulted with them on this case, but he couldn't bring himself to make that call.

There were only a few doctors at The Island Clinic who actually knew that Jackson and Sheryl Edwards were his parents. They'd worked on many A-list clients just like Merriam Blankenship. But Merriam didn't want to do this under the spotlight of Los Angeles, and he couldn't blame her.

So putting Sasha firmly out of his mind, he headed to the elevator and the second floor, where The Island Clinic's newest high-profile patient was waiting.

Sasha was taking a break in the staff lounge, eating a forbidden Danish when Nate walked in. She tried to banish the look of guilt that she knew was splashed across her face.

"Hey, can I have a word?"

She still had a big bite of the pastry in her mouth, so forced herself to chew. And chew and chew before finally swallowing. If this had to do with what had happened in the sea yesterday, she was going to wish she'd choked on that Danish.

"Um sure." She glanced at the chair next to her.

But Nate didn't sit down. He just stood there for a

minute. The sugar in the pastry she'd just eaten soured in her stomach.

Another doctor came into the room and took one look at them and quickly grabbed a water and excused himself.

Great. Just what she wanted. To look like she was having some cozy interlude with the chief of staff from The Island Clinic.

A place she'd scoffed about to Patty.

But hadn't she had that cozy interlude? Down by the beach?

Yes. But she didn't want anyone else to know about it. Not even Patty. Surely he hadn't…

"Er…no one knows about…"

"I was just going to ask you the same thing." His face held a seriousness she hadn't seen since they'd operated on that accident victim at The Island Clinic.

He thought she'd told someone? "No, I haven't said anything. To anyone."

"You didn't come to the meeting last night, and your mom said something odd to me."

"She did?"

"I just wanted to make sure it didn't have anything to do with what happened."

What had her mother said now? "I didn't say anything to her. At all. And I won't."

"Okay, thanks." A beat went by. "Do you think we could have lunch? Where no one from the hospital has a chance to overhear?"

Great. He was going to make sure she knew that the sea sex meant nothing.

Sea sex. That sounded like something out of an old tongue twister. *Susie sells sea sex by the seashore.*

Sasha laughed, but it came out half-choked. That damned Danish! That's what she got for sneaking stuff she wasn't supposed to have.

Like Nate?

Her laughter dried up in a hurry. "Sorry. I just always seem to get caught doing something I shouldn't."

"We...didn't get caught."

"Not that. This." She pushed the plate forward. "I swore off sugar."

"Ah." He actually smiled. "So if I offered to buy you a sugarless lunch, would you accept?"

"Why?"

"I just wanted to make sure we're on the same page about things."

She stiffened her back. "I'm pretty sure we are." Was he expecting her to cry and beg him not to throw her away?

Too late. She'd already done that with Austin. Without the begging part. She was not anxious to repeat that mistake. Which was why she *should* go to lunch with him. If only to assure him that she had no designs on his person or anything else.

Liar. She did have designs on his person. But only in the physical sense. As for the emotional sense she was free and clear. At least she hoped she was. If not, she was going to make sure she reached that point. So maybe she should hear him out. It would drive home the fact that he was not interested in her.

"Maybe. But I still would like to go somewhere where we can have a little privacy. I have something for you."

He did? Her heart leaped in her chest. *Stop it, Sasha! He doesn't mean it that way.*

"This was actually supposed to be my lunch break. So maybe somewhere 'sugarless' would be better."

"Okay, I know a place down the street that pretty much fits that bill."

A few minutes later they were seated in a place that was known for its conch soup and fried seafood. She wasn't sure it qualified as being healthier than her Danish, but it was delicious. And she'd eaten here more than once. She was actually surprised that Nate hadn't taken her somewhere fancier. Someplace that fit in with his fancy clinic.

She frowned at the thought, pushing it from her head.

Studying the menu for a minute, she chose a bowl of the soup and half a sandwich, while Nate ordered the soup plus a plate of fried clam strips and chips, with a side of cocktail sauce.

When their food arrived, Nate pulled a small paper bag out of his pocket and handed it to her under the table. "I needed to return this, but didn't want to do it at either of our hospitals."

"Return…" She placed the bag next to her plate and started to open it, when he placed his hand over hers. "I don't think you're going to want to do that in here."

Suddenly she knew what it was and her face blazed with heat. She'd totally forgotten about them, had assumed they'd been swept away with the tide. Evidently, he'd retrieved them, somehow. Or had they appeared on the beach near the clinic later? The heat in her face turned into an inferno. "Um…thanks. I'm glad I didn't litter. You could have just tossed them though." She shoved the bag in the deepest darkest recesses of her purse. Had he washed them? The thought of him pulling them out of the washing machine was even worse.

Or of them being plastered against his own laundry and him having to slowly peel them apart. More heat drummed at her temples. A very different kind of heat.

"I thought about it, but then wondered if you'd worry about what happened to them. Or the thought that you'd 'littered'..." he smiled as he reused her term "...or that they'd reappear somewhere more public. And you walked back to the clinic so fast afterward that there was no time to hand them to you."

He was right. She had made a beeline all the way back to the boardwalk and beyond. Once her senses returned, she hadn't wanted to dissect what had happened, just figured if they didn't talk about it, they were both free to let it drop.

Like she'd done with her underwear.

Sayè!

"Okay, well, thanks." Her appetite had suddenly deserted her. "Is this why you wanted to bring me here?"

"Partly. But I also wanted to apologize."

"Oh, please. Don't." He'd already apologized for the other stuff. She couldn't bear it if he went into some huge monologue about how badly he felt about them tumbling around in the waves too. "I don't regret what happened. Any of it."

Really? *Really?*

Hadn't she regretted it so much that she hadn't been able to show her face at the meeting last night, afraid she'd be undressing him with her eyes the whole time? She hadn't actually gotten to see much of him in the water. But the parts that she'd felt...

"I don't regret it either. But I also don't want it to affect our working relationship. And I certainly don't want to be the reason why you..."

He seemed to be struggling to say something. But he needn't bother. "Listen. I went into that water knowing exactly where things stood, if that's what you're trying to get at. I don't expect anything of you, and I don't think you expect anything of me. I haven't been with anyone in a long time, and things just got…carried away. But it was nice and I…enjoyed it."

The words were ludicrous. She made it sound like she'd read a pleasant book.

His lips twitched. "Good to know it was *nice*. But I also wanted you to know that I don't make a habit of sleeping with colleagues. I know how messy that can get. How much it can hurt when things don't turn out the way you expect them to."

Something in his face. The way he was avoiding her eyes right now. Was that…pity?

Oh, hell, no. "Exactly what did my mother say to you?"

"Say?"

"Don't even act like you don't know what I'm talking about."

His smile was crooked. And worried. "You two are far too much alike, did you know that? She made me promise to keep it to myself."

This took the cake. Actually she should have finished that Danish. She could use a shot of sugar right now. "Did she guess about…you know? Is that why she said something?"

"I don't think so. I thought at first maybe you'd told her and that's why she brought up Austin."

At the sound of that name, her soup curdled in her stomach. "I'm pretty sure she would have confronted me, if she'd guessed."

"Well, I came to the same conclusion, that it was a genuine slip of the tongue. It came out after she mentioned your dad and how hard his loss was."

Sasha took a deep breath, her anger dissipating immediately. "Yes, I can see her linking the two. I'm just embarrassed that she brought him up. I was stupid and naive, back then, and had never been around men with money before."

"Whether he had money or not shouldn't have made any difference. What the man did was wrong. And I wanted to make sure I hadn't inadvertently hurt you, as well."

It *had* been pity. But hadn't she felt a trace of that when he'd told her about Marie? About how broken he'd been by her death?

Maybe it wasn't pity. Maybe it was just…compassion. Understanding.

"You didn't hurt me. I knew what was what when we went into that water. Now, if you had professed your undying love for me only to retract it a few days later, I might have cut you up and fed you to the fish. But you didn't. And I didn't. So it's all good."

Even if he *had* said he loved her, she wouldn't have believed him. She was far too wise to be taken in by pretty words nowadays. Fortunately he'd not tossed any her way.

That made her smile. "Did your wallet end up being ruined?"

"More or less. It was fun explaining to my bank and creditors how my credit cards got lost in the sea."

"Will they reissue everything?"

"Yep. I should have them in a few days."

"I'm glad. And your shoes?"

"They dried out. A little buffing, and they should be passable again."

Her smile widened. She felt kind of like his shoes. A little buffing here and there and she should be passable again too. Right now, though, she still felt just a little vulnerable and quick to jump to conclusions whenever he said something. "I'm glad. And I'm very glad that part of the beach is so private."

Which made her wonder if he'd towed some other woman over to his "secret spot" and done the same thing. Except his earlier words made her think that he hadn't. At least not one of his colleagues. For that she was glad.

And if that first wave hadn't hit, they probably wouldn't have wound up in the predicament they had. At least they had an excuse for both of them returning soaked. She was pretty sure they weren't the first people who had been surprised by one of those crazy waves.

Luckily, once Nate had caught up with her, he'd sneaked her into one of the hotel rooms and let her dry her clothes and hair with one of the handheld hair dryers. She assumed he'd done the same in another room. Of course they did have an apartment block for the staff, from what she'd heard, so maybe he lived in one of them. Although he'd been wearing the same clothes when he came back to check on her. She'd driven her car over, so she'd hurried away before he had a chance to say much.

"I am, as well. And that we opted not to put cameras on any of the beaches out of respect for some of our more sensitive patients."

Yikes, she hadn't even thought about cameras. Surely he wouldn't have carried her into the water if there had been any. Of course it would have saved her from the embarrassing moment of having her underwear passed to her under the table.

But she'd told him the truth. She didn't regret going into that water. The experience had been exhilarating—freeing in a way she couldn't describe—and she'd probably never do anything like it again. Someday when she was a granny she'd probably think about that day with pride.

Unless she was never a grandmother.

Okay, Sasha. Not something you need to think about right now.

She spooned the last bit of conch soup into her mouth. Funny how what had tasted like cardboard a few moments earlier now tasted pretty darned good.

"How was your conch?"

"It's never failed to please."

The words *And how was I?* sang through her head. But of course she was never ever going to ask him that question.

"My mom actually gave them the recipe for the soup."

His brows went up in a way she was beginning to recognize. "You're kidding."

"I'm not. I hear she's planning on making it for the gala. It was my grandmother's recipe, originally."

He leaned forward. "Listen. I really need to thank you for suggesting we hire out to local companies. I think this year's fund-raiser is going to be a big hit with the folks who attend."

"I hope so. I wondered after I suggested it. I hope they don't hate it all. You're taking a risk by agreeing."

"I think I can safely say the people who come are

going to love everything about it. Some of them might never want to leave Saint Victoria."

"Like you?"

He smiled. "Yes. Like me."

And just like that, they were on ground that felt more stable and less like quicksand. Somehow knowing that he never wanted to leave made her heart feel lighter than it had in the last couple of days. There'd been a tiny part of her that wondered what his plans for the future were. Well, it sounded like he had every intention of staying for the foreseeable future. "You know, I hear they have a great crème brûlée here."

"I thought you were swearing off sugar."

"I am. But since I already ruined my resolution with the Danish back at the staff lounge, I might as well hold off on renewing that vow until tomorrow."

He raised his hand to signal their waiter. "And that sounds like the best plan I've heard all day."

CHAPTER SEVEN

WAS THAT LACY underwear still in her purse?

Nate spied Sasha just as he was wheeling Bill Waddel, their heart attack patient, through the double doors of the ER.

"They said you were coming through here. I'm so glad to see you."

The low, husky words should have made his chest tighten, except Sasha's eyes weren't on him, they were on Bill.

"I'm feeling much better. I wanted to thank you and Dr. Edwards for everything you did."

She smiled. "I think the cardiologist over at The Island Clinic is the one you should thank. We were short-staffed when you arrived and our cardiologist was stuck in surgery. It looks like they got you all patched up though."

"Two stents later, yes. I still have to go through cardiac rehab. I'm sure losing weight and eating better will be on the menu, but I'm willing to do anything to make sure I live to see my first grandchild who's due next month."

Only then did she glance up at Nate. The smile was still on her face, but she seemed a little more stiff than she had at the restaurant. It had been a couple of days since he'd seen her, though; he'd been busy trying to get things for the gala nailed down. And he'd heard that Marcus Warren, the doctor from Saint Victoria Hospital who'd been taking care of an ill relative, was back at work as of yesterday, so they hadn't needed him as much.

"Don't let me forget. I have something for you," she said.

She did? Those were almost the exact same words he'd used when he'd talked to her a couple of days ago. He hadn't left a piece of clothing in the sea, though.

Just the thought sent memories sliding through the deepest recesses of his brain. With it, came a question. Had the condom done its job even with everything so… wet? As in the sea water?

It had still been in place afterward, so everything pointed to it having effectively done its job, but it was new territory for him. He'd never dragged anyone into the ocean before. Not even Tara.

"Okay. I was just taking Bill to meet his therapy team here at Saint Victoria Hospital, since it's closer to where he lives."

"That makes sense. Our cardiac team is really good at what they do, including rehab."

Was there a note of defensiveness in her voice? She'd seemed wary that first day he'd come in to help, but he'd thought they'd made it past all of that stuff. There had been that kiss. And the sea.

So why was he feeling like they'd taken several steps backward? The hospitals weren't in competition with each other. He wanted The Island Clinic to be an enhancement of what Saint Victoria Hospital was doing.

An addition. Not take the place of it. Maybe that was something he needed to work on.

"Good to know," Bill said.

His voice was still a touch weak, but after what he'd been through it was to be expected.

Nate glanced at her. "Do you have time to walk with us?"

"I do. Let's go. Cardiac Rehab is on this floor actually, so you won't have to worry with elevators or anything. And there's a separate entrance, so you'll be able to park near it and walk in. I'll show you where."

Nate had forgotten that the unit had its own entrance. Since it was at the back of the hospital, it made sense that they wouldn't want patients with more vulnerable health issues having to walk long distances.

They headed down the long corridor, making two turns before reaching glass doors with a sign reading, "Welcome to Saint Victoria Hospital Rehab. We'll kick your behinds…in the best possible way." It was punctuated with a smiley face sitting at some kind of weight machine.

Bill laughed. "I'm not sure how much kicking I can take. But I'll give it a shot."

While Sasha opened the door, Nate wheeled Bill in, heading for the reception desk. They got checked in, and he made sure Bill had someone picking him up. Sasha leaned down and gave their patient a hug. "Don't be a stranger. Let me know when you're here, and if I'm free I'll drop in to see you."

"I will. Thanks again for everything. Both of you."

Nate waited until Sasha caught up with him. "So you said you had something for me?"

"My mom sent over some conch soup. It's in the refrigerator of the staff lounge. So it'll need to be heated up, obviously. She wanted you to taste it to make sure it's suitable."

"I already had some the day we went out to lunch. She doesn't have to send over a sample of everything. But I'll enjoy the soup. Tell her thank you."

"I will."

"So, I wasn't sure if you were worried about the aftermath of what happened. But I wanted to let you know that everything was still in place afterward."

"Still in place?"

"The protection." He lowered his voice.

"Oh." Her eyes widened. "Ooh. I didn't even think about it. But thanks for letting me know. I probably should be on the Pill, but I don't…well, there's not really a need as I…"

"I get it. It's okay. I just didn't want you panicking. But if for some reason, you are…late…"

She nodded. "I'll let you know. But like you said, as long as everything was still there it should be fine. There were no oils or sunscreens involved."

"Right."

He decided to change the subject. "You know you don't have to defend Saint Victoria Hospital every time I'm around."

"Defend it, what do you mean?"

"Just that when you were talking about the cardiac rehab center, it sounded like you wanted to make sure I knew that it was up to snuff."

Her eyes squinched just a bit. "It came through, did it? Sorry. It's just a habit. Sometimes I wonder if people see us as second best."

"I've never heard anything but good things about the hospital, or I wouldn't have invested so much in it."

She gave a half shrug. "I think I know that up here," she pointed at her head, "but in here, I'm not always so sure." With that, she pressed her hand to her chest.

He found the gesture touching somehow. And it had probably been hard for her to admit that. And he really did know what she meant. Firsthand, actually. "I get it. Sometimes you can feel that way regardless."

"What do you mean?"

Hell. He wasn't sure why he'd said that, except at her words, the image of his parents presenting that plaque came to mind. And their expressions when he'd been forced to tell them that he wasn't ever going to join their practice because he wasn't going to specialize in plastic surgery. They'd had this look on their faces. Like they suddenly weren't even sure he was their child.

"Nothing, really. I'm sure we've just all felt that way at some time or other. Not good enough, I mean."

"Yes, I'm sure we all have."

She drew the words out on a little sigh. Was she thinking of the man she'd dated at Harvard? What was his name? Austin, right? In trying to take the spotlight off himself, he may have just reminded Sasha of a painful time in her life.

Before he could try to think of a way to pull the words in a different direction, she spoke up.

"I actually have the next week off. I was wondering…" She shook her head. "Never mind."

"No. What?"

She stopped and looked up at him. "Well, you mentioned me sounding defensive about Saint Victoria Hospital. Maybe it's not so much defensive as it is protective. So…maybe I could spend a few days at The Island Clinic and see how things work over there. Like you did over here. Well…you didn't do it for that reason, but if there's something I could help with, maybe it would—"

"Help you see us with different eyes."

"Exactly."

He liked the idea. Not because it would give him more time to spend with her. Not at all. But they'd often had doctors from the hospital come over and work with them. He had a feeling that Sasha could be a powerful voice in their favor if he could win her over.

"I think that's a great idea. Let me know when you want to start and how many hours you want to put in each day, and we can put you somewhere…trauma, maybe?"

"How about Monday. I can float around. Maybe see a couple of surgeries done."

He was pretty sure one of Merriam Blankenship's reconstruction surgeries was coming up next week. It might be a good one for her to see. "We have a couple of nice observation areas. And I think I know a good one for you to watch. A melanoma that infiltrated a woman's cheekbone. She'll need pretty extensive repair work."

He'd have to get Merriam's permission for her to watch but as long as he assured her that it was educational and had nothing to do with her fame, she would probably be okay with it. Not even his parents' practice could afford patients the amount of privacy that The Island Clinic did. There were no cell phones allowed in certain areas of the clinic, even by staff members. And there were rigorous background checks and waivers that everyone signed. There was also a one-strike-you're-out policy. Nate would not hesitate to prosecute anyone who violated patient confidentiality.

The Island Clinic's very existence depended on its ability to keep its promise to its patients.

"That sounds interesting. I would love to watch."

"I'll join you. Let me find out exactly when it is, and I'll get back to you. In the meantime, if you want to come in on Monday, I can take you on rounds."

"Perfect. What time are rounds?"

"Eight. Do you want me to send the shuttle?"

"It's okay. I'll drive over. It'll make it easier on everyone."

They stopped at the staff lounge. "Let me get that container of soup for you."

"Thanks. Much appreciated." As he watched her duck into the room, he was buoyed by the thought of her seeing the clinic. It would be the perfect opportunity to see all that was right about his medical facility. And to change her mind about it, once and for all.

On Monday morning, Sasha went through the front doors of The Island Clinic and was met by the sound of screaming and people running in all directions. What the...?

Out of habit she started to race toward the sound, only to be stopped by someone at the reception desk. "I'm sorry. Can I help you?"

Of course she couldn't just jump in. No one knew who she was. "I'm Dr. James from Saint Victoria Hospital. I'm supposed to go on rounds with Dr. Edwards this morning."

"Oh, of course, he told me you were coming. Let me see if I can page him." The young woman was calm and serene, acting like there wasn't something terrible going on less than a hundred feet from her station.

"Can I help with something?"

This time the woman bit her lip. "I'm not sure… Let me see if I can find out." She put her ear to the phone and spoke in low tones to whoever was on the other end. Then she hung up.

"Dr. Edwards is on his way."

Still no reply to her original question. But the sounds were also dying down. She had to remember, this wasn't Saint Victoria Hospital. She couldn't just walk in and take charge like she was used to in her ER. But it was hard to shut off the part of her mind that said *run*! when she heard sounds of distress.

Nate came down the hallway, motioning her forward. He nodded at the receptionist. "Thanks, Jen."

Impressive. He knew her name. Although Saint Victoria Hospital's administrator probably knew most of the names at their hospital, as well. She just always expected to be met with snootiness here at The Island Clinic. So far she'd been proven wrong at every turn.

"What's happening?"

The screams had reduced to muffled crying.

"They're doing bandage changes on the melanoma patient that I told you about." He paused. "For someone who makes a living off her appearance… Well, it would be a shock to anyone."

"I can imagine." So it had to be someone famous. Patty had mentioned that a lot of well-known and well-heeled people came through The Island Clinic's doors. "Does that happen often?"

"Surgery?"

"No…screaming. Your receptionist was as cool as could be about it."

"No. It doesn't happen often. No more than any other hospital."

Touché. Saint Victoria Hospital had had its share of patients and families whose emotions got the better of them. And some for good reason. The hospital was not the happiest of places most of the time. Except for maybe in the obstetrics wing.

Which made her wonder. "Do you have obstetrics here?"

His eyes narrowed. "We do. Why?"

Too late, she realized he was probably remembering their earlier conversation about condoms. "I just wondered."

"Does this have anything to do with what we talked about?"

"Not at all." She decided to explain. "I was just thinking about how hospitals aren't necessarily a place of laughter. Except the maternity ward."

"That makes sense." His shoulders sank in what looked like relief. Well, why wouldn't he be relieved? He probably wouldn't be thrilled if someone he'd had a brief encounter with got pregnant. Visions of Austin came to mind. Would he have stayed with her, if she'd been expecting his child?

She couldn't think of a worse reason to be with someone you didn't love. And he hadn't loved her. That much was obvious. And looking back, it was probably for the best, although at the time she had felt used and humiliated.

"Let me peek in on Mrs. Blankenship and make sure things are okay."

"Mrs. Blankenship as in…"

He nodded. "Now you see why she might be upset."

Merriam Blankenship was beautiful in an elfin way, with high cheekbones and delicate features. She was one of the top-paid actors in the States, from what Sasha understood. "I'll wait here."

"I'll be out as soon as I can."

"No, take your time."

Nate went down a couple of doors, then with a quick knock he went inside. The sounds of crying intensified when the door opened, but muted again as soon as it swung shut. The soundproofing was obviously better here than at Saint Victoria Hospital. Then again, she couldn't remember ever getting a patient like this one.

She could see how Nate might have to perform a balancing act that she didn't have to deal with in the ER. Sure the island had its own wealthy population, but it wasn't on the scale that one found in other places in the world.

Nate stuck his head out. "Sasha, could you come in here please?"

That surprised her. But she braced herself to treat the woman like any other patient as she went into the room.

Merriam Blankenship's tear-stained face met her, lids swollen and her lashes plastered together.

"Merriam, this is Dr. James from our sister hospital in Williamtown. I just want her to have a look at you."

She wasn't a specialist in oncology or plastic surgery, so she wasn't sure exactly what Nate wanted to do, but there was a reason he'd called her in here. She just didn't want to mess it up. There were three other medical personnel in the room and a man who sat holding the woman's other hand. He must be her husband.

Moving toward the woman, she was surprised when Merriam reached her hand toward her. Sasha didn't stop to put gloves on; she knew there was healing in skin-to-skin touch that you couldn't get in other ways. She would glove up and sanitize her hands before she examined her.

"Do I look horrid?" Merriam turned to look at her fully, revealing the cause of her distress. There was a large hole in the woman's cheek, some of the packing still wedged in it. According to what Nate had told her earlier, part of the cheekbone had to be removed.

Still, the question shocked her. Beneath Merriam's tears, Sasha could see real fear in her eyes. For someone who was used to looking gorgeous and idolized by millions, this would be a very hard blow. "No. Of course you don't." There was a stool next to the examination table where Merriam sat. Sasha sank down to be near her. "It looks like it does now because of the swelling and bruising. But Dr. Edwards only has the best of the best here at the hospital. I've seen wounds much, much worse than this have a good final result."

"Will I...look like me?"

She glanced up and Nate nodded to another man in the room, before he spoke up. "Dr. Seldridge has some renderings drawn up. Do you think you can look at them right now?"

Merriam's fingers went to Sasha's cheek, and she held very still to let her explore. "You're beautiful. You could be an actress too."

Sasha smiled. "No, I'm afraid I couldn't. My real feelings show far too easily. I'm not good at pretending to be someone I'm not. You have a rare gift."

"Thank you." She glanced at Nate and then Dr. Seldridge. "I'll look at what you have."

Sasha gave Merriam's hand a squeeze and got up to give the other doctor room to sit with his tablet. They went through the stages of the reconstruction process and Sasha was seriously impressed. This man had done his homework.

Then again, he would have. Nate would have made sure of it.

"How long?"

"Total, including healing time? Probably six months to a year."

Merriam glanced at her husband and whispered, "Can you check on when *Marriage of the Swans* is set to start filming?"

The man took out a device and scrolled through what looked like a calendar. "Nine months."

She blinked. "Will most of the work be done by then?"

"I can't promise, but I imagine so, but there may still be some redness from scarring."

"Makeup will cover scarring as long as the skin is smooth." She seemed to muse to herself. "It's not my best side and I can ask filming to take that into consideration."

Her husband smiled. "See? Not a tragedy."

"You got clean margins?"

"Yes. We'll want to scan you to make sure nothing lights up, but we're optimistic it hasn't spread."

"Thank God." She nodded. "Okay. Let's get this show on the road. I have a schedule to meet."

And for the first time since she'd come into the room, Merriam smiled and reached out to hug her husband.

His whispered words reached her ears. "You're always the most beautiful woman in the room."

Sasha wasn't offended. Because the words were said in love. Merriam could be disfigured for life, and she was positive the words her husband uttered would have been exactly the same as they were now. She couldn't imagine being loved like that. Except for by her mom.

Her gaze went to Nate and found him looking at her. She quickly averted her eyes to the wall behind him hoping he just saw it as a passing glance that meant nothing.

Because it did. It meant nothing.

Three minutes later, they were on their way down the hallway. "Thanks for coming in. I just felt that if a woman she'd never seen before could come in and not flinch or recoil, it would help her feel better."

"It kind of helps that I'm a surgeon and an ER doc and have seen almost everything."

He laughed. "Yes, it does. But you're also compassionate. And that came through in droves."

"I'm glad."

The emergency had broken the ice and made meeting him here a little easier. Except for his reaction to her question about the clinic having an obstetrics department. She could see how that might have sent him into a panic.

"Hey. I just want you to know that even if I had somehow wound up pregnant—which I don't see happening—I wouldn't expect anything out of you. I don't believe in partnering with someone for reasons other than love."

"Sometimes you don't have a choice."

"There's always a choice."

He didn't say anything, just quickened his step enough that she had to hurry to keep up. He realized almost immediately and slowed back down with an apology. Something she'd said had struck a nerve. Had he found himself in exactly that situation at one point and been forced to provide support?

But he'd said he didn't have children. Unless someone had manipulated a situation or lied.

Although she wasn't going to ask him, if he didn't want to talk about it. She decided to make small talk instead. "So you know about my dad and have met my mom. What do your parents think of you starting your own clinic?"

He stopped and turned toward her. "What made you ask that?"

"No reason, really. I was just curious. They must be proud of you."

"Not so much." He took off walking again. "Our first patient is just ahead."

And that subject was evidently *entèdi*, as well. Fine.

But why on earth would he think his parents wouldn't be proud of him? He had accomplished so much.

As much as his response stung, she found her heart aching for him. What child didn't seek the approval of his mom and dad? Her father, even though he'd died far too young, had been proud of her accomplishments and had never been shy about telling her.

"So who is this next patient?"

He paused outside a door. "A forty-five-year-old man who was just diagnosed with amyloidosis."

"That's young, isn't it, for that kind of diagnosis? Is it someone from Saint Victoria?"

"Yes. He'd been complaining of gastrointestinal issues for a while. They thought it was IBS, but then some other symptoms came up. Swollen tongue, etc. They referred him here from Saint Victoria Hospital three weeks ago. Testing shows the ATTR form."

Meaning it was the hereditary form of the condition.

Amyloidosis was a devastating, incurable disease. It was also rare. She hadn't run into a case of it during her entire career. At least not that she knew of. It was also notoriously hard to diagnose, so like with this patient, it was often mistaken for other conditions.

"Is his heart affected? Lungs?"

"No, not yet. It's still early enough that we have some treatment options. His hematologist will be in a little later today."

Nate pushed the door open, and she followed him in. She put on her professional smile and glanced at the patient. She blinked. Blinked again. Her smile faded.

"Sasha, *nyès*, what are you doing here?" the patient asked.

Nate's glance went from one to the other. "You two know each other?"

Bondye, this couldn't be happening. Tears welled up in her eyes, but she forced them back, running a thousand words over in her mind, but rejecting them all. Instead she asked, "Why did you not tell us?"

"I couldn't. Not yet, anyway. Plus, I did not want to alarm anyone."

Too late. She was officially alarmed.

She looked at Nate and nodded. "This is Art James. Art is my uncle."

CHAPTER EIGHT

ART JAMES WAS Sasha's uncle?

Hell, he should have realized the second he heard the last name.

Sasha sank onto the stool beside the man, just like she had when talking to Merriam Blankenship. But there were none of the smiles or compassion. There was just confusion.

"How could you not tell us you were coming here for tests? We had no idea. At least Mom never mentioned it."

"I didn't tell her. I wanted to see if treatment worked. If it does, it will buy me more time. Years maybe."

She swallowed. "You shouldn't be going through this alone."

Art had said he wasn't married and had no children. He'd made it sound like he didn't have any close relatives at all, which was another reason the name didn't click. Then again, Nate and his parents weren't close, so maybe they were estranged. But Sasha didn't act like they were.

"I don't want your mother to know. Not yet. She's been through enough. But I would have had to tell you. They said this form can be inherited. In a gene. Maybe your dad—"

"Let's worry about that later. Right now, I want to concentrate on you." She turned to Nate. "When does he start treatment?"

Art answered. "I do an infusion tomorrow. They said they want to knock this thing back on its ass." He grinned. "Well, they didn't quite use that language."

"I imagine they didn't."

Nate smiled. "We're going to use melphalan and dexamethasone. Hopefully we can achieve remission, and he'll start to feel better."

There was no cure for amyloidosis, but if they could slow the rate that amyloids were deposited in the tissues, the body could heal some of the damage done. Patients sometimes lived fairly normal lives for years to come.

"That's why I'm here, today. To make sure everything looks good for the infusion tomorrow."

Nate leaned closer to Art. "Now that she's here, can I share what we're looking at? I'm pretty sure she'll want to know. And there's no more hiding it at this point, since you can't make yourself invisible."

"Are you sure about that?" Art chuckled, then got serious again. "Tell her what you told me about the gene test we did. About the fifty percent chance."

"Let's deal with you, first." He softened his response with a smile.

Normally they worried about the inherited form of amyloidosis in children of the patient. But Art had no children. Although Sasha had also said her dad died of a heart attack. Due to undiagnosed amyloidosis?

Hell. He hoped not. His chest contracted at the thought. But he needed to concentrate on this patient right now. They could deal with those other questions later.

Nate sat down with them and went over the particulars. What he could expect from treatment. Some of the side effects he might face from the chemo drug.

"How long will he be here?"

Sasha's question wasn't unexpected, but there wasn't a simple answer. "We'll want to keep him overnight after his infusion so we can monitor his immediate reaction to it. Then we'll send him home."

Sasha looked at Art. "I'll come and check in on you at home, the first couple of nights. Do you want me to stay with you?"

Art shook his head. "No. I'll be fine. I'm a pretty tough old goat."

"I know that for a fact." She smiled. "We will need to discuss when and where we tell my mom though."

At this, her uncle's chin jutted out just a bit. "We can discuss it, but no promises."

"It's a deal." She got up and hugged him, kissing the top of his head. "I love you, Uncle Art. I'll be here for your infusion."

Art frowned. "You don't have to work?"

"I'm actually off this week, so I asked to put in some hours here at The Island Clinic."

"Are you sure you want to spend it sitting with me?" asked Art.

"I'm positive."

Once they left the room, Sasha turned to Nate. "My dad was almost fifteen years older than his brother. Everyone assumed he'd just had a heart attack. Is it possible…"

He knew what she was thinking. If her dad had amyloidosis and they'd found it, maybe he could have been treated.

"Do you want to take a genetic test, just to rule out that you inherited it?"

"I do. Just so I'll know the risks of having children. And what I might be facing someday." There was a frown that said she really was worried.

He reached out and squeezed her hand. "Hey, he's not your father, so the chances of you having the markers might not be as high."

"No, but I just have this gut feeling, Nate. I think my dad had it. And just didn't know it. My mom is going to be asking the same questions. If my test comes back negative, it'll take one worry off her."

She could very well be right. And he didn't agree with Art about keeping this from his family.

Maybe it was because his parents had kept their plans from him until it was almost too late. So when they did finally tell him, the damage had been done and trust was broken. Hopefully it hadn't quite gotten to that point with Art, Tessi and Sasha.

And if Sasha had inherited the gene?

Something in his gut rebelled against that thought. But the only way they would know was if they pulled her blood and sent it in.

And if he hadn't worn a condom in the water? If she'd gotten pregnant? Damn.

"So you want to be tested? You're sure?"

"I am. Can you pull the blood?"

"I can, but we have phlebotomists who are very good, if you want me to call one."

She shook her head. "I'd rather you do it, if that's okay. The sooner the better. It's just the shock of seeing him in that room. I never suspected…"

"I know. And if I had realized exactly who he was, I wouldn't have taken you in there."

She stopped and looked at him. "So if you had known

that Art was my uncle and that he had an inherited form of amyloidosis, you would have kept it from me?"

Would he have? What if Art had chosen never to tell any of his family and Sasha went through her life without knowing and developed it. When it was too late to do anything about it?

"Ethically, I should say yes."

"And if I had a child who later developed it?"

"I said ethically. What I would have probably done was talk to Art and try to convince him that you deserved to know, the same as if he'd had Huntington's or any other of the familial conditions."

"Okay. I can handle that. I'd like to think my uncle would have eventually decided to do the right thing." She touched his arm. "He's a good man."

"I know. I've sat and talked to him for a bit. I think he was telling the truth. He wanted to wait and see what form he had." He paused. "I'll take you to my office, and then I'll retrieve the items needed to do the blood draw."

"Will he be okay alone?"

"The hematologist will be there in a minute. And I'll check in on him, as well."

He unlocked his office door and ushered her inside. "Have a seat wherever you'll be most comfortable, and I'll be back in a minute."

Sasha wandered around Nate's office for a minute or two, not really seeing anything. Had her father had amyloidosis? It was surreal that he could have died from something that had been eating away at his system for years. But then the early signs tended to be vague, and her dad had always been pretty stoic about his health.

By the time of his heart attack, though, he had to have been feeling bad. And yet he'd said nothing.

"Why, Papi? You could have been here with us longer."

But it wasn't his fault. He hadn't known what he had, or he would have tried to get treatment. She caught sight of the doll on Nate's shelf. Her dad wasn't to blame, just as that child's parents weren't to blame for her death. They couldn't have known. And Sasha's dad didn't know, of that she could be sure.

That helped a little. She had no idea how her mom was going to react. But Sasha felt strongly that she needed to know. And it wasn't up to her to make decisions for other people.

And if she had it? God, she could kind of understand why Art might hesitate to let her mom know. He'd want to save her the worry. Sasha could see herself wanting to do the same. But that wasn't fair to her mother.

And what about kids? Did that mean she'd never hold a baby in her arms? Her chest tightened until it was hard to breathe. And marriage? Could she see putting her husband through the pain of watching her slowly waste away if she developed a severe form of the condition?

She went to the couch and sank into the deep leather cushions. They smelled clean and masculine. Like Nate's scent when he'd held her on that beach. She breathed deeply, allowing it to calm her spirit, to bring her back from the panic that had welled inside her. As a surgeon, she knew that treatments for amyloidosis had drastically improved. It couldn't be cured, but it could be managed. Sometimes for a relatively long period of time.

She sighed. Why couldn't things be simple? Like

Nate's lingering scent that clung to his couch. But they weren't. And neither was Nate.

Even by virtue of his offer to go and get the supplies needed to draw her blood. Not just anyone could take it on themselves to do that. Only someone with clout…or money, could bypass the normal protocol of things like that. She'd seen that in Austin in a lot of little ways. When he went to a professor to ask something, that professor almost always made himself available. It had impressed her at first. But then she started to question the way it reinforced feelings of entitlement and being above the rules that others had to follow. And the way Austin could just move to New York with never a thought as to what it would do to Sasha. He'd just done it because…he could. Because he took it for granted that he could always find someone else.

And yet, in asking Nate to draw her blood, wasn't she falling into the same trap? Using her familiarity with him to gain a favor? So wasn't she just as guilty?

Probably. And it made her slightly nauseous. She didn't want to take advantage or use people for what she could get from them.

He came back in with a carry tray and a couple of vials, before she could go very far down that avenue of thought. "You're sure."

Now would be the time to say she'd made a mistake and ask him to please call one of the phlebotomists. Or say that she didn't want to be tested. But she didn't. Instead, she nodded.

Then he slowly knelt in front of her and took her hand in his.

She swallowed. Would she ever have children? Would someone kneel in front of her like this and ask her to marry him, if it turned out she'd inherited the condition? Would they even want to, knowing the possibilities? Damn! She needed to get a hold of herself. All of this speculating was doing her no good.

"Which arm?"

"Right one." He wasn't proposing to her. Nor would he ever. And she didn't want him to.

"Make a fist."

She stretched out her arm, watching as he pulled a piece of rubber strapping tight around her upper arm. He tapped the crook of her elbow, looking for a likely vein. Then he slid the needle home, getting the right spot on the very first try. Clicking a vial onto the end, he let the suction pull blood into the container.

"Release your fist." When the first vial was full, he popped it off and put the second one on. And yes, he definitely smelled like his couch.

The vials were already labeled with her name. "What's your date of birth?"

She told him and he printed it on the sides of both tubes of blood. "I'll take these down to the lab, so they can send them off."

"How long will it take?"

"Two to four weeks. I'll put a rush on it."

She gripped his wrist. "No, don't. Please. Just send it off as you would anyone else's blood."

His head cocked as he looked at her, but he nodded. "Okay, but we ask for lab tests to be rushed all the time."

It reminded her of when he'd offered to have the helicopter pick her up at Saint Victoria Hospital. Her answer was just the same now as it was then. "I'd rather save that option for the people who really need it."

Maybe he remembered that incident too, because he

gave a slight shrug and climbed to his feet and left the room, taking the tote with him.

Two to four weeks and she would know if she was likely to develop amyloidosis. She almost wished she'd opted to remain in the dark. But that would be unethical, especially if she met someone someday who actually wanted to have children with her. It was an autosomal-dominant trait, so all that was needed was one copy of the gene to pass it on. Her copy. So her children would have a 50 percent chance of inheriting the mutated gene. The odds were bad enough that she might not risk having children if she was a carrier of the trait. Unless she was willing to take a prenatal test and consider terminating the pregnancy if the fetus carried the gene. The thought of making a decision like that...

Maybe she should tell him to forget about sending her blood off until later, when her emotions had settled down.

But it was too late for that. Besides, she'd rather know now...start treatment early.

He was back in a minute or two, sans the blood kit. "Thank you for doing that for me. I probably shouldn't have asked."

"Yes, you should have. And I know it's a shock. But there's a good chance you don't have the gene."

"If my dad had it, there's a good chance that I do."

He sat down beside her. "Let's just wait and see what the findings are."

"Okay." She forced herself to shake off the sense of melancholy that had enveloped her. "Are there other patients to see?"

"I had someone else take over rounds this morning."

Something else he had the option of doing because

of his position. And yet, again, it was because of her. "I'm sorry. I've disrupted your whole routine. I think I should go."

"You haven't disrupted anything. I normally do rounds just because I feel a duty to the clinic to follow up on its patients."

That made sense.

He went on. "Your uncle never married."

"No. He was engaged once, but it didn't work out. Her parents had very high standards and didn't think he was good enough for her. And even though she didn't agree with that assessment, they succeeded in putting a wedge between them. They were embarrassed that their daughter might marry someone from a poorer background. Can you imagine a parent acting like that? Shouldn't they have wanted her to be…happy?"

When she glanced up at him, she saw that a muscle was working in his jaw. Surely he didn't agree with Corinne's parents. "My uncle actually did very well for himself. I think maybe their contempt spurred him to work extra hard just to show them what he was made of."

"And did it work? Were they at least sorry for coming between them?"

"I don't know. He and Corinne were broken up by that time, so it didn't really matter. It was kind of ironic, because as far as I know she never married either."

"They never got back together?"

"She broke my uncle's heart. I think he found it hard to trust anyone after that. He poured himself into his job, instead."

He muttered something she didn't catch. "Sorry?"

"Nothing. Just I can understand that. You spend a large chunk of time thinking you know someone, only to find out you don't, when it really matters."

He could have been talking about her and Austin. Maybe he was, in fact. "I know what you mean."

"Your ex?"

"Yep. I think everyone must have an ex they can look back on like that."

"I think most of us can."

"You've had a serious relationship?"

One of his brows went up and he leaned back against the sofa. "It depends what you mean by serious. I've never been engaged, but I was dating someone I expected to someday marry."

She hadn't known that about him. What had happened to break them up?

"I wasn't engaged, either," she said, "but five years sure seemed serious, at the time."

"I would consider that a serious relationship too."

She sighed. "My mom always hoped to be a grandmother. I don't know if that will ever happen, now. Do yours feel the same?"

"Doubtful. My parents were always about looking young and healthy."

She remembered his attitude when she'd asked about his parents before and didn't want to push it. But the little glimpses he'd let her see of his parents didn't impress her. In fact they sounded just a little bit like Corinne's parents. Sasha doubted that she would have measured up to their expectations, either. Not that she needed to worry about that. Still she was curious.

"You said you doubted they were proud of you when I asked earlier. Have they ever come here?"

"No. I haven't seen them since I moved to Saint Victoria."

Wow, that shocked her. "I would think they would

have wanted to come and see The Island Clinic, since you founded the place."

He laid his arm over the back of the couch. "I don't think they're really interested."

His parents weren't interested in what he'd accomplished? That was just strange. She knew they were wealthy, because the rumors were that Nate had started the clinic using the money from his trust fund. It had been a hefty amount. He'd had a helipad built for Saint Victoria Hospital, after all.

"If that's true, then I'm sorry."

"It's true. And don't be sorry. I'm doing what I want to do. That's all that's important to me, right now."

So his relationship with his folks didn't count as important? Sasha couldn't imagine being estranged from her family. But not all families were like hers. Some were like Corinne's, destroying their child's chance for happiness. And from what it looked like, they'd had no regrets about it.

Could Nate's folks really be that bad?

"I get it. I'm doing what I want to do, as well. What makes me happy. Fortunately I'm doing it with my mom's blessing." Her mind went back to her uncle. "So if the chemo treatment works, how long will he have? My uncle, I mean."

"I figured that's who you were talking about. It's hard to put a number on it. But if we achieve an early remission, he has a chance of living ten years, maybe more."

"That's longer than I thought." She relaxed in her seat a bit. She'd been thinking one or two years max, so to hear it could be longer was a relief.

Maybe she should call Corinne. How would Sasha

feel if someone she'd cared deeply for had a terminal illness and no one told her?

Not very good.

And yet, should she interfere? She saw the woman periodically at the store and they smiled at each other, but neither of them mentioned Art. She figured it was their business. It still was. But she'd been hurt to find her uncle had kept his condition from his own family. Well, she could decide about that later.

First she had to tell her mom about it. Or rather, they did, since she'd promised Art she wouldn't say anything about it right now. And she needed to keep that promise. Art didn't need any added stress at the moment.

She found her mind drifting for some reason and came to with a start when she realized her head had fallen back against the backrest of the sofa. She must have drifted off. It must have been because of the late night she'd had at the hospital last night. She'd been called in unexpectedly and had worked until after one in the morning. "I'm sorry. I really should go."

"No." He stood. "Why don't you stay and take a little nap. You've had a shock. I have some work to do behind my desk, so you'll have complete quiet."

She should just get up and drive back to Williamtown, but she was totally exhausted, even though it wasn't even noon yet. She didn't want to nod off on the drive home. But how did she feel about Nate watching her sleep? Not as embarrassed as she might have been, if she were wide awake. "Are you sure?"

"Yep. Positive." He went over to a closet and retrieved a pillow and a light blanket, smiling when he noticed her glance. "I sometimes sleep in here if I get tied up for too long. Pop your shoes off."

He set the pillow on the end of the couch that was nearest his desk. Sasha did as he asked and toed off her shoes, leaving them beside the sofa. Then she lay down and stretched out her legs, immediately wishing she hadn't when his scent rose up from the pillow against her cheek. He had slept on this very pillow, his head cradled in its softness. But other than jump up and race out of here, she had no choice but to pretend she didn't notice.

Nate shook out the blanket and draped it over her. "Okay?"

She wasn't sure it was anymore, but she needed to do her best to pretend she was just fine. "Are you sure you don't mind? I worked later than I expected last night, but I still shouldn't be this tired."

"Like I said, it was probably the shock of seeing Art in that room. Just rest. And then maybe we can sit down and talk a little more about the gala."

"That sounds like a plan. And I want to check in on my uncle in a while anyway before I leave."

"Okay."

With that, Nate ducked out of sight and headed back to his desk. Somehow it was comforting to know he was not far away. Would be clicking away at his computer or something.

For the first time in a long time, she let her muscles relax and snuggled deeper into the blanket—the one that also carried Nate's scent.

And she let herself drift away.

CHAPTER NINE

"I CALLED YOUR father for a consult. I hope you don't mind."

It took Nate's brain a second to compute the meaning of the words. A quick wave of anger rose inside him. Totally unjustified, but it foamed and frothed in the background anyway. He'd been thinking of seeing Sasha curled up on his couch a few days ago, and hadn't been able to erase the image from his skull. She'd been sweet and totally relaxed, one arm hanging off the cushions, the other one tucked under her head. And that snore...

Well, it wasn't exactly a snore. More like a tiny snuffle that periodically pulled his attention from his paperwork.

Not that it was ever fully on his work.

"I'm assuming this is in regard to Merriam Blankenship's upcoming reconstruction surgery."

A surgery Sasha was supposed to come and watch tomorrow. It would be the last day she would be working at The Island Clinic.

Dr. Seldridge nodded. "I've been here since the day this place opened, and I feel in some ways that the newest procedures have passed me by. Ones I might have heard about if I'd stayed in the States."

"I've always told the staff to take some time off, if needed, to go explore new protocols or take a furlough."

"I don't think I've been here long enough to warrant that, but I sent over the pictures of the surgical site and—"

"You withheld the name and blocked out features of her face, I'm hoping?" He could see his parents deciding to somehow use this to further their own practice.

And how cynical was that? In days gone by he would never have even had such a thought. But now? He himself had been the target of them trying to expand their horizons. And when he hadn't cooperated? They'd cut him off. But he didn't want to tell Frank any of that. There was no need.

"Of course. They offered to come over and consult in person, but I turned them down, saying it was a sensitive case."

When Frank had first started that sentence, Nate had tensed so hard his jaw ached. How he'd longed for his parents to come and visit his clinic. At first. Until it was obvious they were simply not interested. Or they were angry. But three years was a long time to harbor that kind of grudge.

He knew from experience. Because he'd done the exact same thing.

"I think you made the right call. Mrs. Blankenship came over here for the exact reason that she didn't want anyone to know about the surgery."

"I did get her permission to ask Jackson...your father."

Nate smiled. "I know who he is. And thank you for getting permission."

"I really want her to have a good outcome." Frank dropped into one of the chairs flanking Nate's desk.

"I do, as well. Was the call able to reassure you?"

"Yes. Your dad said he would take the exact multipronged approach that I planned to. He seemed very interested in what we do here."

He decided to ignore that last sentence. "I never had any doubt that your approach was the right one. It's why I worked so hard to bring you here." As uncomfortable as it made him to know that his father had probably heard Nate's name mentioned in conversation, he couldn't fault Frank for calling him. In his place he might have done the same. He held not only a person's looks, but their livelihood in his hands. And while it was true, you couldn't always work miracles, plastic surgery was one of those specialties where people seemed to expect just that. He'd heard that time and time again from his parents. It was part of what had turned him off to going into plastic surgery. Their conversations about who had done what, or who had done a terrible job on someone's face or body had rubbed him the wrong way. The emphasis wasn't on the quality of life, or helping people, but about outdoing their fellow surgeons.

Nate had interviewed his prospective staff members carefully, for just that reason. He did not want that kind of competitive spirit at The Island Clinic. He wanted the focus to be wholly on helping their patients and supporting Saint Victoria Hospital.

He hoped even Sasha was beginning to see that. Everything about his clinic was geared toward that, from the huge bronze statue of a little girl out front, her hands outstretched with a sign at her feet promising We Are Always Here to Help, to the clinic's five-star restaurant that not only fed the rich and famous, but also provided free meals to family members of patients who couldn't afford to pay.

Frank had definitely fit the profile of what the clinic looked for in a doctor. Even his calling Nate's dad bore evidence of that. He wanted a good outcome…for the patient, not for himself. *That* was why he had called Jackson Edwards.

"So you're not upset I called him? I felt like I needed to tell you."

"I'm not upset." It was true. He'd been pretty angry when he first realized what Frank had done, but now that he'd had time to really think it through, he agreed with the decision. Hadn't Nate even thought about calling his parents to do the exact same thing Frank had? And if he had, he wouldn't have blamed Frank for being upset at him for going around him, since Frank was the specialist.

And he was very glad his parents weren't coming to Saint Victoria. As he'd watched Sasha sleeping on his couch, for a split second he wondered what it might be like to have a life like other people had. To be able to love and be loved and not wonder if there was some kind of motive underlying those expressions of love.

And who would this mythical person be?

Sasha's face flashed across his mind's eye.

No. Frank's confession just brought home all the reasons why he didn't trust love. Didn't trust his own ability to read people. Because he'd been so very wrong about his parents. One thing he hadn't been wrong about, though, was moving to this island. This felt more like home than anywhere he'd ever been. Even when Sasha had looked at him with suspicion that first day.

Because it just made him want to show her and anyone else that his motivation wasn't to puff himself up and make himself look important. He didn't care how he looked. He just wanted to do good.

"Everything still a go for the surgery tomorrow? Mrs. Blankenship is more optimistic?"

"I don't think that I would use the word *optimistic*. But she's no longer in a state of panic. She knows that if she left the tumor, it would eventually spread farther and kill her. I think her husband convinced her that all he cared about was having her with him."

Nate's chest tightened. He'd never experienced that type of love. Not from his parents. Not from Tara or any other woman.

"Good." Nate glanced at the other doctor. "I have Sasha James coming to observe tomorrow, is that okay?"

"She's the one who came in and calmed Merriam down?"

"Yes. I wanted her to see how we do surgery here at The Island Clinic." He smiled, remembering the day he met her. "When I first met her, she was a little less than impressed by what she thought we were doing here."

"Why?"

The question was fair, but Nate could see the other side of it. With wealthy people flying in and off the island for quiet, private procedures, it could seem like they were using the island just for privacy and to make money. He believed she was changing her mind. At least he hoped she was. He wasn't sure why it mattered so much to him, but it did.

Because they'd had sex? Maybe. But it was more

than that, although he didn't really want to examine it too closely.

"I think some people might see the Merriam Blankenships sliding in and out of the hospital and think this is just a money-making operation."

"Really? I think that statue out front makes it pretty plain that's not the case."

"She'd never even visited the clinic up until a couple of weeks ago. I'm hoping the gala will bring more people in to see what we're about—what we're *really* about."

There was a little part of him that hoped maybe Sasha's mom was going to rub a bit of the gilt off the trappings and make The Island Clinic a little more…homey? Was that the right word? Not quite. Maybe *inviting.*

He hoped Sasha herself would be able to convince those who still thought they were here for nefarious reasons that it wasn't that at all. Nothing was more convincing than a person who had herself been convinced.

At least he hoped that was true. And with Sasha's mom and her "small army" of local vendors heading things up, this fund-raiser would be even more spectacular than if they served truffles on alabaster plates.

As if he'd read Nate's mind, Frank said, "I think you're doing the right thing having this catered locally."

He'd been hearing that from person after person. "I'm hoping everyone else sees that as a good thing, as well."

Frank paused. "Speaking of Dr. James. Is she involved, do you know?"

"In the gala preparations?"

The surgeon shook his head. "No, I'm talking more in terms of romantic involvement."

Nate's mind froze in place for several seconds. When he could think again, the word *yes* hung on his lips only to be swallowed back. She wasn't involved.

He knew that how? Because she'd slept with him? Because she'd had a terrible experience with that Austin person?

She wouldn't have a bad experience with Frank though. He was sure of that. The plastic surgeon was a good man.

But damn, Nate did not want him to ask her out. At all. Someone was bound to at some point, but at least if that happened, he probably wouldn't know who it was. Would just hear about it in some roundabout fashion. Wouldn't have to watch Sasha come over to The Island Clinic and…kiss someone.

"I really don't know. You'll have to ask her that question."

"Maybe I will. Just thought I'd ask and see if you knew anything."

Nate could always tell him he'd had wild sex with her just down the beach from the hospital. But he was pretty sure Sasha would kill him if he breathed a word of that encounter to anyone.

So why didn't he want her dating Frank?

He had no idea. But the faster he got the other doctor out of his office, the better. Because the last thing he wanted to talk about with another man was Sasha James.

Nate dropped into the seat beside her.

Sasha's insides knotted the second she saw him. She was a little surprised that he'd opted to observe the surgery with her. Surely he had more important things to do than to babysit her. But who said he was there to do that?

She'd been at the clinic on and off over the last week, but had barely seen Nate since she'd fallen asleep on his couch. She'd come to sit with her uncle when he'd had his infusion, but Nate hadn't appeared that day, either. She'd wondered if he was avoiding her, in fact. And yet here he was suddenly appearing at Merriam's surgery.

Well, this was a high-profile case. It probably had nothing to do with her at all. He probably had to be there for the ones who could line the clinic's pockets. She immediately pulled herself up for the thought. Because the clinic was supporting Saint Victoria Hospital in a very real way. It was why her uncle was able to receive his treatments, probably at minimal or no cost.

"Are they running late?" she asked.

The patient wasn't in the room yet, but this was the time that Nate had given her when he last saw her. Actually that was the morning she'd slept in his office after being floored by her uncle's presence at the hospital.

And looking back, she couldn't understand why she'd let herself do that. If it had been any other doctor at this hospital or at hers, she wouldn't have. Would have forced herself to wake up and get a grip on her emotions. Was she letting her guard down around Nate without realizing it?

Oh, she hoped not.

"Yes, a few minutes. Frank wanted to go over the procedure with Merriam and her husband one last time before she went under sedation."

"I can't blame him. Any patient would be lucky to have him. He's incredibly thorough."

Nate stiffened beside her. "Yes. He is."

There was something about the way he said that, almost as if there was something wrong with that observation. But what?

"I don't know him personally, but he's a very good doctor, from what you've said."

He settled back in his chair again. What on earth?

"He's got a good plan for this patient."

Just then the doors opened and in came a gurney. It was wheeled over to where the surgical team was assembling. Various people spoke to the patient who nodded, then a nurse moved to set up the drips.

"Will Frank be in before she's under?"

"You seem to have gotten the hang of calling everyone by their first names. Even those you don't know very well."

Touché. But then again, she hadn't liked Nate very much when he'd first asked her to use his.

And now? She swallowed. Well, now she might like him just a little too much. That, in and of itself, should send alarm bells pealing in her head. But there was nothing in there but the periodic chirp of a cricket. And a low hum of awareness.

This man had seen her at her most vulnerable. She should be a ball of nerves even sitting beside him. Instead, along with awareness, there was this subtle undercurrent of excitement. Anticipation. A woozy sense of euphoria, even.

But why? If she was hoping to repeat that scene in the ocean, she could forget it. That was not happening. They'd both made that promise. And yet this man had a way of getting under her skin and making her do unexpected things.

Just like Austin had?

She hoped not. That had been a huge disaster. This might even be a bigger one, seeing as they had to work together. Seeing as her mother was almost heading up his gala single-handedly. And seeing as she might have the gene for amyloidosis.

Her heart squeezed in her chest. Sasha needed to be careful. More than careful. If not, she could mess this up for a lot of people, including her mom. Including herself.

"Well, you kind of insisted I call you by your first name. I just assumed that went for everyone that worked here."

"You're right. It does."

But there was still something in his tone that worried her. "Is something wrong?"

"No, nothing." He nodded at the scene in front of them, where Frank had just come into the room. "There he is now."

Within minutes the patient was under general anesthesia, and they had a couple of work drapes set up. One at Merriam's hip area and one at her cheek. "Will he do the bone graft first?"

"Yes, he'll kind of have to, since he needs to set up the scaffolding on which to rebuild her cheek. They'll take a sliver of bone from her hip and set it in place. The bone should build density as it heals. Then they'll add muscle and a layer of fat tissue. Finally, they'll harvest skin from the same area they're taking the bone from, since the skin there is often a similar texture to what is on the face. They'll turn it into a mesh that they'll lay in place." He glanced at her. "There will be several revision surgeries to minimize any scarring and make sure the tissue is covering the way it should. There are always cheek implants that can help with that, as well."

Sasha was a surgeon, so knew a lot of the mechanics, but this was microsurgery. There were nerves and fine work that she didn't need to worry about. Yes, she tried to be aware of scarring when she stitched someone up, but her first concern was function. Aesthetics came second to that. And if it was something delicate, like a lip margin that had been sliced through, she normally called in a plastic surgeon just to make sure things were lined up the way they should be.

A shiver went over her. If only people worked like that. If only they could be lined up so they matched perfectly, so that just the right couples found each other. But that wasn't how things were in the real world. Relationships were messy and ugly and sometimes they were treacherous. And sometimes you never found the right person with whom to share your life. Or circumstances prevented it from becoming a reality.

Except… She was very aware of Nate beside her. Aware of his breathing, his movements, his posture. He was now leaning forward, elbows planted on his knees, fingers steepled as he watched what was happening below.

There was no doubt the man was gorgeous—he probably had women swarming around him. He had good looks and far too much charisma. And his physical features were put together in just the right way.

Ha! Kind of like what Frank was trying to accomplish in the surgery happening below.

And the way Nate made love…

Her eyes closed for a second as a wave of remembered sensation went over her. The water on her body, his warm hands stroking over her.

She sucked down a quick breath and sat up as emotions from that day threatened to pull her under.

"Everything okay?"

God, no, it wasn't. But she didn't know how to turn off the scenes playing in her head.

"Yes, fine." She stared straight ahead. "W-what's he doing now?"

"He's remodeling the remainder of bone in the cheek so he can fit what he's harvested in there."

She knew what the surgeon was doing, but it was the only thing she could think of to say that would force back the tide in her skull. Did Nate ever think about that day? Or had he been able to just sweep it away and forget about those tiny moments that went into what had happened between them?

Moments like laughing at the wave that had swept over them on the beach. Moments like handing her the paper bag that held her underwear.

Oh, what a mess she'd made by having sex with him.

And there was no way to undo it. Just like there'd been no way to undo what had happened with Austin.

All she could do was push through it and move on to the next chapter of her life.

Except all those chapters contained Nate in some way, shape or form, unless he decided to leave his position at The Island Clinic. And she didn't see that happening. He loved it here.

So she forced her attention back down to what was happening in the room beneath them. Frank was moving from one step to another, his hands steady. She couldn't see his face, but she imagined it was just as calm and methodical as his fingers.

If only Sasha could be the same. Maybe she could

though. She could move through these next days, these next months with methodical deliberation. She would walk with her uncle through his treatments, wait on her own diagnosis. And do her best to enjoy life. Enjoy her job. Even enjoy these moments next to Nate. Because life sped on by no matter what came your way. You couldn't go back and redo any of it.

So make the best of it.

And if she made the mistake of sleeping with Nate again?

Well, mistake or not, life would move on down the road, right? She wouldn't be stuck in those moments forever. So she should enjoy them while she could.

Nate's phone buzzed. He glanced down at the readout and frowned. Dragged a hand through his hair. When he looked her way, Sasha was careful to act like her attention had been on the surgery below.

"I need to go outside and deal with this. I should be back soon."

"Okay."

If it was anything to do with her uncle he would have told her, right? So apart from that, it was none of her business who was calling him. Probably something about the gala.

Or maybe it was a woman. Someone else he'd been with.

He left the room and Sasha forced her mind off the disturbing thought of Nate having a girlfriend and back toward what was happening below. She could hear Frank's voice as he called out for instruments or spoke a summary that would mark part of the official transcripts of the surgery. From what she could make out, all was going according to plan.

Nate was back within five minutes. The frown was still there.

"Is everything okay?"

He dropped back into his seat. "I'm not sure."

How could you not be sure everything was okay? "Anything I can help with?"

"Not unless you know of a magical way to deal with relatives."

She forced her eyes to go wide. "You have met my mom, right?"

"I'd take a thousand of your moms over dealing with my parents."

His parents! Not some woman waiting in the wings.

Nate had said his parents had never visited the clinic. Had all but said that they weren't proud of what he'd done. "Was that them on the phone?"

"Yes, Frank mentioned he'd called my father to consult with him on Merriam's surgery."

That surprised her. "I thought they weren't interested in The Island Clinic?"

"They're not. Unless they can get something out of it."

He made them sound pretty awful. "Was the phone call about the surgery?"

"Actually no. It was about the gala. They've decided to come to it. Out of the blue."

Maybe people could change.

"That's great." She looked at his face and reconsidered. "Isn't it?"

"I'm not sure." He rubbed his palm down his face. "I don't know what their angle is yet."

"Maybe there's not one. Maybe they realized they needed to make amends."

"I don't think that's even possible at this point. There's too much water under that particular bridge."

"But why? Do you want to talk about it?"

He stared straight ahead for several long moments. Either he hadn't heard the question, or he'd decided to ignore it. So she pretended she'd never posed the question.

Then Nate turned toward her. "Actually, I think I would. Do you want to grab a coffee, or would you rather stay here until the surgery is completed?"

She glanced down where the operation was still going strong. "I think they're going to be there for a while." Frank was still working on the bone graft. She imagined this could take close to eight or ten hours. "So we can go and always come back if there's time."

There was a relief on Nate's face she'd never seen there before. All of a sudden, she was glad she was there. Glad he was willing to confide in her—or at least tell her about whatever was bothering him.

They stood and Nate opened the door for her, and together they headed down the hallway toward the cafeteria.

CHAPTER TEN

NATE WASN'T SURE why he'd told Sasha he wanted to talk about his parents, but he did want to. Maybe because she was from Saint Victoria Hospital and he wouldn't have to face her day in and day out, like he would Frank or his other colleagues. Or maybe it was because she'd shared stuff about herself that he was pretty sure not everyone knew.

They went into the coffee shop and found a quiet corner and sat down. "What would you like?"

"A cappuccino, if they have it."

"They do."

Her brows went up. "I figured they did."

He thought there might be an undercurrent there, but if there was, she was hiding it pretty well. Maybe she was just being polite back in the observation room. He couldn't imagine anything worse than seeing her eyes glaze in boredom as he spilled out the sordid details of the rift between him and his parents. "Listen, don't feel like you have to sit here and listen to—"

"I'm the one who offered." She laid her hand on his arm. "Go get our coffees. I'll be here when you get back."

He turned to go, the words she'd just said sliding over him. *I'll be here when you get back.*

Did she know how that sounded? Whether she did or not, he wasn't prepared for the wave of emotion that washed over him at the words. He went up and stood in line, mulling over what it would be like for someone like Sasha to be there for you, no matter what. To never have to wonder if she was telling the truth. To never have to wonder if she was sizing up what you could do for her.

To just be there…for you.

He liked it. Liked the idea of someone being there when you got home. Of someone being there to hear about your day and to tell you about theirs.

But unfortunately that wasn't in the cards for him.

Or was it?

He glanced back at where Sasha sat, and found her watching him, her beautiful face soft and accessible.

Hell. What if that "someone" was… Sasha?

His mind went to hell all of a sudden, various parts of his brain going to war with the other parts. Maybe it was just the fact that she was willing to listen. Once he told her about his parents, he would likely change the dynamic between them. Did he want her to feel sorry for him? Hell no. That was the last thing he wanted.

So he would just tell her and go from there.

He ordered their coffees and when they were ready he threw some packets of sugar and sweetener on the tray before carrying it back to the table. "I wasn't sure what you took in yours."

Picking up two of the yellow packets, she ripped them open and hesitated as she looked at her coffee. "I always hate messing up the pictures they draw with the frothed milk."

There was a heart with what looked like an arrow going through it. He stiffened. Had the barista done it on purpose? Nate had had coffee in here with various other people, but he didn't think he'd ever brought anyone who was more than just a colleague in here.

"I'm sure they're used to it."

Sasha dumped the packets in. "I'm sure they are, but it still seems sad." She stirred, removing all traces of the image. Just as well, because he was starting to get some very strange thoughts going through his head.

He took a sip of his espresso, very glad there was no room for pictures or anything else in the tiny demitasse cup. Just solid black liquid. He glanced at her. "How is it?"

"Perfect." She smiled and propped her elbows on the edge of the table, her cup cradled between her hands. She was lithe and beautiful and her attention focused solely on him. "So. Tell me why you don't want your parents to come to the gala."

"I didn't say that."

"You didn't say it outright, but it was there in your body language. Or am I wrong."

Oh, she wasn't wrong. But it was a little disconcerting that she could read him so well. Could everyone else? He'd always considered himself a pretty tough nut to crack. The people who'd tried normally pulled back pretty quickly when they realized he wasn't interested in cozy little tête-à-têtes about his personal life. Stuff about the clinic? Fine, he welcomed that all day long. But his relationships were off-limits. To everyone.

Until now.

He had a decision to make. He could put a halt to this before the conversation began, or he could continue and accept whatever consequences it brought.

"You're not wrong," he said.

"But why? They're your parents."

"They are, but we haven't spoken in years. Since I came back from my tour with Medicine Around the World."

She took a sip of her coffee, licking off a tiny fleck of cream that stuck to her lip. His stomach twisted when her tongue darted back into her mouth. He remembered the slide of her tongue against his as they kissed in the sea.

"Was that after Hurricane Regan, when you came to Saint Victoria?"

"It was. I arrived home to a press release and a ribbon-cutting ceremony at my parents' clinic."

She blinked, and he couldn't blame her confusion.

"Before you ask, the problem wasn't the ribbon cutting. The problem was, I was expected to specialize in plastic surgery and join their practice. And they announced it without consulting me. There were photographers and reporters, and cameras were flashing and…"

"And you were in shock." She reached across the table. "Oh, God. That was after Marie…"

"Yes. I found out what the diagnosis was just before boarding the flight. I had the doll in my hand."

A jumble of tangled emotions went through him as he remembered the horror of that sight. Of his parents' and Tara's wide smiles as they handed him a glass of champagne. One he took, still not understanding exactly what was happening. He set the doll on a table beside him, only to have his mom pick it up and look at it, an expression of utter disgust coming into her face, and make a nasty comment.

He'd taken the doll from her and set his glass on the table. As photographers continued to snap their pictures he turned to them and caught sight of the plaque on the wall.

No, he'd said. And he turned and walked away from the clinic, catching a cab and taking it back to his apartment.

"They evidently didn't take it well when you told them you were planning on coming back here instead of joining their practice."

He gave a rough laugh. "You could say that. They called me, accused me of being selfish and insensitive. Of embarrassing them in front of everyone. Said that if I went through with coming to Saint Victoria, I was no longer welcome in their home."

Her fingers squeezed his. "They actually said that?"

"Yep."

A look of anger came over her face. *"Modi. Paran ou yo se moun fou."*

He knew what that first word meant, but had no idea about the rest. "Translation, please?"

"You don't want to know." She gave him a smile. "Let's just say it wasn't very complimentary toward your mom and dad."

He laughed. Somehow her saying that put into words all the things he hadn't said during that terrible time. Even if he didn't quite understand it. "I probably made them sound worse than they were."

"Did they say those things?"

"Yes."

"Then no, they're even *worse* than you made them sound."

He sighed. "I think they were hurt. They'd built this up into a huge deal. And part of it was my fault. I never explicitly told them no. But when Marie died, I knew I wasn't going to be happy with just sitting in an office consulting with plastic surgery cases all day. I wanted to do more with my life than that. Not that there's anything wrong with what my parents do. It just isn't for me. And what I'm doing isn't for them. My mom would hate living so close to the beach."

She took another sip of her coffee, watching him over the top of the cup. "And yet you don't hate the beach. Didn't you say you go out there a lot?"

"I do. It's one of my favorite spots in the world."

More so now, after what they'd done there. The only problem was, it was hard to go out there without seeing Sasha lying on that beach laughing, her clothing soaked, looking up at him with those dark eyes and even darker lashes. Of seeing her as she let go of him and lay back in the water.

His body reacted, just as it always did.

"It's one of my favorite spots in the world too."

He had a feeling she knew what he was thinking.

She set her cup down and looked at him. "What are you going to do about your mom and dad? Are you going to let them come?"

"I think so, yes. I don't need their approval, but I would like them to see why I couldn't join their practice."

"Do you think they'll understand?"

Unfortunately, he didn't think it would change a damned thing. But he somehow wanted them to acknowledge that there were other paths. Other ways to find fulfillment in life. "I don't know. Most of me doesn't think so, and part of me isn't exactly sure why they want to come."

Sasha's eyes softened. "Maybe they've realized that they misjudged you, Nate." She paused. "Just like I did."

His chest filled with some strange emotion that defied explanation. "You did?"

"I think so. I thought you were just some rich *monché* with a savior complex."

"Monché?"

"Dude…man…"

He laughed. "I don't think I have a savior complex, at least I hope I don't. I just want to help people, Sasha. Truly."

She gripped his hand. "I know that now. Truly." Her head tilted. "That statue in front of the clinic, is it…"

"Yes. It's Marie. I asked her parents if I could erect it there, and they gave me permission."

"I like that." She gave a visible swallow. "While her death should never have happened, I'm glad that we can now saves lives like hers."

He leaned closer and took both of her hands. "Thank you for that. I never really told anyone who that statue represented, and you're the first person to see the connection."

"I doubt I am. I'm just not as polite as other people. I tend to say what I think."

"That's one of the things I…" His mind switched tracks just in time. "That I like about you."

Her mouth quirked up on one side. "Well, my mom might disagree with you. I can't tell you the number of times she had to shush me as a kid. The thing she doesn't get is that she's just like me." Sasha laughed.

"No…" He feigned a surprised look.

She let go of one of his hands to swat at his arm. "Watch it, *monché*."

His heart was lighter than it had been in a long time. He loved sitting here sparring verbally with her. Loved the way she spoke her mind, no matter what her mom might have thought. Loved…her.

Hell. Had he just said that aloud?

No. Her eyes hadn't rounded in horror. She hadn't pulled back in disgust. He'd only voiced the words in his head. But it was enough. Enough to set them in concrete.

Was it possible?

She did tend to say what she thought. So, unlike his parents, she was easier to read. Easier to get a straight answer from. Something else that he liked. Suddenly he wanted his parents to meet her. Wanted them to see how different Sasha was from them.

"I think you're right about my mom and dad. I'm going to invite them. Whether they like what we've done with the clinic or not is immaterial. But they deserve to see where my trust fund has gone and that it's doing good things. That whether or not they care, the money they put into that fund is helping others."

Sasha smiled again. "I think that's a very good thing. You're not responsible for what they think or don't think. You're only responsible for you."

For once he believed that. Believed in the possibility of something outside the walls he'd built around his heart.

His fingers found her cheek. "Come back to my apartment, Sash."

"Are we having drinks? I drove my car here."

His thoughts were spiraling way too fast for him to keep up with. Before he quite realized what was happening, he said, "What if you just left your car here all night and picked it up in the morning?"

Her eyes came up and found his. "Leave it here in front of the clinic?"

"Yes."

"And pick it up in the…"

He nodded.

Her smile was slow in coming, but when it appeared, it lit up her whole face. "Why, Dr. Edwards, are you asking me to spend the night with you?"

"Would you say yes, if I were?"

"Mmm, let me think…"

Just when he thought she was going to come up with some excuse about needing to be at work the next day or telling him it wouldn't be a good idea, she gifted him with a kiss on the palm of his hand.

"I say yes."

There was no road leading back to the housing complex, just a wide sandy path set with bamboo torches. Since it was early afternoon, the lights hadn't come on yet. "Are these gas lamps?"

"No. Electric. I didn't want any danger of something catching on fire."

He took her hand and twined his fingers in hers as they walked. She needn't have worried about anyone seeing them, since it looked like the area was deserted. "Do all of the clinic staff live here?"

"Not all. Some of the doctors do, but some of the other staff members already have housing in other parts of the island."

They came into a clearing of domiciles that were replicas of each other. But they were lovely. The outsides were painted in the same pale green tones as the inside of the hotel. It blended into the greenery around them. "How many homes are there?"

"Twenty right now. If we expand our staff at all, we'll have to add a few more."

Normally she might have balked at that, but the spots were so tastefully made, and it looked like they'd done their best to preserve the nature around them. "There are no cars back here?"

"No. We have a couple of golf carts that we can bring back here and the odd truck when someone moves in or out, but for the most part we just try to keep things quiet and peaceful."

"It really is." She scuffed at the path. "What would your mom think of all this sand?"

He laughed. "She would absolutely hate it."

They made it to the very back of the buildings, and around the corner there was only one house. And behind it was a stand of palm trees and low shrubbery. "This is yours?"

A hammock was stretched between two of the trees, and it wasn't just some tourist decoration. There was a plastic cup sitting on the ground beside it as if he'd used it very recently. She glanced up at him. Nate surprised her in a lot of different ways.

And it scared her just a little bit.

The sand turned to river rocks as they reached a small path leading up to his front door. A very practical way of losing the sand from your shoes as you walked toward the entryway. "This is beautiful."

"Thank you. I wanted the staff who live here to have a quiet place to come home to once they finish at the clinic."

"And you didn't want a nice quiet place to come to this afternoon?"

He used their still clasped hands to pull her against him. "No, not this afternoon. Maybe not even tonight."

She hadn't gotten to see all of him the last time they were together, but this time?

Her mouth watered at the thought. They would be totally alone. Totally cut off from any possibility of being caught, since his house wasn't attached to any of the others. She assumed there were wives and children in here somewhere, but right now, it was quiet, as if this were their own little oasis of space.

And in a very real sense it was true. Someone would have to purposely skirt some obstacles to get back to his home.

As if reading her thoughts, his arms went around her waist and he walked her backward, up the rock path, under the overhang, against the front door. The wood was solid and smooth against her back, the cool surface a welcome contrast to the heat radiating off his body.

He propped his forearms on either side of her, leaning in, touched his nose to hers. "Are you wearing them?"

His fresh breath washed over her face, and she shivered at how close he was. How his words were making her squirm against him. "Wearing what?"

He dipped closer, his cheek brushing hers as he moved to her ear. "The same panties?"

Confusion went through her until she realized what he was talking about. The underwear from their other encounter. "I can't remember."

She remembered very well, but wasn't going to stand here and describe them. They weren't the same pair, but they were from the same maker. A silky black undergarment cut deep in the back. And she wanted him to slide them slowly down her legs.

His mouth moved across hers, a light touch that drove her crazy with need, one leg coming between hers and pressing hard against her.

That felt so good. Familiar. Her arms went around his neck, as she tilted her head to deepen the kiss. Except he pulled away.

"Nate?"

"I don't want it out here. And if I keep kissing you, that's exactly what's going to happen."

"Mmm, does it matter?"

He leaned back and pulled his lanyard over his head, reaching beside her to press the key card to something. The door clicked open suddenly, and if he hadn't been holding her, she would have fallen through the entryway. As it was, the momentum caused them both to lurch through it, Sasha giving a slight shriek as she almost tumbled backward.

Somehow they stayed upright, Nate kicking the door shut behind them.

He said something and lights came on around them. He must have an automated wireless system, a luxury on most parts of the island. Something squelched inside her, but she pushed it back as he kissed her again.

Soon, her thoughts zeroed back in on the man and his palms sliding down her arms, her loose sleeveless dress rippling against her body as his fingers touched portions of it. "Let me take my shoes off," she murmured against his mouth.

He stood and watched as she kicked her white thong-style sandals off on the tiled floor. The flooring extended into the living room where pale sand-colored walls gave the place an open, spacious feeling. Then his arms were back around her. "Are you hungry?"

"No."

"Thirsty?"

She smiled. "No."

He leaned down until his arms were just under her bottom and he picked her up so that her face was at the same level as his. "Good." He kissed her, walking with her to some back part of the house. Down a short hallway and through another door.

His bedroom.

He walked over to a massive carved four-poster bed and turned to sit down, her feet touching the floor. She didn't wait for an invitation; she scrambled onto the bed, her legs straddling his hips, her hands cupping the back of his head.

"Hi," she whispered.

He kissed her. "Hi yourself."

She could feel him against her, hard and ready, and they'd barely touched. It made her smile, because it matched the ache that was growing inside her, waiting for him. How could that be?

It had been very different with Austin. Something she didn't want to think about right now.

Nate bunched her dress in his hands, sliding it up her thighs as she raised up a bit to help. Then it was around her waist and she was that much closer to him. His fingers explored her underwear and she shivered as his palms smoothed over the skin he found at the edges of the elastic.

God, she wanted to be next to him without any barriers between them. She reached down and found the hem of her dress, pulled it up and over her head, tossed it onto the far side of the mattress.

When she reached behind her to unhook her bra, he stopped her. "Let me."

He found the clasp and the rush of air against her back was a heady experience. Closer. She needed to be closer to him.

As if reading her mind he dragged off his polo shirt, letting it drop to the floor in the same spot he'd discarded her bra.

She couldn't help herself. She mashed herself against his chest, her nipples instantly hardening at the unexpected friction from the dusting of hair she found there.

One of his hands slid up her back in a steady move until he reached her nape, fingers sinking deep into her hair.

"Hell, Sash. I didn't think anything could be better than last time, but…"

She understood exactly what he meant. "I know."

His lips pressed against the side of her neck, trailing up and over her jaw, peppering tiny kisses along her cheek until he was back at her mouth. Then he was right where he needed to be, teeth and tongue and mouth devouring hers in a way that made her breathless and so very needy.

She squirmed against him, lifting and sliding in a way that mimicked what she wanted to happen. Needed to happen.

When she couldn't stand it anymore, she climbed off him, her lips leaving his as he groaned.

"Just a minute," she whispered. "I need to…"

She stripped off her underwear, as Nate's eyes followed her every move. "I can't believe you're here with me."

"I am. I'm right here."

Then she reached for his trousers and popped the button free.

CHAPTER ELEVEN

NATE WAS ON fire as Sasha tugged his pants down his hips, taking his boxers with them. Then he was free, the air from the room sluicing over him like the waves in the sea.

"Come here." His voice was rougher than he'd meant it to be, but she evidently didn't mind, because she just laughed.

"Not quite yet." She pulled something from the back pocket of his slacks and tossed it to him. "New wallet?"

"Yes." He took it and opened it to where he'd put a new packet, took it out and then tossed the wallet onto his night table. He started to tear it open, but she stopped him.

He looked at her in puzzlement, until she pulled him to his feet and turned him to face the bed, while she slowly sat on it. She reached her hand out for the condom, but when he gave it to her, she set it on the bed next to her hip.

"I thought this might be just the perfect height. And I was right." Her smile held a secret knowledge.

He had no idea what she was talking about, until her hands reached for him and drew him slowly toward her.

Hell! The second her mouth slid over him, he wondered if it was all over. The wet heat took him by storm, destroying his defenses. He buried his hands in her hair in an attempt to gain some semblance of control over the situation. But it wasn't happening. Sasha was doing what Sasha did, being as direct with her actions as she was with her words. He loved it. Feared it. Wanted it more than anything he knew.

All he could do was somehow show her. His fingers stroked her face, brushed her hair off her forehead even as his eyes closed and he allowed himself to take in every sensation she let him have.

There was no sense of selfishness in this woman. No taking whatever she could get. And he was coming very close to…

His eyes opened with a start and he pulled free. "No. Not like this."

She sat back on the bed, licking her lips with a smile. "What? You didn't like it?" She reached for him again. "I could just finish—"

"It's my turn." He ripped open the condom and slid it over himself before bearing her down onto the bed and covering her body with his. "God, I want you so much it hurts."

It was true. His body ached. But so did his chest. His eyes. Parts of him that he never equated with sex. Because it wasn't just about sex. This was his first time making love and knowing that it actually was about more than just the physical act. So he showed her. Loved her. And when he finally parted her legs and entered her, it was a spiritual experience. A sharing he'd never experienced with any other woman.

Sasha wrapped her legs around him, like she had in the water, but the solidness of the bed held them up without them needing to put any effort into that part. Instead, he could just concentrate on the push and pull of their bodies as the inner waves began to build.

And when she breathed his name, he knew it was time. Reaching between them, he found that sensitive spot that he knew she liked. Stroked it, teased it, while kissing her and whispering how much he wanted her, how good it felt to be inside her. How he needed to feel her let go against him.

He quickened his pace, their bodies tangled together in a heap that he hoped he could never unravel. He thrust harder, touched her with more urgency until she was arching against him, gasping for him not to stop. He didn't. Drove home with all he had.

And then he felt her give way beneath him, her hips moving frantically as she came. He could hold back no longer, pouring everything he had into her with a fury that surprised him. He buried his face against her neck and rode out wave after wave of sensation, trying to draw it out as his pumping got slower, less frantic.

Then he was still, enjoying the feeling of being joined with her in the soft aftermath, as her hands stroked up and down his back.

Surely she'd felt what he'd felt. He opened his mouth to say the words, but something stoppered them in the back of his throat. He wasn't sure what it was. Or why.

This was all happening too fast. They'd known each other what? A few weeks?

She'd had one terrible relationship; he didn't want to do anything that might scare her off. So maybe it was best just to let things ride. They could take it slow. He could take her to the gala as his date.

Introduce her to his parents.

Was he kidding? They didn't even come into the equation when it came to Sasha.

He felt her shift beneath him and realized a lot of his weight was on her.

"Sorry." He rolled off her, only to have her come onto her side, her fingers playing in the hair of his chest.

"Don't be. That was…delicious."

He laughed. Leave it to her to come up with a term that was so unexpected, and yet so perfect. It was why he lo… No. Don't jinx it. Take it slow, remember? "It was, was it?"

He dragged her on top of him, kissing her, then smoothing her hair back so he could look into her face. "Now, I'm hungry. So I'll fix us something to eat. Then," he slid his mouth down the side of her jaw, "then, once it's good and dark, and the rest of the world is in bed, I want to take you outside and rock you to sleep in that hammock that's sitting under the trees."

She bit his lip. "And if I don't want to go to sleep?"

"Oh, sweetheart. The sleeping won't take place for a very long time."

Sasha didn't wake up in the hammock. But true to his word, he had rocked her to sleep out there. Her face heated at all the things they'd done out in the open air. She had no idea you could do that many things in a rocking bed. A flash of worry went through her that she quickly banished. It didn't mean he'd learned those things with some other woman.

The thought of him spending time in that hammock with someone else made her slightly nauseous. Maybe because of the way it molded to your body in a way that a mattress didn't. It was close and intimate, and so very sexy.

Don't think about it.

She turned her head to find him already awake, his hair wet from a recent shower. He was lying on the bed propped on his elbow watching her. And he smelled divine.

It made her feel kind of sweaty and grimy and she wasn't sure why.

And when he smiled and bent down to kiss her, she ducked out of the way. "I haven't brushed my teeth yet."

"I don't care."

She laughed. "Well, I do. It's not fair for you to be all clean and fresh. Let me get a shower, then we'll talk."

"Okay. First I want to ask you something."

Something about the way he said that made her blink. "What is it?"

"It's about the gala."

She relaxed. "Can't it wait until after I shower?" For some reason, she really needed to be on an equal footing with him.

"Sure. I'll get you a towel." He got off the bed and waited until she'd scrambled off as well before moving out of the room. Now that she could actually look around without the thrill of kisses and distractions of lovemaking, she was surprised by how large the room was. It was probably twice the size of her bedroom. She wasn't sure why that felt important, but it did.

She fidgeted and then looked for her clothes, not finding them. "Nate?"

He reappeared holding a thick beige towel. Her clothes were folded neatly on top of it.

"Did you wash these?" Austin had never done anything like that. It would have never even crossed his mind. But somehow it made her feel guilty. How long had Nate been up?

"It was no problem. There is shampoo and soap in the bathroom. Help yourself."

"Thank you." She padded to the bathroom that she'd briefly seen between lovemaking sessions and closed the door behind her. The decor was in keeping with the island feel, but it was well-appointed, just like his bedroom. And the curved faucets were pricey.

She frowned. *Why does it matter, Sasha?*

Nate wasn't pretentious. At all. In fact, the fancy decor seemed a little out of character with the Nate she'd grown accustomed to. Maybe these apartments also served to house families of patients in case the hotel filled up, like he said happened during the gala.

That made sense. She relaxed and turned on the shower, allowing the warm water to flow over her body and soothe the slight aches of muscles that she hadn't noticed last night. Nate was certainly…active…in his lovemaking. But, *oh* it had been wonderful and almost overwhelming.

She soaped her hair and then let the water sluice over it, rinsing the suds. She smiled. She was going to smell like him.

No, not like him. Because there was no scent known to man that could smell as good as he did. Her hands trailed down her stomach, shivering as she remembered his touch. His body covering hers.

Oh, she was getting worked up all over again. She needed to get out of here and get home. Where she could unpack everything that had happened last night.

Finishing up, she turned the taps off and stepped

out of the shower onto the thick mat. After toweling herself dry, she wrapped the towel around her hair, while she got dressed. Glancing at the bathroom vanity, she frowned again when she spied a new toothbrush wrapped in cellophane and a tiny tube of toothpaste next to it. Also new and unused.

The thoughts of him bringing other women here slithered back into her head. For once, she wished she carried a toothbrush in her purse so she could leave those on the counter untouched. But she didn't, so she ripped open the package and brushed her teeth as quickly as she could, rinsed her mouth. She held the toothbrush there for a minute and looked at the holder where he kept his.

No way.

She went over to the small stainless-steel trash can and stepped on the lever to open it. Then she tossed the brush and toothpaste into it.

She wasn't sure what she was getting so uneasy about. It was a nice gesture. Just like washing her clothes.

But then she thought she'd known Austin too. Except he'd never showered her with these little touches either. She unwrapped her hair and dragged her fingers through it, arranging the curls the best she could. Thank heavens he hadn't set out a new hairbrush, as well.

She looked at herself in the mirror. The woman staring back at her looked wide-eyed and unsure of herself. She recognized that person from another time in her life and quickly turned her back on her.

Gathering her composure, she counted to ten before opening the bathroom door and reentering the bedroom.

Nate was nowhere to be seen now. Thank goodness. But she was going to have to face him sometime.

The smell of bacon and eggs reached her nose and her stomach took a swan dive. She had no idea what was wrong with her. She had not felt like this the first time they made love. But they hadn't been in his house, where the trappings of luxury surrounded her. It had just been her and Nate and the ocean. And she'd felt on equal footing with him.

She didn't want to sit at a table with china plates and try to think of what she could say to him. But if he'd made her breakfast, she didn't very well see how she could refuse without hurting his feelings. And really, he'd done nothing wrong. He was still the same person he'd been when he'd first come to Saint Victoria Hospital that day.

So she moved into the living area and forced a cheerful smile on her face. "Good morning."

He came around from the kitchen, his feet bare, wearing dark jeans and an unbuttoned shirt. The dusting of hair on his chest narrowed and slid in a smooth trail past his waistband.

. This man was any girl's fantasy. And maybe he was.

"Safe to kiss now?"

What could she say? No? She held her face up and his lips brushed across hers, familiar and warm. Her uneasiness subsided a bit.

"Everything okay?" he asked.

"Fine. It's a little later than I expected."

He glanced back at the stainless-steel clock over his sink. It matched the rest of the appliances. "It's barely six."

"I know, but I kind of want to head home before a lot of other people are up."

A frown puckered his brow, but he nodded. "Of course."

"Oh, you wanted to ask me something about the gala. Is it about my mom? As far as I know she has everything under control. I'll be there helping her serve, of course, along with a whole slew of other people."

"You're planning on serving?"

"Yes, why?"

He paused as if trying to figure out a way to say something. "Does she not have enough help?"

"I'm sure she does, but she's my mom, and I want to pitch in."

The slithering thoughts about him being here with other women morphed and changed into something else. "Is there a problem with that?"

"No. I just thought it might be nice if a member of each of our hospitals greeted the guests. I was going to ask you if you would be Saint Victoria Hospital's representative."

"And who would be the clinic's representative?"

"I would be."

Memories of her time with Austin resurfaced, ugly and eerily similar. He had cared about where they went for dinner, what she wore, one time even buying her a dress to wear to an opera he wanted to go to.

So Nate didn't want her serving food to his rich guests? The nausea that had disappeared with his kiss resurfaced. Would the Nate wearing a tuxedo at his gala be a total stranger to her? Would he wander regally from group to group asking if they had everything they needed while her mom and the rest of her crew waited hand and foot on them?

Suddenly she didn't want to find out. Knew now why she'd avoided going to the gala in the past. She'd already visited in the circles of the very wealthy during her time with Austin, and in the end found out that it was nothing like its glitzy facade. What she'd seen of Austin's world was shallow and entitled, and the people were used to having things handed to them.

Sasha was used to working her ass off for everything she'd accomplished. Did she regret her time at Harvard? No. The school had been wonderful, and she was truly grateful for being gifted with that education. It had allowed her to do what she loved most in this world. But she couldn't bear it if Nate turned out to be exactly like the man she'd once imagined him to be, the man she'd been avoiding for the last three years.

"Nate, I can't. I'm sorry. I told my mother I was going to help her, and that's where I need to be. I'm sure the hospital administrator over at Saint Victoria Hospital, or any number of people would be happy to help you greet your guests."

His frown deepened. "I understand."

But he didn't. She could see it in his face. Sense it in the stiff formal posture he'd settled into. This was wrong. She never should have come here. Should have left things as they were with the rosy image of what they'd had that day on the beach.

She found her sandals in the entryway and somehow managed to stuff her feet into them, even though her eyes were gritty and difficult to see through. "I really do need to get home, Nate—I'm sorry I can't stay for breakfast."

"I'll walk you to your car."

"No!" If she had to travel down that sandy path with him, she wasn't going to make it without bursting into tears. History really did repeat itself, and Sasha was finding out just how stupid she was for believing the distance between them could be spanned. It couldn't. Her heart was sitting there telling her it was possible, but her mind... Her mind was telling her what she'd known all along. She and Nate were on different courses. A geometry term popped into her mind and she grabbed at it.

Asymptotes.

They were asymptotes. He was a line and she was a curve that got closer and closer to him, but never quite reached where he was. She would never be a part of that world. Didn't even want to.

It was better that she found out now than later, when her emotions had become too tangled up in him.

Weren't they already?

Oh, she hoped not. Couldn't bear it if she actually fell for him.

A whispering in her mind circled around, but she chased it away, horrified when she realized her hands had actually gone up and followed the thought.

"Sasha, what is it?"

His voice came through a fog, but she was shaking her head telling him she was fine, she just had some things she needed to do. Without waiting for him to say anything else, she fled out his door, hurried down the sandy path and somehow made it to her car.

Once there, she buried her head in her arms against the steering wheel and cried until there were no more tears. Thank the Lord he hadn't followed her. And since it was still really early, there was no one around to see her start her car, back out of the parking spot and head down the road. Away from The Island Clinic. Away from Nate.

In her rearview mirror, the bronze likeness of Marie stared mournfully after her, arms outstretched as if pleading with her not to go. But she had to. For her own self-preservation. And to hold on to what good memories she still had of her and Nate's time together. Because she knew deep down, there was no chance of it ever happening again. She would make sure of it.

Nate sat at his desk, toying with his cell phone, before finally tossing the thing into a drawer. He hadn't seen Sasha in a week. He'd tried calling her, but he was always sent straight to voice mail. And the two times he'd driven over to Saint Victoria Hospital, he'd been told by Patty, a friend of hers, that she was in surgery and she had no idea when she would be out.

He finally got the message. She was avoiding him. He wasn't sure why. Unless she'd sensed that he cared for her, and she didn't return his feelings. The look on her face when he'd asked her to stand with him to greet guests had sent a chill over him. She'd looked… stricken. That was the only word he could come up with to describe it. Was it that repugnant to her to actually be seen with him in public?

He swallowed. Why not? His parents had pretty much avoided being seen with him once he told them he wasn't interested in joining their practice.

Well, damn.

It wasn't like he hadn't been through this before. He should be well used to it by now. But Sasha had seemed so caring and understanding when he'd talked about his devastation over losing Marie, and when he'd shared from his heart about his parents and how hurt he'd been by their behavior.

Had it all been an act?

Again. Why not?

She'd been quick to offer her mom's services when she'd come to that meeting about the gala. She'd been there what, ten minutes, and then her hand went up and she asked why they didn't use local businesses.

But she'd slept with him after he offered the catering to her mom. There was no way those two things could be connected. Could they?

He didn't think so, but his mind was so screwed up right now that he was no longer sure of anything.

Dammit all. This was why he didn't do relationships anymore. He had no idea what was what…what was true and what wasn't, when it came to other people's emotions. Or his own.

Well, he wasn't going to call her again. If she didn't want to talk to him, then so be it. If she didn't want to stand beside him, that was all well and good. To prove that point, he called Saint Victoria Hospital and got hold of Maurice, the hospital administrator—he refused to believe it was because that was who Sasha had suggested—and found the man was more than willing to help him in that endeavor. So even if she came back and offered, he'd tell her he already had it covered.

She wouldn't though. He knew it in his soul. When she'd walked out of his apartment, she'd done so with the intention of never coming back. And he had no idea why.

But he hadn't begged his parents not to turn their

backs on him all those years ago, and he wasn't going to beg Sasha not to do so now. He just didn't have it in him. Not today. And probably not tomorrow, either.

When he saw her at the gala tomorrow night, maybe he'd get a better sense of what was going on with her. He'd just wait and see if her attitude changed. Maybe she just needed time to process what had happened at his place.

But something told him otherwise.

Well, hell, he didn't have time to worry about this. Not with the fund-raiser already on his doorstep. He took Marie's doll down from the shelf and set her on his desk. This was what he needed to keep in front of him. This was his entire reason for coming to Saint Victoria. It hadn't been for Sasha or his parents or anyone else. It had been because of the way a young child had touched his heart and challenged him to make a difference.

That motivation had been enough years ago.

And it would be enough to get him through the next day or week or year.

CHAPTER TWELVE

"WHAT DO YOU MEAN, you don't feel well? Do you have a fever?"

Sasha stood at her door in pajamas and shook her head at her mom. There was no way she could go to that gala. She thought she could. Thought she could hold her head up high and face Formal Nate, all decked out in his finest garb. But she couldn't.

"Sasha, you're scaring me. Did you get the results back from the test?"

She'd convinced her uncle Art to tell her mom about his illness, but there was a string attached. She had to come clean about the genetic test she'd taken.

But she wished now that she'd waited until after the gala was over. Her mom had been obsessed and worried and had almost said she couldn't do the catering. Sasha had panicked and begged her to please go through with it. It would mean a lot to the island and a lot to her. Besides, her mom needed something to keep her mind off things she couldn't control.

"I didn't. But this has nothing to do with amyloidosis. My stomach is just in knots. It was a hard day at work, and I'm exhausted." That last part was a lie, but the part about her stomach was very true. But it was in knots from nerves and heartache over what had happened with Nate. She probably should have taken his calls and just come clean about her feelings, but the grinding sense of despair had kept her from doing that. She hadn't wanted to believe the worst about Austin, only to find out it was very true. It crushed her to think that Nate might be cut from the very same cloth.

Wasn't it better to assume, thereby avoiding having the actual facts slap her right in the face?

She didn't know, but she was running on fumes right now, and the gala wasn't the place to tackle those hard questions. Maybe after it was over, she'd make an appointment to see him.

Make an appointment.

God, she'd made love to the man, and yet she didn't have the courage to march into his office and tell him she needed to ask him a question. Whether or not he was the person she hoped he was, or whether he was the person she feared he was.

"Is this about Nate?" Her mom's voice cut through her musings like a knife, slashing into emotions that were already raw.

"What? Of course not."

Her mom stared at her, then grabbed her arms and led her over to the sofa. "Oh, honey, tell me. Are you afraid of the diagnosis?"

Sasha couldn't suppress a laugh that quickly turned to a gasping sob. She hadn't been. It hadn't even crossed her mind since that day at his cottage. Until now. And no matter how many times she'd told herself otherwise—told herself to think rationally—it was like one more nail hitting the coffin containing her hopes and dreams. She somehow got hold of herself. "No. That's not it."

"Then what?"

How could she say the actual words? She couldn't, so she simply said, "He's rich."

Tessi looked into her face. "Oh, honey. Nate is not Austin."

The bottom of her chin trembled as she took in those words. "But what if he is?" The question came out in whispered tones.

"I can't answer that question. All I can do is tell you to search your heart. Deep down, you know the truth. But until you believe it, until you pull it into your soul and hold it tight, you're not going to listen to what anyone says." She patted her cheek. "I have to go. But think about it. What I will say is don't wait too long to come to a conclusion. Because you might just find out you missed a chance at something that doesn't come along every day. Something like I had with your dad."

With that, Tessi stood. "I need to get going. Call me if you need anything. I'll answer, even if it's in the middle of the gala." With that she let herself out the door, going to the very place where Sasha should be going.

Nate spotted Tessi over by one of the long banquet tables setting out hors d'oeuvres. He went over to her. When she saw him, she put the lid on the tray she was holding and smiled. "Your guests will be arriving soon."

"Everything looks wonderful—thank you so much." He hesitated. "Is Sasha here? She mentioned she would be helping you serve tonight."

"No." She fixed him with a look. "She was feeling under the weather and decided to stay home."

That wasn't like Sasha. If he knew anything about her, it was that she was serious about her commitments. Was that why she'd run off like she had the last morning they were together? Was she afraid of being pressed to make a commitment she wouldn't be able to keep? Well, she wouldn't have to worry about that anymore. He wasn't going to press her for anything.

"Is it something serious?"

"I'm sorry, but I need to get back to the catering."

Real worry crawled down his spine. "Tessi, what's wrong with her?"

She looked at him for a minute, then shook her head. "That's not for me to say." She started to walk away, then stopped and turned to face him. "Do you think there's a difference between those of us who are here to serve food and those who come to eat that food?"

He frowned, not sure what she was saying. "No. Of course not."

She smiled. "That's all I needed to hear." With that she turned and moved to another long serving table, her hands working over it with a grace and elegance that reminded him of her daughter's hands as she'd stitched up their accident patient.

He had no idea what she'd meant by her question, but sensed it was important. Critical. And that it had something to do with Sasha.

Do you think there's a difference between those of us who are here to serve food and those who come to eat that food?

Sasha had told him she was going to help her mom serve the food. And when he'd asked her to help him greet guests, instead, something in her face had changed. A wariness had come over her. When he'd pressed her, she'd bolted.

Why?

He stood there, his mind mulling Tessi's words until they were burned into his brain.

Then something sliced through him like a hemostatic scalpel, cutting and cauterizing as it went. And he knew what was wrong. At least he thought he did.

Austin.

The rich boyfriend she'd had at Harvard who'd cast her aside after five years of dating. She'd said enough about him that Nate knew that relationship had wounded her deeply.

What had Sasha said to him one time? *I'm hoping I was wrong about you.* Nate had told her he hoped she was wrong too.

Maybe she'd taken his request for her to greet guests the wrong way. He'd never meant to imply that helping her mom serve was any less important. Tessi was a smart woman. She'd asked him that question for a reason.

Hell, in trying to go slow, in trying to court her, he'd sent a message he'd never meant to send.

So what was he going to do about it?

He was going to go see her and confess to his real crime. That he loved her and had been too much of a coward to tell her that last night they were together. And if she kicked him out of her house?

Well, then he'd know he was wrong. That she really didn't love him. And he would accept it and go on. But there was no way he was giving up without at least trying.

He made his way back over to where Tessi stood. She

glanced over at him as if she knew. And she smiled. "I forgot to say you look very nice. Very...*sophisticated.*"

Nate took the heavy tray from her. "Where is she?"

"At home." Tessi rattled off an address that Nate committed to memory.

He then bent down and kissed her cheek. "Thank you for everything. For doing such a wonderful job here. And for teaching your daughter to be the incredible woman she is." He motioned to the tray. "Where do you want this?"

"Those happen to be extras. Why don't you find someone to share them with?"

He laughed. She was not very subtle. But then she was like her daughter. Direct. Sometimes blunt. But with a heart of gold. A heart he wasn't sure he deserved.

But he was damned well going to try to win it.

"Thanks for the food. I'll return the tray." He could not believe he was about to run out on a gala that could very well provide another year's worth of funding for both The Island Clinic and Saint Victoria Hospital. But Frank Seldridge had been his backup for the last two years and would do an admirable job of holding down the fort. He found his friend talking to one of the early arrivals. Nate greeted them with a smile, his chest tight with the need to get away, to go find Sasha.

He murmured to Frank, "I have somewhere I need to be. I really need you to step in for me tonight. Can you do it?"

The surgeon, who was well on the way to working a miracle on Merriam Blankenship, could perform just as big a miracle tonight. The man took one look at the covered silver tray in Nate's hands and glanced up in his face. Whatever he read there must have convinced him. "Go. We'll be fine."

"Thanks."

"Oh, and Nate…" He chuckled. "Best of luck."

He appreciated it, because he was going to need it.

He hurried down the front steps, only to run smack-dab into his parents. He'd totally forgotten they were coming tonight. But he didn't have time for this right now.

"Nathaniel, how nice to see you," his father said. "Nice little place you have here."

Was he kidding? Before he had a chance to respond, his mom took him by the shoulders and gave him an air kiss on the cheek. "Why are you holding that tray, dear?"

Said as if everything between them was perfectly normal. Well, he wasn't going to stand around and chit-chat. If they wanted to talk to him, they could get in line. Behind the person who meant more than anything in this world to him. "I'm taking some food to a… friend."

What else could he call her? He certainly didn't know if she was going to kick him out on his ass the second he showed up at her house.

He gave them both a smile that he hoped looked genuine enough and said, "I'm sorry. I'll talk to you later, but please stay and see what it is I've been up to for the last three years."

With that, he turned and headed out to the parking lot.

Nate drove as fast as he safely could, although the ride to Williamtown still seemed to take forever. But then he was entering the main street of the town, glancing at the address he'd scribbled onto a scrap of paper. He drove slowly down a side street that was less than a mile from the hospital. The white house was modest but neat, a tended garden out front boasting a colorful array of flowers, while a huge bougainvillea sprawled over an archway, behind which was a dark red door.

He felt a little stupid standing there in a tuxedo holding a silver tray. But he had a feeling words were not going to be enough right now. He knocked on the door.

He waited for a minute, wondering if she could see him and would refuse to open the door. Then he heard the sound of a lock snicking. The door opened.

Sasha stood there in an…evening gown? Then she tilted her head and stared at him, her glance trailing over him. "Nate? What are you doing here? You're supposed to be at the gala."

"I'm playing hooky."

"You're playing what?" Her eyes widened. "Is that my mother's tray?" Her hand went to her mouth, then a string of Creole words poured out, searing the air around them. "Did she *send* you here?"

"No, she didn't. And I won't ask you what you just said."

Her lips twitched the tiniest bit. "Good. Because you might not like the answer."

"Can I come in? Your mom's tray is rather heavy."

She glanced down at herself. "I was just getting ready to go to…"

He realized why she had the dress on. "You were coming?"

"Yes. I decided I had some unfinished business."

A flare of hope surged through him. Sasha stepped

aside and let him in, directing him to set the tray on a pass-through counter that divided the living room from the kitchen.

"I like your house."

"Thanks."

The furnishings were clean and comfortable, and she had a flare for decorating. The room pulled you in and invited you to stay.

He realized how cold his own house might have appeared with its more formal furnishings. But the houses were all decorated alike, in case they needed to be pulled into service as extra places to house guests.

But looking at it after what he'd figured out, he could see how it might have seemed to Sasha. And his request that she greet guests… Hell. He wasn't sure how to make it right. Except she was dressed in formal wear, the green fabric of her dress hugging her slender curves to a tee. She said she'd been getting ready to come to the gala. That she had unfinished business.

With him?

She seemed to gather her composure. "Why are you here?"

"This is where I should be. Where I needed to be. But let me ask you this. Why are you here, rather than at the gala?"

"I was late in coming to a decision."

He took a step closer. "Care to tell me what that decision is?"

"I—I…"

Taking one of her hands in his, he said, "Okay, I'll go first. I have something I need to tell you."

"You do?"

"Yes." He led her over to the couch. Then his gaze

held hers as he prepared to pour out his heart and soul. "I don't know what you think of me, Sash, or what you think you know of me, but… I'm not rich."

"What?" Shock went through her face.

"It's true. I sank every penny of my trust fund into the clinic. I earn a salary as a doctor and as the chief of staff, but it's not a hefty one. Because that's not what I want. That's *not why I'm there*." He drew the words out very slowly.

"But your house…"

"It's a cookie-cutter house, made just like all the rest of them. We made everything to pull double duty, if necessary."

Her eyes traveled over his tuxedo, touching the collar, sliding over his bow tie. "You look very nice."

"So do you. But then you're beautiful no matter what you're wearing. Or not wearing." He smiled and took both her hands, doing his best not to get sidetracked this time. "I need you to know that even if I were wealthy. Even if I had all the money in the world, I would still want to be on this island, doing exactly what I'm doing. I would still be the same man who's sitting next to you right now."

"I figured that out just a little while ago. It's why I'd decided to come to the gala." Tears welled in her eyes. "I misjudged you again. I'm sorry, Nate."

"I realize now how I might have come across at the house. I wanted you to be with me to greet the guests because… I love you, Sasha. Not for any other reason."

"And I thought you—"

"I know."

"My mom?"

He paused. "Not exactly. She was careful not to say

very much. But it was enough that I realized how my words might have come across. I promise—I want nothing more from you than a chance to be with you. For the long haul. Not just for five years." He let that sink in for a minute before going on. "Not for ten years. But for the rest of our lives."

She leaned against him, putting her head on his shoulder. "I feel like such a fool. My mom told me you were nothing like…"

"Austin?"

"I was so afraid to believe, to just listen to my heart."

"I know. Me too." He wrapped his arms around her, pulling her closer. "Looks like we both have some growing to do. As individuals. And as a couple."

"You never entertained other women at your house? The toothbrush, the toiletries?"

"All in case a guest needed to use the house unexpectedly. I would have vacated and slept in my office."

"Of course." She drew in a deep breath. "Can you forgive me?"

"There's nothing to forgive, although my parents seemed pretty peeved at my leaving them standing on the steps of the conference center."

She sat up and looked at him. "You didn't?"

"I did. And I don't regret it. If they really want to reconnect, they'll try again. If they don't, then…" He gave a shrug.

Her face got very still. "Wait. We can't. Not until I find out the results of my test."

"Do you really think that would change things?"

"It should. You don't have to—"

He stopped what she was going to say with a kiss.

"Yes. I do. I love you. I don't want to live without you. That is, unless you don't…"

"I do. But then I'm sure my very discreet mother already let that cat out of the bag too."

"Actually, she didn't. But she did hint that I might want to take that tray and make a beeline for your house."

Sasha laughed, the sound lighter and more carefree than anything he'd heard in a while. And it was sweeter than the finest symphony.

"Well, it's a good thing. Because if you hadn't, I would have stormed that gala and yelled at the top of my lungs until someone found you and brought you to me." She sighed. "I realized what a mistake I was making. I love you too, by the way."

"Thank God. And if you'd shown up, I would have been honored to have you standing by my side or to have you helping your mom with the catering. You're my other half, Sasha. The one I didn't realize I was missing."

"How about if neither of us goes to the gala. What if we both stay right here?"

"I like the way you think."

She toyed with his bow tie, giving it a playful tug. "Think they'll miss us?"

"It wouldn't matter if they do." He smiled at her. "Why? Do you have something in mind?"

This time the tug on his tie was serious and succeeding in loosening the knot enough that it hung free around his neck.

"I'm wondering how long it takes to get a very handsome man out of his tuxedo?"

He growled, pulling her toward him. "You'd better be talking about me."

"No one else, my love. No one else. I'll miss the hammock, but we'll have to make do with a bed that's a whole lot narrower than yours."

He kissed her long and hard. "Believe me, Sash. There's not going to be enough room between us to tell the difference." With that he scooped her into his arms and carried her into the interior part of the house. A place where they would pledge their love and become the asymptote that defied all the odds, when it dared to intersect and join lovers as one.

EPILOGUE

Two years later

NATE LOWERED HIS baby girl into her crib. "Good night, sweetheart."

She was already sound asleep, her belly full. He was finding he loved these middle-of-the-night feedings. It was a time when the world was still and quiet, when he could take the time to reflect on how utterly happy he was.

He reached into the pocket of his robe and felt something. Damn. He'd almost forgotten. He pulled the object free and walked over to the shelf that flanked the white crib. Placing the doll carefully in the spot he'd chosen, he touched its hand.

Arms encircled his midsection, and warm lips tickled his neck. "I have a lot to be grateful to her for."

Nate didn't ask who she meant; he knew. "It's still hard to think about her death."

"I know. But there's an awareness out there now, that our island is not exempt from things like schistosomiasis. And you're watching for it now. It won't take you by surprise again."

She was right. They'd treated three more cases over

the last couple of years, all of them children. All of them had lived. Maybe Marie was somehow looking down on them, watching over her island and its inhabitants.

Sasha turned him around to face her. "Guess who I saw in town today?"

"Who?"

"Uncle Art."

Two years after his diagnosis, treatment had put him into remission. He would live with the condition for the rest of his life. But he was making the most of whatever time he had left.

"You did?"

"Yes. He was with Corinne."

He cocked his head, trying to place the name. "You mean *the* Corinne? The one whose parents broke them up?"

"Yep. And they looked pretty chummy." She reached up and cupped his face. "Wouldn't it be great if they got their happy ending too?"

"It would, indeed." Sasha's amyloidosis test had come back negative for the gene. They'd both been relieved, and while they'd already talked about having children, it had erased any lingering doubts. Dayna Marie Edwards had made her way into the world kicking and screaming and letting everyone know she was taking after her mama. She still was. Their baby was direct and to the point about what she needed and when she needed it. And Nate couldn't love her more. Couldn't love her mother more.

She glanced up at him. "Your mom called today. They booked their flight for next week."

Nate frowned. "Are you sure you're up to this?"

"I'm looking forward to it."

This would be his parents' third visit. The first time was at the gala, when he'd been too busy wooing Sasha to spend time with them. The second time was at their wedding a year ago. The fences weren't completely mended, but they were working on it. Thanks to Sasha's wisdom and her canny knack of moving chess pieces into just the right spot.

He still couldn't believe she was his. And he was hers. But he was never going to take her for granted. Never going to take their love for granted. They could have so easily lost it all.

But thank God they hadn't.

"Hey, come on." He leaned down to kiss her. "You need your sleep. I'm hoping she won't wake up again."

But if she did, Nate would come get her and bring her in to nurse so that Sasha wouldn't have to make the trek. It was the least he could do, and he did it with a grateful heart. He had the family he thought he'd never have.

The family who'd stolen his heart and then given it back. The family who showed him every single day how loved he was. And that was worth more than money to Nate.

It was…everything.

* * * * *

CARIBBEAN PARADISE, MIRACLE FAMILY

JULIE DANVERS

MILLS & BOON

To Charlotte, who always sees the potential.

CHAPTER ONE

"COME ON, MAISIE! Kick! You can do it!"

Willow Thompson clung to her three-year-old daughter's chubby little hands as Maisie did her best to keep herself afloat in the shallow water. The beach behind their home on the island of St. Victoria was an ideal place to learn to swim, as the water curved into a sandy cove that provided refuge from the strong waves of the Caribbean Sea.

Willow could have chosen to live at the accommodations provided by her workplace. She was a nurse at the Island Clinic, a private clinic in the Caribbean that specialized in providing top-notch medical care to some of the wealthiest and most well-known patients on earth. The clinic prided itself on its ability to provide patients with luxury almost as much as its ability to provide quality health care, and the clinic's extravagance extended to its staff quarters.

But as much as Willow enjoyed elegance, she enjoyed balance between her work and personal life even more. The small cottage she'd rented on the beach offered privacy for herself and her daughter, and gave Willow the separation from work that she needed. As much as she loved her job as a nurse, part of the reason she'd taken the job was so that she could put work behind her at the end of each day and focus on spending time with her daughter. And living apart from the clinic gave Willow the chance to fully immerse herself—and Maisie—into island life. Willow wanted her daughter to take advantage of all that growing up in the Caribbean had to offer. Which, at the moment, included swimming lessons.

Most island children learned to swim almost before they could walk, but Willow and Maisie had only moved to St. Victoria in the past year. As Maisie paddled in the gentle waves, Willow thought, for what felt like the hundredth time, of how right she'd been to move from their dreary North London flat to the sun-drenched Caribbean islands. In London, swimming lessons would have been impossible on Willow's budget. In fact, just about everything in London was a strain on her budget. Between her modest income as a critical care nurse, and the small amount of money her grandmother had left in trust for Maisie before she passed, there was never much left over after accounting for rent and childcare.

Willow had lived her whole life in Islington, raised by her grandmother. Though they didn't have much, she'd never once felt poor, because Gran had always made her feel loved. But becoming a single mother had opened Willow's eyes to just how wide the divide was between the haves and have-nots. She constantly had to deny Maisie all the little "extras" that her preschool classmates were able to enjoy. Worse, after working all day, Willow only had time to spend a few exhausted hours with Maisie each night. She'd ached to have a child for so long, but felt as though Maisie's childhood was passing her by. The final straw came when she'd picked Maisie up from day care and learned that her daughter had spoken her first word. Willow was devastated that she hadn't been there to hear it. That very night, she decided that she and Maisie needed a change. She hadn't been certain, at first, of what that change would be, but she knew that it needed to be as different from North London as possible.

St. Victoria certainly fit the bill. The vast turquoise waters and boundless blue sky of the island were a stark contrast to London's relentless clouds and smoke. Their little house on the beach was small, but cozy. Like many homes in the Caribbean, it was raised on stilts to protect against flooding and hurricanes. The back door opened directly onto the beach, which was a toddler's delight. There was plenty of sand for Maisie to play in, a network of tide pools to explore and miles of clear, gentle water, perfect for swimming.

Of course, one would have to learn how to swim first. Maisie furrowed her brow in concentration as she kicked her legs in the water.

Living on the beach as they did, Willow had known that she'd need to teach Maisie to swim as quickly as possible. But they'd hit a snag almost as soon as they'd started: Maisie was unwilling to submerge her head under the waves. She could kick her legs, but she refused to put her face into the water. As Maisie began to huff and puff, Willow stood her daughter up in the waist-high water.

"Look, darling. You must put your face into the water if you are to learn to swim."

"Don't want to." Maisie's lower lip began to pout, an expression Willow knew all too well.

"Mummy can do it. See?" Willow quickly dunked

her own head under the water and then broke the surface. "It's not hard. It feels lovely."

Maisie's lower lip began to tremble, and Willow knew that tears were likely to come next. Maisie was usually a very agreeable child, rarely protesting against Willow unless she felt anxious or in need of reassurance. So far, tantrums were a rare event in their little two-person household by the sea. But Willow knew that once the tears started coming, there would be no closing the floodgates again until Maisie had had a good cry. What had started as a pleasant day could turn to tears and storm clouds if Willow pushed Maisie before she was ready.

Perhaps they'd had enough of the sea for one day. Willow wanted swimming to remain a fun experience for Maisie, so the girl would feel confident in the water. Pushing Maisie any further today might spoil it.

"All right, then. Maybe that's enough swimming for this morning. Run up to the house and get your sand toys. Show me what kind of castle you can build on the beach."

Maisie's face broke into a smile, and she sprinted ahead of Willow onto the beach.

As always, it brought Willow joy to see Maisie happy. But she also felt a pang of uncertainty that was becoming all too familiar as Maisie grew. Had she done the right thing, giving in so easily when Maisie didn't want to put her head under the water? She never wanted Maisie to feel pushed to do anything she was afraid of. But on the other hand, children needed to be challenged. If she always gave in at the first sign of Maisie's lip trembling, wouldn't that create its own set of problems later on? Willow wanted her daughter to be resilient. If she was too soft on Maisie, her daughter might begin to think she could avoid anything unpleasant simply by crying.

Oh, who am I kidding, she thought. *Maisie's already got me wrapped around her little finger, and she probably knows it.*

Willow wondered if her fate, as a single mother, would involve forever questioning whether she was pushing Maisie too hard, or not enough. Although she had never regretted her decision to raise Maisie on her own, one of the hardest parts about single parenting had been learning to trust her instincts. Her grandmother had passed away shortly after Maisie was born, and Willow had no other family she could ask for advice. At times like this, when she found herself questioning whether she'd given in too easily, she longed for someone who could offer support. Someone she could trust, and who she could rely on to watch over both her and Maisie.

It was a nice dream, but Willow was a practical person. Any dreams of a partner for herself, or a father for Maisie, were unlikely to ever become more than dreams.

She'd always wanted to have children. As a nurse, she'd had so many chances to see firsthand the joy that new babies brought to their parents. Moreover, she'd seen the support that families brought to one another when going through hard times. But Willow had always felt like an outsider as she watched families comfort one another through hardships. At home, it was only herself and Gran. But when Gran had passed away, there had been no one to comfort Willow.

Growing up with Gran had felt special, because it

was just the two of them, but it had also felt lonely at times. Willow had always wondered what it would be like to grow up in a large family, with siblings and cousins to share joys and sorrows. Since she couldn't change her own childhood, she decided that she would do the next best thing by having plenty of children of her own. For many years, she'd dreamed of starting a family, and she'd always thought that Jamie, her childhood sweetheart, was dreaming along with her.

Jamie had always agreed that he, too, wanted to get married and have a big family—but he wanted to wait for the right time to start. For eight years, Willow waited with him. She waited as Jamie went through career changes, as he started and dropped out of educational programs and as she watched many of her friends get married and start families of their own. Finally, after her best friend's wedding, she decided she'd waited long enough. She confronted Jamie and asked exactly when they were going to get married.

"What's the rush?" he'd asked. "We've got all the time in the world for that sort of thing."

But Willow knew that wasn't true. As a nurse, she knew that a mother's age had an impact on an infant's health, and newer research was showing that the age of the father had an impact, as well. Even though she'd seen plenty of women give birth to healthy babies well into their forties, she wanted to avoid any increased risk. If she and Jamie were going to have children, she wanted to start soon.

That was when Jamie had dropped his bombshell. He didn't want children. *Any* children. He'd never really been interested in starting a family at all. And when she'd asked him why he'd never shared this rather important information with her, his easy explanation left her breathless.

"You've been talking about having children for years," he'd said. "How was I supposed to tell you that I realized that I didn't want kids? I thought you'd break up with me if you knew the truth. It just seemed easier not to say anything until it was too late. You can't blame me for keeping quiet. I was just trying to keep us together."

His explanation made things so much worse. Jamie hadn't just changed his mind about wanting children. He'd *never* wanted children, and for years he'd told her otherwise because it was what he'd thought she wanted to hear. She felt as though her dream of having a large family was slipping though her fingers, but worst of all, she felt manipulated and betrayed.

After the breakup, she'd despaired of ever having a child. She'd never dated much before Jamie. He'd been her first serious relationship. And now, after eight years with one person, she felt clumsy and awkward on the dating scene. It didn't help that her trust in men—and in herself—felt irreparably shattered. She was certain she would never be able to trust anyone enough to be in a relationship again.

But even though she was done with relationships, she wasn't done with her dream of having a family. She couldn't be. Her heart ached to even think of it.

And so she'd decided to take a different path. If there was one thing Gran had taught Willow, it was to not let obstacles stop her. There were many ways to have a family, and Willow wasn't going to let one broken dream get in the way of another.

Gran had wholeheartedly approved of Willow's decision to have a child via donor insemination. Willow was unfazed by the idea of using an anonymous sperm donor, because she knew how carefully clinics screened donors for potential issues in their health history. The more she thought about it, the more confident she became that she could be a single mother.

There had been one small, unexpected snag in her plan. Shortly after the insemination process, an extremely apologetic director from the fertility clinic had called her to let her know that there had been a mistake. Instead of using a sample from a carefully vetted donor, the clinic had accidentally used sperm from a man who'd had cancer and had frozen his sperm due to the effects that chemotherapy could have on fertility.

At first, Willow had been alarmed at the news. She was shocked that the clinic could make such a mistake, and she was concerned that the donor hadn't been vetted for hereditary health issues. But the clinic informed her that the donor had been diagnosed with melanoma, a nonhereditary form of cancer. Willow's child would not be affected. Still, not only did Willow need to know what had happened, but they would have to inform the donor, as well.

Willow felt uneasy at the idea of the donor having any kind of involvement. But she knew that if their situations were reversed—if she had a child, somewhere out there, who was biologically hers—she'd want to know about it. There was nothing she could do to change the mistake the clinic had made, and the donor, whoever he was, probably felt just as shocked as she did. There was no use in casting blame, and ultimately, the only thing that mattered to her was that she had a healthy baby. She decided to give permission for the clinic to share her contact information with the donor, in case he wanted to discuss their extremely unusual circumstances, and in case he wanted the chance to get to know his child.

But the donor had never shown the slightest interest in meeting her. Not then, and not several months later, when she'd given her permission for him to be informed of Maisie's birth. As far as Willow was concerned, the donor had no interest in being part of their lives. Which was fine with her. It was how she'd planned it all along.

Aside from that one small mix-up, Willow's pregnancy had gone remarkably smoothly. She and Gran had both been completely besotted with Maisie from the moment she was born, and Gran had even put all of her savings into a trust fund for Maisie before she passed away. Willow had known that with Gran's good example to go on, she'd be able to provide her child with a loving home.

And as she watched Maisie traipse down the back steps with her bucket of sand toys, she couldn't imagine having done motherhood any other way. She wouldn't trade anything for the chance to meet the tiny person growing day by day before her very eyes. Maisie brought more joy to Willow's life than Willow could have ever imagined.

Willow thought that she and Maisie were getting on rather well in the world. Moving to the Caribbean had changed their lives for the better in every way. It might be far from all that was familiar in London, but London was fraught with memories of Jamie that Willow was happy to leave behind.

Willow's search for a change had led her to the Island Clinic on St. Victoria. At first, she'd been skeptical about the idea of working at a medical center that

catered to celebrities. She'd become a nurse to practice medical care, not to tend to the whims of the A-list
crowd. But she was drawn in by the clinic's commitment to helping its community, even providing care free
of charge to island residents. And the motto fit with her
own values—*We are always here to help.* Of course,
it didn't hurt that the salary was more than twice what
she was making in London.

As soon as she and Maisie had settled into their
beach house, Willow knew she'd made the right decision. Their days were full of light and laughter, and
Maisie was learning more about the world around her
growing up on a Caribbean island than she possibly
could have by spending her days in a North London
day care.

She might not have the large family she'd always
dreamed of, but she had Maisie, and that was enough.
And on an island like St. Victoria, it was almost impossible not to know everyone. In many ways, her neighbors were like a family unit. Mrs. Jean, her nosy but
well-meaning next-door neighbor, was always happy to
watch Maisie along with her own grandchildren, and
the island provided a sense of community Willow had
never known anywhere else. At work, Willow's colleagues never failed to let her know that she was indis-
pensable. She felt so close to her work friends that they
seemed like a kind of family, too.

As for love… There were many different kinds of
love, Willow thought. She certainly felt loved by the
small circle of people in her life. But when it came to romantic love…well, she'd tried that, and it hadn't worked
out very well. Willow still felt a pang in her chest when-

ever she remembered Jamie's words: *I thought you'd break up with me if you knew the truth.*

How could she ever tell if someone was just saying what they thought she wanted to hear, the way Jamie had? There was no way to know for sure. The only guaranteed way to protect herself was to decide that she was done with relationships, once and for all.

Willow had accepted that romance wasn't going to be part of her life. But not everyone on the island seemed as willing to accept that Willow had sworn off relationships.

Case in point: her neighbor, Mrs. Jean, was gathering rosemary from her small porch-side herb garden. Mrs. Jean seemed to feel it was her mission in life to see Willow settled in a relationship, and had a habit of willfully ignoring Willow's hints that this wasn't going to happen.

"Good morning," Mrs. Jean called as Willow approached. "I noticed that you and Maisie slept in a little."

Willow smiled. Maisie was a notoriously early riser. "Sleeping in" meant up by eight a.m. for the two of them. "Maisie was up a little later than usual last night, so we both needed some extra rest this morning."

Mrs. Jean's eyes twinkled. "Oh. I thought maybe you had a hot date and were sleeping in afterward."

"If your definition of 'hot date' is playing four games of Candyland in a row and then trying to wrestle an overtired three-year-old into the bathtub, then I'm guilty as charged."

Mrs. Jean snorted. "You spend all your time working and looking after Maisie. You need to take a little time for yourself once in a while."

"Ooh, is this an offer to babysit?"

"You know that Maisie's welcome over anytime. Why don't I watch her this Friday night and give you a break?"

"That would be great. I could really use a chance to catch up on some paperwork at the clinic."

Mrs. Jean gave her a pained expression. "I'm not offering to watch Maisie so you can do some paperwork. I want you to go out and have some *fun*. Go down to Williamtown and meet some young men. That's what I would be doing if I were your age."

Willow had her doubts about that. Mrs. Jean had eight children of her own, and numerous grandchildren. Even if she didn't know about the heartbreak Willow had faced, she should at least be able to understand that Willow didn't have time for dating between her full-time job and taking care of Maisie.

"Mrs. Jean, even if I had time in my life to date, you know as well as I do that there aren't too many single people to choose from on St. Victoria. I can't imagine how I'd meet someone new on an island this small."

At this, Mrs. Jean's eyes gleamed, and Willow realized too late that rather than ending the conversation, she'd given Mrs. Jean an opening.

"What about one of those nice doctors you work with?"

"Absolutely not. I could never date one of my colleagues. My job is important to me, and relationships make everything too complicated."

"Then what about one of those celebrities who are always coming to your clinic? Didn't that big Hollywood action star just have his gallbladder removed? You must have at least tried to get his number."

Willow couldn't help laughing. "If I don't want to complicate my job by dating a colleague, then I *definitely* don't want to complicate things by dating a patient. It'd certainly cost me my job."

"Who needs a job if you can snag yourself a movie star or an oil sheikh?"

"Mrs. Jean!"

The older woman rolled her eyes. "All right, I get it. You have principles, or some such nonsense. No dating patients. We'll just have to think of someone else for you."

"Sorry, Mrs. Jean, but even if I did plan to date again, I'm afraid it would be a hopeless case. Everyone on the island is either already taken or someone I work with. Or they're a neighbor or a friend."

"I wouldn't be so sure about that. What about that tall drink of water coming up the beach?"

Willow turned in surprise. Newcomers hardly ever came by the secluded stretch of beach she lived on. Yet less than twenty feet away, a tall man with light brown hair was picking his way over the sand. His crisp white shirt and tie were decidedly out of place in the Caribbean sunshine, and she could tell from his pale skin that he was unaccustomed to the sun. He was barefoot, with the ends of his trousers rolled up around his shins, and he carried his shoes and suit coat in one hand, and a briefcase in the other.

As the man approached, Willow noticed that his features were not altogether unattractive. His brown hair grazed his forehead in a way that made Willow want to sweep it from his eyes, which were a pleasing hazel. His frame was thin, but his gait suggested that he was used to carrying himself with the stance of a more muscular man. Willow found herself wondering if he were recovering from a long illness. Or perhaps he was simply unused to walking on hot sand—his pale skin suggested he didn't spend much time on the beach.

When he looked up at Willow, he smiled in greeting, and it was his smile that sent a jolt through Willow that she wasn't expecting. There was something about his mouth that caught her attention, although she couldn't quite put her finger on what it was. Perhaps it was the shape of his jaw—or maybe the way his chin curved— that made him seem extremely…kissable.

"Not bad, not bad," muttered Mrs. Jean.

The sound of Mrs. Jean's voice brought Willow back to reality, and she chided herself for having absurd thoughts about a complete stranger. As the man bent to speak to Maisie, her maternal instinct kicked in.

"Maisie," she called. "You know better than to talk to strangers."

She tried to make her voice sound stern, but she was terrible at being stern with Maisie. And strangers were such a rarity on this part of the island that her voice came out with more curiosity than sternness.

Now that she was at close range, Willow could see that the man looked more out of place than ever. Despite his pallor, she couldn't help noticing again that his hazel eyes were a striking complement to his sandy brown hair.

She wondered if he was a lost tourist, looking for directions to Williamtown. But in his stiff white shirt, he looked more like a solicitor than a tourist.

"Sorry to intrude," he said as she approached. "I was just complimenting this little one on such a fine sandcastle."

Willow recognized the clipped cadence of a North

London accent, and things began to fall into place. Her first guess—that the man might be a solicitor—might be correct, after all. The trust that Gran had left for Maisie wasn't large, but it had been enough to ensure that Maisie would have a little bit of money to rely on if anything should ever happen to Willow. Back in London, a solicitor from the firm would check on Maisie once a year to ensure her well-being. Gran had felt that this was only practical, given that Willow and Maisie were alone in the world. She'd wanted to be sure that Maisie would always be supported, no matter what. After moving to the Caribbean, Willow had assumed the firm would simply do these check-ins through video conference calls, rather than sending someone all the way out to the islands. But then, Gran had been a formidable woman. She'd probably threatened to haunt the firm from beyond the grave if they didn't do their due diligence where Maisie was concerned—and no one who'd ever met Gran would deny that she was capable of it.

"You must be from Camden," Willow said, naming the North London borough where her grandmother's firm was based.

He seemed surprised, but replied, "I am indeed from Camden. Theo Moore. I'm looking for Willow Thompson."

"Well, here we are. I'm Willow, and this is my daughter, Maisie."

For just a moment, Willow could have sworn the man was at a loss for words. She wondered if he was somewhat new at his job. Or perhaps he was simply tired from a long journey. But then he swallowed hard and seemed to recover. "Maisie," he said quietly. "You chose a beautiful name for her."

Willow couldn't help smiling. She loved saying Maisie's name. "We both think it suits very well, don't we, Maisie?" she said as the little girl gave a firm nod.

Theo paused for a moment, as though trying to recover himself. Willow realized that he must be exhausted.

"Did you come straight from the airport?" she asked.

"I did indeed. I'm terribly sorry to intrude in this way. I should have found some way to notify you that I was coming, but I only knew that you lived somewhere on St. Victoria. It did take a bit of detective work to track you down."

"I'm surprised to hear that. I thought I'd updated my new address with the firm when we moved."

He gave her a quizzical look. "The…firm, I suppose…had your old London address. I learned from your former neighbors that you'd moved."

Out of the corner of her eye, Willow could see Mrs. Jean approaching. "Why don't you come inside for some lemonade?" she said quickly. "Camden's a long way away, and I'm sure you're tired from your journey."

Again, he looked surprised, but said, "I'd love that. There's much for us to discuss, and it's probably best that we go over it all inside."

Willow couldn't imagine what there would be to discuss, as Maisie's yearly check-in visits were usually quite brief. She supposed that since this Theo Moore had traveled all the way from London, the visit would be longer than usual in order to justify the expense.

To her surprise, Maisie slipped her hand into Theo's

as they walked toward the house. Theo didn't seem to mind. In fact, he appeared to be quite charmed.

Willow felt her heart do a flip-flop in her chest. *Settle down*, she told herself. She'd known the man for all of forty seconds, and yet here she was, ogling him like a teenager at a school dance. She forced herself to tear her eyes away from him and turn toward the house, hoping that he hadn't noticed her staring at him.

As they passed Mrs. Jean, she gave Willow a pointed look that Willow interpreted as *Don't screw this up*. Willow shot back a look that she hoped Mrs. Jean interpreted as *Quit making such a big deal out of everything*. The older woman snorted and sashayed back to her house.

Willow, Theo and Maisie stepped through the back door of Willow's beach house and into the kitchen, and Willow pulled a pitcher of lemonade from the refrigerator.

"I can help pour," Maisie said.

"The pitcher's too heavy, love. But you can take three big glasses from the cupboard." She glanced at Theo. "Maisie's at the age where she loves to help."

"I can see that," he replied as Maisie strained to reach the plastic glasses from a high cupboard. "I like to help, too. May I lift you up, Maisie?" He glanced toward Willow, who nodded her permission.

Maisie nodded, too, and Theo lifted her just high enough so that the little girl could take three glasses from the cupboard and set them on the kitchen counter.

"She must like you," said Willow. "Normally she's very big on doing things all by herself."

"I'm told I make a great first impression," he said, and Willow felt her knees weaken a bit as he smiled again.

She pulled a chair from the kitchen table to steady herself. "Why don't we sit down? I'm sure you'd welcome the rest after coming such a long way."

"Thank you." He sat beside her at the table and sipped his lemonade. "This is very kind of you. I haven't had anything to drink since the flight."

"It's no trouble at all. We Londoners have to look out for one another."

He waved at the beach outside the kitchen window. "This is a far cry from London."

"Yes, that was the idea."

"It's an interesting choice, to raise a child so far away from home."

She stiffened. It seemed an awfully forward thing for a solicitor to say. Strikingly attractive or not, this man had no right to judge her decision of where to raise Maisie, even if he was involved in managing Gran's trust. Willow was the sole person responsible for Maisie's care, and although she often wished she had more help, one of the benefits of being a single mum was that Willow didn't have to put up with anyone's judgment of her parenting. "St. Victoria is our home now," she replied. "It may be unconventional, but I believe the experiences Maisie has here are far more educational than anything she could get out of an overpriced day care in the city."

"I'm sure you're right," he said. "I simply meant that you do seem to be so far from family, here in the Caribbean."

"Family?" she said, looking at him quizzically. "What are you talking about? I thought the firm that managed Gran's trust knew perfectly well that Maisie and I haven't any other family."

Now it was his turn to look confused. "Trust?" he said. "What trust?"

"Gran's trust… Vera Brown's trust, that she had set up for Maisie before she died. Isn't that what you're here to discuss? Aren't you a solicitor from the firm? A moment ago, when I mentioned the firm, you said they had my old London address."

"I'm afraid I wasn't entirely sure what you meant by 'the firm.' I thought you might be referring to the fertility clinic. The one you went to…to have Maisie."

Willow's stomach went cold.

"I've been searching for you for months," he said. "The clinic gave me your last known address, but it's been a few years, and it seems you moved a few times. I eventually learned that you lived on St. Victoria, and once I arrived, some helpful locals pointed me to the right beach. They said if I just started walking, I'd run into you eventually."

She already knew the answer, but she forced the question out, anyway, in a dry whisper. "Why have you been searching for me for months?"

"Because I needed to meet my daughter."

She shook her head. "You can't be saying what I think you're saying."

"Yes. I'm Maisie's father."

CHAPTER TWO

WILLOW SAT AT her kitchen table, head spinning, as she tried to absorb Theo's words. She couldn't fit them in her mind in a way that made sense. Maisie didn't have a father. Maisie had Willow, the way Willow had had Gran when she was growing up. Their family was small, but special. And it did not include a father.

Even though she was sitting, she clutched the edges of the kitchen table to steady herself.

"I'm sure this is a lot to take in," said Theo. "I did ask the clinic to let you know that I was trying to get in touch, but all of the contact information they had for you was out of date. I suppose that's not surprising. It has been several years, after all."

Maternal instinct overrode Willow's shock, and she stood up and pulled back Maisie's chair. "Run along and play in your room, love. Mr. Moore and I need to talk."

"Can I bring my lemonade?"

"Yes, but hold the glass with both hands so you don't spill." Maisie took her glass from the table with two sturdy hands, her brow furrowed in concentration as she carried it to her room.

Theo gave Willow a pained expression. "You don't want her to see me."

Willow was surprised to feel a twinge of sympathy for this stranger in her kitchen. But she barely knew this man. Even if he were Maisie's father, she had no intention of letting him near Maisie until she knew a lot more about him. "It's nothing personal, Mr. Moore. It's just that I don't know anything about you, or why you're here."

"Please, call me Theo. I know that me showing up here must come as a shock. But I can explain everything—why I've showed up here so suddenly, and why I've stayed away for so long. Just hear me out, and afterward, if you want me to leave, I'll go. I'm just asking for a chance."

He'd kept his voice fairly steady, but as a nurse, Willow was used to listening to people in pain. She hadn't missed the note of anguish in his voice, and it touched her heart. She didn't know what had brought this man here, but she could see that, to him, it was a matter of desperate importance.

But she couldn't imagine what would be so important that he had to be here now, in person, when he'd never bothered to contact her before. Unless… Her heart rose in her throat. The clinic had told her that they'd used sperm from a donor who'd had a history of cancer, but they'd assured her it was nonhereditary. But what if there was some other, newly discovered health problem that Theo had come to warn her about? Something that could affect Maisie? She told herself not to panic. Whatever Theo was so desperate to speak about with her might be important, but there was no reason to assume the worst. Not yet, anyway.

He took a manila envelope from underneath the suit coat he'd been holding. As he moved, she thought she noticed again a slight awkwardness, as though he was used to moving with more bulk. Another worry crossed her mind: Was he here because something had changed with his own health? Had the cancer, perhaps, returned? His skin was so pale. On the beach, she'd thought he had the look of someone recovering from a long illness, and now, as she examined him with a professional eye, she wondered if that illness had been quite recent. Or perhaps was still ongoing. Despite having just met Theo, she felt a pang of concern for him. She might not know him at all, but his hazel eyes seemed so kind. Now that he was sitting across from her, he was close enough that she could make out flecks of gold in them.

Shocked as she was to see him here, she had only to look at him to see that he'd been through some suffering. And yet, she couldn't help noticing that for all his awkwardness his hands were steady and graceful as he opened the manila envelope and removed several documents. His eyes met hers, and their expression was hopeful, but determined. And he'd come such a long way. It couldn't hurt, she thought, to at least find out why he was here.

"All right, Mr. Moore," she said, gently emphasizing her use of his last name. "Why don't you start by proving that you're who you say you are."

His relief was palpable. "Easy enough," he said, handing her the documents from the envelope.

She took the papers with trembling hands, and spread them before her on the table.

Among other things, there were letters from the fertility clinic where she'd undergone treatments explaining the whole mix-up: how they'd intended to use sperm from a vetted donor, but had accidentally used Theo's frozen sperm instead. She remembered those letters all too well. She'd received very similar letters herself, with their apologies and explanations.

Willow remembered how shocked she'd been upon first learning that the clinic could make such a mistake. If she'd have wanted to she could have pursued legal action, but in the end, she'd decided that having a healthy baby was all that mattered, all she wanted. She didn't need to complicate that. And Theo's choice not to get in touch made that even easier. Once she'd learned that the insemination had been successful, she'd even given the clinic permission to contact Theo. And again, when Maisie was born, she'd given her permission for Theo to meet her. But he'd never responded.

Although she could see that the clinic had followed through: the envelope held a copy of the letter to Theo, informing him that he was the father of a healthy baby girl. There was even a copy of an ultrasound picture that she recognized. She had the original picture, framed, in her bedroom.

Even if Theo hadn't brought along all of this documentation, Willow would have known that he was telling the truth about being Maisie's father. All she had to do was look at Maisie. The little girl shared so many features with Theo that seeing him was like seeing the missing pieces of a puzzle. Willow kept her eyes fixed on the documents: there was a copy of a photo ID of Theo, a work badge that identified him as a research oncologist at Regent's Hospital in London. He had longer hair in the picture, which made the features that he and Maisie shared even more evident. Willow had always thought that Maisie got her wavy hair from her, but the color, a light, sandy brown, was clearly Theo's.

And Maisie's height—now there was another mystery solved. At three years old, Maisie was already half a head taller than every child in her preschool class, and as she took in Theo's frame, Willow could see why.

Theo was, indeed, Maisie's father.

Or at least, he was her biological father. He was a sperm donor, she reminded herself. Not a father.

She looked again at Theo's work badge from Regent's Hospital. "You're an oncologist?"

"Yes. I mainly do research, though I like to work with patients when I can. But there've been certain… unexpected changes that made clinical work difficult. In a way, I suppose that's how this all starts."

"Go on," she said.

"About four years ago, I was diagnosed with melanoma. That's why I froze my sperm in the first place. My doctors advised that I take that step because chemotherapy can sometimes have an effect on fertility. I've always known that I wanted to be a father, so freezing my sperm was a safeguard."

Pieces were beginning to fall into place. She'd known, from the staff at the fertility clinic, that Theo had cancer, but his choosing not to get in touch meant she had no idea how he might have been getting on. And looking at Theo now, it was clear that the cancer wasn't far behind him. She estimated he was about thirty pounds underweight for his height and frame, and his sandy brown hair was quite short, as though it were just starting to grow back. She couldn't help feeling sympathetic. Cancer could be devastating, and the treatment took almost as much of a toll on the body as the illness itself.

"When I got the call from the clinic, informing me

of the mix-up, I didn't know how to feel," he continued. "At first, I was outraged. It was such a grave mistake on their part. But then, as I got used to the idea, I realized that it might be for the best."

For the best? For a moment, she wondered if the Caribbean heat was affecting him. But then she recalled all the times she'd had that very same thought over the past three years. The mix-up was for the best, because if things had happened any other way, she wouldn't have Maisie.

But Theo couldn't have that perspective. He'd barely met Maisie, by his own choice. "How could you think such a serious mistake was for the best?" she asked.

"I know it sounds strange. But I'd always wanted to have children, and at the time, there was no way for me to be certain of whether that would ever happen. It might not have been how I'd ever pictured becoming a father, but it meant the world to me to know that she existed."

This definitely didn't fit with the impression of Theo she'd formed over the past three years. She'd pictured a man who wanted to put the clinic's mistake as far behind him as possible, dealing with the situation by ignoring it, and eager to avoid any commitment she might ask of him. He certainly didn't need to worry about that: legally, he had no claim to Maisie; his name wasn't on her birth certificate. His lack of contact with her had informed that decision. Willow needed nothing from him. But he spoke as though Maisie meant everything to him, even though he'd chosen not to know her.

She wondered if she would have felt differently if she'd known he was fighting cancer all this time. But that, she thought, was the heart of the problem. Theo had never reached out to explain his situation at all, until now.

"I wish I had known all this sooner," she said. "The fertility clinic told me about your medical history, but that didn't explain why you didn't reach out. As I never heard from you, even after you'd had two opportunities to be involved, I assumed you either didn't want a child, or didn't want Maisie." She tried to keep the note of accusation out of her voice. She sympathized with Theo's situation, she really did, but part of her wondered…what kind of man ignored his own child for three years? Even under the most extenuating circumstances?

"I can see why you might think that," he said, his voice tinged with emotion. "I hadn't planned to be involved, even though I wanted to be there very much. Staying away from Maisie is one of the biggest regrets of my life."

"Then why didn't you ever try to meet her? You could have explained your situation at any time during the past three years."

He gave an emphatic shake of his head. "No, I couldn't. It was hard enough being sick. I couldn't stand the thought of an innocent child—*my* child—being exposed to that much stress. And if treatment didn't… go well, then I didn't want to put my child through the grief of losing a parent."

He seemed to be trying to speak with a casual air, but Willow noticed the catch in Theo's voice as he acknowledged the possibility that treatment might not have been successful. There was so much unpredictability over the course of cancer treatment, so many times where all anyone could do was wait to see what happened next. Theo had been afraid for his life, she realized, and he'd had to make a difficult choice.

"I can't imagine what it would be like, to deal with cancer and then to learn you'd unexpectedly had a child," she said. "You made the decision you thought was best. So why come here now, after all this time?"

"Because I'm finally in remission. I started looking for you and Maisie as soon as I learned the good news."

A wave of relief washed over her upon hearing the word *remission*, and she realized she'd been anxious to know if his treatment had been successful. The relief she felt was real, even though she'd only known him a few moments.

But her thoughts were in turmoil. Everything Theo said was in direct opposition to the assumptions she'd made about him over the past three years. On the rare occasions she'd thought of Theo, it had been with cynicism and some resentment for his complete lack of interest in Maisie. It wasn't that she necessarily wanted his involvement; it was simply that his apparent dismissal of her daughter amounted to a rejection of the person she held most dear in the world. And now she was learning that his circumstances hadn't been what she'd thought they were. For if what Theo said was true, then he hadn't been ignoring Maisie. He'd been trying to protect her.

And now, three years later, he was in remission, and he was here, hoping for…what exactly? Did he expect to have any sort of relationship with Maisie? His next words confirmed her fears.

"I want to get to know my daughter," he said. "I know I have no legal recourse, but I am her father, and

I came here hoping to find some way to be involved in her life."

She was overtaken by a wave of feelings, including protectiveness toward Maisie, and jealousy at the thought of anyone else involved in their close bond. When she'd become pregnant, she'd never imagined sharing Maisie with anyone else. The thought of having another parent involved in her daughter's life was completely at odds with everything she'd envisioned for the future. She certainly hadn't imagined having to deal with a man she barely knew arriving, unannounced, and declaring himself the father of her child. Not someone who, while pale and underweight, also had a devastatingly handsome smile and a pair of clear, hazel eyes that reminded her of the green and gold pebbles in the tide pools on the beach outside her home.

But no matter how interesting Theo's eyes were, his presence on the island would only be distracting for her, and for Maisie. Theo was a complicating factor that they didn't need.

Her life was proceeding just as she'd planned, and she didn't need any surprises now. Theo was right: he had no legal standing as Maisie's father. His name wasn't on her birth certificate. If she told him to leave, he'd have to go.

But Theo seemed so hopeful, and he'd been through so much. A part of her wished she could tell him that after all he'd been through, *of course* he was welcome into her and Maisie's lives. But however much she might sympathize with his situation, it didn't change the consequences of his decision. She had to think of her daughter first. Theo Moore was, by his own choice, a complete stranger to Maisie, despite their biological connection.

Still, he'd been in such an awful position, suffering all the uncertainty that came with facing a deadly illness. She didn't want to crush him completely, especially when he'd been in such a hard situation. She decided to let him down as gently as possible.

"I can understand why you feel it's important to get to know Maisie," she said. "It sounds as though it was very hard for you to stay away from her, although you did ultimately make the choice not to be involved."

"Because I wanted to spare her from any grief."

"I understand you were trying to do what you thought was right. But…it doesn't change the fact that Maisie is three years old now, and has no idea who you are. How would you even explain your relationship to her?"

His jaw tightened. "I'm her father."

"You might see it that way, but how can she? She doesn't know you at all."

"Which is exactly why I'm here. To form a relationship with her. To *be* the father I haven't been able to be all this time."

"But how would that even work? Practically speaking, I mean. Maisie and I have our lives here, on St. Victoria. Your life is waiting for you back in London. Four thousand miles away."

"I will find a way to make it work. I came here planning to do whatever it takes to be in my daughter's life."

"I can appreciate your determination, Mr. Moore. But you aren't thinking through the practicalities. How long were you even planning to stay in the Caribbean?"

"My return ticket is open-ended. I can stay for as long as necessary."

"But how long were you *planning* to stay?"

"I wasn't sure how you'd react to my arrival here. I thought perhaps…a week?"

"And then what? You'd fly back to London, while Maisie grows up here. You'd see her, perhaps, once or twice a year. I don't want to be harsh, Mr. Moore, but I have to protect my daughter, and I don't want her getting attached to someone who's just going to leave after a few days. And I really don't want her to get the impression that a father is someone who visits once a year."

"Then I suppose the way forward is clear. There's no other choice, really."

She breathed out in relief, glad that he could see how impractical it all was.

"I'll simply have to move to St. Victoria."

Her eyes widened. "You can't just decide to move to the Caribbean on a moment's notice."

"Why not? You decided to move here yourself."

"Yes, but I had researched positions abroad for nearly a year, and then chose the situation that I thought would be best for raising my daughter."

"And I'm trying to do the same. I've spent the past three years trying to do what's best for my child by staying away from her. And now that I'm finally in remission, I'm not going to waste my chance to be part of her life. This isn't an impulsive decision, it's an *easy* decision."

Theo was either reckless, crazy or…or, perhaps, he was as desperate to be involved in his daughter's life as he claimed to be.

He could also simply be telling her what he thought she wanted to hear, just as Jamie had. But Jamie's eyes had never blazed with determination the way Theo's did now, and his jaw had never been set with the same firmness.

She'd trusted Jamie, because she'd known him for years. But even though he'd said he wanted children, he'd never taken any action to back up his words. Theo, though, had tracked her down with limited information, and had flown four thousand miles with nothing more than hope for a chance to know his daughter. And even though it was hard to reconcile his presence now with his decision to stay away for so long, having cancer was one hell of an extenuating circumstance.

But could she trust him to be reliable? To be a suitable person for her daughter to have in her life? Without knowing him at all, how could she be certain of anything?

She thought it over for a long moment. Finally, she asked, "Why is Maisie so important to you?"

"What do you mean, '*why*'? She's my child."

"But do you know for certain that she's your only chance to have a child? Now that you're in remission, you could take a fertility test. Suppose you learned you could have other children? Would you really want to spend your life on a small island in the Caribbean, when there might be other options for you?"

He held her gaze for a long moment. "First of all, regardless of any children I *might* have in the future, Maisie is here now. Even if I were to have other children, she'd still be my daughter, and I'd still be determined to have a relationship with her, in whatever capacity you might allow.

"Second, the results of a fertility test won't be reliable until I've been in remission for at least a year. I don't know if Maisie is the only child I'll ever have, or if I'll get another chance. But I don't need to wait another year to decide if I want to know my daughter. I've already had three years to think about her growing up without me, and I won't spend another minute without her if I can help it.

"And *third*, even though I haven't been with Maisie, she's been with me. Or at least, the idea of her has. Even though it was painful to think of her growing up without me, knowing that she was out there got me through some of the hardest days of my life. No matter what happens in the future, Maisie will always be important to me."

Willow almost believed that he meant every word. Almost. She had misgivings about whether he understood the commitment involved in being a parent, and whether he'd thought through what it would mean to make a permanent move to the Caribbean.

But he seemed determined to give it a try.

He'd had two chances to be involved in Maisie's life, and both times she'd thought his absence had spoken volumes. Could she give him a third chance? Especially now that she knew everything he'd gone through, just to be here, at her kitchen table?

His presence was a complication that she didn't want in her life. But something prevented her from telling Theo to leave. Maybe it was the sympathy she felt for all he'd been through. Maybe it was the determination in his voice and his expression. Or maybe, in spite of all the alarm bells going off in her mind, she wasn't done appreciating the exact shade of hazel in Theo's eyes.

Whatever the reason, she found herself saying, "If you're going to stay here, you'll need to find a job."

"I'm an oncologist."

"That's wonderful. I'm a nurse myself. But oncology is a profession, not a job. How are you going to earn a living here on St. Victoria? You'll need to have something that pays a salary and gives you a reason to stay here."

"Maisie is my reason for staying here."

"That's fine for right now, but what about next week? Next year? Island life isn't for everyone, and St. Victoria is small. How long before you get tired of the beach and start to miss your family and friends? How long before you start to resent Maisie for keeping you away from other work opportunities, other life opportunities, that you could have in London?"

"That would never happen."

Willow's mouth became a firm line. "The job is a deal-breaker. I need to know that you could see yourself living here long-term."

"You don't trust easily, do you?"

"Where my child is concerned, I don't trust anyone unless I have a good reason."

"Done. I'll get a job."

"And somewhere at least semipermanent to live."

"I'll start looking immediately."

Willow couldn't help but be impressed by his confidence. "I hope you understand where I'm coming from," she said. "I know you've been through a lot, and I'm so glad you're in remission. But you're a virtual stranger, and you're asking to be involved in my daughter's life. I can't risk her getting attached to someone who just wants to be around once in a while. Children need stability. Consistency."

His gaze pierced her from across the table. "And what about what *you* need?"

She felt disoriented, her heart and stomach doing jumping jacks together. Who cared about what she needed? As long as Maisie was taken care of, that was all that mattered. Except, when she looked into his hazel eyes, she felt a need that had nothing to do with groceries and roof repairs and everything to do with a growing warmth that she'd felt since the moment Theo entered the room.

"I have everything I need," she said curtly.

"What about financial support? You could at least let me help pay for Maisie's schooling, or for any necessities." He looked around the house, as though searching for any repairs he could offer to finance.

"We don't need money. My salary more than covers everything. All I need from you, Mr. Moore, is for you to show that you're someone who can be dependable. In case Maisie ever needs to depend on you."

"She can. I'll prove to her, and to you, that she can."

Willow hoped, from the bottom of her heart, that he was telling her the truth.

"You know what? I think that went about as well as could be expected. All things considered, I think you should feel good about this, Theo. I really do."

Theo pressed his hand to his temples, grateful that his twin sister, Becca, couldn't see the pained expression on his face over the phone. Ever the optimist, Becca had a tendency to stretch reality at times in her determination to put a positive spin on things. Her hopeful attitude had been helpful while he was battling some of his worst days with cancer. But her determination to look on the bright side of life meant that she sometimes didn't understand the magnitude of the obstacles he was facing.

He was back in his room at the Harbor Hotel, a charming, hacienda-style inn filled with tourists. He'd called Becca as soon as he could to tell her about his conversation with Willow. Of all his siblings, only Becca knew that Theo had gone to St. Victoria in search of his daughter, or that he even had a daughter. When Theo had learned he was a father, even though he'd wanted to shout that news from the rooftops, he decided against telling his family because he knew they'd want to be involved. It had been hard enough for Theo not to make contact with his daughter, knowing that if he did, he could potentially put her through the grief of losing a parent at an early age. He knew that he wouldn't be able to withstand additional pressure from his family if they felt he should make contact. And so he'd only shared the news with Becca, the person he trusted most to respect his feelings.

But he wasn't quite sure he agreed with her assessment of what had passed between him and Willow. "You think it went *well*, even though the mother of my child isn't sure she wants to let me into my own daughter's life?"

"I think it's a good sign that she wants you to show you can be consistent and stable first. She wants to know that you're serious about this. Now it's only a matter of time before she sees that you want the best for your child, same as she does. You can't blame her for being careful. I'd feel the same if it were my own child."

He knew Becca was right. But part of him had hoped that, somehow, Willow would trust him right away. He ached to get to know his daughter better. When Willow had invited him inside for lemonade, his heart had skipped a beat as Maisie had casually slipped her hand into his. His daughter's hand. There was nothing on earth that would stop him from holding her hand again.

"It's just that when I saw my daughter today…" He paused, trying to gain control over his emotions. "It made everything so real. Everything the cancer took from me."

"But now you get to take it all back, one step at a time. Starting with the most important part of all—Maisie. Cute name, by the way."

"I like it, too."

"So what's the mum like?"

"She's a nurse. She seems nice, but I think I overwhelmed her by showing up so suddenly. We exchanged our contact information, so I'll call her as soon as I have a firm job offer and a place to live."

"That could take a while. Don't you want to call her a little sooner, just to keep her updated?"

"No. I think I should give her some space, so we can get to know each other gradually. I don't want to screw this up."

"What does she look like?"

"She's beautiful," said Theo before he could stop himself. He instantly wished he hadn't said it. It was a sure way to get Becca to start making assumptions about Willow that had no basis in reality.

"Whoa."

"No, don't get any ideas. I wasn't trying to imply anything, I was just stating a fact. I just meant that she *happens* to be objectively beautiful." And friendly, and warm. Something about her demeanor had instantly put Theo at ease, nervous as he'd been about making his first impression. And she *was* beautiful. The waves of her rich, dark brown hair had framed her face in a way that made him long to pull her silky tresses through his fingers.

But he was here to meet his daughter, and nothing more. The situation was already complicated enough. Whatever attraction he might feel for Willow would have to be ignored.

"Look, I know you're hesitant to get back into the dating pool, but you can't put it off forever," Becca said. "You've always wanted a family. And so unless you want to find someone else who agrees to make use of the rest of the sample you stored in that sperm bank four years ago, you'll have to go on a date eventually."

"I'll cross that bridge when I come to it. For now, I'm not interested in dating anyone, least of all the woman who determines whether or not I'm able to see my own child. Besides, I still look…well, you've seen me. You know how I look."

"Theo. You look fine."

But he couldn't believe it. Every time Theo glimpsed himself in the mirror, it was a shock to see how much his body had changed as a result of his illness and treatment. He'd lost over thirty pounds, and his frame, he thought, looked positively gaunt. His skin was pallid, and his sandy hair had only just started to grow back in the past few months. He couldn't imagine that he would be an appealing prospect for anyone, let alone someone like Willow.

"Your body will adjust back to its old self in no time, now that you're not going through treatment anymore. And any woman shallow enough to let your appearance keep her from seeing your personality probably isn't someone who's right for you."

He wanted to appreciate Becca's loyalty, but she couldn't know how it felt for him to see his own body change so much over the past few years. Thinking about dating and relationships was the last thing he needed right now.

"There's actually something I have to ask you," he said, hoping a swift change of subject would distract Becca from her interest in his love life. "I really hate to put you in this position, but I need to borrow some money."

"Don't give it a second thought," she said. "Just let me know how much you need, and I'll get it to you."

He hated having to rely on his sister for money. It wasn't that he thought Becca would say no. She was a successful financier, and had readily offered her support during his illness. But having to ask for her help was one more reminder of all that the cancer had taken from him. It had been nearly impossible to hold a steady job over the past few years. As an oncologist with a strong research background, he was always able to find a job when he was healthy enough to work. But keeping his bank account in order hadn't been easy. He had enough to support himself, but not enough to find a house in the Caribbean on short notice.

"I'll need at least enough to put down for a few months' rent," he said.

"Of course. And you should get a long-term lease. The mum needs to know you're committed."

"But what if—"

"Theo, no. No more what-ifs. You can't put everything on hold because of what might happen. None of us knows how long we have. Look at Dad. Look at *you*. We've all got to live while we can, which in your case means borrowing some money from your fantastically well-to-do twin sister so you can find a suitable place to live."

"I'll start paying you back as soon as I get a job," he said. He hoped St. Victoria needed oncologists. Not that it mattered. He'd take whatever job he could find if it meant he could be with his daughter.

"I know you will. But in the meantime, I'm actually glad you asked. I think it's good for you to ask for some support once in a while, instead of trying to face everything by yourself."

"Thanks, Becca. I'll repay you for…for everything. Someday. I swear."

"Hey. What are savings accounts for, if not to help your brother move to a Caribbean island? Don't worry about money right now. Just focus on getting your life back to where it's supposed to be. Get things settled with your daughter so I can come and meet her."

"Thanks," he said again, and hung up the phone.

Becca was the only person in his family he'd spoken to in several days, with the result that when he finally checked his phone, there'd been seventeen voice mails waiting for his response. As he'd spent the past week traveling and tracking Willow down, he hadn't spared much time for returning calls. Now, he had messages from his parents, siblings, aunts, uncles and various cousins, all eager to know where he was, what his availability was like for upcoming holidays and whether he had a moment to chat. So far, the only message he'd returned was Becca's. He'd probably have to delete the rest and apologize for not responding later.

He scrolled through his call history and saw that not all the voice mails were from family. There were several from his medical care team, as well. He played the next message to hear the concerned voice of his primary doctor.

"We're all so glad to see you're in remission, but the fight isn't over yet. Get in touch with me as soon as you can so we can schedule your first year of follow-up appointments."

He knew he should return the call, but he wasn't ready to return to talking about cancer yet. Cancer had taken up so much of his time and attention over the past four years. He wanted a moment to himself, to absorb the reality: he'd met his daughter. He'd laid eyes on her, talked with her, seen that she was real. And perfect.

Oddly, though he tried to focus on Maisie, he found that his thoughts kept drifting to Willow. He hadn't wanted to tell Becca, because he knew she'd get carried away, but there had been something about Willow's warmth that had made Theo feel instantly connected to her, even as she had explained her reservations about allowing him in Maisie's life. She'd been frank and straightforward about what she needed with him, and why. There was something about her that made him feel she was innately trustworthy.

Openness was a trait Theo admired in people, because he was terrible at it himself. Growing up in such a large family had made it difficult to have any privacy, let alone any secrets. As soon as one person found something out, everyone else knew. Some of his family took this in their stride, but Theo had always been more guarded than his siblings. As a child, he'd always hated it when something important happened to him and one of his siblings spread the news first, or when family gossip distorted actual events. He was quieter than his siblings, keeping most of his feelings to himself, with the exception of Becca. He'd been lucky that he had a twin to confide in. He and Becca had always been fiercely protective of one another's privacy.

And there were times when he did want privacy, so very much. He'd been diagnosed with cancer shortly after his father had been diagnosed with Alzheimer's, which had devastated his mother and siblings. His father was doing well so far, but Theo knew, when he'd been diagnosed, that he couldn't put his family through the threat of another loss. Not when there was so much to do surrounding Dad's care, and when his mother needed so much support. He'd downplayed the extent of his cancer as much as he could. It was just a touch of melanoma. There was a high survival rate, and no need to worry.

Only Becca had seen past Theo's lighthearted demeanor and recognized it as a coping mechanism. She hadn't pressed him to talk about his illness any more than he was ready to, but she'd stayed over at his apartment on the long nights when the side effects of the treatment were bad, and she called and checked in on him often. She always claimed she was just calling to say hello, but he knew better.

Even though it was hard for him to let people in, he was grateful he'd had Becca. And if he'd chosen to, he'd have had the support of his other family members, as well. He simply hadn't wanted to cause his family any more distress. They had enough to deal with in managing his father's care.

He wondered what had it been like for Willow to be

a single mother for these past three years. Had she had anyone to turn to when she needed support? Had she wanted anyone?

Her green eyes had seemed to light up when she'd first seen him, not knowing who he was, but simply wanting to welcome a stranger and show him kindness. He wondered what it would take to get her eyes to light up like that again.

First things first. A house, a job and then…some sort of plan for his new life in St. Victoria.

He hadn't expected that his stay here would be permanent, but he'd meant it when he'd told Willow earlier that it was an easy decision. His choice had been made the moment he felt the warmth of Maisie's hand in his. If his daughter lived here, then so did he. He was used to life changing suddenly and unexpectedly. At least this time, the changes were in a direction that offered something good.

He decided he could wait until later to return his doctor's call. He deleted the voice mail, stuck the phone in his back pocket and went to ask the hotel concierge about where he could find a good real estate agent.

CHAPTER THREE

WILLOW WAS A little disappointed, but not too surprised, when a week passed without any word from Theo. They'd exchanged contact information with the understanding that he'd call when he got himself settled. *If* he got himself settled. Despite the confidence he'd shown, she couldn't help wondering if he'd given it some thought and decided that he wasn't ready to move his entire life to the Caribbean. She knew that a week wasn't much time to find a job or a place to live, but she'd assumed that if he intended to stay, then he would keep her updated on his progress. Instead, the past week had brought much of what she was used to hearing from Theo Moore: silence.

She hadn't mentioned his arrival on the island to anyone. She'd told Maisie that Theo was a friend who had come to visit, and that she didn't know if they would see him again. As each day passed and she still didn't hear from Theo, she became increasingly confident that she'd been right not to explain things further. For all she knew, Theo might not even be on St. Victoria anymore. Perhaps he'd seen the sense in her words as she'd explained why he couldn't simply burst into their lives out of nowhere.

Still, a part of her had hoped that he would follow through with all the things he'd said he would. He'd seemed so sure of himself, so resolute. But then, she knew from experience that people weren't always what they seemed.

During their conversation, she'd formed the impression that Theo was someone who didn't give up easily. The determination in the set of his jaw, the fire in his nazel eyes…she'd almost fallen for that easy confidence of his. But she'd clearly been right to keep her guard up, because despite his fine words and smoldering expression, he'd made no attempt to keep in touch with her.

She did find it rather grating that, once again, she'd offered Theo the chance to be part of Maisie's life, and his response was complete silence, just as it had been when she was pregnant and when she'd given birth to Maisie. Despite his assertion that he'd frozen his sperm because he'd always wanted children, perhaps he'd decided that the responsibilities involved in fatherhood were more than he was willing to take on.

She told herself it was probably for the best. It wasn't good for Maisie to have an unreliable father figure popping in and out of her life. Willow herself had grown up without a father, and she'd turned out all right. Gran had never dated anyone, and had certainly never suggested that Willow needed any sort of guiding male influence. She smiled to think of Gran dating. It was impossible to imagine. Willow had barely been a year old when her parents passed away in a car accident, and Gran had thrown herself so wholeheartedly into childrearing that Willow had always felt she'd had all the love and support she needed. Still, there were times when she'd wondered what it would be like to have her parents present. When she'd broken up with Jamie, for example, she'd wished she'd had a father she could go to for advice. Gran had been wonderfully supportive, but she couldn't exactly offer a male perspective. And now, with Theo popping up so unexpectedly, she felt again how helpful it would be to have a father of her own to consult.

But Gran had taught her to make do with what she had. And right now, all she had was her instinct that it would be better for Maisie to have no father figure in her life, rather than one who was unreliable.

Willow also thought it might be for the best that *she* did not have much more exposure to Theo, either. Even though she hadn't seen him for several days, her mind had an inconvenient way of recalling how his hair, short but unruly, seemed to spill over his forehead in a way that made her want to push back the locks that just brushed his eyes. And the way his mouth curved up at the corners, as though that warm smile were about to break over his face at any moment.

She told herself that she had *not* been attracted to Theo. He simply had an interesting face, that was all. With a warm smile. As shocked and confused as Theo's visit had left her, she hadn't been able to stop herself from thinking about that smile over the past several days. Which left her all the more relieved that he hadn't contacted her again.

Between working full-time and raising a daughter on her own, Willow had always told herself that she was too busy to find a place for love or romance in her life. It was just as well that she hadn't felt an attraction to anyone in years, because work and Maisie kept her very busy. Not just busy, but safe. She'd never questioned her decision to be done with relationships after the breakup with Jamie. She'd trusted him for years, and in the end, not only had she been deeply hurt, but all of her dreams for the future had almost been lost. She couldn't risk that happening again, especially now that she had a child.

She felt another burst of irritation with Theo. What kind of a person confidently agreed to the conditions under which he could see his own child, and then disappeared without any communication for a week? Even if he'd decided to leave, he could have at least called to let her know he'd changed his mind.

She could understand if he was disappointed to learn that being involved in Maisie's life might be harder than he'd thought. But unless he had a place to live, a job and a plan for how he was going to be consistently present for Maisie, then Willow couldn't allow him to see her. Parenting was a huge commitment. Willow knew that none of the things she'd asked Theo to do were easy, because *she'd* done all of those things. She'd been doing them from the moment Maisie was born. And that really was the point. She knew what it took to be a parent, and she couldn't accept anything less for her daughter.

Of course, she could understand all he'd been through. Cancer wreaked such havoc and destruction on people's lives. She was so glad he was in remission. But that didn't mean he was ready to take on the reality of raising a child.

As she walked into work, Willow decided that she wasn't going to worry about Theo Moore any longer. She was tired of waiting for an update from him, and of worrying about the impact his presence would have on her life and Maisie's.

It's been over a week, she thought. *Surely if he were going to stay, I'd have heard from him by now. It's time to stop worrying about it, and to let things get back to normal.*

And she did, indeed, have a wonderful sense of normalcy as she headed into the nurses' station. She loved her job, and throwing herself into her work was one of her favorite ways to take a break from worrying about her own problems. She'd always found that when she was immersed in a medical procedure, her own worries drifted away as she focused on the task at hand. A few routine procedures were just what she needed.

When Willow had taken her job at the Island Clinic, she'd been looking for a way to make a drastic change in her life. She'd hoped that the job would allow her to have better work-life balance, and more time with Maisie, but she'd never dreamed that she would end up loving her job as much as she did. Willow had always been a caring and compassionate nurse, but in North London, she'd also been overworked, burned out and struggling to make ends meet. Most of her colleagues were in the same position. Now that she was working at a clinic where the salary more than met her needs, and where her colleagues were excited to come to work each morning, Willow discovered a new sense of enthusiasm for her profession.

At first she'd been nervous about whether she'd fit in at the Island Clinic. She was a practical person who had entered nursing because she wanted to care for those in need. But at the clinic, some of the clientele had faces that were almost as familiar to Willow as her own. Patients routinely arrived with an entourage and lists of extremely specific demands, including everything from dietary preferences to the kind of music played in exam rooms.

But even though the clinic catered to the well-known and the wealthy, it also strove to meet the needs of the island's residents, as well. The staff took the clinic's mission statement seriously: *We are always here to help.* No patient was ever turned away from the clinic due to their inability to pay. The clinic often shared patients with nearby St. Victoria Hospital, taking on difficult cases or patients whose care might be too costly for the hospital. Willow was more than willing to put up with the quirks and demands of entitled celebrities from time to time, if it meant that the people of St. Victoria—people who were now her friends and neighbors—had the medical care they needed.

As she began to review the day's medical charts, she had to admit that after more than a year of working at the clinic, she was coming to appreciate many of its perks. The same luxury experiences the clinic strove to provide to patients tended to spill over onto the staff. Willow could and had worked under all kinds of conditions, and she didn't need luxury to be an effective nurse. But she certainly didn't mind that the coffee she sipped during her chart review came from a French press, or that the lunches she ate with her colleagues each day were prepared by a chef who'd earned three Michelin stars. In fact, she was almost starting to get used to it.

She looked up from her chart to take in the view from the big picture window outside the nurses' station. She'd never get used to the constant presence of white sand and palm trees, and she was glad of that. The view of the ocean was every bit as breathtaking as it had been the day she arrived.

She heard a buzz of voices as three nurses headed toward the station, deep in excited conversation. "Willow!" gasped Talia, a fellow nurse. "Have you heard? There's a rumor that Roni Santiago is on her way to the clinic!"

Willow couldn't help raising her eyebrows. Even though she was used to celebrity patients by now, Veronica Santiago—or Roni, as she was known by nearly everyone on earth—would be one of the most famous patients ever to arrive. Roni had begun her media career decades ago as a daytime talk show host. Her program was known to delve deeply into serious social issues, going far beyond typical sensationalism and fluff. She developed a reputation for bringing out deep emotions among her program guests and audience members. She'd also been known, and perhaps especially loved, for her frequent giveaways. Once, she'd gifted her entire studio audience with a weeklong cruise on the Baltic Sea. Since then, she'd founded a global nonprofit organization as well as her own media empire. There was a Roni magazine, a streaming TV channel and a lifestyle website where members could engage directly with Roni and with each other.

"Isn't it exciting?" said Talia. "My mother and I used to watch her show together after I got out of school. I've always wanted to meet her."

Under other circumstances, Willow might have shared in Talia's excitement. But she'd been hoping to get wrapped up in some straightforward medical procedures. A few days of setting broken bones and mending lacerations would help her to get her mind off the turmoil that Theo's arrival had caused. She'd been in charge of coordinating celebrity care before, and in her experience, it usually meant not much medicine and a lot of babysitting. A guest with as big a name as Roni's was bound to arrive with her own list of special demands in addition to the luxury the clinic already offered. Willow hoped that she would be able to stay out of Roni's way and focus on providing medical care, rather than meeting the needs of a celebrity who was likely used to getting her own way most of the time.

Those hopes were dashed moments later when her boss, Dr. Nate Edwards, arrived at the nurses' station.

Nate was chief of staff at the Island Clinic, and Willow had developed tremendous admiration for him over the past year. When she'd first arrived in the Caribbean, his warmth and patience had helped Willow overcome any lingering doubts about her decision to move to St. Victoria. When she'd first read about the Island Clinic, she'd been intrigued by the location and the high salary. But it had been Nate's personality that confirmed for her that she was going to take the job. Nate's demeanor, driven yet down to earth, had convinced her that the clinic was sincere in its mission to help. She'd worked with him long enough to know that she could always trust him to do what was best for the clinic, the staff and their patients.

Which was why she felt her heart sink when he said, "Willow, I was wondering if you'd be willing to take the lead on coordinating Roni Santiago's care when she gets here."

"Are you sure you don't need me somewhere else?" she asked, desperately trying to think of an excuse.

"Wouldn't I be more use in surgery? Or in the infectious disease wing?"

"I know looking after celebrities isn't your favorite part of the job. But Roni is in a somewhat unusual situation. She began chemotherapy for breast cancer a month ago, and since then, someone either in her entourage or on her treatment team has been leaking information to the press. A lot of it has been sensationalized—the tabloids make it sound as though she's on death's door."

"That's terrible," said Willow. "I had no idea Roni Santiago had cancer. And I'm sure the reports in the news aren't good for her physical or emotional health."

"I'm surprised you haven't heard—it's been all over the tabloids."

"I never pay much attention to those," she said. That, and she'd so been preoccupied with thoughts of Theo's visit that she hadn't had much time to think of anything else.

"The paparazzi have been a serious problem. They're hounding Roni at every turn. She and her doctors agreed it would be best for her to come here, for the sake of security and privacy. We'll all need to be extra careful. I want her to be able to focus on rest and recovery."

"Is there any danger of the press finding out she's coming here?"

"The director of her previous cancer treatment center has assured me that no one at their end could *possibly* have revealed that Roni is headed our way, so we should be able to maintain her privacy without worrying that we'll be inundated by paparazzi. Still, caution is important. The press has been relentless."

"I'm sure that doesn't help with her emotional state." It was crucial for cancer patients to keep their spirits up. Still, Willow had been hoping for a brief respite from celebrity nursing. "Are you certain you need me to be the one to coordinate her care?" she asked Nate.

"If you don't mind. For one thing, you live off-campus. In the unlikely event that the paparazzi become a problem, it'll be less pressure for Roni and the staff if those involved in her care are able to leave at the end of the day."

Willow nodded. Being able to leave her work at work was one of the primary reasons she'd opted not to live in the clinic's on-campus housing.

"To tell you the truth, I have some ulterior motives in wanting Roni's care to be coordinated by one of our best nurses."

Willow couldn't help smiling at the compliment. She cared about what Nate thought of her, and it meant something to be held high in his regard.

And she didn't have to think very hard about what his ulterior motives might be. Nate was passionate about the clinic's mission to serve the island, especially to provide care to those who couldn't afford to pay. Even though the high fees paid by celebrities helped to offset the clinic's outreach work, Nate was always on the lookout for opportunities to encourage donations from high-profile patients.

"You're hoping she'll make a donation, either to us or to St. Victoria Hospital," she said.

"I certainly am. In fact, if Roni can see all the potential she has to help people on the island, then I'm hoping she'll consider sending some people from her nonprofit foundation out here, to help support the community even further. And…there's something else, too."

Willow waited. Nate looked around to make sure that

no one else was listening. Then he turned back to her and said, "The thing is… I'm a huge Roni fan."

"What?" Willow laughed, not at Nate, but because she was surprised. He hardly fit the profile of Roni's core fan base, which tended to be a bit older, and mostly female.

"It's true. I grew up watching her show. Our house-keeper had it on every day when I came home from school. My family wasn't especially into big emotional discussions, or really *any* emotional discussions. So when I saw Roni's show, I was instantly hooked. Her guests and the people in her studio audience didn't even know each other, and yet they talked more about their feelings in five minutes than my family did in the average month. And Roni always tackled the real issues. There was nothing she shied away from. I think Roni Santiago might be personally responsible for a good ninety percent of my emotional development as a teenager."

"Wow," said Willow. "I'd never have taken you for a Roni fan."

"One of her biggest." Nate tapped his messenger bag. "This bag was on Roni's list of Favorite Fall Must-Haves two years ago. I've been using it ever since. Her recommendations never let me down."

Willow couldn't help smiling. "All right. If this one is important to you personally, then it's personal to me, too. I'll do everything I can to make sure she has a good experience here."

Nate beamed in gratitude. "I know you will."

"Meanwhile, I haven't seen a chart for her yet. Is her previous treatment center faxing her medical records?"

Nate pulled a chart from his bag and handed it to

Willow. She thumbed through it, mentally gathering the essentials. "This is her second bout with breast cancer?"

"Yes. She had a bout of it eight years ago and went into full remission."

"It looks like she got lucky the first time. Just surgery to remove the tumor, and a few rounds of radiation. No chemo."

"The tumor was less than one centimeter, fully encapsulated when they caught it. Things are still looking good for her this time. They caught it fast, and she's already started chemo. In addition to the extra privacy, she and her doctors thought that a relaxing setting like ours would be helpful for her. Chemo takes a toll on the body, after all."

Willow nodded. Chemo was a terrible treatment, but if one absolutely had to undergo chemotherapy…well, she couldn't think of a better place than an island paradise with world-class doctors on call.

"Actually, there's one other piece to this that I wanted to talk over with you. We've just hired a new oncologist, and naturally he'll be the attending physician on Roni's case."

Willow felt a sudden sense of dread. *No*, she thought. *It's not possible.*

She held the edge of the counter at the nurses' station for balance as her knees had suddenly become unreliable and threatened to give out from under her. She swallowed hard, forcing herself to get the words out. "A new oncologist? What about Dr. Armstrong?"

"She's been talking about retirement for a while. She wants to cut back on her hours so she can spend more time with her family. This new guy is the perfect solution—he wants to focus on research, so both he and

Dr. Armstrong can work part-time. It's win-win for everyone—we get a top-notch cancer researcher, Dr. Armstrong gets to cut back on her hours and we're still able to meet our own patients' needs while taking on those from St. Victoria Hospital. Also, he's pretty nice. I think you're going to like Theo Moore."

As if on cue, Willow saw the double doors behind Nate swing open, and Theo walked in.

He strode toward the nurses' station, nodding at Nate. His eyes widened as he saw Willow. Willow steeled herself, trying to maintain her outward veneer of calm, even though she felt as though the room was spinning. Somehow, when she had told Theo he needed to get a job, it had never crossed her mind that he might work *here*. She hadn't even known the clinic was looking to hire a new oncologist.

And if she had, would she have told Theo? A firm *no* welled within her in response. She couldn't possibly work with him. There was the complicating factor of his relationship to her as Maisie's biological father, which put him in the unusual position of being a complete stranger, yet also connected him to her.

And then there was the matter of his eyes. They were quite problematic, standing out as they did from the few locks of hair that fell from his forehead and just brushed against them. Why didn't he simply push the hair out of his eyes? Her fingers gave an involuntary twitch as she fought a momentary impulse to do it for him.

She reminded herself that she was a very busy single, working mother who didn't have time for distractions. She could understand how some women might find Theo attractive, but she was too busy to care about the way Theo's tousled hair fell over his forehead.

She definitely didn't have any attention to spare for his mouth and the way it creased up at the corners.

Then he smiled, and she caught her breath.

Dammit, she thought. No matter how busy she was, there was no way around it: Theo was an undeniably attractive man. And now, apparently, he was her undeniably attractive coworker.

Theo hadn't meant to get a job at the same clinic as Willow. The moment he stepped into the clinic and saw her, he was gripped with the fear that he might have made a terrible mistake. She'd told him she was a nurse, so it was a fair guess that she worked at one of the major medical centers on the island. But the past few days had been a whirlwind of job searching and house-hunting for Theo, and he'd never stopped to consider the possibility that he and Willow could end up working together.

He'd inquired about a job at St. Victoria Hospital first. Their head oncologist, Dr. Burke, had explained that they didn't have the budget for an additional oncologist, but had introduced him to Nate Edwards. Nate had been thrilled to meet Theo, and he was even more thrilled when he learned about the cancer research that Theo had been involved in. As the head oncologist at the Island Clinic wanted to reduce her hours before retirement, Nate offered Theo a position that would involve research and part-time clinical work at the clinic.

At first, Theo had been hesitant about working at a clinic that catered to celebrities. But as Nate explained it, he'd also be expected to take on patients from St. Victoria Hospital when needed. And the research component of his job would allow him to create grant proposals and research trials that would expand the treatment offered by the hospital. Theo liked the idea of having ample time to do research and pro-bono work, and he also liked the clinic's mission to ensure that no one was turned away, regardless of their ability to pay.

But Willow's presence was a complicating factor that he hadn't accounted for. All of the excitement he'd felt at the thought of calling to tell her he'd found a job drained away the moment he saw her at the nurses' station.

"Theo!" Nate clapped him on the shoulder. "We were just talking about you. Come meet one of our best nurses."

"We've met," said Willow, her clipped tones confirming Theo's worst fears.

"Really? How——" But at that moment, Nate was paged overhead to the trauma wing. "Duty calls. I'll have to let you two catch up with each other on your own. We can touch base on the Santiago case later. And I want to hear about how you already know each other!" Nate flashed a grin and sped off.

Theo took a deep breath and tried to smile at Willow. "That should be an interesting conversation. What should we tell him?"

"Maybe first you can tell *me* what you're doing here!"

Theo gestured toward his white coat. "You said I needed to find a job. Well, here I am."

She closed her eyes, and Theo said, "Look, I understand. I had no idea that you worked here, and if I'd known, I would have turned the job down and figured out something else. But I think there's a strong upside to this. You're cautious about introducing me to Maisie because I'm essentially a stranger to both of you, right?

But if we're working together, I won't be a stranger for very long. We'll get to know one another in no time."

"Yes, but…that's just it. You coming here…wanting to be in Maisie's life…and now *working* at the same clinic—it's just a lot to take in all at once. And you haven't even tried to get in touch with me since last week."

Damn. Becca had been right; he should have called Willow sooner.

"I'm sorry," he said. "I didn't want to bother you with too many updates before I had everything settled. And I wasn't sure how often you'd want to hear from me. I didn't want it to seem as though I was trying to force myself into your life. Although…" He waved his arm at the clinic. "I guess my plan to give you space didn't work out the way I hoped it would."

She sighed. "It's not your fault. I should have seen this coming. If I'd given it any thought, I would have realized that you were bound to end up here or at St. Victoria Hospital. I was just so shocked when you arrived that I didn't even think of the chance that you could end up working here. But I would have appreciated some updates over the past week. When I didn't hear from you, I thought you'd decided to leave."

He could feel his stomach roil in protest. Leave? When he'd barely begun to get to know his daughter? Willow didn't know him at all.

But then, that was the problem. The fact that Willow didn't know anything about him was the biggest obstacle he faced in getting to know his daughter.

"I'm not going anywhere," he said. "And I promise that working here won't interfere with our personal lives. I'm just here to do my job, and I'm sure you are, too."

She was about to respond, but at that moment, there was a burst of activity through the hospital's main doors. A throng of reporters surrounded a woman in a wheelchair as she was being pushed into the clinic. Each reporter shouted their questions so loudly that it was impossible to hear any of them clearly. Cameras snapped and chaos erupted as the press was shooed away by medical staff, only to swarm back toward the woman in the wheelchair while members of her entourage tried to protect her. Amid it all, a small French bulldog ran in circles, barking wildly.

Roni Santiago had arrived.

CHAPTER FOUR

WITHIN SECONDS, THE lobby of the clinic was packed with reporters, medical staff and members of Roni's entourage. A TV news crew was attempting to set up a camera in one corner, ignoring the arguments of a nurse, and the woman pushing Roni's wheelchair had to shove at reporters to keep them away.

"Call security," said Willow. Another nurse, who'd wisely decided to cower behind the nurses' station, nodded and began dialing. Willow headed toward Roni, but not before a reporter stuck a microphone in front of her face. "Miss, what's it like to have Roni herself at the Island Clinic? Are the rumors that she has a deadly, inoperable cancer true?"

So much for maintaining Roni's privacy. There was either a leak in Roni's entourage, or someone from her previous treatment center had revealed her transfer to the Island Clinic. Either way, the press had followed her here, and now it would fall on the clinic staff to control the damage.

"Our patients' medical histories are confidential, and you need to leave, now," said Willow, barely concealing the irritation in her voice.

To her absolute shock, as she tried to move toward

Roni, the reporter grabbed her arm in a tight grip and shouted, "Just a few more questions, please!" She tried to shake him off, but his grip was like a vise, and she nearly lost her balance trying to twist away from his grasp.

Theo moved so quickly that she barely saw him. One moment the reporter had hold of her arm; the next, his microphone had clattered to the floor, and Theo was holding the reporter's shoulder in a firm grip. Theo twisted the reporter's arm behind his back and steered him away from Willow. The expression on Theo's face was so furious that Willow wasn't sure what might have happened next had a uniformed security guard not arrived to take hold of the reporter.

More security officers arrived to herd the press back outside the clinic. Willow could see that Roni was barely conscious.

"We need to take her back to an exam room immediately," she muttered to Theo.

"I'll show you the way, if you can get us through this crowd."

Theo put one arm around Willow's shoulders to protect her as he cleared a path through the crowd. She appreciated his tall frame, which provided shelter from the mob. As the security officers pressed the reporters back, Theo and Willow made their way to the woman who was pushing Roni's wheelchair.

"Are you family?" Theo asked her.

"I'm her best friend. Siobhan."

"All right, you take the dog, I'll take over wheelchair duty." Theo and Willow guided Roni's chair into an exam room as her friend picked up the French bulldog, which immediately stopped barking. Roni seemed as though she could barely lift her head, and as Willow began her examination, she could see that Roni was drifting in and out of consciousness.

"How long has she been like this?" Theo asked Siobhan. Willow noticed that his voice was firm but calm, with no trace of the fury she'd seen in his expression a moment ago.

"About fifteen minutes. We were talking on the plane, and then all of a sudden she just started…drifting off. I thought she was losing consciousness, but she comes around every couple of minutes or so. I can't believe the press followed us here. The whole point of coming was to have some privacy."

"Security will get things under control," Willow reassured her. "Roni will have the rest and privacy she needs."

From her wheelchair, Roni gave a low chuckle. "Thank God for that."

"Roni?" said Willow. "Can you hear us?" But Roni had once again dropped her head to her shoulder and closed her eyes.

Willow nodded at Theo. "Mild seizures, possibly in response to high fever."

"Give me the history," he said.

"Latina woman in her early sixties, current diagnosis of breast cancer, recently started chemotherapy. No known allergies. Presents with seizures and possible high fever." Willow checked her thermometer. "Temperature of one hundred and five. Seizures are persistent but seem to have slowed. Shall we order testing? It could be a seasonal flu, or a bacterial infection she picked up while traveling."

He paused. "She's already started chemo?"

Willow glanced at the chart. "According to her records, she started a few weeks ago. It looks as though she was about halfway through the first planned round of chemo before she decided to transfer her care here."

"Then let's order the testing, but start her on a fever reducer and antibiotics right away."

Theo leaned in toward Roni's wheelchair. "Roni?" he said gently. "Can you hear me?"

Roni's eyes fluttered open.

"Roni, you most likely have a case of febrile neutropenia. That means your body is having a strong reaction to chemotherapy, and it hasn't been making enough of the white blood cells you need to fight off a bacterial infection. The good news is that your friend got you here fast enough for us to start antibiotics within two hours of your fever, which means that you should begin feeling better right away."

"Sounds like I got here just in time," Roni croaked.

"Not a moment too soon," Theo agreed, and Willow noticed again the way the corners of his mouth seemed to tug upward as he spoke. "We still need to wait for the test results to be sure, but we're going to start the antibiotics right way. Odds are good you'll be feeling better very soon."

Of course, Willow thought. Febrile neutropenia. No wonder Theo hadn't wanted to wait for test results. Starting a patient on antibiotics within two hours of the outbreak of a fever could have a significant impact on treatment outcome. Thanks to Theo's quick thinking, Roni was probably going to be fine.

She considered what he'd said only a few moments ago—that working together might allow them to get to know one another more quickly. She still wasn't certain of how she felt about that. But she was glad of the chance to see that Theo was a competent doctor. And although she was certain she could have handled the situation herself, she did appreciate the way he'd pulled that reporter off of her without a moment's hesitation.

So far, Theo had proved that he knew his field well, and that he had her back. She grudgingly admitted to herself that both of those were qualities she valued greatly among her coworkers.

She just wished her stomach wouldn't do flip-flops as she watched him write orders in Roni's chart.

"There's a suite waiting for both of you, but we need to keep her in the exam room for a few hours of observation," she said to Siobhan, trying to pull her focus back to her patient. "You're welcome to stay with her until then."

"Can she keep the dog with her?" asked Siobhan.

Willow hesitated. Dogs typically weren't allowed in exam rooms, but Roni's French Bulldog had settled down considerably, curling quietly into her lap. She smiled and touched a finger to her lips. "I suppose it's fine. But keep it quiet."

As they left the exam room together, Theo said, "Wow. Is it typically like this, with the press?"

"Actually, it's extremely rare. We all take discretion very seriously here. My guess is that someone on Roni's team leaked the information that she was coming. It may not even have been an intentional leak. Some of our patients get so much scrutiny from the press that a careless word, dropped at the wrong time, can tip off the news media to things they aren't supposed to know. Fortunately, we do have excellent security personnel. They're very good at keeping the sharks away. As are you apparently. I want to thank you for helping me out with the reporter back there."

His eyes grew stormy again, and for a moment she thought she saw a trace of the anger that had clouded his face earlier. But it quickly passed as he said, "The important thing is that you're all right." He searched her face carefully. "You *are* all right, aren't you?"

"I'm perfectly fine." Despite herself, she rubbed her arm. It did still hurt a bit. The reporter's grip had been firmer than she'd realized. She hoped she wasn't going to have a bruise.

Theo frowned. "If they're going to be that bold, we should talk to Nate about increasing security for the staff as well as for Roni."

"Certainly, if it makes you feel better. But I know Nate. He won't tolerate an intrusion into a patient's privacy without swift action." And then, in spite of herself, she laughed as she remembered her own first week at the Island Clinic, just over a year ago. "If you think that was bad, you should have been here last year. We had an entire K-pop group."

"K-pop?"

"Korean pop music. Picture five teenage boys, all on the verge of international stardom. Some of the dance moves they do are pretty complex, and apparently they'd been attempting an illegal pyramid formation on a high stage that collapsed, resulting in multiple compound fractures. Their manager didn't want word getting out that they'd been practicing moves banned in Korea, so he had them flown here for absolute privacy."

"But word got out they were here?"

"Through no fault of ours. One of the boys posted a picture of the view from his room online, and a fan from the island realized he was probably somewhere on St. Victoria. It's a small island, and with every woman under twenty on the lookout—well, it was only a matter of time before they determined by process of elimination that the band members were here."

"It was bad, huh?"

"Never underestimate the detective work of teenage girls. Every young woman on the island started trying to get a glimpse of them at the clinic. One of them actually succeeded by disguising herself as a delivery driver. But don't worry. After a while you'll see that these kinds of incidents are really extremely rare."

"I see. So...does this mean you've come around to the idea of us working together?"

She told her stomach to stop doing flip-flops. "I suppose it won't hurt to give it a try. You made a good call with Roni back there. And I liked how you discussed her treatment with her."

"How's that?"

"You told her that the odds were good that she would feel better soon, but you didn't make any false promises. You were confident, without overselling or twisting the truth."

He nodded. "That's important with cancer patients. Everything's about what the odds are. You have to talk about chances, rather than promises. And you have to talk about statistics without making a person *feel* like one."

She was certain he was speaking from his experience as a patient. How important it must be to him, she realized, to be able to use his firsthand knowledge of how it felt to have cancer to help his patients.

Nate's words from earlier that morning came back to

her: *I think you're going to like Theo Moore.* She wondered if that could possibly turn out to be true.

She broke from her reverie to notice that he was staring at her.

"What is it?" she asked. She looked at her nurse's coat, trying to see if she'd spilled coffee somewhere.

"It's just…" He took a deep breath, and his words came rapidly, as though he were forcing himself to push them out. "Speaking of statistics. I was wondering. What are the odds you might have dinner with me later this week?"

For one brief, wild moment, she almost thought that Theo was asking her out on a date. But then she realized that couldn't possibly be the case. Given the circumstances between the two of them, a date was out of the question.

Still, it couldn't hurt to clarify. "When you say, 'have dinner with me,' what exactly do you have in mind?"

He gave her a quizzical look. "Well, I suppose by 'have dinner,' I'm anticipating that there'd be food involved, most likely eaten in the evening, and the 'with me' part implies that it'd be the two of us, eating that food together."

She rolled her eyes. "Yes, but it's *just* dinner, right? It's not…a date?"

"Oh, no, not at all," he said without any hesitation. "I hope it didn't sound as though I was suggesting a date. Especially considering our situation. My priority is getting to know Maisie, after all."

She blushed. *Of course* he hadn't intended to suggest a date. He'd traveled four thousand miles and uprooted his life for the chance at being involved with his daughter; the last thing any reasonable man in his situation would do was put everything at risk with romantic entanglements. And she had no reason to believe he was attracted to her.

She was glad he couldn't read her thoughts, because in spite of the fact that she knew perfectly well that it would be a mistake to date Theo, her spirits had plummeted when he'd explained he was asking her to dinner with no romantic intentions whatsoever. While she wished he hadn't jumped to clarify his lack of interest in her quite *so* quickly, it was probably fortunate that his intentions were strictly platonic. She was too busy, and the risks were far too high. Life was complicated enough without adding heartbreak. Not to mention how confusing things could be for Maisie. Even if Theo had been interested in her, he'd have been off-limits to Willow for that reason alone.

But Theo was right about one thing. She needed to get to know him better. He was clearly making a concerted effort to build a life for himself on St. Victoria. If she intended to give him a fair chance, then she'd need to see him more often.

Maybe dinner wasn't such a bad idea.

"I suppose it couldn't hurt," she said.

"I should hope not. Who knows? It might even be fun."

Dammit. His hazel eyes positively twinkled when he smiled like that. Despite herself, she smiled back, even as her mind continued to resonate with phrases like *off-limits* and *totally inappropriate* and *probably not even interested, anyway.* She told herself to listen to the wisdom of those words.

"What time?" she heard herself say.

* * *

Four days later found Theo trying, desperately and unsuccessfully, to remove dog hair from his suit trousers.

He didn't have a dog, but he did have an unexpected guest. When he'd leased the house, a large, energetic dust mop that he suspected was a Labrador-poodle mix had been making itself comfortable on the porch. The real estate agent had explained that the Caribbean had a serious problem with strays, and had offered to call animal control. But Theo had a soft spot for dogs, and this one was friendly. And there was something about the dog's thin frame that touched his heart. The dog needed to get its strength back, just like him. He'd taken to feeding it each morning, although he wouldn't let it into the house. As much as Theo was determined to make his life on St. Victoria work, he didn't want the dog to get too attached if he had to leave.

The dog had no such reservations. His enthusiastic greetings had left Theo's one good pair of trousers covered with fur.

Theo wanted to look presentable for his dinner with Willow, but so far, his attempts were not going well. His once wavy hair still stuck out at odd angles around his head. Except, of course, for the persistent spray that seemed to insist on falling directly over his forehead and into his eyes, no matter what he tried to do with it.

He told himself that there was no reason to be so nervous. It wasn't as though he was getting ready for a date. He was glad he'd clarified that with Willow from the start, although he still cringed at the awkward way his words had come out.

She'd lost no time in making certain that their dinner

was not a date. He knew she'd been wise to do so, and he'd kicked himself for suggesting dinner in the first place. Why not lunch? Why not a coffee after work? Either of those would have accomplished his goal of getting to know Willow better, thereby bringing him that much closer to getting to know Maisie.

But his words—*What are the odds that you'll have dinner with me?*—had spilled out before he'd had time to think of something that might sound less like a date.

His feelings, especially his unspoken attraction to Willow, had betrayed him. He couldn't think of a worse idea than becoming romantically involved with Willow. His relationship with Maisie was completely at her discretion. After years of not knowing if he'd ever see his daughter, he couldn't allow anything to put his chance to get to know her at risk. Which meant that he had to ignore what he might feel for Willow. He'd already spent the first years of his daughter's life without her. If he and Willow were involved, and things became complicated, he couldn't risk losing Maisie again.

He wondered if things could have been different if he and Willow had met under more normal circumstances. He couldn't deny that he was physically attracted to Willow. He was entranced by the way the waves of her dark brown hair fell against the curve of her neck. And she held herself with such presence: though she had a petite frame, she projected a quiet authority that he imagined she'd developed over her years as a nurse. But it was her warmth, more than anything, that had led him to feel more attracted to her than to anyone he'd met in years. Granted, he'd gone on a very scant handful of dates since his illness was diagnosed four years ago. But even before the diagnosis, he couldn't remember being so struck by any woman's warmth and gentleness. Even back in her kitchen, when she'd been in the middle of explaining that she wasn't certain if he could see his own daughter, she'd expressed such genuine compassion. There was so much he wanted to know about Willow. He wanted to learn where that compassion came from, and who else in her life she might turn that compassion toward. From what he could tell so far, she shared it with everyone.

He was afraid that the more he got to know Willow, the more certain he would be that he wanted her in his life. And no matter how much he wanted her, Maisie was the priority. Even if Willow felt something for him—and he didn't think she did—but even if she was as interested in him as he was in her, he was certain she would agree that their daughter had to come first.

He caught a glance of himself in the mirror as he threw on a crisp, white shirt and did up the buttons. He'd always been on the muscular side, but now his body looked positively gaunt, the missing muscle all too evident after years of treatment. Pale skin, uncontrollable hair. It felt like a cancer survivor's body, but it didn't feel like *his* body.

He wished it didn't feel as though there was so much riding on this dinner. He reminded himself, for what felt like the millionth time, that this wasn't a date. And yet the nervous feelings he had were so similar to the worries he typically had before a date. What if he couldn't think of anything to say? What if she hated the restaurant he'd picked? What if she decided she hated him, and he never got to know Maisie?

Stop panicking, he told himself firmly. *You got through cancer. You can get through this.*

* * *

He still hadn't returned his doctor's message from when he'd first arrived on the island. He'd been too nervous thinking about his upcoming dinner with Willow to spare a thought for checking in with his doctor. And he wanted some time to enjoy being in remission, before getting into a routine with his follow-up appointments. He needed to live his life. Which, at this moment, meant screwing up his courage and heading to the French Indian fusion restaurant in Williamtown where he was meeting Willow.

He took a deep breath and stepped out onto the veranda. The dog padded toward Theo with hopeful eyes, and leaned against his legs.

"I suppose a little more fur can't make a difference now," said Theo, scratching behind the dog's ears. "Wish me luck, old fellow."

In response, the dog thumped his tail twice on the porch. Theo decided to interpret this as a good sign. He was going to need all the help he could get.

Willow couldn't remember the last time she'd felt so nervous. Her mouth was dry, and as she sat across from Theo and tried desperately to think of something to say, it was all she could do to keep her hands from shaking.

Relax, it's not a date, she tried to tell herself. But somehow, it had the feeling of one.

Theo looked perfectly comfortable in his white, button-down shirt, while she'd simply thrown on an old sundress with a light shawl. But even on an un-date, as she referred to it in her mind, it was horribly awkward trying to think of something to say. She couldn't imagine how they would begin to feel comfortable with each other.

It didn't help that his hair, once again, fell just over his forehead. *Just try not to look at his hair, and control yourself,* she thought. It might have been a while since she'd had an evening out with another adult, but she had a feeling running her fingers through Theo's tousled hair in the middle of a crowded restaurant wouldn't do anything to reduce the awkwardness she felt.

When she'd first met Theo, his smile had caught her attention. Later, she'd found that she was quite taken with his eyes. But now, as she watched him peruse the menu, she realized that his hands were quite slender. Steady, careful hands.

Dammit, she thought. Was there anything about him that wasn't attractive?

She racked her brain for something besides his appearance to talk about. *Work. Ask him how work is going.*

It was difficult, because she felt as though her mouth was full of cotton, but she managed to squeak out, "How are you adjusting to the clinic?"

He seized upon the question with an eagerness that made Willow suspect that he'd probably been searching for something to talk about, as well.

"It's fascinating. Although I'm not sure I'll ever get used to working with celebrity patients. I have to admit that it's not exactly the clientele I'd always imagined working with."

"Well, you've made quite an impression on Roni Santiago. Providing health care to the rich and famous might just be your calling."

"Perhaps. I suppose life is full of surprises. Speaking of which…sorry, again, for taking a job at your workplace. I never meant to make you uncomfortable."

She shrugged. "Don't worry. It was a surprise at first, but I should have anticipated it. There aren't too many options for oncologists on one small island."

He seemed to relax a bit at her words. "I'm glad you feel that way, because I think I might really like working at the Island Clinic. With so many unexpected changes, it hasn't always been easy to move forward with my career."

She realized that he was referring to the cancer. "I'm sure it couldn't have been easy to hold down a job consistently while you were ill."

"It wasn't. It's why I've mostly been in research positions, even though my passion is working directly with patients. One of the best things about the Island Clinic is that I get to do some clinical work on the side."

"You couldn't find something like that in England?"

"Oh, I could. But then, you see, I learned that my daughter had moved here. Finding her was the priority."

His jaw had that determined set to it again. Willow felt a twinge of guilt at having treated him with such suspicion at first. She didn't trust him yet. But she found that she wanted to.

"Is it hard to live so far from the rest of your family?" he asked.

"There's no other family. My parents died when I was very young, so I was raised by my grandmother, who passed away just after Maisie was born."

"I'm so sorry."

"It's all right."

He gave her a rueful smile. "Now there's a phrase I know all too well. Along with 'It's fine' and 'Don't worry about it.' That's my set of typical stock phrases for when someone asks a big question without realizing it, and then tries to apologize."

"Does that happen often?"

"Speaking as a cancer patient, it happens all the time. Sometimes all people can say is 'I'm so sorry,' and then all you can say back is 'It's all right.'"

She thought about that for a moment. Her response to Theo's question had been automatic. He was right; it was what she almost always said when people found out about her parents. And she was certain it was what he usually said when people learned he'd had cancer.

"I suppose I've been an orphan for so long that it just doesn't feel unusual to me," she said. "My parents died in a car accident before I was even a year old. Growing up, I did often wonder what they were like. I was lucky that I at least had Gran to tell me about them. But then, I always felt lucky to have Gran."

"So she was there to fill their shoes."

"In a way. She didn't replace them. She'd have been the first to admit that she never could have taken their place. But she made me feel loved enough that our tiny family felt much bigger than it actually was."

She hadn't expected to open up this much to Theo. But she found that she enjoyed talking to him. No one had asked much about her family, or about Gran in particular, for years.

She couldn't help thinking about the parallels of her own life to Maisie's. Her daughter had only one other person in the world to rely on, just as Willow had, growing up. As a child, Willow had missed having the presence, the advice, of a father at times. As a mother, she often wished she had the ability to give Maisie a large family. In addition to enriching Maisie's life, it would have brought Willow peace of mind to know that Maisie would have other family if anything happened to Willow. She wondered if Maisie would begin to wish for more family as she grew older, just as Willow had.

Willow was sure Theo couldn't have known that her thoughts would turn in this direction when he'd asked about her family.

"What about you?" she asked. "Do you have much family back in England?"

"Four siblings, one of them a twin sister." He launched into a detailed description of the advantages and drawbacks of having a large family. In addition to his siblings, he seemed to have an extensive network of aunts, uncles and cousins who were all very involved in one another's lives. As they spoke, Willow realized that she was growing more comfortable. It had been so long since she'd spent an evening with another adult that she'd forgotten it could actually be fun.

But just as she was starting to relax and enjoy herself, a crash came from a few tables away. An older man was at the center of the commotion, surrounded by concerned waitstaff and restaurant patrons. Willow heard a faint cry of "Is anyone a doctor?"

"Looks like we're on call tonight," Theo said.

They approached the man, who was heavyset and seemed to be in his late sixties. His skin was beet-red, and his breathing was shallow and rapid. His forehead was hot to the touch, and his heart rate was elevated. He was conscious, but his words weren't making sense.

"He could be having a stroke," Theo muttered into her ear. A woman—presumably the man's wife—fluttered frantically about him in tears. "Does he have any neurological issues?" he asked her.

Willow turned to a waiter. "Get me a large pitcher of ice water," she said, ignoring Theo's quizzical look.

The man was wearing a heavy wool sweater, far too thick for the weather. "Help me get this off him," she said to Theo.

"It was a birthday present," the man's wife said through her tears. "He wanted to wear it even though I told him it was far too hot."

"Has he had any heavy exertion today?" Willow asked.

"We played tennis for a few hours, then I gave him the sweater and we came down here for a few drinks."

"How much alcohol has he had?"

"Two, maybe three drinks."

Willow nodded. "He's overheated. Don't worry—heatstroke can make people crash hard, but recovery is quick if we act fast." In fact, the man had already begun to come around as she rubbed his neck and forehead with ice.

"Drink this," she told him, lifting his head so he could sip a glass of cold water. "And no more alcohol for you today. Overexertion plus alcohol is a recipe for heatstroke."

Someone had called the paramedics, and the man was already sitting up on his own by the time they arrived on the scene.

"Will he be all right?" his wife asked.

"I'm sure he'll be fine," said Willow. "But he should go to the hospital to get checked out."

The woman thanked them profusely and proceeded to berate her husband. "I *told* you to take it easy," she

scolded as she packed herself into the back of the ambulance with him.

"I'm impressed," Theo said. "I never thought of
something as simple as heatstroke. I was thinking it
was some sort of neurological condition. But then, I
tend to overthink things."

"As a good researcher should," she said, smiling.
"I've seen heatstroke a hundred times since moving to
the island. Tourists aren't prepared for the heat of the
Caribbean and don't realize how quickly they can over-
exert themselves."

As they headed back to their cold entrees, a waiter
approached and let them know the cost of their meal
had been compensated, to thank them for their help with
the medical emergency. Willow thanked the waiter as
Theo poked at his cold food.

"It's very kind of them, but I'm afraid this evening
is a bit of a bust, isn't it?" said Theo. "Why don't we
take a walk outside?"

They headed out to the boardwalk along the beach,
where the sun was just beginning to set, illuminating
the beach in tones of red and gold.

"I know this might sound strange, but I'm almost
grateful for the medical emergency," Willow said. "It
was nice to feel competent for a moment, after getting
so nervous about our dinner together." She was careful
to avoid the word *date*, even though, somehow, it was
starting to feel like one.

"You were nervous? I would never have guessed."

She laughed. "Come on, you must have noticed how
hard it was for me to talk at first."

"Maybe I didn't notice because I was nervous, too."

They stopped walking, and he gazed at her intently.

She felt an unexpected wave of heat wash over her, a flush that had nothing to do with the warmth of the Caribbean air.

It's time to go home, she thought to herself. *Time to wrap that shawl around your shoulders like a respectable woman, and go home to take care of your child.*

But then Theo traced her arm, lightly, and her shawl slipped even lower on her shoulders. And somehow, Willow found herself not moving to put it back where it belonged. He was standing close to her, and she took in just how very tall he was. Her head fit just under his chin.

"How's your arm?" he said. For a moment she didn't know what he meant, but then she realized he was referring to when the reporter had grabbed her.

"Oh," she said distractedly. "It's fine. It's nothing… it barely left a mark."

The determined set to his jaw was starting to become familiar. She felt one of his arms circle her, protectively, and she didn't resist as he pulled her close against his chest.

She turned her face up toward his and lost herself in his clear, hazel eyes. He bent his head to hers and kissed her, softly at first, but then more deeply as she let her body melt against his. Things were moving far too fast, she knew, but she was also powerless to resist the sensation of his lips on hers. His arms enveloped her, one tight around her waist, the other caressing the waves of her hair that fell against her shoulder.

A current of heat ran through her entire body. It was agonizing to pull away from him, but she made herself do it. Not because she wanted the kiss to stop, but because she knew she'd reached the end of her resistance.

If she didn't stop now, she never would. And there were so many reasons to stop. The primary reason was at home with Mrs. Jean, waiting for Willow to return and read her a bedtime story.

Theo held her for a moment longer, until she forced herself to step out of his arms.

The sun had gone down, and they were shrouded in darkness. There were only a few lights from further up the beach. After they'd walked together for a moment or two, Theo broke their silence.

"I'd give anything to know what you're thinking."

She wasn't sure how to begin. Or where to begin. She wanted to explain to him that she had sworn off relationships. She had responsibilities. She couldn't risk getting hurt again. And there was Maisie. She wanted him to understand.

But more than anything, she wanted him to kiss her again.

She was about to say that they'd made a mistake, but then she stopped. Honesty was important to her. "That was nice," she admitted.

His eyes were afire. "I can show you more than nice."

She was willing to bet that he could. But she had a daughter. She had to be cautious.

"I think, for now, we might have to leave it at nice," she said firmly.

"Because of the reason I think you're thinking of?"

"That's probably the main reason, yes."

He nodded. "Because no matter what we might be feeling for one another, those feelings have to be put on hold. We can't risk whatever happens between us affecting Maisie. Because that's the right thing to do."

She gave him the smallest of smiles. "I think you're

starting to understand what it means to be a parent, Theo Moore."

He let out a long breath. "I think so, too. So nothing can happen between us."

She knew she should leave it at that. She should go home, without saying one thing more. She knew enough of who Theo was by now to know that if she never said another word about it, he would never bring up any of this again, out of respect for her.

But she couldn't accept that she'd had her last kiss with him.

She couldn't help herself. She blurted out, "Not for now, anyway."

He'd been looking out at the ocean, and now he whirled toward her. *Dammit.* His eyes did light up when he smiled. "Wait a minute. When you say, 'for now'… does that mean that there could be a *later* in our future?"

"I can't pretend to know what the future holds. But I think I can safely say that there could be a 'later' for us. And when that *later* time comes, I might be interested in more."

He smiled, and she was glad it was dark, so that he couldn't see her resistance melting away. "I can handle later," he said. "I've been waiting a long time for my life to start. I can wait a little more."

CHAPTER FIVE

"EVERYTHING LOOKS GOOD," said Willow, flipping Roni's chart closed. "Your prognosis is looking very strong, despite what the tabloids might say. I'll come back to start your next round of chemo in a few hours. Until then, keep resting, and let me know if you have any pain."

Roni scratched her French bulldog behind the ears. "I know the drill. I think Buttons and I will head up to the rooftop patio for some rest and relaxation in a few minutes. Then we'll take a little pre-chemo nap up there in the sun, so that we'll be well-rested for our post-chemo siesta this afternoon."

Willow smiled. "You've got the idea. The more you rest, the better your body is able to recover."

"Sounds logical enough, but I can't get used to all of this lying around. I need to work. I can't remember the last time I had so much time off. At least by doing chemo here, I can make it feel like a proper vacation." She fixed Willow with an eye. "Any chance you can have someone send up a mai tai while I'm on the roof?"

"If you like, but it'll have to be virgin. You know you shouldn't drink right now."

"Honey, I don't even want the alcohol. I just want to hold one of those big tropical drinks for the *effect*.

I want to lean back on one of those lounge chairs and sip on something delicious, something decorated with tiny umbrellas and twenty different pieces of fruit and a flower or two."

"I'll put a note in to the kitchen and ask them to send up something ostentatious."

"That would be lovely. I want a drink that says, 'Screw you, cancer, I'm still living my life.'" Her expression grew sober. "That's the point, you know. Some of my friends thought that I should keep doing my treatment at home. I told them I needed more privacy, but that's not all it was about. This might sound silly, but I wanted to *show* cancer it hadn't beaten me. And I thought that if I could pretend that I was here by choice, as though I were on some sort of vacation, then no matter what happens with my treatment… I still win."

Willow impulsively reached out for Roni's hand. "There's nothing silly about that. Maintaining a positive attitude is crucial for treatment."

Roni gave Willow's hand a little squeeze. "I'm glad you understand. It's not denial. I'm perfectly aware of my situation. It's just my way of coping, and it helps to be in a setting where everyone's agreed to play along." She traced her bulldog's ears. "Having a little company doesn't hurt, either. Back home, they wouldn't let me keep Buttons next to me during treatment."

"Technically, we don't allow it, either, so make sure to keep him under that sheet." According to clinic rules, the dog was supposed to stay in Roni's suite, but Willow had agreed to overlook his presence. Roni was so attached to the dog, and he clearly helped to lift her spirits.

Willow's initial reluctance to oversee Roni's care had

quickly melted away as they got to know each other. Willow had been relieved to find that Roni was just as down-to-earth as she came across on television.

In fact, the most complicated part about working with Roni had nothing to do with Roni at all. It was Theo.

Several days had passed since their un-date. And their kiss.

The kiss was a problem, because it had been perfect.

The way his arms had enveloped her, holding her close to him. He was tall enough so that her head fit just under his chin, and when he'd bent his head to hers, she'd felt an excitement she thought she'd forgotten after all those years of having sworn off romance.

She'd felt very safe, very protected, in his arms. But the problem was that it wasn't safe at all. Kissing Theo, trusting Theo, *feeling* things for Theo…all of it put her in a very vulnerable position.

She might feel safe with Theo, but she couldn't trust her feelings. She'd felt safe with Jamie for years. And all that time, he hadn't really been himself with her. She'd nearly lost her dream of having a child because of his inability to tell her the truth about what he really wanted.

And now there was so much more at stake. Not just her own happiness, but Maisie's, too. One of the main reasons she'd sworn off relationships, aside from her own heartbreak, was her fear that Maisie could become attached to someone, and could be confused or even hurt if things didn't work out. But what if things didn't work out between Willow and a man who happened to be Maisie's father? She couldn't put her daughter through that.

She wanted to believe that she could trust Theo to

protect her heart as much as she could trust him to protect her child. In the short time she'd known him, she'd noticed that he had a knack for saying just the right thing. But how could she trust that he was sincere? She'd already been with one man who'd said what she wanted to hear, rather than telling her the truth.

And so the kiss was a problem. Because no matter how perfect it had been, it didn't change the host of other issues she had to worry about. In fact, the more she thought about it, the more she became convinced that the kiss was a problem *because* it had been so perfect. If it had been a bad kiss, she could have forgotten about it by now and moved on.

Instead, it seemed determined to linger in her memory.

"Hey. Earth to Willow." Roni's voice brought Willow back to the present with a start.

"Oh, sorry. I must have spaced out for a minute. Let me just take a quick look at your lab results." She picked up Roni's chart.

"You just did that a few minutes ago, remember?"

Willow blushed, flustered. She *never* got distracted at work like this. "You're right. I don't know where my head is today."

"Maybe you were daydreaming about that hot date you had a few days ago."

Willow's eyebrows shot up her forehead. "You know about that?" Her chest began to tighten. Who else knew? Was it all over the clinic? "It wasn't exactly a date."

"Of course I know about it. Theo checks in on me every day. No, don't look like that," she said, noting Willow's affronted expression. "He didn't say a word to me about it. I heard him ask you to dinner the day I got here. I may have been feverish, but the two of you were just outside the door. Come on, dish. What's he like?"

At least there weren't rumors flying all over the clinic about the two of them. "It's…complicated."

Roni rolled her eyes. "Isn't it always."

"No, I mean it's really complicated. Theo is working here under a rather unusual set of circumstances, and even though I like him–"

Roni's gaze met hers. "You like him."

"Well, everyone seems to like him, so far."

"But not the way you do."

Willow was beginning to see how Roni had always got the guests on her show to open up so quickly about their most personal issues. The woman was relentless. "Theo and I are in a very unusual situation. Surely you'd rather rest than hear all the details," she protested weakly.

Roni chuckled. "I've got nothing but time to fill, and I need a good distraction. Besides, you can't leave me in suspense after all this talk about 'complications' and 'unusual situations.' What's the story with you and Dr. Moore?"

Willow was about to demur, but Roni's eyes seemed to plead for excitement. Suddenly, she realized that Roni might be the perfect person to talk to. She couldn't tell any of her friends from work because *they* all worked with Theo, too, and revealing her connection with him could create the very kinds of problems she wanted to avoid. And her friends outside of work were so eager to set her up with someone that they would probably ignore all of the problems that her feelings for Theo entailed. Roni was the perfect neutral party, and Willow had a feeling that she could trust Roni not to contribute to any gossip.

She took a deep breath. "You see, about four years ago, I decided to have a child on my own. But there was this mix-up." She went on to explain everything about the confusion at the clinic. She'd meant to just stick to the facts, but as she talked to Roni, she found herself opening up more and more about how conflicted her feelings were. Even though she didn't necessarily agree with the decision Theo had made to stay out of Maisie's life, given his circumstances, she could understand why he'd made the choice he did. She felt that after all he'd been through, he deserved to have a chance to get to know Maisie, especially as she was starting to believe he was serious about making a life on St. Victoria. But she also felt that she was putting Maisie's happiness at risk.

"That's the real problem, isn't it?" said Roni. "This isn't just about letting him get to know his child. I think you're afraid of him getting to know *you*."

Willow blushed again. "I don't know what to do. For the past three years, everything in my life has been about what's best for Maisie. I can't change that just because of an attraction to someone I barely even know."

"Even if that someone happens to be the father of your child?"

"*Especially* because of that. What if it doesn't work out? Where does that leave Maisie?"

"I hear you. But here's a thought—what if it does?"

Willow hesitated. "That's the other problem. I want to trust him, but I still don't know if I can. I'll admit that there's a lot I like about him. But…he ignored his daughter for three years. Supposedly, he's always wanted children, but if that were true, then shouldn't he have made every effort to be in her life when he had the chance?"

"Cancer, though," said Roni. "It's a hell of a mitigating circumstance."

"I know. And I want to be sympathetic to his situation, I really do. Except all these warning bells keep going off in my mind, telling me to be on my guard. But then, when we kissed, it felt so right." She clapped a hand over her mouth. She hadn't meant to tell Roni about the kiss.

But the look Roni gave her was full of understanding. "You've been hurt before, haven't you?" she said.

Willow nodded. Tears welled to her eyes, and she hastened to wipe them away.

"Then there's your answer," Roni said. "You don't have man problems. You have trust problems."

"What?"

"Please. I didn't host the highest-rated talk show in the world for fourteen years just to not be able to tell when someone's hiding from themselves. Your problem isn't with Theo at all."

"Of course it is. If he hadn't shown up here, I wouldn't have to be dealing with any of this."

Roni waved her hand in dismissal. "That's just details. Date him, don't date him, it's your call. Although I have to admit that I'm biased toward you dating him. He did save my life, after all."

Willow couldn't disagree with the latter part of Roni's statement. However she might feel about Theo, his abilities as an oncologist were clear.

"My point is that he's not the cause of your problems. It's the memories of this person who hurt you, not Theo."

Willow wasn't sure she agreed. None of the turmoil she'd experienced lately had started until Theo had shown up. She'd never once questioned her decision to swear off relationships until Theo had started flashing that warm smile of his in her direction.

"But how can this not be about him?" she said. "He's the one who decided to show up here. He's the one who got a job at the same clinic I'm working at."

"Maybe he doesn't want to waste any more time. Look, I don't know what happened to you before, but I can say that cancer gives you a different outlook. You start looking at life differently, see all the opportunities you didn't take."

"Wait, Roni Santiago is talking about roads not taken? Surely you can't have any regrets in life. Everyone in the world knows your name."

"There's more to life than just career. I'm talking about roads not taken in relationships. Opportunities of the heart. Maybe this Theo Moore is thinking of missed opportunities, too."

Maybe Roni had a point.

"So you think I should give him a chance?"

"Oh, no," Roni said, to Willow's surprise. "I think you should give *yourself* a chance. I think you should try to let go of the memories of whoever hurt you, if you can. And if, while you were doing that, you happened to also let yourself see where things might go with Theo…who knows? You might even have some fun. He's pretty easy on the eyes, after all. A little on the pale side. Needs some building up. But nice to look at overall. If I absolutely have to go through cancer, it doesn't hurt to have a handsome doctor to get me through it."

Willow pretended to look scandalized.

"Hey, I'm allowed to make the best of a bad situation."

Willow snorted. "I'll admit that it's not a *great* situation, but it's certainly not as bad as the tabloids say." She stood up from Roni's bedside and turned to leave. As she reached the door, she looked back and said, "Roni... I'd appreciate it if you didn't tell anyone about our conversation."

Roni motioned to Buttons and said, "If you can keep my secrets, I can keep yours."

"Theo? Do you have an update on the Santiago case?" Nate's voice cut through Theo's reverie.

Theo pulled his attention back to the meeting. He was in a case conference with the clinic's senior staff members, reviewing updates on pressing clinical issues. His mind, though, kept drifting back to the kiss he'd shared with Willow several days ago.

But pleasant as it might be to reminisce, those thoughts weren't going to help him make a good impression at his new job. This was his first chance at a clinical position after he'd entered remission, and he wanted to shine. He forced himself to focus.

"Roni's prognosis is very good. She's had quality care before she arrived, and the plan is to continue her chemo regimen here. She has about two months left of her full course, at which time we'll reevaluate and update her treatment plan accordingly."

"Sounds like things are going smoothly," Nate replied. "Moving on—"

"There is a problem, though," Theo continued.

"With her treatment?"

"No. With the press." Theo threw a tabloid paper onto the conference table. Its headline read Roni Santiago Fights Mysterious Deadly Illness! "For one thing, these headlines are wildly misleading. It seems like in the absence of any real information they're just making things up."

"Nothing we can do about that," Nate replied. "We can't reveal any confidential information about our patients, and Roni wants utter privacy."

"That's not all, though. The press corps camped outside the clinic has been pushy and aggressive since the day they arrived. I'm worried about how they're responding to staff. One of them already grabbed Willow's arm when she tried to walk away from him." Theo felt a twinge of guilt, as Willow had said there was no need to mention the incident to Nate. Still, seeing the throng of press outside when he arrived at work every day was unsettling. They seemed to be constantly pushing back against the security staff.

"Is Willow all right?"

"She's fine. But I'm concerned that things could have been more serious. I've never seen reporters act in such a way."

"It's because it's not just press, it's paparazzi," another doctor chimed in. "They'll do anything to get a compromising photo of Roni. Theo's right, though. We should do something about it before the situation escalates."

Nate nodded. "I'll talk to the clinic security staff about ways we might need to change procedure. Everyone should feel safe coming here, no matter what.

But don't worry, Theo. We've dealt with these kinds of situations before."

"Yes, I heard about the K-pop band," Theo said, and everyone laughed.

"*That* was a fiasco," said Nate. "I think every single teenage girl on the island faked an illness or injury in order to come here and catch a glimpse of those boys."

Most of the doctors were still laughing as they left the conference room. Theo was glad that he seemed to be fitting in well. But as he headed back toward his office, he found himself wishing that he knew where he stood with Willow.

They'd had ample opportunity to see each other over the past few days, as they were both part of Roni Santiago's medical team. She'd been warm, but professional, and he'd tried his best to respond in kind. He always seemed to find himself tongue-tied around her.

Though, for some reason, he hadn't felt nervous at all during their kiss. It had seemed like the most natural thing in the world to bend his head to hers and to feel her mouth yield to his, with nothing but the gentle lapping of the waves on the beach to keep him from getting utterly lost in the moment, in *her*.

He understood why she'd pulled back from him. If he knew one thing about Willow, it was that she was protective of her daughter. There was no way for the two of them to become involved without acknowledging the fact that it could be confusing for Maisie. He hoped Willow knew that he'd agreed with everything she'd said about wanting to put their feelings on hold because of Maisie. He thought it was for the best, too. Complicating, or even losing, his chance to get to know

Maisie was out of the question. But losing the chance to kiss Willow again…well, that was also a grim prospect.

After she'd pulled away from their kiss, he'd thought, for a moment, that Willow would say that they had no chance at all. But he'd been relieved that she'd kept the door open for…something.

He wasn't sure what that something might be, or just how far into the future she envisioned "later" to be. He was still trying to think of a way to bring it up with her when he arrived at his office and found a sticky note stuck to his computer screen. It was from Willow, inviting him to meet her for lunch in the cafeteria.

He arrived to find her already nibbling at a chocolate croissant.

"Interesting choice," he said, sitting across from her. "A cafeteria staffed by Michelin-star-quality cooks, and yet you're opting for a coffee and croissant for lunch."

She closed her eyes in pleasure as she took a bite. "Clearly you haven't yet enjoyed the magic of the Island Clinic morning pastry table. There are hardly any leftovers by lunch, but I managed to snag this one today."

"I'll have to try one soon."

She gave him a mock glare and pulled the croissant toward herself. "Don't get any ideas. This one's mine."

He held up his hands. "Your croissants are safe with me."

She took a long sip of coffee, and he had a feeling she was gathering her thoughts. He was bracing himself for whatever she might say next. He hoped, more than anything, that she wasn't about to tell him that they couldn't see each other, because of Maisie. And yet if she was, well, then…he might not like it, but he could understand.

"I really enjoyed having dinner with you," she said. He noticed that she seemed as careful to avoid the word *date* as he was. "It was my first night out in a long time, and it was fun."

"Even with the medical emergency?"

"Especially with that. It gave me a chance to show off a little."

He sighed. "I can't help but feel that there's a 'but' coming."

"Theo, honesty is extremely important to me. Which is why I want to tell you that I had a good time the other night. And... I am enjoying getting to know you. I've been thinking a lot about roads not taken, and if it were just me, if I were completely on my own, then this would probably be a road I'd want to explore. But I'm not on my own."

He reached across the table and covered her hand with his, and she didn't move away. "I appreciate your honesty, and I understand. And just so you know, you're not in this alone. Protecting Maisie is important to me, too."

"I can see that. And that's why we need to take things really, really slowly."

His world stopped for a minute. He wasn't sure he'd heard correctly. Once again, he'd been so certain that Willow was going to tell him that she couldn't be romantically involved with him at all. But if she were talking about taking things slowly, then that meant he had a chance.

"We need to take our time," she continued. "We've both been through some very sudden changes lately, and we need some time to adapt. If it were just me, I might be ready to jump in with both feet. But I don't want to throw lots of sudden changes Maisie's way."

Her hand was still under his, on the table. Cautiously, without breaking eye contact, he turned his hand so that he was holding hers. "So just to be clear, this isn't a full stop, but a slowdown."

She held his hand as firmly as she held his gaze. "I need you to be okay with slow."

He couldn't stop the relieved grin that broke over his face. "Are you kidding me? I am *thrilled* with slow. If slow is my chance to get to know my daughter, and you, then slow is my new favorite speed."

She gave his hand a squeeze before she took hers back. "I hope you can understand."

"Willow, I do. I meant it when I said that you're not in this alone. Protecting Maisie will always be my first priority."

She nodded, but he wasn't sure if she understood what he meant. How could she? He hadn't yet had a chance to explain to her what having children meant to him.

"When I was diagnosed with cancer, I worried that having lots of children would be one of many dreams that I'd have to put on hold. I didn't know if it was ever going to happen. Having my sperm frozen was my last chance. But even with that, there was no way to be sure that I would ever have children. All it did was help to increase my chances a little. And so when the clinic had their accident and Maisie was conceived…to me, it wasn't an accident. It was a miracle. And even though I don't know her, she's very precious to me, because she represents part of a dream I once had. There's nothing I wouldn't do for her. Including taking things slow."

Willow was staring at him intently. Theo hoped his words had made sense. He hoped he hadn't come on too strong, but even if he had, he didn't think he could have put it any other way. He'd meant every word.

But then she smiled. "I know a little something about feeling like your dreams are being taken away. Maisie represents a dream for me, too."

He realized that she must be referring to the reason she'd had Maisie via donor insemination. It was such a personal decision that he hadn't yet had a chance to ask her about it, but he was curious.

"What kind of dream did you have?" he asked gently.

"Oh, nothing too uncommon, I suppose. I didn't grow up in a big family like yours. But I was always envious of people who did. I imagined having a large family of my own. And I thought my ex did, too. He'd said he did. Until, after eight years together, he decided he didn't."

Theo winced in sympathy. "It's an awfully big thing to change one's mind about."

"The worst part is, I could have forgiven him a long time ago if he'd simply changed his mind about it. But he always said that we'd have children someday, when the time was right."

"And the right time never came?"

She shook her head in frustration. "At first I was furious with him. All that time, he could have told me the truth, instead of saying the things he thought I wanted to hear. If he had, then maybe we could have parted as friends. Maybe we could have both found people who wanted the same things we did. But now I think I was just as angry with myself, for not seeing the truth sooner. Of course Jamie wouldn't want children. He didn't even *like* children. He never wanted to spend any time with his young nieces and nephews. He'd even complain if we went to a restaurant and there were children nearby."

"It sounds as though you two were rather badly matched."

"To say the least of it. I can see now that we weren't right for each other. But we started dating when we were very young. I'd never broken up with anyone before. And the worst part wasn't just losing the relationship. It was losing that whole dream of having a family."

"And so you decided to have Maisie."

"Exactly," she said. "So you see, Theo, I do know how it feels to worry that your dreams are slipping away."

Theo realized that he and Willow might be more similar than he'd thought. They'd both had to find creative ways around life's obstacles. He found his respect for her growing even more.

"I had so much of my future built up around Jamie, and so when we broke up, I knew that I never wanted to put myself through that pain again," she continued. "Especially once Maisie arrived. And so I swore off relationships for a while. I guess what I'm trying to say is that I'm pretty out of practice with…certain things."

He smiled. "So we go slow."

"Yes."

He tried not to let his expression betray his thoughts. *She* was out of practice? He hadn't been with anyone for nearly four years. His body was such a shadow of what it used to be after chemo that it was hard enough for him to look at it, let alone anyone else.

But when he'd kissed Willow on the boardwalk, his

body had seemed to know just how to respond when he'd felt her hot skin against his, out of practice or not.

He wanted very much to find some secluded place with Willow now, where they could finish what they'd started on that boardwalk, and catch up on whatever practice they needed after taking the past few years off from relationships.

But they were trying to take things slow. And so instead, he said, "I found a house to rent last week. I decided to decline the staff housing here, in favor of increased privacy. Would it be going slow enough if I invited you and Maisie over to see the house this week-end? We could make it a bit of a housewarming party. I could spend some time with her, and you can see if the house meets with your approval."

"You have a house already? You've only been here three weeks."

"It turned out to be much easier to find a place to rent than I thought. It even came with a dog."

"I...didn't know that was typical."

"The landlord said he'd been living on the porch for months. He's very friendly. Do you like dogs? Does Maisie?"

"She'll be over the moon. She's been pestering me for one for ages, but I was going to wait for her birth-day next year."

"You'll come, then? It's a...date?"

"It's a start."

CHAPTER SIX

THE HOUSE THEO had rented turned out to be on a stretch of beach just outside Williamtown, about a twenty-minute walk from Willow's home. Willow was grateful for the walk, as she wanted time to collect her thoughts. This would be the first time Maisie would have any amount of interaction with Theo, and she was nervous about how it would go.

Willow had simply told her that they were visiting a friend. The plan was to have a picnic lunch on the beach, and Maisie chattered excitedly from her stroller about the dog Willow had said would be there.

Maisie, Willow knew, would be fine, no matter how this afternoon went. After all, as far as she was concerned, this was just another day out. To Willow, it was much more. Her conversation with Roni had been spinning in her head all week. She knew that she hadn't had feelings like those she felt for Theo in a long time. But despite all the reasons *not* to start anything with Theo—and there were so many good reasons—maybe Roni was right. Maybe all of those reasons were nothing more than Willow's way of hiding from herself.

Swearing off relationships had let her feel safe. For years, she'd told herself that she could be content with just herself and her daughter. But then, she'd never encountered anyone like Theo over the past few years. Someone who gave rise to the first stirrings of a desire for something more.

Or perhaps "first stirrings" was a bit of an understatement. She still remembered the way Theo's hand had brushed her neck when they kissed. The way her shawl had dropped down from her shoulder.

She'd wanted so much more than just a kiss.

But she'd also meant what she'd said, about wanting to take things slow. The attraction she felt for him had disrupted her calm life and left her feeling thrown off-balance, because she knew the heartbreak that could come if things went badly.

She'd felt encouraged by the conversation they'd had in the cafeteria. But then, Theo always knew what to say. It was whether he followed his words up with actions that mattered.

They approached Theo's house, where he waved to them from the porch. Like their own house, it was built on stilts to protect against hurricanes. Maisie hopped out of her stroller and they traipsed down the narrow pathway, until Maisie came to a dead stop.

"No," she said.

"What is it, love?"

Maisie pointed a chubby finger. "No dog."

A large, curly-haired dog sat placidly next to Theo on the porch. As Willow and Maisie stared at it, it placed its head on Theo's knee and gazed at him with brazen adoration.

"This is Bixby," Theo said, scratching the dog behind its ears as Bixby closed his eyes in ecstasy. "He came with the house. He lives out here on the porch, and seems very determined to stay."

Maisie stepped back, and peeked out from behind Willow's skirt. "What's wrong, Mais?" Willow asked. "I thought you were excited to meet the doggy."

"That one's too big."

"He is a big fellow, isn't he?" said Theo, rubbing Bixby's sides. The dog stood up and shook, and Maisie cowered behind Willow even more. Willow guessed the dog was some mix of Labrador and poodle. He seemed to resemble the average dust mop, with about the same amount of coordination.

"Here's the great thing about big dogs, though," Theo continued. "They're big enough to hug, which is important when you've got a dog with as much fluff as Bixby here. And they're clever. Bixby and I have only known each other a few weeks, but he can do all kinds of tricks."

Maisie's lower lip began to pout, and Willow knew where this was going. "She doesn't have much experience with dogs," she said to Theo. "I think she was expecting a small puppy."

"He's very well-behaved," Theo said.

"Yes, I can see he's perfectly calm, but it's not him I'm worried about." She jerked her head toward Maisie, whose lower lip was now trembling. Willow was certain tears were on the horizon. Her protective instincts were on the alert. Bixby clearly wasn't a vicious animal— at the moment, he was trying to lick Theo's face—but she didn't want her daughter to feel afraid. "It might be best to take the dog inside," she said.

"Let's just try one thing more," Theo said. Willow grit her teeth. Theo might mean well, but he didn't seem to understand that Maisie was about to implode. He needed to take the dog inside before she had a full meltdown.

"Look at what he can do," Theo said. "Shake, Bixby." The dog sat up, alert, and extended his paw.

Willow began, "I don't think that's going to—" But to her surprise, Maisie had stuck her head out from behind her skirt.

"What else can he do?"

"Oh, lots of things. He can give me a high-five." Theo and Bixby demonstrated. "But *this* is my favorite. Let me show you."

Maisie watched intently as Theo showed her a tennis ball and three paper cups. Willow watched Maisie just as intently. Only a moment ago, her child had been showing classic signs of an imminent Maisie Meltdown, and Willow had been determined to rescue her from anything that could cause her a moment's fear. Now, she was taking tentative steps toward the porch, all traces of tears gone as she watched Theo and the dog.

Theo hid a tennis ball underneath one of the paper cups, and switched the placement of each cup in front of Bixby. "Go on, Bix. Find your ball."

The dog knocked over one paper cup, then another. Neither hid the ball. He placed his paw on the third cup and looked expectantly at Theo.

"Sorry, boy," Theo said. He turned the cup over to reveal that it, too, had been empty.

"You tricked him!" Maisie shouted. "Poor Bixby, that wasn't fair!"

Theo tossed the tennis ball to Maisie, who caught it with both hands. "Maybe you can be a better playmate for him. He loves fetch. He'll bring that ball back to you as many times as you're willing to throw it."

Minutes later, Maisie and Bixby were running back and forth together on the beach.

"I don't get it," Willow said, trying to wrap her head around what had just happened. "Look at her. One minute she's about to go into full-on tantrum mode, and now suddenly they're the best of friends."

"Well, Bixby's easy to make friends with."

"No, it's more than that. I was ready to jump in and protect her, even though she clearly didn't need it. But you gave her a chance to see that there was nothing to be afraid of."

"She just needed a little time to adjust to a new situation, that's all. Children sometimes think they're scared, when really, they just need a moment to get used to something new."

"How do you know so much about children?"

"I had a large family, remember? I spent my teenage years looking after my younger cousins. It taught me how to tell the difference between real tears and an attempt to escape a situation."

Theo had set up a picnic blanket on the beach where they could have lunch and watch Maisie play. As they filled their plates with grapes and cheese, Willow heard Maisie shriek with laughter from further down the beach.

It had always been important to her to be protective of Maisie, but she realized that her daughter did, indeed, need to be pushed to face her fears. If she'd had her way, Maisie would still be huddled behind her skirt, instead of running on the beach, playing with a dog. It was the swimming lessons all over again, only this time, someone had given Maisie a chance to be brave, instead of giving in at the first sign of a trembling lip.

"I know I should be firmer with her," she said to Theo. "I'm probably lucky that Maisie's well-behaved most of the time, because I'm not great at standing my ground with her. The first sign of tears, and I'm usually ready to give in."

"I'm sure it can't be easy, being a single parent. You've got no one to back you up, or reassure you that you're on the right track."

"Intellectually, I know it's not easy, but it's hard to remember to give myself a break. I chose this life, so I feel like I should be better at it. I should push her more. I want her to be brave and open to adventure."

"Didn't you push her by moving her out here in the first place? That was a bold and adventurous move."

"I suppose. But I think Maisie would have me wrapped around her little finger no matter where we lived."

"Was it a hard decision, to leave London?"

Willow shook her head emphatically. "No. It was a careful decision. It was a big change, but nothing about it was hard."

"Really? Surely there must have been some difficulty adjusting. You moved thousands of miles from everything you knew. And London has so much to offer a child. It must have been hard to take Maisie away from all those experiences."

"Hardly. Maisie was missing out on much more in London. She was always being watched by someone else, stuck at daycare or with a neighbor. I was so busy all the time, and yet on the salary I was making, I could barely make ends meet. I grew up in Islington, and it was all I knew. But Maisie deserved more. At the very least, she deserved to have her mother around."

"It must have been hard on you, too."

"I was missing so much of her life. And then…" She paused, because it was still painful to think about, but she pressed onward, anyway. "I missed her first word."

"No!"

"Yes. She was about one year old, and the daycare workers mentioned that she'd been saying 'horsie' when she wanted her stuffed horse at naptime. They thought I already knew. Apparently she'd been saying it for weeks. I was so upset that I'd missed it. And sad, of course, that it wasn't 'Mummy,' although I suppose that's silly. Children say all kinds of different things for their first word. But I couldn't help feeling as though it meant something. That if I'd been around more, maybe her first word *would* have been 'Mummy,' and maybe she'd have said it to me."

"But you *were* there for her. Maybe you weren't physically with her as often as you wished you could be, but you were doing the best you could to support her."

"I was. But it wasn't what I wanted. And when I found the job here…well, that was the first time I started to hope that maybe I *could* have it all. I could support our family and spend lots of time with Maisie, too."

"And it…wasn't as though you had any family you were taking her away from."

"No. I mean, I'd assumed you didn't want anything to do with her." She could see that her words caused him some pain, but it was the truth. And even though she didn't want to hurt him, it did mean something to her that he was feeling the weight of all that he'd missed. She touched Theo's arm lightly. "We can't change the past. I can't change that Maisie and I have built a life here, just as you can't change that you weren't able to be part of our lives for the past few years. What matters is what we want the future to look like."

"Speaking of the future, there's something I've been meaning to talk about. You don't have to make any big decisions about it yet, but I wanted you to know that there's lots of family in England, for Maisie, if she ever wants it. Some of my brothers and sisters have children. She has cousins her age, and grandparents who would be delighted to spoil her rotten."

The thought gave Willow pause. Somehow, she hadn't considered what Theo's large family might mean for Maisie. Since Maisie's birth, she'd envisioned life with just the two of them. But now Maisie had cousins. She didn't know what that would be like. She'd never had a cousin.

She recalled the brief surge of jealousy she'd felt when Theo first arrived on the island. The idea of her special bond with Maisie changing to include anyone else had been inconceivable. She'd just got used to the idea of Maisie spending any time with Theo. It felt strange to consider that there might be a whole host of other people who also wanted to be in Maisie's life.

"Do they know about her?"

"No. The only person I've ever told is my twin sister, Becca. She's very good about privacy. Telling the others would only complicate things."

"How so?"

"For one thing, most of my family members, whom I love dearly, are not the best with boundaries. Half of them would swarm into your life the moment they became aware of your existence. They're not big on personal space. It's their way of showing love, but it can be very overwhelming. I think it should be your choice whether they become part of Maisie's life or not."

Or Maisie's choice, she supposed, when Maisie got older. Willow thought of all the times that she had seen families support each other through difficult diagnoses and medical emergencies. She'd always been touched, and a little envious, when she saw family members come together through tough times. Willow was proud of her own independence, but there were many times when she wished she had more family to rely on for support. And even though she might not ever have the support she wished for, it might be possible for Maisie to have family members who would be there for her when she needed them. It brought a strange, bittersweet ache to her heart to think about it. As much as she wished she could meet Maisie's every need, she knew there were some shoes she could never fill.

Losing her own parents at an early age had taught her that lesson well. Gran had loved Willow with all her heart, but she'd never been able to give Willow the large family she'd longed for. And sometimes love wasn't enough. There had always been the danger that if something happened to Gran, Willow would be all alone. But Maisie wouldn't have to face that risk, with Theo and his family involved in her life. No matter what her daughter faced, she could have the family support that Willow had always longed for.

"Even if they're intrusive, it must have been comforting to have your family around you while you were going through cancer," she said. "They must be so glad you're finally in remission."

He looked away, and she thought she saw a guilty expression in his eyes. "What is it?"

"I may have somewhat downplayed my cancer to them. They never really knew how bad it was."

"How on earth would you do that? *Why* would you do that?"

"My father was diagnosed with Alzheimer's shortly before I started chemo. He's still doing all right, as far as his health goes, but his mind is very different from what it used to be. It's been heartbreaking for my mum. Watching her go through that, I knew I couldn't burden her with everything I was going through, too. So I downplayed everything. I emphasized the cure rate for melanoma, and I never mentioned my treatment unless someone asked about it. I hid the side effects from everyone, except Becca. I tried to act like I had more energy than I did, and I stayed away from everyone on the worst days."

She couldn't believe what she was hearing. Theo had something she'd wanted for her entire life: a family that could support him through tough times. And yet when he'd needed them most, he hadn't reached out to them at all.

"I'm surprised you could keep such a secret from your family, if they're as pushy as you say they are."

"It wasn't easy, believe me. But everyone was very upset about my father. I was determined not to burden them any further."

"With the truth? Don't you think they would have preferred to know what was going on?"

"I didn't lie to them."

"But you put on a facade. You told them what you

thought they wanted to hear, rather than being honest with them."

She could see that he was uncomfortable with this interpretation of events. "I wanted to do what was best for them," he said. "I love my family. I couldn't bear to see what my mother was going through. She was just starting to realize that she was losing my father just a little bit more, every day. I couldn't stand to think that she'd have to worry about me, too."

She could see that his intentions came from a good place, but she worried that the results of his choices left people feeling shut out. For three years, she'd thought he hadn't cared about Maisie at all because of his silence. And even recently, when he'd arrived on St. Victoria, he'd been silent for that first week because he'd said he hadn't wanted to bother her, while she'd begun to think that he'd left the island and given up on fatherhood. She believed that Theo meant well, but she wondered if he realized that by keeping his feelings so far inside, he was shutting himself out from people who might care about him.

And if Theo was so used to shutting people out, then would he shut her out? Or Maisie? She needed to know.

"What about now?" she said. "I hate to suggest this, but what if the cancer comes back? How can I know for sure that you're not just downplaying anything that's wrong so that I'll feel better?"

"That's not going to happen," he said.

"But how do I know?"

He thought for a long moment. "I suppose all I can do is promise to tell you if anything changes," he said.

"And will you?" she said. "You'll tell me at the first sign of any problems?"

"Yes. Only there aren't going to be any problems."

"How can you possibly say that? Surely you must worry about the cancer coming back. How could you not, as an oncologist *and* a recovering cancer patient."

"I worry about it sometimes, in an abstract way."

"No." She shook her head. "I don't believe you. You're scared about it, I can tell."

He raised his eyebrows. "Scared?"

"Absolutely. And it's completely understandable. Anyone in your situation would feel the same way. I even feel a little scared, thinking about your health."

"Willow, there's no need to worry. I'm fine."

She shook her head. "I don't need you to reassure me that you're okay. I need you to be real with me about how you're feeling."

"And you believe I'm feeling scared."

"I know you are."

"How?"

She nodded toward where Bixby was running on the beach. "Because that poor dog lives on your front porch."

He looked more confused than ever. "Bixby? But he's happy there. I've bought him a bed, and toys."

"You've even taught him a few tricks. Anyone can see that you love that dog. So…why the porch, Theo? Why doesn't your dog live in the house?"

His shoulders slumped in defeat. He'd seen where she was going. "Because I don't want him to get too attached. He's just a dog. If anything happened to me, he couldn't understand. Who would take care of him if the cancer came back?"

They sat together for a while, watching Maisie play on the beach. After a long while, he said, "I suppose you're right. I am a little scared about the cancer coming back. But my prognosis is looking very good. There's really no reason to worry."

"Besides the fact that cancer is just generally a scary and worrisome thing?"

"Besides that, yes."

"Good."

He looked quizzical. *"Good?"*

"Yes. Not that your cancer could return. That's sad to think about, and I hope you don't ever have to face that. But we've just been talking about how you kept the extent of your illness hidden from the people closest to you, and I need to be able to trust that if you were dealing with something serious, you'd tell me. So I'm glad that you could finally admit that you're scared. Because the things that happen to you won't just affect you, they'll affect Maisie, too. So I need you to be open about what you're going through."

She wasn't sure how to put it into words, but Willow also knew that *she* would be extremely upset if anything were to happen to Theo. She didn't want to be taken by surprise, if possible. And more than that, she wanted to know that Theo wasn't the kind of person who shut other people out of his life during difficult times. The whole point of family, as she'd always seen it, was to support one another. She needed to know that Theo could be emotionally accessible. He might claim to distance himself in order to protect his loved ones, but she didn't think that was the whole story. He'd talked about his family having poor boundaries sometimes, and she wondered if he'd grown overly cautious about how much he allowed himself to depend on people.

Well, they certainly had that in common. But if Theo

couldn't let a dog that he was clearly fond of into his own home, what did that say about his ability to get close to his child?

But Theo had promised to be open with her. And she did believe that he was sincere in his desire to protect those he cared about. She might not agree with his past choices, but it seemed that he was doing his best to change his future. After all, he was here now. And she was more than willing to give both Theo, and herself, a chance.

She allowed her body to relax into the crook of his arm, letting herself enjoy feeling him circling her, protecting her.

He buried his nose in her hair and murmured, "Think she'll notice if I steal a kiss?"

"Later," she murmured back.

Hours later, Willow had left, an exhausted Maisie asleep in her stroller.

Theo waited until Bixby had settled down on his porch bed, and then went inside to sink into an armchair.

He should have felt flushed with accomplishment. And in many ways, he did. The day had offered him exactly what he'd hoped to find when he came to St. Victoria. He'd spent time with Maisie and had found that even at just three years of age, his daughter had a personality all her own. She was funny and bright, fond of tickles and delighted to show him interesting objects she'd found on the beach. It had warmed his heart to find her so eager to connect with him, even though he and Willow had agreed that she wasn't old enough yet to understand who he was in relation to her.

But his joy was bittersweet. Getting to know Maisie had shown him the stark reality of all the things he'd missed by staying away from her for these past few years. Willow's voice had sounded so pained when she'd spoken of missing Maisie's first words. But he'd missed all of it. The more he spent time with her, the more he began to regret his choice to stay away from her. And from Willow. The most beautiful woman he'd ever met, the warmest, kindest woman he'd ever known, had been right there in London all along. All he'd had to do was call her.

But he couldn't have. Not then. Not while he was facing the worst of the cancer. If he couldn't bear the thought of burdening his family with an accurate picture of his illness, then he certainly couldn't have shared that information with the mother of his child.

He'd stayed away for their own good. But the cost of the choice he had made hit him harder today than it had in three years. It made his heart ache to think that Willow had struggled with her finances in London. He should have been there to help.

If he were faced with the same decision today, he wondered, would he still make the same choice he'd made more than three years ago? Now that he knew how much he cared for both of them, it would be far, far more difficult to stay out of their lives. At the time, he'd been so certain he was making the right choice, because he was doing it to protect them. But had it been the right choice? Suppose the worst happened, and he had to go through all of it again. Would it be better for him, to have Willow and Maisie there to support him? More importantly, he wondered if Willow was right; if it would be better for the two of them to know what he was going through.

He couldn't change the past. All he could do was move forward.

He glanced at his phone and felt a twinge of guilt. He'd promised Willow that he'd be open with her about the cancer. And so far, he had been. His doctors had all been extremely positive about his prognosis now that he was in remission. But he hadn't responded to a single message from any of his doctors since he'd arrived in the Caribbean a few weeks ago.

As a doctor, he knew his avoidance was foolish. The best thing he could do was call his medical team back immediately so that he could arrange to have oversight of his care transferred to doctors in St. Victoria. Still, he hesitated. For the first few days, he'd told himself he was busy, that he was waiting to get settled in, and that he'd call when he had the time. But now Theo's doctors were calling every day, and he was deleting their messages without listening to them first.

It wasn't that he was afraid of what those messages might say exactly. It was more that he simply wanted a break from being a patient. He wanted one part of his life that wasn't touched by cancer. He was enjoying the sense of finally, *finally* starting the life he wanted. He didn't have to schedule his work life around medical appointments. He was starting to connect with his daughter. And he might have a real chance at a relationship with Willow. He just wanted a moment to enjoy all of that, without the next medical appointment looming over his head.

But the moment was turning into days, which were turning into weeks. Soon, it would be months, and Theo would have to acknowledge that he wasn't just taking a break. He was hiding. And Willow had been right, on the beach: he was scared.

But he couldn't hide forever. It was time to call his doctor back. Not just for himself, but for the people he cared about. He wanted to keep the promise he'd made to Willow, and be honest with her.

He checked his watch. It would be just after eight p.m. in London if he called now. His doctor wouldn't be in the office, but he could leave a message. For a moment he wondered if he should wait until the next morning, so he could speak with his doctor directly. No, he thought, best to get it done now. Who knew how he might feel in the morning. If he waited any later to make the call, he might change his mind.

To his surprise, his doctor answered the phone. "Theo!" Dr. Raida greeted him. "Where have you been? I was getting worried."

Theo's heart sank. He liked his doctor, but until that moment, he hadn't realized how much he'd been hoping that Dr. Raida had gone home for the evening. He'd wanted to leave a quick message and then hang up, but hearing his doctor's voice brought back all the memories he'd been hoping to avoid.

"I'm sorry, Doc. I've been incredibly busy. As are you apparently, if you're working after eight p.m. tonight."

His doctor *tsked* over the phone. "I had a few emergencies this morning and decided to stay late to finish up with some paperwork—and a good thing, too, or I'd have missed your call. You of all people should know how important it is to keep close contact with your treatment team. What kind of oncologist drops off the face of the earth the moment he's in remission?"

"I noticed that you've been trying to get hold of me."

"Yes, and thank goodness I finally did. We need to do another biopsy."

Theo's stomach went cold. "What?"

"I'm sorry, Theo. I know that's not something you want to hear. But I was looking over some imaging from your case just before you left. You remember that skin lesion we took a picture of? I wasn't too worried about it at first, but I've talked it over with some colleagues, and we agreed that we should take a tissue sample to rule out cancer."

Theo held his forehead in his hands.

"This is just a precautionary measure. Just to be on the safe side. Don't get too concerned yet. By all other indications, your prognosis is very good. But we want to be absolutely sure everything's okay."

"I can't leave the Caribbean right now." He tried to keep his voice from cracking.

"That's all right. Have you set up care with any doctors there?"

"Not yet. I'll get to work on that right away."

"Do that, please. We'll fax your records over as soon as we can and talk about coordinating care."

"Sure thing," Theo said as he hung up the phone.

Amid all the devastation, turmoil and fear that flooded his mind, one thought emerged, clear as day: he could not tell Willow about this.

Things were just starting to go well, both with her and with every other area of his life. He couldn't let cancer screw everything up again.

He remembered what he'd told her on the beach.

And he remembered what she'd said about her ex, in the cafeteria. How he'd just told her what he thought she wanted to hear, instead of the truth.

But this was different. For one thing, nothing had really changed about his situation. He didn't need to update Willow about anything, because there was nothing new to report. Just because his doctor was ordering a biopsy didn't mean that his remission status had changed. There would be nothing new to tell Willow until after he had the test results. And why mention it before then? What if the test results were clear, and he'd worried her for no reason?

And another thing: he wasn't trying to deliberately mislead Willow. He just wanted to protect her. The same way he'd tried to protect his family from the full knowledge of what he was facing. The way he'd tried to protect Maisie from the loss of a parent. Willow might say that she wanted him to be open with her about what he was going through, but she probably didn't understand the magnitude of what she was asking.

He'd start setting up appointments tomorrow, he decided. Not at the clinic, but at St. Victoria Hospital. They might not have the resources of the Island Clinic, but they should be perfectly capable of coordinating with his care team in London. With no danger of the information getting back to Willow.

CHAPTER SEVEN

OVER THE NEXT few weeks, Willow's life began to settle back into an easy routine of work, caring for Maisie and spending time with Theo. She realized that over her past year on St. Victoria, she'd never had any visitors, and it was fun to play tour guide and show Theo all that the island had to offer. For Maisie, that meant hours showing Theo her favorite dolls, her tea sets and her rather alarming collection of small dried crustacean bodies gleaned from the tide pools near their home. For Willow, it meant visiting various hiking spots and music venues on the island. Although neither of them said it outright, many of their outings felt suspiciously like *dates*, although Willow expected that, if pressed, she and Theo would both describe their time together as simply "getting to know each other."

Maisie became attached to Theo just as quickly as Willow had feared. She'd tried to remind herself that she couldn't focus all of her energy on how Maisie might get hurt if things didn't work out. She recalled her conversation with Roni: What if things *did* go well? What if Maisie and Theo had a perfectly lovely time together, and rather than being scarred for life by disappointment, Maisie simply formed some positive memories?

She had to admit that it was nice to have someone willing to help with Maisie, without having to impose on her neighbors. After their first visit to Theo's house, he'd begun dropping by Willow's place on weekends to check in on Maisie and to see if Willow wanted some time to herself. At first, Willow was hesitant to leave Maisie and Theo to their own devices, but Maisie was always thrilled to see Theo, especially when he began to bring Bixby on his visits. And there were certain days, especially after a long workweek, where it felt positively decadent to have time for a nap or some reading on weekend afternoons.

They'd had to set some ground rules at first. Theo had thought it might be fun to give Maisie some cooking lessons.

"Maybe start with something small, like pouring a bowl of cereal," Willow had suggested.

"Don't worry about it," said Theo. "We've got this." Maisie had outfitted him in a number of Mardi Gras beads, and was herself wearing a long feather boa. She seemed to delight in dressing Theo in the most garish accessories she could find from her dressing-up box, and Theo submitted to this with good humor.

"Are you sure?" Willow said.

"It's fine. I've been teaching my nieces and nephews to bake since they were toddlers. I'll be doing most of the work, and Maisie will help."

"She does love to help," said Willow, bemused. She'd taken a lovely nap, and forty minutes later awoke to pancake batter on the kitchen ceiling.

"We made pamcakes!" Maisie announced, bursting with pride. Theo's expression was somewhat more shamefaced.

"Things…got a little out of hand," he said as Willow

surveyed the wreckage. Cracked eggs on the linoleum floor, seven different mixing bowls in various stages of cleanliness and batter coating the stove, ceiling and cupboards.

"I would say so," she said, shaking with silent laughter. "It looks like you let Maisie help a lot."

"Oh, yes. Every step of the way, in fact."

"Well. As long as you had fun."

"We did," Maisie said, her eyes shining. "Try the pamcake, Mummy. I made it."

Theo's eyes were shining, too, and Willow could see how happy it made him to have made something with his daughter. Even if the kitchen now held more mess than it did pancakes.

But after he'd cleaned her kitchen, it smelled even nicer than before they'd started, so she didn't mind.

She was a little nervous, but mostly pleased, to see that he and Maisie were getting on so well together. As for Theo and herself…she never thought she'd regret their decision to proceed slowly. But as they continued to spend time together, she was finding it increasingly difficult to hold back. She wanted him. Her skin felt afire every time he touched her. If he put an arm around her or helped her with her coat, it was all she could do not to burst into flames. But the rational part of her was able to maintain a tenuous control, just enough so that she was able to keep herself from making any decisions she'd regret. She had responsibilities. She couldn't let physical desire override her judgment.

She threw herself into her work, hoping she could distract herself. Of course, Theo was at work, too, so it wasn't as if he wasn't on her mind there, as well. But then again, he wasn't around as much as he'd been at first. She supposed that made sense. He only did clinical work part-time, after all, and the rest of the time he did research. He'd begun setting up a number of research studies through St. Victoria Hospital so that patients who couldn't afford treatment could be part of research trials and have their care supported by grant funding. Setting up the research trials took up much of his time, he said, and so he was often away from the clinic and working late hours.

With Theo so busy, they didn't have much time to talk at work. He always seemed to be rushing off to St. Victoria Hospital for one appointment or another. But Willow didn't mind. She was glad that Theo was starting to fit in at his new job, and she was proud that he was doing research he was passionate about. She did miss seeing him as often as she'd used to, though. Just a few weeks ago, she'd never have thought she could miss seeing him at work. Yet here she was, thinking about his presence, his smile…his hands, steady and strong, pressing against her waist as they stole a moment together.

"Willow. Are you thinking about Theo again?" Roni's eyes twinkled from where she lay on her gurney, Buttons curled up beside her.

"Nonsense. I'd never let my personal life distract me at work," Willow said, lying through her teeth. She smiled and whispered, "Keep it down! We don't want anyone at work finding out just yet."

"But I need details! Have you two done the deed yet?"

Willow was about to protest, but then gave up, knowing that Roni was relentless in her pursuit of information. "We're taking it slow."

"Slow!" Roni scoffed. "Youth is wasted on the young."

"Besides, he's been very busy lately. He has to do a lot of running back and forth between here and St. Victoria Hospital. So we haven't been able to see each other much."

Roni frowned. "What could possibly be more important to this young man than spending time with you?"

"Oh, no, it's not like that! I just know that it's a lot of work to adjust to a new job, and Theo is still figuring out how to manage everything."

Roni still looked perturbed, and in an effort to change the subject, Willow said, "Your prognosis is still looking very good, despite what the press might say." The doom and gloom headlines about Roni's treatment persisted, with the press claiming that Roni was practically at death's door.

"I suppose telling everyone that I'm dying sells more papers than the truth."

"Still, you might want to think about having one of your assistants give them a little information. They could send out a press release, or at least give a quote about your condition."

At first, Roni and the clinic staff had agreed that as the press was so pushy, they shouldn't be given any information. Everyone had hoped that if the press realized there was no information to be had, they would simply go away. But the press encampment outside the clinic property had only got larger over the past few weeks, and the misinformation they were printing had become increasingly egregious.

"Hmm. I suppose they've stewed long enough. I'll hold a press conference. That way I can update them on my condition and announce the donation I'm making, as well. I think pledging a few million to support health-care programs for the residents of St. Victoria should be enough to distract the press from their obsession with my health, and focus on that story instead."

"Roni, that's wonderful. The island will be able to do some wonderful things with that kind of funding."

"Least I can do. St. Victoria is a special place. And while I do love coming here to beat cancer in style, I'll love it even more knowing that everyone has access to the help they need." Roni threw back her blankets and sat up. "Time to get back to work. Let's set this press conference up and give the sharks their feeding frenzy."

Theo turned his car up the long parkway toward the clinic's main entrance. Most days, he spent his mornings at St. Victoria Hospital, where he set up research studies, and then headed for the Island Clinic in the afternoon to work with patients. He found that he liked the variety of his work a great deal. He also didn't mind traveling the short distance between both medical centers every day. His schedule was flexible enough that the brief commute didn't add any pressure. But more importantly, he was able to attend his own medical appointments at St. Victoria Hospital as often as needed, without drawing anyone else's attention.

When he'd set up his medical care at St. Victoria Hospital, he'd done so with the express goal of not wanting to alert Willow that there was anything amiss. He'd worried that he would face questions from other doctors about his decision not to use the Island Clinic's resources, but apparently plenty of clinic staff got their care at St. Victoria Hospital, and vice versa, both as a professional courtesy and to minimize conflicts of interest. So the care team at St. Victoria Hospital hadn't been surprised that he was arranging for his care there at all. He'd had the biopsy done, and now had only to wait the typical four to six weeks for the results. His medical team had been reassuring that all signs continued to indicate that he was still in remission. The important thing was to keep his spirits up while they waited for the results.

He'd heard it all before. Cancer was all about measuring and waiting, and keeping morale high while one measured and waited. He tried not to think about it, but he did worry that Willow might have noticed that he was hiding something from her. He'd had to slip out of the clinic frequently over the past few weeks in order to establish care with new doctors, and then had to work late to make up for lost time. He'd told her that he was still adjusting to his new job, but he worried she might suspect it was more than that.

He still felt guilty about breaking his promise to Willow. But technically, he was within the letter of the law. He'd promised to keep her updated about any changes in his health, but really, a test wasn't a change. It was just a procedure to find out whether there *had been* a change. So there was no need to put Willow through the stress of waiting to get the biopsy results with him. If it turned out they were clear, he might not ever need to tell her about it at all.

The closer he became to Willow and Maisie, the more certain he was that he didn't want to tell Willow about the biopsy. The days he spent with Maisie were everything he'd hoped they would be. He delighted in spending time with his daughter, doing all the little things he'd imagined doing with a child of his own.

They'd baked cookies together—with extremely careful supervision and somewhat less helping from Maisie, after the pancake fiasco—took long walks on the beach discovering interesting shells and pebbles and had dress-up tea parties. He was loving every minute of it.

But as he felt himself growing closer to both of them, he also wondered, again, if he could let himself have a family of his own. How could the three of them ever be a real family when the threat of cancer loomed over him? When he'd gone into remission, his doctors had reminded him to take things one day at a time. But it was hard not to focus on his worries and fears about the future when he was awaiting biopsy results. Did he have the right to ask Willow to join him for a lifetime of worrying that the cancer might come back someday? There was no way to know if he would have multiple cancer scares throughout his life, or if this most recent biopsy would be the last time he'd have to go through this. With such little certainty, could he allow himself to get close to Willow, knowing that there was a chance he'd have to rely on her for much greater support in the near future? He wasn't sure if that was fair to Willow, or to Maisie.

As he drove up the Island Clinic parkway, he saw Roni standing on the edge of the clinic grounds, with a few of the staff behind her. He could recognize Willow's petite frame, even from this distance, because she was a head or two shorter than the rest of the staff. She was surrounded by a phalanx of press, and she was holding a giant, oversize check. *Good, a press conference*, Theo thought. About time. The press was getting out of control with the amount of unsubstantiated rumors they were printing. And it looked as though Roni was announcing a donation, as well. Nate should be pleased. Theo also noticed that there was a heavy security presence. He was glad Nate had taken his caution about the overzealousness of the press seriously.

As he parked and stepped out of his car, he heard an uproar from the crowd. Roni's French bulldog had somehow broken away from her—Theo couldn't see clearly, but he thought it might have been lured away by one of the reporters—and was running across the lawn. One of the reporters lunged for the small dog. To his horror, he saw that Willow had chased the dog and was leaning forward to pick it up, out of the reporter's grasp. But the reporter, who was fairly large, had gathered too much momentum to stop running, and moments later, he was tackled by an even larger security guard.

Theo watched in horror as they all went down together—the reporter falling on top of Willow, who collapsed to the ground as the security guard fell on top of both of them. The dog had made its way safely back to Roni, but Theo barely had time to register this as he sprinted across the lawn. Both men were slowly getting to their feet as he arrived, but Willow wasn't moving. Under other circumstances, Theo, who had never been violent in his life, might have felt compelled to beat both the reporter and the security guard to a pulp, but at the moment, all his attention was focused on Willow.

After what felt like years, he finally reached her. Gently, he turned her over. He'd been alarmed that she was so still, but her eyes fluttered open. She motioned to her throat and made a strained noise, and he realized she'd had the wind knocked out of her. "Easy," he said. "You'll be all right in a few minutes. I'm going to take you inside so we can make sure you're okay."

He scooped Willow into his arms and headed toward the clinic. He couldn't believe the utter carelessness of the other two men, the blatant disregard they'd shown for Willow's well-being.

Once inside, he took Willow into an exam room and sat her down on the exam table. Her breathing was already easier; she was sitting upright on her own.

He began to feel her limbs, gently, to check for any other injuries, but she stopped him and shook her head. He cupped her cheek with his hand, stroking her hair, as they waited for her breath to recover.

Finally, she said, "I'm all right. Just winded."

Relief flooded through him, to be quickly replaced by anger. "*Just* winded? That reporter should be in jail. That security guard should be fired."

"It was an accident. No one was hurt."

"*You* were hurt." He resumed his examination, palpating her shoulders, her collarbone.

"Stop. Theo. It's all right. I'm fine." She reached up and turned his face toward hers. "I'm fine."

He found he was trembling. At first he'd thought he was shaking in anger, but now he realized that it was fear, as well. When he'd seen Willow lying on the grass, so still, he'd thought the worst. The idea of Willow being hurt, of losing Willow, was unbearable.

Without thinking, he pulled her close to him, her head against his chest. "I was so worried," he said. "I thought I'd lost you."

"Nonsense," she said, tilting her face up toward his. "I'm right here."

He gave her a light kiss, meant to reassure them both. He needed the comfort as much as she did. But his lips lingered, just before he pulled away, and then he didn't

pull away at all. Their kiss deepened, her mouth yield-
ing to his, her lips soft and pliable. His tongue began
to explore her mouth, and he noticed that she tasted of
honey, cinnamon and something else. Something that
was indefinable yet tantalizing all the same.

She reached up from where she sat on the table to
put her arms around his neck and pull him closer to
her. He wanted to tell her that if they didn't stop now,
he wasn't sure if he'd be able to, but then his nose was
buried in the rich, dark hair that fell just so against the
crook of her neck. His hands went to her waist, and
then, gently, he traced the rise of one breast, just below
the top of her blouse. *Go slow*, he reminded himself,
we agreed to go slow.

But holding Willow in his arms stirred every feeling
that had been reawakened since their first sunset kiss
on the boardwalk. For weeks he'd been trying to pace
himself, using every last bit of willpower to keep himself from asking for anything more than she was willing to offer. It didn't help matters much that he'd barely
touched a woman during the four years before he'd met
Willow—and now, restraint was nearly impossible as
he drank in the warmth of her body, her hands raking
through his hair.

There hadn't been a day that went by since his arrival
on St. Victoria that he hadn't dreamed of holding her
in his arms, just like this. To stop now would be agony,
and yet…they'd agreed to go slow. Somehow, he managed to pull himself away from her just long enough to
whisper, "Should we stop?"

Willow's eyes met his, her lips wet, her breathing
heavy. In response, she shifted herself toward the edge
of the table so that her body melted into his. He shiv-

ered, then groaned as he felt her press against him, and he began to feel himself grow hard. Now there was a new kind of agony as he became enveloped in the sensation of her: the smooth skin of her thighs beneath his hands, the sweet citrus scent of her hair and the heat of her lips on his. He was surrounded by the warmth of her, and yet still he burned with wanting her.

He had no thought, no awareness, beyond the softness of her skin against his hands, the smell of cinnamon enveloping them both and the warm curves of her body that seemed to meld into him. And so it came as surprise when he heard a knock on the exam room door.

"Hello?" called one of the nurses from the hallway outside.

They broke apart in a panic. Theo tucked his shirt back in and smoothed the wrinkles, while Willow did up the top buttons of her blouse.

"Theo? Willow?" It sounded like Talia's voice.

"Just a minute," Willow called back.

"We just wanted to check and make sure that Willow was all right," Talia called again.

"I'm fine," Willow replied. "Just a little winded. A little out of breath. Just give me a couple more minutes and I'll be right out."

There was a rather long pause, and then Talia said, "Okay. Just let me know if you need anything."

They were both silent until they heard the sound of Talia's receding footsteps, and then Willow erupted into laughter.

"I don't know how you can possibly laugh right now," Theo said. He couldn't believe what he'd just done. After all their talk of taking things slowly, he'd gone and acted like some sort of caveman, practically taking Willow right on the exam room table. What must she be thinking of him?

Seeing her knocked to the ground out on the lawn must have activated some sort of primal urge in him. And he'd been so relieved to see that she was all right that he'd got carried away with his feelings.

Fortunately, Willow didn't seem to mind. Far from it. "Do you think they know?" she said, jerking her head toward the door.

"Well, we've been trying to keep our relationship a secret, so I'm certain the whole clinic knows about it. As for whether they know about what we were doing just now…let's hope they trust in our professionalism."

Willow bit her lip. "Let's hope so indeed."

As she stood up to leave, straightening her skirt, Theo put his hand on hers. "Wait."

He was about to apologize. But then he remembered how much Willow valued honesty. And he would never, ever be sorry for the moment they'd just had.

"Do you think you can get a sitter for Maisie tonight?"

"Why? Do I have plans for tonight?"

"I very much hope you do."

Mrs. Jean was all too happy to watch Maisie for the evening.

"Don't even think about it," she said when Willow tried to apologize for the short notice. "It's about time you started getting serious about someone. Shall I assume it's that doctor I've seen coming over to your place all month?"

"His name's Theo. We've only been seeing each other a little bit, but…it's going very well."

"I would hope so. He's over here often enough. Why don't you pack an overnight bag for Maisie, so you can pick her up in the morning? That way you don't have to worry about rushing home early tonight."

"Oh, that's not necessary. I'm sure I'll be home by eleven."

"Sweetheart. Pack Maisie a bag. And maybe one for yourself, too. If you come back tonight, fine. But if you do end up spending the night with this young gentleman, then at least you won't need to worry about rushing home." Willow nodded in agreement, and the older woman cackled. "That's what I thought. Tonight's the night."

Willow was so flushed with excitement that she couldn't even fend off Mrs. Jean's insinuations. Besides, Mrs. Jean was right, if that moment with Theo in the exam room was any indication of his intentions. Tonight *was* the night.

For the first time in years, tonight was the night.

As she packed her things—a toothbrush, a change of clothes for work tomorrow—she could barely keep her hands from shaking. That exam room kiss had turned into something more so rapidly that she hadn't had time to think. But then Theo had suggested that she come over tonight so that they could do things properly, without the worry of unlocked doors and the hundreds of other things that could go wrong with intimacy in a workplace setting.

She'd immediately agreed, but then she'd spent the rest of the day thinking about it. And worrying about it.

She was so out of practice. What if Theo noticed?

In the exam room, she hadn't had time to think. It had happened so suddenly that instinct had just taken over. But now she'd spent an entire day thinking about what awaited her in the evening. Her skin burned with a heat she hadn't felt in ages. She'd almost forgotten what it felt like to want someone so badly that it seemed almost impossible to get close enough to them. In fact, she wasn't certain if she'd ever wanted anyone the way she wanted Theo.

She hoped she wouldn't embarrass herself. But she also knew that it didn't matter. Nothing, not even potential embarrassment, was going to stop her from feeling Theo's hands on her skin again. She could still feel the warmth where he'd cupped her cheek.

She decided to drive the short distance to Theo's house, just in case she did end up spending the night.

Once again, he and Bixby were waiting on the porch.

She got out of her car, hoping he couldn't see her knees knocking. Why was she so nervous? It was Theo, she thought. He'd become so familiar to her over these past few weeks. Most of the time, his presence was warm and comforting.

Perhaps, she thought, she was nervous because she didn't want warmth just now.

She wanted flames.

She somehow made herself walk up the porch steps. He slipped an arm around her waist and held her close, and she let herself lean into his arms. Nervous as she was, she was grateful for the support. Then a flicker of light inside the house caught her eye, and she looked over his shoulder, through the doorway.

"Oh, Theo," she breathed. "It's beautiful."

The lights inside the house were dim, and dozens of small candles dotted the front entryway and living room. White and red rose petals were scattered everywhere, including a trail to the bedroom.

He leaned in close and murmured into her hair. "Four years."

"What?"

"That's how long it's been for me. Longer, in fact, although I never kept an exact count. I haven't been with anyone for four years. And you said that it had been a long time for you, too. So I thought, since it's the first time in a long time for both of us, that I should do something to make it special."

She raised a hand to his cheek, feeling the faint stubble there. "Tonight's already special."

He kissed her, a gentle, searching kiss that quickly deepened. She felt the warmth that had kindled deep within her begin to spread, and as he traced her arm with one finger, she shivered.

"Are you cold?" he said.

"Not exactly."

He smiled. "Maybe we should go inside all the same."

He led her up the rose petal path to the bedroom. There were only a few candles there, casting dim shadows on the walls.

It was very romantic. But it was also very dark. And Willow thought she might know why.

"Theo," she said, "are you nervous about me seeing you?"

He let out a long breath, and she realized he must have been even more nervous than she was.

"I should have known you would guess," he said.

"Tell me." She waited in the darkness.

"I've lost a lot of weight from the cancer. My body's

changed. I don't look like me anymore. At least, not how I remember myself. No one's really seen me since before I started treatment. This is my first time doing *this* the way I look now, and I'm not sure what it will be like."

She kissed the corner of his mouth, right where it always seemed about to pull up into a smile. "I know you've been through some changes. And that we're both scared. But let's not hide from each other tonight."

The candlelight flickered, catching at the gold flecks in his hazel eyes. "What could you possibly have to hide from me?"

She swallowed. "That it's been such a long time since I've done this that I might…lose control. And that I'm afraid of what you might think, if you see me like that."

Now his eyes were ablaze, and she didn't think it was just from candlelight. "I think I might like to see you lose control."

"I think you almost did, earlier this morning."

"Mmm. And it was almost every bit as lovely as I might have hoped."

"Almost?"

"Well, we were constrained by our circumstances. And caught up in the moment. I didn't, for example, have the opportunity to do this." He leaned her against the back of the bedroom wall and kissed the hollow of her throat. She tilted her chin upward to give him greater access, her skin humming against her.

"Or this," he said as his hands went to the back of her neck to undo the clasp of her halter dress. Once undone, the top fell to her waist, her breasts exposed. He cupped one of them, his fingers caressing, then gently pulling and teasing one nipple. She arched her back, moaning, to press herself more firmly into his palm.

He knelt before her, kissing between her breasts, her stomach, as he made his way downward. "Or, of course, this," he whispered, pulling her dress from her hips. There was a soft crumple as it hit the floor. He gazed up at her, his chin level with the tops of her thighs, and slowly slid her panties from her hips.

She could feel his soft breath against the tuft of hair between her legs, and then, almost before she knew what was happening, he'd buried his face in the warmth there, and she felt the slow strokes of his tongue. She tried to tell him that he didn't have to, that no one had *ever*, but somehow her words were lost, and all that came out were gasps of air. Her knees were shaking; she didn't know how she could keep standing upright, but then she felt his hands on her thighs, holding her in place as he continued on with what he'd started. She began to see starbursts in front of her eyes, dark as the room was, and she moaned his name and told him she couldn't hold back.

He lifted her to the bed then, and she heard him racing to remove his clothes. There was the sound of a foil wrapper; she knew she could trust Theo to have planned on protection.

And not a moment too soon. Her body ached with a primal need; her skin was aflame, and she felt the yearning that had begun deep within her threaten to overwhelm her entirely. She could feel his body next to her on the bed. "Now," she breathed, and a moment later he had fully embedded himself in her. Her hips rocked upward to meet his, and he pushed himself into her, again and again, their bodies joining in a dance as old as time itself.

With each thrust, she felt herself getting closer to the

point of no return, to the loss of control that she feared, and yet desperately craved. She felt his pace quicken, felt herself pushed to the brink, and then suddenly she cried his name again and let herself go. Her consciousness shattered into a thousand pieces, and for a moment there was nothing beyond his breath and hers, the sensation of their bodies moving together. And then, at last, there was the feeling of lying together, replete and exhausted, their limbs tangled together, their bodies apart.

How strange, she thought dreamily as her eyes began to close. A moment ago, she'd felt shattered into pieces. But now, somehow, she felt…whole.

CHAPTER EIGHT

THEO WOKE THE next morning to see Willow fast asleep on the pillow beside him. He slipped out of bed quietly, so as not to wake her. She worked so hard. She deserved her sleep.

Especially after the night before. What a way to break a four-year dry spell. He smiled, remembering how nervous they'd both been at the start. Clearly, neither of them had had anything to worry about. Or at least, Willow hadn't. Theo was certain he'd never felt the things he'd felt with Willow with anyone else before. He hoped the night had been all she'd wanted it to be. And if it hadn't, he hoped they could practice until they got it right.

He headed toward the kitchen, wondering what Willow might like for breakfast. As he was pulling a loaf of bread from the refrigerator, his phone rang.

It was Becca. He listened to her chatter away about family concerns. She mentioned that his father had had a yearly checkup, and his Alzheimer's appeared to have plateaued, which was very good news. After a while, though, Becca noticed that he wasn't saying much.

"What's going on?" she said. "Why are you being so quiet?"

"I'm not," he said, trying to keep his voice low so that he wouldn't wake Willow in the other room. "I'm just listening to you."

"No, you're hardly saying anything. And now you're *speaking* quietly."

He was about to protest, but at that moment, Willow came tiptoeing down the hall, already dressed.

Sister, he mouthed quietly, pointing at the phone. Willow nodded and headed toward the door.

Damn. He didn't want to tell Becca about Willow, because doing so would undoubtedly result in shrieks of sisterly joy that he didn't want his ears subjected to this early in the morning. On the other hand, he didn't want Willow to leave without having breakfast. Or at least without saying goodbye.

"Hold on," he said into the phone. "Just give me one minute."

He caught Willow just as she was about to walk out the door.

"I was hoping you'd stay for breakfast."

"I can't. I have an early shift today. I should have been up an hour ago. I don't even have time for toast."

"You should have told me! I would have set the alarm earlier this morning."

"No, I needed the rest after last night. It's all right. I'll pick up a chocolate croissant when I get in."

"When can I see you again?"

"In about thirty minutes. I'm going to work, remember?"

"No, I mean when can I *see* you again?"

She gave him a quick kiss, just at the corner of his mouth. "As soon as possible."

He watched her leave, and then turned his attention back to his phone, where he could hear Becca's voice screeching.

"Who was that? They sounded female. What was a woman doing at your place this early in the morning?"

He sighed. Becca would find out eventually. And now that he had some coffee going, he thought he might be able to handle her reaction.

"That was Willow. She was just leaving."

"But isn't it, like, seven in the morning in the Caribbean? Why was she over just now?"

"She, ah…spent the night."

He had to hold the phone an arm's length away from his ear as Becca gave an excited shriek.

"So what's the story with you two? Are you an item? When will the family meet her?"

"Not for a long time. We're taking it slow and seeing how it goes."

"You can't be taking it *that* slow. You've been there, what, a month and a half, and she's already sleeping over? When did this start?"

"Look, I'd be happy to fill you in on the details, but for right now, I don't want you to get overexcited, okay? This is a very new situation for both of us, and it's complicated, because it could affect Maisie. We don't want to add any more pressure than there already is."

"Okay. Got it. No pressure. But can I at least be happy for you?"

He couldn't help smiling. "I'm happy for me, so I guess it's okay if you are, too."

"You deserve it, little brother."

"Becca. We're twins."

"Yes, but I'm the five-minutes-older twin. Which makes me five minutes wiser, too. You've had plenty of tough stuff in your life. I'm glad you get some brightness, too."

He knew she meant well. But his sister could be very...effusive at times.

"Speaking of the tough stuff," she continued. "Did you get those biopsy results yet?"

"Still waiting. It usually takes four to six weeks, so I should get them any day now."

"How's Willow handling it? I'm sure she must be nervous."

"Um. Actually, I haven't told her about it."

"What? How could you not tell her?"

"The test results might be clear. I didn't see any reason to worry her unnecessarily."

"I don't believe it. This is so you. You're doing exactly what you always do."

"Which is what?"

"You're pushing people away, especially the people who could help you the most. You're distancing and cutting yourself off from people under the guise of protecting them."

"Well, that's just completely not true."

"I've seen you do it before. With the family. With Mum and Dad especially. Downplaying your cancer, being secretive about how your treatments were working out. Pretending that you weren't that tired or that the side effects weren't that bad. The way you were acting, anyone might have thought you had a touch of flu, rather than a life-threatening illness."

"That was different. Dad had just been diagnosed with Alzheimer's and Mum needed our help. She didn't need to worry about what was happening with me, too."

"I hate to say this, but what if things hadn't gone

well? What if Mum had learned that you'd died suddenly, and she didn't have any time to prepare for it?"

Theo shifted uneasily. "I never lied to her about anything."

"Sure, but you never volunteered information, either. You made it sound like cancer was a matter of a few chemo treatments and then you were done, rather than a four-year struggle for your life. We didn't even get to celebrate that you were in remission, because more than half the family didn't realize you'd had cancer in the first place."

"Which was as I wanted it. Being in remission was enough good news. Yes, it would have been nice to have everyone celebrate with me, but making sure no one knew the full extent of it was more important."

"Yes, but what you don't realize, Theo, is that I was the one everyone went to when they were trying to figure out how serious your cancer was. And I couldn't tell them anything, because I knew you'd never forgive me for it. It was so stupid, because everyone just wanted to help you. You could have had so much more support if you'd only let people in."

"Now hold on. That's exactly why I tried to keep everyone from finding out the full extent of what I was dealing with. You know how our family is. Everyone wants to know everything. Gossip flies fast, and if people get even the tiniest shred of news, suddenly our third cousin in Ibiza knows about it. I didn't want anything to get out, not just for my own desire for privacy, but because I also didn't want one of the aunts or cousins to call Mum and start telling her all about how I was struggling with the side effects."

"Look, I get why you did it, even if I don't necessarily agree with it. But if you keep shutting people out like this, eventually someone's going to get hurt. I know you do it because you want to protect everyone, but it comes off as though you don't want people involved in your life."

"It doesn't matter," he told her. "You don't know what it's like to have a serious illness. It's hard enough to deal with cancer without having to know about how much other people are worrying."

"Are you serious?" her voice cried from the phone. "I don't know what it's *like*?"

He instantly regretted his choice of words. Becca was the only person in his family that he'd confided in during the worst of the cancer, and he'd just been completely dismissive of her support. "I didn't mean that the way it sounded," he said, not quickly enough.

"I hope not." He'd never heard her sound so angry. "Because I was the one who was there on those nights that you supposedly didn't need to worry anybody. I was the one keeping your meds organized and driving you to the hospital when your fevers got too high."

"And I feel terrible that you were in that position."

"I wanted to be in that position! I'm your sister, Theo. Even if you don't want me, I'm going to be there for you. That's what family does—they stick by each other when things are tough. Not just for the good times, but for the difficult bits, too. And I'm certain that Willow will want to be there for you through this."

"I'll think about it," he said, because he knew Becca wouldn't let this go unless he at least pretended to acknowledge changing his mind. In any other situation, he might have agreed with her. But she just didn't understand how he felt. She couldn't, unless she'd been in the same situation herself. He hoped she never would be.

"You do that. Think about it a lot," Becca said. "And... I'll be thinking about you, and hoping your biopsy comes through clear. Because I care about you. In fact, you've got a lot of people who care about you. So don't shut us out, okay?"

They ended their call and Theo went onto the porch to have his toast and coffee next to Bixby. The dog settled his head on Theo's knee, and Theo scratched just the right spot behind his ears.

He felt guilty about what he'd said to Becca, and even guiltier that she'd shouldered so much of the burden of worrying about his health. It had been so hard for him to open up to her that he'd never stopped to consider that she might have appreciated being able to share her worries about him with someone else. But of course, she'd kept his secrets and respected his privacy as best she could, because she was his sister. He felt a wave of affection for her, even though he still didn't think she understood why he had to keep his biopsy a secret from Willow.

When Theo went to go back inside, the dog placed his paw on the door and looked at him with his usual pleading eyes. "No, Bixby," Theo said firmly. "You know you live out here." The dog whined, and Theo rubbed his sides to reassure him. "Come on, you've got a perfectly nice bed and all your toys on the porch."

There was nothing he would have liked more than to bring the dog inside. He'd had a dog as a child, and he'd always wanted one as an adult, but he'd been so busy in medical school that he'd never had the time. And then the cancer had hit soon after, and he could barely take care of himself, let alone a dog.

And now, just when he was trying to prove that he could take care of his own child, he was also facing the worry that his cancer might come back. He couldn't stomach his anger toward the cancer. It ruined everything in his life. The cancer had been the reason he'd stayed away from his daughter in the first place, hoping he could protect her from grief. When he'd entered remission, he'd decided that he couldn't live his life as though the threat of a recurrence of cancer was always in the background. He was tired of letting cancer control his decisions, tired of letting it take away everything he wanted.

He'd missed the first three years of his daughter's life because of cancer. Or because of his desire to protect her from the emotional impact of his cancer. At the time, he'd been so certain he was making the right decision. But over the past few weeks, he'd been faced with the full realization of everything he'd missed. Maisie's deep, full-body chuckle; her preoccupation with the little rocks and shells she found on the beach; the warmth of her hand in his. Now that he knew her, his heart ached at how much he'd missed. For weeks, he'd been wrestling with the decision he'd made more than three years ago. He'd tried to tell himself that there was no use dwelling on it; he couldn't change the past. But he knew now that if he were faced with the same decision today, he could not have made the same choice. It had been hard enough to stay out of Maisie's life without having ever met her. Now that he knew his daughter, he'd never be able to leave her again.

The thought scared him. Because as much as he

blamed the cancer for some of the losses in his life, the cancer wasn't the only thing that had held him back. He'd chosen not to meet Maisie. Just as he'd chosen to cut himself off from his family's support. He'd told himself that he was doing what was best for them, but... was he really? Becca's words had had more of an impact than he'd realized at first. What if his mum had learned he'd died suddenly, without any chance to prepare?

And what if something had happened to Willow, while she'd been caring for Maisie by herself for the past three years? Maisie would have been completely on her own. He recalled that Willow had mentioned her gran had set up a trust for Maisie, but it sounded as though it wasn't much. He felt sick at the thought of Maisie being left so alone. His own daughter, a child with an extensive number of relatives who would happily cherish her, would have been orphaned. Had he really protected her at all by staying away?

Bixby brushed against his legs. The dog had an unabashed love for him. Banishing him to the porch hadn't diminished his attachment to Theo at all. In fact, the only effect it had had was that Theo often found himself rather sad that he couldn't have the dog with him more often. He remembered when Willow had told him that keeping the dog on the porch was a sign that he was scared. Well, that was true enough. He was scared for his health, and he was scared of letting down everyone he cared about.

But if he was too afraid to let a dog into his home, how could he ever allow himself to get close to Willow? Or to his own daughter? He was so afraid of letting them down that he wasn't doing a good job of being there for them in the first place. He was breaking a promise to Willow, right now, by not telling her that he was awaiting biopsy results, and he might tell himself that it was to protect her, but the truth was that he was afraid of making his worst fears real. But keeping the biopsy a secret didn't place him in any less danger, or put him at any less risk of letting Willow and Maisie down.

He had to tell Willow about the biopsy. He just hoped she would understand why he'd kept it a secret for so long.

It had been a long time since Willow had felt this good in the morning.

Oh, she enjoyed most mornings, but *this* one was special. She sipped her coffee as she finished her chart reviews in one of the nurses' offices. Everyone seemed especially friendly as she'd come in to work, and she had a feeling that they might be responding to something they saw in her. There was a kind of lightness that she felt within herself. The day was like any other, and yet it seemed to be full of possibility.

She didn't have to think too hard about what was different. Last night with Theo had been positively decadent. She might not have dated much in her past, but she was certain that she'd never felt the things she'd felt last night with anyone. Theo had been so… She shivered, thinking about it.

If it had been hard to concentrate at work before, then it was going to be nearly impossible now. She would have to find some way to keep her mind off him.

And so she tried to focus on the other things that brought her joy. It seemed as though everything she loved in her life had been turned up in volume, as if her night with Theo had left her with a heightened sensitivity to all that was good in life. Mrs. Jean had texted her a picture of a still-sleeping Maisie that morning, and Willow reveled as always in the chubby hands and full cheeks. Someone had already started the coffee when she got to work, and it was made to perfection. She'd managed to snag a chocolate croissant before they were all gone, and she thought it might be the best bit of pastry she'd ever had in her life. The entire world felt as though it were tinted with a soft, warm glow.

She was thoroughly enjoying her morning, and was just about to wrap up her chart review and begin seeing patients, when the phone rang in the nurse's office.

She picked up; it was a lab technician from St. Victoria Hospital.

They had faxed over some lab work for a patient, and wanted to make sure it had come through. Willow thought that was a little unusual, since the clinic had its own lab and was unlikely to use the hospital's. She found the results on the fax machine and let the technician know they'd arrived.

Normally, she checked the name of the ordering physician on the lab charts and put them in the corresponding file folders. But this time, something caught her eye. The lab tech had mistakenly typed Theo's name in the "patient" section.

It was probably a mistake. Although the staff at St. Victoria Hospital rarely made mistakes. Still, it was an easy enough oversight.

She dropped the lab work into Theo's file. She couldn't help noticing, at a glance, that the paperwork included biopsy results.

A distant alarm began to ring in her mind. She did her best to ignore it. But the thought kept returning to her mind: What if it wasn't a mistake? What if Theo had indeed been the patient?

If he had been, then it was none of her business. She should respect his confidentiality, as she would in any other professional situation.

Except Theo had promised to keep her updated of any changes regarding his remission status. And that fax had contained biopsy results. With Theo's name listed as the patient.

But Theo couldn't have had a biopsy. That was exactly the kind of thing he'd promised he would tell her about.

Unless Theo didn't keep his promises.

Unable to restrain herself any longer, she dove back into Theo's file and retrieved the test results. They were the results of a biopsy that had been done a few weeks ago, confirming that a skin lesion on the patient's arm was benign. The patient was clearly listed as Theo Moore.

The biopsy was clear. That fact rang within her head. She wanted to be relieved. *Was* relieved. Except her heart was breaking. Why wouldn't Theo tell her he was waiting on biopsy results after he'd promised to keep her abreast of any changes regarding his health? Didn't he think she cared about him? Didn't he want her to be there for him, no matter what he was facing?

And worst of all, if that was how he felt—if he didn't want her to be there for him—then why had he promised to keep her informed?

He'd just been telling her what he thought she wanted to hear. Just like Jamie. Rather than the truth, he'd said what sounded good in the moment.

She heard footsteps at the doorway and looked up to see Theo standing there.

"Those are my test results," he said.

"I know. Your biopsy was clear." She needed to tell him right away. She could deal with the tears that she was struggling to hold back in just a moment. But Theo must have been agonizing over these results for weeks—all the while, of course, not telling her that he was worried—and he should learn the results as soon as he could.

"Well, that's a relief."

"Yes, I'm sure it is." The anger was coming into her voice now, despite her attempts to hold it back. "When were you going to tell me that you had a biopsy done?"

"Just now," he said. "I came here to tell you about it."

"Oh, well, that's very convenient. Because the results were faxed over from St. Victoria a few seconds ago. So that's interesting that you were just about to tell me, just now."

Her head felt very strange, and she realized a headache was beginning. The kind that started when she was trying not to cry.

"Congratulations," she said, trying muster her emotions. "You're healthy." She was trying so hard to feel the relief she should feel. This was good news. She should be happy. They both should be. Except why hadn't Theo told her about it in the first place? Why had she found out about this by accident? Had he *ever* been planning to tell her about it?

"Oh," he said, his smile small and forced. "That's good news, isn't it?"

The tears welled in her eyes, and she blinked furiously to hold them back. "How long have you been waiting for these results?"

"A little over a month."

"A little…" She couldn't finish; she was too overwhelmed by disbelief. "And you never thought to tell me about it?"

"I hoped I wouldn't have to. I know you're a worrier. And I didn't want you to have to worry about this."

"This is why you've been running back and forth between the clinic and the hospital so much, isn't it? You told me that you were just adjusting to your new job and your new schedule. But it's also because you're probably getting your medical care there. It makes sense. You've only just gone into remission. It stands to reason you'd have to attend plenty of follow-up appointments. But what does not make sense, Theo, is why you would ever try to hide that from me. Why you wouldn't just be open about where you were going and what you were doing."

"Because I wanted to spare you from all that! It's bad enough that I have to deal with all the stress of it. I didn't want to put that on your shoulders, too. Especially because I hoped that the biopsy would be clear. I thought, what was the point of worrying you if it would all turn out to be nothing?"

"The point, Theo, is that you promised me that you'd let me know of any changes with your health."

"But does it matter, now that we know the results are clear? Nothing's changed. I was in remission a few weeks ago, and I'm in remission now."

"Yes—after weeks of worrying about the biopsy, without ever giving me a hint of what you were going through. I'm glad you're healthy, Theo, but I'm very, very concerned you didn't tell me. I could have been there for you, instead of you having to wait for these results alone. Didn't you *want* me to be there for you?"

Asking the question almost broke her heart. She'd thought she meant something to Theo. But if he couldn't be transparent with her about something like this, then maybe she wasn't important to him at all.

He rushed forward and grabbed both of her hands. "I wanted to protect you."

"By shutting me out? That doesn't make me feel protected, Theo. It makes me feel like I don't matter."

"That's not true," he said. "There is *nothing* that matters to me more than you."

"Really?" she said. "Is this how you treat the people who matter to you? By being secretive? Withholding crucial information? That's not how you deal with a relationship, Theo—if this even is a relationship."

"I just wanted to spare you any stress. I had to hide everything, because I didn't want you to be upset."

She'd heard it before. It was Jamie all over again. Theo wasn't telling her the whole story because he didn't want to hurt her, when she was hurt far more by not knowing the truth. All this time, she'd thought they were growing closer, when in fact he hadn't even been able to tell her that he was waiting to hear whether he'd have to suffer the return of a life-threatening illness. How could he have kept such an enormous secret from her? Worse, how could he have acted for weeks as though nothing was bothering him? That was what upset her the most. She didn't want to be in a relationship with someone who kept her at arm's length and put up a facade.

Her dream of a family had always involved having a group of people who supported each other through tough times. But if Theo had thought it best to go through this alone—to put up a front, and shut her out from everything he was really feeling—then being with him put her further away from that goal than ever. It was that simple: if he couldn't be open with her, then he wasn't the right person for her.

Tears fell from her eyes despite her attempts to blink them back. This was exactly why she had sworn off relationships in the first place. She'd wasted so much of her life waiting for Jamie to be ready. She'd waited for an engagement, for marriage and for the family she'd believed they both wanted. But she couldn't wait any more. She had a life to live, and a daughter to take care of. Theo was never supposed to have been part of any of it. He'd simply arrived, without warning, and stirred feelings that she'd thought were long dormant. She was furious with him, but she was even more furious with herself for not realizing straightaway that those feelings would only lead to heartbreak.

"I think I understand," she said. "When you made that promise, you were telling me what you thought I wanted to hear."

"What I thought would be the least painful."

She shook her head. "I can't believe you're still trying to justify it."

He tried to put a hand on her shoulder, and she twisted away. "No," she said. "You promised you wouldn't do this. You know how important honesty is to me. I thought it was important to you, too. But instead, you hid things and kept secrets. You let me know only the information you thought would make me feel better, rather than the whole truth."

"I'm sorry," he said, and she could see that he meant it. He was beginning to blink back tears, too. "I'd do anything to change this. Anything to go back to a month from now and make a different decision. If I could do it over again, I'd tell you about the biopsy, I swear. My

God, Willow, there's so much in my life I'd do differently if I had the chance."

She wished she could believe him. But over and over again, he'd shown her who he was.

"I don't know if that's true, Theo. Isn't this kind of what you do?"

He looked as though she'd slapped him.

"Think about it. You stayed away from Maisie, missed the first three years of your daughter's life, because you wanted to protect her from grief. You kept the extent of your cancer a secret from your family because you didn't want them to feel sad. You can't even let a dog into your house because you're worried about it getting attached to you. If you can't do that, then how do you expect to let a child into your life? You can't be a parent unless you're willing to put your whole heart into it. But your heart, Theo, is a secret. You *claim* to be protecting the people you care about, when all you're actually doing is hiding the truth from everyone, and keeping yourself emotionally cut off!"

She was shaking with emotion. Theo's face looked absolutely heartbroken, and it broke her heart to think that she was hurting him. But he'd hurt her first. And if he could hurt her that way, then she couldn't see any future with him. No matter how painful it might be to see her dreams fade away, she had to let them go. Because she couldn't be with someone who wasn't transparent with her.

"It's time to ask yourself who you're really protecting," she continued. "Because I sure as hell don't feel protected. I just feel lied to. Maybe this has nothing to do with protecting other people, and everything to do with protecting yourself."

"From what?" he whispered.

"I don't know. Maybe from getting close. Maybe from getting some of the things you want, only to have to be afraid of losing them again. But those are questions for you to ask yourself, Theo. I can't get hurt again while I'm waiting for you to figure them out."

"What are you saying?"

"I'm saying that this isn't working. It can't work. We're not…" She swallowed, trying to force the words out. "We're not right for each other. We'd just keep going around in circles. You'd keep hiding things from me, and I'd keep feeling betrayed."

"And what about Maisie?"

"This is exactly what I didn't want for her. I didn't want her getting attached, and then getting hurt."

"I never wanted that, either. But does it have to be that way?"

"I'm sorry, but it does. I think it's for the best if we don't tell her you're her father." The look on his face was absolutely devastating. It tore her heart into pieces to think that she was hurting him this much.

But she did not want her daughter to have an emotionally distant father. She had to protect her child.

"Please," he said. "Don't do this. I can change. I'll do anything to prove it to you."

She couldn't stop the tears that streamed down her cheeks. "It's too late."

Willow knew that one of the most important parts of getting through work in any medical setting was finding a good place to cry. Even when one wasn't going through personal heartbreak, her profession offered plenty of opportunities for tears. Losing a patient, an altercation with a colleague or just the simple stress of balancing home with work necessitated a thorough knowledge of all the quiet, private spaces that might be available if one ever needed a good cry.

Most of the nurses at the clinic shared their space, so she didn't have an office of her own. But she knew of a quiet nook in the clinic's courtyard that would afford some privacy. She often went there when she needed a quiet moment. The nook held a simple concrete bench, and was shielded by walls on two sides and by the tall flowers of a butterfly garden on the other. She went there now, hoping for some peace, and hoping to simply let her tears fall without having to worry about holding them back.

She had trusted Theo. Even in the face of all the signs not to, she had believed him when he'd said he would be honest with her. She'd felt that he deserved a second chance, after all he'd been through. And then she'd developed feelings for him, allowing herself to hope that maybe, just this once, growing close to someone wouldn't lead to heartbreak.

But here she was, in the same situation all over again. Only this time, it was worse, because Maisie was involved.

Maisie was clearly very attached to Theo. She loved visiting his house, loved playing with Bixby. And she loved playing games with Theo. This was exactly the situation Willow had wanted to avoid: Maisie getting attached to someone who would then leave her life.

But was keeping Theo from Maisie the best option? A moment ago, she had been certain. By keeping his biopsy a secret, and acting as though everything was normal for several weeks—she shook her head, still unable to believe it—Theo had shown her that he couldn't be emotionally available. But she thought about Theo's extended family. If she didn't tell Maisie that Theo was her father, would she essentially be denying her daughter the chance to be someone's cousin, someone's niece? Someone's granddaughter? Willow's own gran couldn't be here for Maisie, but she still had a chance to have a grandmother. Reluctantly, she wondered if she might rethink her decision regarding Maisie's relationship with Theo. She didn't want her daughter to have an emotionally distant father, but nor did she want to keep her child from the opportunity to have close family relationships. She'd have to figure out what that would look like later. For now, she was still reeling from Theo's decision to lie to her.

He'd treated her just as Jamie had. He'd told her the things he thought she wanted to hear, rather than the truth. And then he'd tried to justify it by explaining that he'd held his silence because *she* would have been upset, a justification that only made everything much worse. As though she'd ever be upset by knowing the truth. Lies had caused her much greater pain than the truth ever could.

What was *wrong* with her? Was she simply drawn to manipulative men?

As much as she hated what Theo had done, it wasn't the worst part. The worst part was that she was so relieved that his biopsy had been clear. She wanted to celebrate that with him. But she couldn't. Theo had taken that chance for joy away from her because he'd shut her out.

She rubbed her temples, her head aching, as she again thought of what he'd said about protecting her. It made her so sad, to think of Theo carrying that lonely burden all by himself. He must have been so scared while he was waiting for the test results. It scared her, too, to think of losing him. But how much scarier to go through that alone. If she and Theo stayed together, she might not be able to trust him to keep her informed about everything. What if she lost him unexpectedly, without time to prepare, because he'd withheld important information in a misguided attempt to "protect" her? Some people might prefer it that way, but it wasn't what Willow wanted. She thought she'd been clear about that. She *had* been clear about that. Theo just hadn't listened.

As much as she feared the thought of losing Theo, the thought of being kept in the dark was even more frightening. She was a critical care nurse. She knew that there were many things in life that were scary. She didn't want to hide from them; she wanted to find someone she could trust, so they could be together through all the scary things. It broke her heart that that person wasn't Theo.

CHAPTER NINE

THEO DIDN'T KNOW how he was able to get himself to work over the next few days, but he managed somehow. He might have felt as though his heart had been ripped from his chest were it not for the occasional pangs that shot through it, letting him know that his heart was indeed still there, still beating and still broken.

He hadn't seen Willow for several days. He knew nothing of the details of her absence, only that she'd taken a few days off. He hoped that she wasn't alone, in pain, because of him. When he'd first gotten to know Willow, he'd been struck by how independent she was, and also how alone. He, at least, had Becca to talk to, and if he'd wanted to, he had more family anytime he needed them. Who did Willow talk to about her heartbreak? Was she feeling heartbreak? He didn't know what would feel worse, the thought of her getting over their relationship quickly, or the thought of her grieving by herself, with no one to give her comfort or support.

He should be that person, giving her support. Instead, he was the person who'd caused her pain. Something he promised himself he'd never do. But then, it seemed he was in the habit of breaking promises these days. Even to himself.

Even though it was hard to focus at work, he was grateful for the distraction that his patients and his research provided. Shifting his attention to his clinical work helped to ease his heartbreak a bit, although of course it was always there, waiting, when he was finished for the day.

He found himself lingering at the clinic after his shifts were over, reluctant to go home with just Bixby for company and face the emptiness there. He spent extra time checking in with his patients, who seemed grateful for his concern, albeit a little surprised by the late hours he was keeping.

One patient was especially blunt.

"Shouldn't you be home by now?" asked Roni. Theo had been taking his time in wrapping up his rounds for the day, and had checked in on Roni more than once.

"I'm staying late tonight to get through some paperwork and thought I'd check in," he responded. "Didn't mean to bother you."

"It's no bother. I just thought that all doctors hit the golf course after four p.m. Glad to be proven wrong."

"I hear you'll be leaving us soon," he said. Roni had her final dose of chemotherapy scheduled within the week, and all signs indicated that her tumor was shrinking. "You'll need to be closely monitored to make sure things continue to go well. But if the cancer cells continue to recede for at least a month, we'll be able to officially say that you're in remission."

"Well, that's good news. I won't miss being sick, but I will miss this place."

"Are you sure you don't want to stay here, where we can keep an eye on you?"

She sighed. "As nice as that sounds, it's time for me

to get back to the real world. This has been a very nice pretend vacation. And I do think pretending to be on vacation was just what I needed to get through chemo. But I'm ready to get back to my life, and my work. What about you, Doc? Are you ready to face reality yet?"

"What do you mean?"

"No offense, Doc, but your expression says a little more than 'I'm bummed to be at work late.' You look positively mopey. If I didn't know better, I might wonder if you're here late because you're hiding from something."

He forced a smile. "It's nothing."

"Nothing you want to talk about with me, anyway. That's fine. You know who's a good person to talk things over with? My favorite nurse. Who I'm pretty sure was *your* favorite nurse, up until a few days ago."

He winced. "How much do you know?"

"She hasn't told me anything. But I know a lovers' quarrel when I see one. Did you do something stupid?"

"Yes, I think maybe I did."

She sighed. "That's very unfortunate. I haven't seen her for a few days, and I miss having her around."

"Me, too."

"What happened?"

"I really screwed up," he said, and then found he simply couldn't continue. His voice caught in his throat. He'd made the same mistake so many times. He'd done it with Maisie, keeping himself out of her life so that she wouldn't be hurt by the loss of a parent. He'd meant to protect her, but instead he simply hadn't been there for her. And then with Willow, by doing the same thing that her ex had done to her. And now he might have lost Willow forever.

It can't be too late, he thought. *It just can't be.*

Roni was waiting patiently. He didn't feel pressured to speak, but he had the distinct impression that she was willing to listen, if he wanted to talk.

"I promised I'd always be open with her," he said. "And then I wasn't. I kept a secret, to protect her."

"Sounds like she wanted the truth more than she wanted to be protected."

"I guess you've gotten to know Willow pretty well during your time here."

"I think so. She's a special one, isn't she?"

"Yes," Theo said, trying without success to keep the emotion out of his voice. "She is."

"I'm going to miss how luxurious this place is, but I'm going to miss my conversations with her most of all. Don't let her get away."

"I think I already have."

"That's possible. We have to let people go when they need to leave. But I've seen how red her eyes are. I don't know if she'd have so many tears if she didn't still have some feelings for you."

His heart twisted itself into knots at the thought of Willow in tears. He wanted to take hope from Roni's words, but Willow had left him feeling certain that she didn't see a future for the two of them.

And even if there was some way that they could get back together, it wouldn't solve the other problem.

The fact was, that even though he'd made a terrible mistake, he had done it to protect Willow. And no matter what happened to change his role in Willow's life, he would always want to protect her. Whether he was her lover, friend, coworker... Even if he became nothing more to her than a distant memory, his first priority would always be her protection.

But Willow didn't want protection. She wanted honesty. How was he supposed to be honest if it hurt her?

And what if something serious did happen? This time, the biopsy had been clear. But what if the cancer came back? Or what if some other, unforeseen disaster befell them? Life was full of surprises, and not all of them were pleasant. He wanted to be someone who could offer Willow shelter, not someone who would add to her worries.

"Even if she does still feel something for me, it doesn't change that there's always the threat of something else looming over us. Cancer, or something else. Something even worse could go wrong."

"Now you're just being ridiculous."

He jerked back in surprise.

"Seriously. What you're saying is absurd. Unexpected problems can arise at any time. That's part of life, Doc. You of all people should know that, both as a doctor and as a cancer survivor. You sound like someone who's just trying to protect yourself from getting hurt."

Her words reminded him so much of what Becca had said, what Willow had said. He thought for a moment, trying to explain how he felt. He looked at the little dog, Buttons, nuzzled close at Roni's side. "Don't you ever worry about what would happen to Buttons if you couldn't take care of him anymore? Wouldn't you do anything to protect him, even if it meant giving him up?"

"Well. You're asking a billionaire with a full-time house staff, so take my answer with a grain of salt. I know that Buttons would be well cared for if anything happened to me. But even I didn't… I could never pass up the chance to have Buttons in my life, even if I didn't have two pennies to rub together. He's been such a comfort to me. And I would rather focus on enjoying the dogs—and the people—who are in my life now, rather than worrying about what might happen later."

He said, a little sheepishly, "I've wanted a dog for a long time, but with the cancer… I was always worried about what would become of it if I couldn't take care of it anymore."

"That's your problem, if you don't mind me saying so, Doc. If you spend your life waiting until it's all smooth sailing, then you'll never get anything you want. You've got to grab your life with both hands and make the future you want for yourself. Cancer be damned. Change is going to happen no matter what. You might as well enjoy yourself while you can."

"But what if someone gets hurt? I just wanted to keep Willow from feeling any sadness. What if I just end up causing her more pain?"

"I don't know. But it seems like you're unilaterally deciding for yourself who should or shouldn't have to feel anything. Maybe she should be part of that decision, too."

He knew Roni was right. Once again, he could feel a dream slipping away from him. Years ago, he'd had the same feeling when he'd been told that he might not be able to have children. He'd done something about that, even though he'd known that freezing his sperm wasn't a guarantee that he'd have children someday. But it had brought him peace of mind, knowing that the option was there. And then Maisie had happened, not so much an accident, but a miracle in his opinion.

But this time, it was Willow who was slipping away, and the dreams he'd already begun for their life together. He'd known her for such a short time that he hadn't realized just how powerful those dreams had become. He hadn't even noticed, until now when he was faced with losing her, that every vision of the future he had included her. And yet now that dream was ending almost as soon as it had begun, and this time it wasn't the fault of some outside force. He couldn't blame this on the cancer. He realized now that the situation was entirely his fault, because of the choice he'd made to withhold information from Willow.

He'd been so stupid, he thought. He could have prevented all of this, if only he been paying attention. Willow had told him what she wanted. Even Becca had tried to warn him that he was making a mistake. And he could see now what he could have done differently, but he was very afraid that Willow had been right when she'd said it was too late.

Willow watched Theo and Roni from the hallway. She couldn't hear their conversation, but she could see Roni's smiles. Theo was so good with patients. There was something about his warm presence that they responded to immediately. She certainly knew how it felt to experience Theo's calm, earnest demeanor. Regardless of the difficulties that had arisen between them, no one could deny that Theo had a sincere desire to help his patients. Willow had always been impressed at how Theo approached each patient with exactly the same warmth. He was the same person with billionaire Roni

Santiago that he was with any patient from St. Victoria. It was one of the things she had liked best about him.

It was still a trait that she appreciated, which was probably a good thing. She was glad she could still like Theo as a doctor, if not as a person.

She could see that he was a good doctor, a good man. Seeing the way he worked with cancer patients had shown her just how well Theo understood the fear and anxiety that came with a life-threatening illness. Her heart still ached for all he'd been through. And a part of her wanted, more than anything, to throw her arms around him and tell him that her feelings hadn't changed. But she couldn't trust that part of her. It might be nice, for a brief moment, to fantasize about holding Theo and telling him that they could have a future, and whatever that future brought, they'd face it together. But that fantasy would never come true, because Theo wasn't the kind of person who wanted to face things together. He'd shown her that clearly enough.

It had been very difficult to go into work each day. So difficult that she'd decided to take a few personal days, just to clear her head. She was glad she'd taken the time off. It had given her the space she needed to gain some clarity about what to do next.

At first, continuing to work in the same place as Theo had seemed impossible. How could she possibly stand seeing him every day? She'd thought briefly about leaving the Island Clinic and taking a job at St. Victoria Hospital. The pay would be far lower, but that might be less painful than seeing Theo.

She'd also considered asking Theo to leave, but that didn't seem fair. He'd come to St. Victoria to meet his daughter. He'd fulfilled every condition she'd set forth, and more. Their time together had simply been an unexpected diversion. He was a good doctor, and he cared deeply for Maisie. St. Victoria and the Island Clinic needed him. And Maisie needed him. She'd decided she couldn't deprive her daughter of the chance to feel connected to an extended family. No matter how heartbroken Willow might be, Maisie deserved to have the family support that Willow had always dreamed of.

She waited for Theo to finish up with Roni. As he turned away from Roni's bedside, she saw his face light up in recognition as he saw her standing in the shadows of the hallway. She noticed that it still hurt to see the way the corners of his mouth tugged up, as though his default expression were to smile. Dammit, she thought. It has to stop hurting someday. She just wished she knew when.

She motioned to him to step out into the hall with her, and they found a secluded corner.

"I'm so glad to see you," he said. "Are you here for a shift?"

"No," she said. "I'll come back officially tomorrow. But I'm here now to see you. I thought it would be good for the two of us to have a chance to talk, face-to-face, before I start again. So that we're both clear on where we stand with one another."

"Please," he said. "Can't I just have one more chance to explain?"

She closed her eyes. She knew she shouldn't listen. But she couldn't bring herself to stop him, either. She wished there were something, anything, that he could say that could make everything better.

"I don't want to let this go. To let *us* go," he said. "There has to be some way to fix it."

"I wish there were."

"You were right, you know. When you said that this is something I do. I do push people away. Usually the people I care about most. Part of it's because my family is so close-knit. I love that, but I love having privacy, too. And when my dad was diagnosed with Alzheimer's, it almost broke me to see all the pain they were going through. I couldn't stand the thought of adding to it."

He took her hand. "And then you became someone who was close to me, too. And when I think of the pain my family went through… I knew that I never wanted to put anyone I cared about through something like that. Not if I could help it. And so I was desperate to spare you.

"But I know that wasn't right. You didn't want to be spared the truth. I should have told you, right away, what was going on. I should never have tried to hide anything from you. Please, I'd do anything to have another chance. To show you I've changed."

She took her hand back. "No. I think we're just going to go around in circles." The words were hard to say, but it would have been harder still to have left them unsaid.

He took a long, slow breath. The look on his face cut her to the core. Then he said, "So what do we do now?"

"Well. That's what I came here to talk to you about."

It was as though a light had dimmed from his eyes. She could see that it was painful for him to speak. But better that they were having this conversation now, rather than later.

"Under other circumstances, I might offer to leave," he said. "I hate the idea of you feeling uncomfortable when we see each other here at work, or anywhere on the island. My leaving would probably make everything less complicated for both of us."

The words sent a jolt through her. It was a possibility she'd considered, but to hear him say it out loud made it real. There was something almost *wrong* about those words.

But then he continued. "I can't, though. Even if you never want to see me again, I can't leave. If you don't want me to see Maisie, I'll understand. But I have to be here for her, in case she ever needs me."

"I know. You're right, you should stay." His eyes widened, and she clarified. "You can see Maisie. Your relationship with her shouldn't be contingent on what happens with us. I need a little more time to pass before I'm ready to set up anything regularly. I'm just... not ready for that conversation yet. But I wanted you to know that eventually we'll figure out some way for you to spend time with her."

The relief on his face was evident, and she felt another wave of warmth toward him. He cared so much for Maisie. But at this moment, warmth was not a helpful feeling. She needed to stay firm in her resolve.

"Getting to know you has been good for Maisie. I can see that. And I want her to know her extended family. I don't want anything that's happened to us to take that from her. And we've both always said that we didn't want her to get hurt as a result of our involvement with one another."

"Thank you, Willow. This means more to me than you can possibly imagine."

"As far as work goes, I know that you're usually at St. Victoria Hospital in the mornings. So I'll just stick to morning shifts, and I can't imagine we'll have to deal with one another too often." She couldn't believe the way her words were coming out: cool and professional. There was no hint of the emotions that had been roiling within her over the past few days. But then, perhaps it was simply because the heartbreak had pushed her to a place beyond feeling.

"I could leave the Island Clinic and get a job somewhere else," he offered.

"Where? You already tried St. Victoria Hospital, and they sent you here. There are no other medical centers on the island. Where else would you work?"

"I…don't have to be a doctor."

"Are you saying that because it's true, or because it's what you think I want to hear?"

"I'm saying it because I mean it. Because even though being an oncologist is important to me, your well-being is more important. And I'm saying it because even though you might be all right with the two of us working together, *I* don't know if I can handle it."

She gave him a watery smile. "Don't you dare decide you're quitting medicine. You've got research studies that are about to start at the hospital. People are counting on those for their care. You're a good doctor, Theo. And you've never had the chance to really shine in your career, due to circumstances outside of your control. But I know you could. And I know that the patients here need you. They need someone who understands the fear, who's been where they've been. You belong here."

Now it was her turn to reach out for his hand. Probably for the last time. "I hope you understand what I'm saying. That I can understand how much you want to be in Maisie's life, and that I think we can work together."

"And nothing more."

She steeled her resolve. She'd come this far, and if she gave in now, she'd never be able to get through this conversation again. "You've earned the right to be here. And to be in Maisie's life. But as far as I'm concerned, you and I are through."

CHAPTER TEN

WILLOW SAT ON her sofa at home, the soft patter of rain tapping out a comforting beat on her roof. She'd packed Maisie off to Mrs. Jean's for a few hours so that she could have some peace and quiet. Or at least some quiet. Peace had been hard to come by for the past several days.

It was one thing to know, in her head, that she and Theo were over. But her heart didn't seem to have caught up. Even though she'd only been with Theo for a short time, signs of him were everywhere. She had photos of him on their phone from hikes they'd taken together. There was a recipe for his great-aunt Myrtle's chile taped to the front of her refrigerator. A small vase he'd bought for her still rested on her kitchen countertop, a single lily protruding from its mouth. She hadn't been able to bring herself to put it away. It was amazing, she thought, how quickly the individual moments of a relationship turned into memories. Even after just a few weeks, there were so many objects strewn across the landscape of her life, each one bringing up a different memory, a different feeling.

It was hard, too, when Maisie asked to see him. Theo had made an impression on her child quickly. Certainly

Theo was very good with children, but Willow wondered if it wasn't so much about Theo's skill as something Maisie needed. Hard as it was to admit, Maisie was growing up. The swimming lessons that had once been a source of anxiety were now simply part of everyday life. Willow loved to see Maisie growing more confident in the water, but there was an ache, too, when she thought about how her child was growing a little taller and a little more independent every day. She needed more than just Willow in her life.

Willow knew that someday soon she would need to find a way to explain to Maisie who Theo was to her. She wished that Gran could be around for that conversation. It wasn't that she had any trepidation about raising the topic with Maisie. She knew that, ultimately, her child would simply understand that she was loved. But Gran always had such a precise way of putting things. She could always find the right words for any situation.

She often found herself missing Gran the most on rainy days. Gran had loved the rain. She'd found it soothing. But then, Gran had never given the appearance of needing much soothing. She'd been a tough, independent woman who never seemed ruffled, even when times were hard.

Willow wondered how Gran had done it all. She'd held down a job as a librarian, raised a daughter and lost her own husband, Willow's grandfather, many years ago. And then, just as she was planning to retire, Willow's parents had passed away, and Gran was left to raise Willow on her own. She must have known moments of loneliness and frustration, but Willow could not recall a moment when her grandmother hadn't been cheerful and loving. Gran had done it all on her own, without ever needing help from anyone else.

And if Gran could do it, then so could she.

She'd been so right to swear off relationships. She'd given romance a chance, and look what had happened. Days spent wallowing in heartbreak, time taken off work to recover and now the extra unwanted emotional turmoil she had to deal with every time she saw Theo at the clinic. Giving in to her attraction to Theo had completely disrupted her life. And she didn't have time for disruption. She was a single mother. She had responsibilities. She recalled that Gran had never once dated for as long as Willow had known her. Gran had understood that being a mother meant that one couldn't afford certain kinds of complications in life.

Willow was certain that Gran wouldn't have faulted her for her decision to date Theo…but she probably wouldn't have made the same decision herself. Gran was far too responsible for boyfriends. *That's where I went wrong*, Willow thought. The whole time she'd been raising Maisie, she'd been trying to follow Gran's example. She should never have strayed. She should have given Theo a firm, decisive "No" the first time he'd asked her out, and thought nothing more of it.

Willow pulled out an old photo album and flipped through the pages. Here were memories of birthday parties and holidays. There were a few with Gran and Maisie, right after Maisie was born. But most were pictures of Willow's childhood.

It surprised her how many were of her and Gran alone. That was only natural, of course. It wasn't as though there had been other relatives to be part of things.

She traced one of her favorite photos with her finger.

It was one of the few pictures of herself and her parents, with Gran in the background, from when she was very small. Underneath, in Gran's spidery handwriting, was the caption "The whole family together."

The words gave Willow a pang. The whole family indeed. She'd always thought that she and Maisie were doing just fine on their own. But that didn't mean that she didn't want more for both of them.

And now her family was small again. Just her and Maisie. But Maisie would have more, through Theo, and that was the important thing.

As she put the photo album back on the shelf, a stray picture fell out. She bent down to retrieve it and realized it was one she hadn't seen before. It must have been stuck behind one of the other photos.

It took her a moment to understand what she was seeing. And as she did, she could understand why she'd never seen the photo before.

It was a picture of Gran. Based on how she looked, Willow estimated that it would have been taken around the time Willow was in middle school or high school. But in the picture, Gran was at a party.

Which was odd. Willow didn't remember Gran ever going to parties. But then, Willow supposed she'd never wondered much about what Gran got up to when Willow was watched by a babysitter, or sleeping over at a friend's house, or at a party of her own. She'd always assumed that Gran was visiting antique markets with her friends, or baking another one of her prize-winning pies, or sitting demurely at home, perhaps…knitting?

In this photo, she was not baking, or knitting, or doing any of the things Willow typically thought of as Gran-like activities.

In this photo, a man was kissing Gran. And she was kissing him right back.

And the man's hands weren't chastely at his sides. One was around Gran's waist. The other…well, Willow could see why Gran might have tucked the photo quietly behind one of the more family-friendly pictures in the album.

She turned the photo over in confusion. To her surprise, Gran had dated the photo in the corner. It must have been important to her; Gran only dated the important ones. And a tiny, neat inscription was at the bottom.

Weekly supper party with Naveen. A tender lover and a better friend. It is love that makes the impossible possible.

A tender *lover*?

Had Gran had a boyfriend?

She turned the photo over and over, as though doing so would somehow give her more information. But the photo remained as much of a mystery as ever.

Or at least, it remained a mystery as long as she ignored the obvious, which was that Gran had had a boyfriend. In fact, judging by the dress Gran was wearing and the people at the party in that photograph, Gran had had an entire life that Willow had known nothing about. A life that didn't seem to focus much on knitting and baking.

It had simply never occurred to Willow to think about Gran's love life. Her grandfather had passed away long before Willow was born, and Gran had kept his picture on the mantel and spoken fondly of him from time to time. As a teenager, Willow had gone through a romantic phase where she'd invented a tragic love story between her grandparents. She believed that Gran, having suffered such a loss, was unwilling to take a chance on love again. She'd told the story to Gran, who had laughed and assured her that her time with Willow's grandfather was a treasured memory, but not a source of constant grief. Still, Willow's adolescent mind had been entranced with the idea of Gran as an epic heroine who'd lost her greatest love too early in life.

As an adult, especially after single motherhood, Willow's assumptions had taken a more practical turn. Gran, she thought, had probably been far too busy with childrearing and work responsibilities to have any time for romance. And Gran's interests had always seemed so innocent. She'd loved trying new recipes and new sewing patterns. True, she occasionally brought friends over to their small London flat, and some of those friends had been men…but it had never occurred to Willow that Gran might have been dating some of those men.

She squinted again at the picture of Naveen and realized that he looked a little familiar. She couldn't recall much, but she was absolutely certain that he was one of the "friends" that had come over to Gran's small flat for occasional drinks and conversation.

She shook her head in amazement. *Gran's boyfriend.* She was surprised to find that it made her happy to think of Gran dating. She'd always thought Gran had given up things like dating and parties in order to take care of Willow. But judging by the photograph, Gran hadn't given up those things entirely. It seemed she'd found a way to fit them into her life, after all.

She thought about the quote Gran had included.

It is love that makes the impossible possible.

Had Gran been in love with this Naveen, then? He was certainly handsome-looking in the photograph. She wished so much that Gran were here so they could talk about it now. There was an entire side of Gran's life that she'd known nothing about.

What would Gran think about what had happened with Theo? Just a moment ago, she'd been worrying that Gran might have disapproved of her choice to date Theo in the first place. But now that she'd seen that photograph, she wondered if Gran might have an entirely different perspective.

As shocked as she was about the idea of Gran having a boyfriend, the more Willow thought about it, the more it made sense. Gran was the kind of woman who'd always invited love into her life. It was stranger to think of her never having a boyfriend.

Gran would probably not have approved of Theo's tendency to avoid pain for himself and others by cutting himself off from everyone. But she might also have suggested that Willow was doing the same thing. By swearing off relationships, she'd been trying to protect herself from all of the pain and turmoil she believed they caused. She'd been trying to avoid all the hurt she'd felt with Jamie.

In other words, she'd been scared. But what if there was no sure way to protect herself from being hurt? What if, rather than protecting herself, she was simply cutting herself off from love?

She'd always believed that Gran had lived her life without love and had gotten by just fine. But now it seemed she'd been wrong about that. Gran hadn't sworn off relationships, she'd just been discreet about them. Willow would give anything for a chance to ask Gran about what had happened with Naveen. But whether Gran had found love or not, she'd clearly been willing to give it a chance. Quite an enthusiastic chance, given how things appeared in the photograph.

Could she say the same for herself? For the first time since meeting Theo—in fact, for the first time in the past few years—Willow realized that she couldn't. Fear, plain and simple, had been holding her back. And that wasn't Theo's fault. In a way, it wasn't even Jamie's fault. Jamie had hurt her, yes. He'd left her feeling deeply betrayed. But she was the one who'd let fear get in the way of opening her heart to the possibility of the one thing she desired most in the world. She was so afraid of losing love. But if she couldn't be open to it in the first place, then she'd never be able to have the family she'd spent her life dreaming of.

It had been right there in front of her. Theo was Maisie's father. And she loved him. She knew that now. The idea of depending on someone, *needing* someone, scared her so much. But the idea of being closed off scared her even more. She'd accused Theo of being unable to access his emotions, but wasn't she just as guilty? She'd convinced herself that she was too busy for love, that relationships could only lead to heartbreak, that she'd get hurt again, the same way she'd been before. But the whole time, she'd just been letting her fear get the best of her. And she'd almost lost what was most important to her.

These past few days without Theo had been nearly unbearable. But not as unbearable as the thought that she might have lost him entirely. She grabbed her car keys from the counter. She had to talk to Theo, had to tell him exactly how she felt, no matter how he reacted. She desperately wanted to give him her heart, but she couldn't imagine what he might do with it.

She might be afraid to give him her heart, but she could give him something else: a chance. Because she loved him. And love deserved another chance.

She'd barely left her front door when she stopped short. Theo was standing in front of her, rain pouring down his face.

"I hope you don't mind that I came over," he said. "I've been trying to give you your space. But I had something I wanted to show you."

"Theo, I need to tell you something."

"Just wait. Please. I'd like to bring you over to my place and show you something. Don't say anything until then. It's just a short drive. Please."

She wanted to explain, to tell him all she felt and hope that they could both give things another chance. But Theo was so insistent.

They made the short drive to his house, and both stepped out of the car.

"Here it is," Theo said.

Willow was confused. "I've seen your house before, Theo."

"Keep looking. Notice anything different about the porch?"

There it was. The dog bed and toys were gone. "What's happened to Bixby?"

Theo stepped forward and opened the door. "He lives inside now."

Willow's face was starting to become very wet. The

rain, of course. It was pattering down steadily. Surely it was the rain that collected in the corners of her eyes.

"You've finally let him in."

"It was time. It should have been done long ago. I should have started letting a lot of people in, long ago."

She couldn't help smiling at him then, though her tears were flowing freely. "Sometimes it just takes practice."

"There's something else I want to show you, as well. Come onto the porch, so you don't get wet."

She stepped onto the porch, and he took out his phone. "Look at your phone, too," he said. "Open your calendar."

She pulled out her phone and looked at the calendar. There were dozens and dozens of appointment invitations awaiting her response. Medical appointments.

"This shows every one of the follow-up appointments I have scheduled so far," he said. "I'm afraid there's quite a lot of them. You know how particular oncologists can be. My medical team insists that I attend numerous checkups to track how my remission is going. And I want you to attend every single one of them with me. I want the person who matters to me most to be there. I want someone who loves and supports me to be at my side, and it would mean everything to me for you to be that person."

She tried to respond, but she couldn't quite speak, whether it was because of her laughter or her tears.

"I want you with me," Theo continued. "I want you to be there because no matter what the future holds, I don't want to go through it alone. I want all three of us to go through it together, as a family. And I want to be a proper father for Maisie. For three years, I was so focused on trying to protect her that I couldn't even be there for her in the first place. But I'm ready to be here for her now. And I'm not afraid of what might happen, because no matter what's in store for us, we can choose to go through it together. And if you'll have me, Willow, then I want to go through it with you. I'll give you my whole self. The good, the bad and everything in between. That is, if it's something you still want. If *I'm* someone you still want. Because I love you. I love you more than I ever thought it was possible to love. I want us to be a family together. But there's one thing I want even more than that."

"What?" she said, breathless, still trying to take it all in.

"I want you to love me back."

A moment later, she was in his arms, his kiss crushing her lips and sending shivers down her spine. She tried to put everything she was feeling into the kiss. It was a kiss that held more than three long years of waiting, her hopes and wishes for the future and all her love for him.

It was the kind of kiss, she thought, that might have made a woman like Gran raise an appreciative eyebrow.

After a long moment, they broke apart, and Theo said, "I don't want to get my hopes up too much. But this seems like a fairly enthusiastic response to my invitation to attend all of my medical appointments."

She reached up to put her arms around his neck and leaned against him. "Some girls get flowers along with declarations of love. I get to be included in your medical appointments. And that's exactly what I want. Because I love you, too, Theo."

"Do you?" he said, his forehead pressed against hers. "Because I was worried that I had ruined everything."

"You weren't the only one who made mistakes. Or the only one who has a hard time being emotionally vulnerable. I accused you of holding back when I was doing exactly the same thing—looking for ways to convince myself that I didn't have room for love in my life, looking for proof that I was right not to trust. I was trying so hard to protect what I had that I didn't even realize what I was missing."

"And what was that exactly?"

She kept her arms around his neck, pulling herself close to him. "A chance to have the family I've always wanted. And a chance to have it with *you*."

He kissed her again, lightly, and before he pulled away, she let her lips brush the corner of his mouth, just where it seemed to curve up into a smile. There was a long silence then, as they held each other and exchanged soft, slow kisses, while the rain continued to pour down just beyond the porch.

After quite some time had passed, Willow spared a quick glance at the calendar on her phone. "This is a lot of appointments."

"Don't I know it. The first year is the worst as far as follow-up goes. They want to do examinations often to keep an eye on things. But then after the first year they start to lighten up a bit, and once you get a few years out it's just once in a while. The five-year appointment is the big one. If you're still in complete remission by then, you're declared cured."

"Five years is a long time." She looked into his eyes, the question left unspoken between them. "It's certainly a long time to be in each other's lives."

He pulled her close. "In a way, we've already been in each other's lives for a long time, because of Maisie. I stupidly thought the best thing I could do for both of you was to stay away, so as not to add any pain to your lives. But now I realize that I shouldn't have just stopped at touching your life. I should have reached out and grabbed on with both hands."

"I'm so glad you finally are."

"This time, I'm not letting go. Because I think the more we reach for one another, the better things will get. I might be wrong, but that's what I believe. Do you want to stay together and see if I'm right?"

"I do."

EPILOGUE

Six months later

"MOMMY, LOOK! I can hold Daddy's laptop and my grape juice *and* three books all at the same time!"

Willow raced into Theo's dining room to assess the situation. Maisie loved to explore more than ever, and her adventures often included tests of her own capabilities that frequently ended in disaster, whether in the form of broken items or bumps and bruises. And now that they were spending so much time at Theo's house, there were even more new things to discover—and, potentially, to break.

Willow was just in time to rescue Theo's laptop as it was about to slip out of Maisie's hands. The little girl had three books tucked under her chin, and was trying to hold on to a cup of grape juice and Bixby's collar in the other.

"Okay, let's not dye Bixby purple," she said, freeing the dog from Maisie's grasp.

"It might be too late for that," said Theo, deftly taking the laptop from her. "I think she got a little on one of his back legs earlier."

"Guess it can't be helped. At least one of us will look

distinctive." She started to comb Maisie's hair, but then caught a look at herself in the dining room mirror and began to brush furiously at her own hair instead. "How many minutes until showtime?"

Theo slipped an arm around her waist. "Just a few, but it won't be the end of the world if we're a little late. You're not nervous, are you?"

She hesitated. "I just wish I'd had a little more time to spend on Maisie's hair this morning. And mine's so frizzy in this humidity. I want to make a good first impression."

"Are you kidding? They're going to love you as much as I do. Well, *almost* as much as I do. And it's not really your first impression. You and Becca never seem to get off the phone with one another. I can barely get a conversation in with her anymore because she's always talking to you."

"But I haven't met the rest of them. And I haven't seen *any* of them face-to-face." She looked at the laptop. "Such as it is."

"Face to laptop. Hey." He pulled her close. "You look absolutely beautiful. And if by some bizarre fluke my family is not completely smitten with you, well…they're four thousand miles away. They can't do much to you from that distance."

Willow called Maisie to her, and the three of them sat in front of the computer monitor as Theo flicked it on. A moment later, Theo's family appeared on-screen.

There was a cavalcade of aunts, uncles and cousins. Willow had got on well with Theo's sister, Becca, but he had three other siblings who were delighted to meet her, as well. Everyone seemed to adore Maisie, who could barely contain her glee as she saw young cousins her own age.

Theo's father was there, as well, seated next to Theo's mother, and surrounded by his own siblings. Though he clearly benefited from the support of those around him, his father appeared to be in good spirits. Willow noticed how tender Theo's mother's expression was as she sat beside him, and she had a feeling that their years together had been happy.

As far as Willow could tell, there were three, possibly four, generations of family in one room. She'd never seen anything like it. Everyone talked at once, but somehow it seemed to work. Willow could imagine what it might be like to be in the room with these people: everyone talking over each other, full of energy and excitement. Everyone seemed to have a family story to share, but they made certain that Willow was included, too. Theo was able to tell his family that he was now in complete remission, with no detectable amount of cancer in his body, and cheers went up in London and the Caribbean.

It was getting to be evening by the time they ended the call. As Theo switched off the computer, Willow quickly wiped a tear from her eye.

"What's this?" he said. "You did great. They absolutely loved you, just as I knew they would. And it seemed as though you were having a good time, too."

"I was. I loved meeting them, all of them. Becca's even funnier in person. And your mother was so warm and kind. It was wonderful."

"Then why the tears?"

"I've always wanted a family like that. Growing up, it did get lonely at times, with just me and Gran. I'm so glad to see that Maisie gets to have so much family in her life."

"Willow." Theo pulled her up from her chair and put his hands around her shoulders. "They're not just Maisie's family. They're going to be your family, too."

He pulled a small box from the mantelpiece behind them. Willow hadn't noticed it before, but as she saw it in Theo's hands, her heart began to race.

Theo knelt down. "Willow Thompson," he began.

"Yes!" she cried, and threw her arms around him. He stood up and kissed her.

"There's something you need to know about this ring," he said.

Willow gently traced her finger over the ring's intricate setting. "The filigree is so detailed, this must be an antique."

"Yes. It belonged to my grandmother. At first, I was planning to look for something new. But the more I thought about it, I realized that I wanted to propose with my grandmother's ring. I talked it over with her, and with all my siblings and cousins who aren't married yet, and they all agreed with me that you should be the one to have it. Assuming you like it, of course."

"Oh, Theo. It's beautiful."

"This isn't just about the two of us, my love. I wanted you to have something that would show you, every day, that you're joining a huge family you'll be part of forever, no matter what happens to me. I want this ring to be a reminder that our family will be more than just the three of us."

"Well. I already knew it would be more than just the three of us."

He stared at her, stunned. "Willow. Have you been keeping a secret from me?"

She smiled. "I suppose it's time you knew. I'm pregnant."

Unmitigated joy broke over his face. He pressed his forehead against hers, and pulled her close to him. "Who would have thought that I'd get a second chance at having everything I wanted," he said.

"I'm so glad you're happy."

"Are you joking? I'm thrilled. How could you imagine I'd feel any other way?"

"Well, you know. Unexpected surprises aren't always easy to deal with."

He buried his nose in her hair. "Thank goodness for unexpected surprises," he murmured. "This time, I'm going to be there for everything, no matter what might come our way."

* * * * *

MILLS & BOON

Coming next month

ISLAND FLING WITH THE SURGEON
Ann McIntosh

"I'm going in," Zach said, after he'd arranged the cooler and towels to his specifications and adjusted the umbrella for maximum shade. When he pulled off his shirt, Gen bit back a groan of pleasure, seeing his bare torso in all its glory for the first time. "Are you coming?"

"Sure," Gen said, her heart going into overdrive as she stood up and unzipped her cover-up, aware of Zach standing just a step or two away, waiting for her.

Oh, she hoped he felt the same way looking at her as she did at the sight of those magnificent pecs and his firm, ridged abdomen.

She didn't look at him as she shrugged the sleeveless dress off her arms and stepped out of it, before bending to pick it up and fold it carefully.

Then, with the long strides she'd learned during her pageant days, she walked past him toward the surf.

He wasn't beside her as she ran the last few steps into the water before doing a shallow dive beneath an incoming wave.

When she came up and turned back toward the beach, wiping the salt water from her face, he was still standing where she'd left him. When their gazes collided, despite the distance between them a shiver of longing ran up her spine.

Then he was in motion, not running but following

her with decisive, intentional strides. He didn't dive into the water, but kept wading until he was standing just inches from where she was bobbing in the water.

"You're trying to drive me bonkers, aren't you?"

It was little better than a growl, and her nipples tightened at his tone, while her core turned molten and needy.

"Is it working?" she asked, holding his gaze, trying to figure out if the gleam there was anger, annoyance or something else entirely.

"Yes," he snapped. "But this…" He waved his hand between them. "This is supposed to be make-believe."

She shrugged lightly. "It doesn't have to be. I'm horribly attracted to you, so if you want to change the rules, we can negotiate."

"Consider this my opening bid," he said, pulling her close, placing his hands on either side of her face and kissing her as though he'd never stop.

Continue reading
ISLAND FLING WITH THE SURGEON
Ann McIntosh

Available next month
www.millsandboon.co.uk

COMING SOON!

We really hope you enjoyed reading this book. If you're looking for more romance, be sure to head to the shops when new books are available on

Thursday 22nd July